# My Bonny Light Horseman

L . A . M E Y E R

# My Bonny Light Horseman

Being an Account of the Further

Adventures of Jacky Faber,

in Love and War

Harcourt, Inc.
*Orlando   Austin   New York   San Diego   London*

www.HarcourtBooks.com

Library of Congress Cataloging-in-Publication Data
Meyer, L. A. (Louis A.), 1942–
My bonny light horseman: being an account of the further adventures of Jacky
Faber, in love and war/L. A. Meyer.
p. cm.—(A Bloody Jack adventure; 6)
Sequel to: Mississippi Jack.
Summary: While trying to run a respectable shipping
business in 1806, teenaged Jacky Faber finds herself in France,
spying for the British Crown in order to save her friends.
[1. Spies—Fiction. 2. Orphans—Fiction. 3. Napoleonic Wars, 1800–1815—
Fiction. 4. France—History—Consulate and First Empire, 1799–1815—Fiction.]
I. Title.
PZ7.M57172My 2008
[Fic]—dc22 2007049582
ISBN 978-0-15-206187-6

Text set in Minion
Display set in Pabst
Designed by Cathy Riggs

First edition
A C E G H F D B

Printed in the United States of America

*Always, for Annetje...*
*and for Joseph W. Lawrence II, Esq.*
*As well as for Marie, Bob, and Stanley.*
*Many thanks to all.*

# My Bonny Light Horseman

# PART I

# Chapter 1

"Is it not a glorious day to be alive, Higgins?" I ask, sitting on the hatch of my fleet little schooner with my back to the aftermast and my legs sprawled out before me, looking up at the trim of the sails. I'm clad in my usual sailing gear of light cotton shirt, short buckskin skirt, bare of lower limbs and bare of feet. The breeze ruffles through the stubble of hair that is regrowing itself on my head and the sun feels good on my face.

"It is indeed, Miss," says my very, *very* good John Higgins, Confidant, Personal Assistant, and Highest-Paid Employee of Faber Shipping, Worldwide. Highest-paid, that is, when Faber Shipping has any money at all to pay anything to anybody. Right now, my corporation consists of two small boats, the *Evening Star* and the *Morning Star,* and the *Nancy B. Alsop,* my beautiful little Gloucester schooner and current flagship of Faber Shipping, Worldwide, on which my bottom now rests.

"However," continues Higgins, nudging, once again, my ankles back together and pulling the hem of my buckskin skirt back down over my knees, over which knees it had crawled up a bit, "you really should stay out of the sun as it is not good for your complexion. I assume you'll be taking your lunch up here on the hatch?"

I nod and smile up at my good friend and protector. "You spoil me too much, Higgins."

"Well, Miss, we must keep you tidy, mustn't we?" says Higgins. He reaches over and runs his hand through my hair, which is now about three inches long. "Soon we'll be able to comb this, which will be a relief. I will be back directly."

I had lost my long, sandy locks in a not-very-pleasant incident on my way down the Mississippi River this summer. To make up for my loss of coiffure, I have purchased, in various ports, a collection of wigs, some rather fancy, some very plain, and I must admit I enjoy prancing about in some of the gaudier ones when we are in foreign ports—I have one especially outrageous long, curly red one festooned with yellow ribbons, which comes all the way down to my bum. Higgins, upon seeing me wearing it for the first time, visibly recoiled and said, "God, that's *ghastly,*" this being the only time I think I have ever moved him to taking the Lord's name in vain, which is something, considering what I have done in the past to offend both his sensibilities and his sense of propriety.

Ah, yes, that was all in good fun, but here, in the sun and amongst my friends who all know me for my eccentricities, I wear no wig at all.

The *Nancy B* is headed south to pick up more sugar in Jamaica—that's what we've been doing during the past few months since we left New Orleans. We haul granite down from New England—it doesn't bring much, but it's good ballast and from what else are they gonna make fine buildings and tombstones down there in Jamaica? Sand? Coral?—and so after we off-load and sell that, we buy sugar and haul it north from the Caribbean to Boston to be made into rum by the many distilleries there. Then we turn around and do it again. And yet again.

Nice and safe and calm—running the *Nancy B* as a coaster, seldom out of sight of land. That's the new level-headed Jacky Faber; no more impulsive plunging into awful situations and then desperately struggling to get myself out of them. Nay, I am doing what I have always said I wanted to do, which is to have a fine ship like this one and haul stuff from a place that's got a lot of that stuff, and take it to another place that ain't got a lot of that stuff and is willing to pay for it, and so prosper. I had thought about sailing across the Big Pond to set up a smuggling operation running the British blockade of France, and maybe after Jaimy gets back to London next year and we are wed, we might give it a try—after all, the stores of Fletcher Wine Company must be getting mighty lean. Maybe I'll write to Jaimy's father and see what he thinks about participating in a little mischief—and tell him about how his son looked when last I saw him on the deck of HMS *Mercury*, all decked out in his new lieutenant's uniform and looking oh-so fine. Maybe I'll write and say...Nay, I won't write to him at all, I know I will not, for I also realize that most of the Family Fletcher has very little use for one Jacky Faber, former privateer, who stole from them not only the affection of their beloved son, but also a good deal of their fortune, at least in wine, that is.

Besides, running a blockade ain't nice and safe and calm, which is what I have resolved to be. Jaimy and I will work out what our lives are to be like when he gets back from Japan and we are united and...

*Ahem.* Back to business. This is the state of Faber Shipping, Worldwide, on this early September day in 1806:

Holdings: The aforementioned two small boats and the *Nancy B. Alsop,* a two-masted schooner, sixty-five feet in length and named after my mother. We've also got nets, traps, and other rigging, plus various armaments. Since acquiring her, we have fitted her with swivel guns fore and aft—I learned about the usefulness of those little pepper pots this past summer when sailing down the Mississippi River on my keelboat, the *Belle of the Golden West.* We've added two standard nine-pound cannons mounted on either side. Sure it's extra weight that could be better used for cargo, but the piece of mind the guns afford outweighs the loss of freight tonnage, for there are pirates abroad in these waters, some of whom I know by name, and many of them do not hold me in the highest regard. After all, I did spend the summer before this one cruising and carousing around the Caribbean on my lovely *Emerald.*

Personnel:

*Miss Jacky Mary Faber,* President

*Mr. John Higgins,* Vice President and Chief Consultant

*Mr. Ezra Pickering,* Esquire, Clerk, Secretary, and Treasurer. From his law office on Union Street in Boston, he manages the books, bails me out of jail (when he can), and makes sure that all is neat and tidy, legalwise.

*Miss Chloe Abyssinia Cantrell,* Freeborn Person of Color, Accountant, toiling in Mr. Pickering's office and under his kind tutelage. She also gives harpsichord lessons to the sons and daughters of the local gentry.

*Mr. James Tanner,* Seaman, Coxswain to the President, and First Mate of the *Nancy B,* where he now stands at the helm.

*Mrs. Clementine Amaryllis Tanner,* wife to Mr. Tanner, newly installed in comfortable lodgings on State Street and employed at the Lawson Peabody School as serving girl and assistant cook to Mrs. Peg Mooney to help pay for said lodgings, till such time as she learns to read and write well enough to be of use to Faber Shipping. Hey, if being a chambermaid was good enough for me, it's good enough for her. Peg reports that she is cheerful, does her job well, and goes about her tasks singing, which is good.

*Mr. Solomon J. Freeman,* newly freed Person of Color, in charge of the *Evening Star* and the *Morning Star,* and the staffing and manning thereof for the purpose of setting and hauling fish and lobster traps in Boston Harbor. He has shown himself to be very good at that. He takes instruction in Language and the Classics from Miss Cantrell, which I think will be to his benefit. Furthermore, he has found outside employment with Messieurs Fennel and Bean in their theatrical productions as both musician and sometime actor. He is becoming quite the man-about-town and is enjoying to the fullest his new life as a free man. I tell him to be careful, but he doesn't listen. Oh, well, when did *I* ever listen to good advice, I ask myself, and the answer to that is seldom, if ever.

*Master Daniel Prescott,* Ship's Boy and Reluctant Scholar. He has been unofficially adopted by Faber Shipping. He is with me on this voyage, as is Jim Tanner and Higgins.

*John Thomas* and *Smasher McGee*, Seamen, Roughnecks, and the rest of the crew of the *Nancy B.*

And that about sums it up, businesswise. Now back to thoughts of Lieutenant James Emerson Fletcher. The sun is on my face and the ankles have drifted apart yet again. *Ummmmm...*

"Daydreaming, are we, Miss?" asks John Higgins, placing a cup of steaming tea in my hands and a tray of bread and cheese next to me as I stretch and lean back against the mast, reveling in both the soaring beauty of this fine early fall day and the beauty of the taut, perfectly trimmed white sails above me as the *Nancy B* rips along.

"I suppose, Higgins." I sigh. "Just counting the days, weeks, and months till we go back to London." I figure we'll cross in the spring, as soon as it's warm enough—I don't like the cold, and I sure don't like ice in the rigging. Jaimy said he'd be back in a year or less, and I do want to be there to greet him.

"I, myself, will not be averse to once again enjoying the charms of that fair city," says Higgins. "I look forward to our arrival there."

"I just bet you do, Higgins," says I, glancing at him with a knowing smirk. "Enough of this colonial life, eh?"

"Boston has had its own charms, believe me, Miss. I have made some *very* good friends over at Harvard College. Many are the nights we have passed discussing various... philosophies," he says with a sly smile playing about his lips, "but it cannot be denied that I will be glad to see London again."

"And I."

"Skipper! Ship, dead ahead!"

I leap to my feet and look up to Daniel Prescott, who's standing aloft in the crow's nest, long glass pressed to his eye.

"What is she?"

"She's just comin' up over the horizon…comin' up now…two masts…it's a brigantine. Heading north, right for us!"

I grab my own long glass from the rack next to the helm, sling it over my shoulder, and climb up the rigging to stand next to the lad. I reflect how quickly Daniel has picked up on maritime lore. I know he much prefers being out here at sea rather than in the classroom, where I force him to be when we are back on land.

Given the fact that we are well armed, considering our small size, the only real danger we face in these journeys up and down the coast of America—aside from hidden reefs, rocky shoals, and the wicked wrath of Poseidon—is from British men-of-war coming upon us and managing to get between us and the land. When we spot them on the open sea, we always run in closer to the shore where they cannot follow due to their deeper draft. It is not danger to myself that I fear from these ships, oh no, for how could they know the ragamuffin they might spy on this schooner dressed in loose cotton shirt and buckskin is none other than the no-torious criminal Jacky Faber, wanted by British Intelligence to answer charges of Piracy and Theft of Royal Property, among some other things? No, it is for my crew that I am afraid—British warships have begun boarding American merchantmen and impressing sailors into their service. In the beginning, they took only British and Irish sailors, but lately they have been seizing Americans as well. This, of course, enrages the United States government and increases the growing tension between the two countries. I fear it will end in yet another stupid war. Hasn't England got enough to do with Bonaparte and the French, without enraging the Americans, too? I will never understand men and their politics.

"It's funny, Skipper," says Daniel, glass still to his eye, "it looks like it's being sailed real sloppy... The sails are flappin' loose and her course ain't straight at all."

I bring up my glass and train it on the approaching ship.

*Hmmm*... he's right. It is strange. I can see that it's not a British warship, which is good. She is certainly leaving a weaving wake, but even so she still keeps getting closer and closer to us in spite of it. As the bark draws near, I can make out figures milling about on deck, and they look to be in a panic.

"On deck there!" I lower the glass and call down, "Look sharp! Uncover the guns and arm yourselves! It might be a trick. Jim, steer in closer to the land in case we have to run all the way in."

"Aye, Missy," sings out Jim Tanner, and the *Nancy B's* head falls off the wind and we head in toward the shore, which lies several miles off. The mystery brig won't be able to follow us very far in, should she mean to trouble us. Smasher and John Thomas trim the sails to accommodate the new course, and I see they've already got their pistols and swords strapped on. Higgins whips the canvas off our cannons and arms the matchlocks.

I lift the glass again and train it on those curious figures. There are arms upraised and waving, as if begging for help. And they seem to be...*women?*"

"What do you make of them, Danny?" I ask, scanning the ship's decks for sign of men but finding none. There is not even anyone at the wheel...'course a ship can be steered in other ways...*hmmmm*...

"I dunno. Looks like a bunch o' crazy ladies to me, Missy," says Daniel, equally mystified.

As the seeming derelict drifts closer, I'm able to make out the costumes the women wear. They seem to be dressed in the North African manner—big, loose, billowy dresses, and shawls and...*veils?*

"Maybe it's the cargo of a slaver that got lucky and over-powered its crew. Maybe it's a plague ship with a disease on board that's taken the men," I muse. I pick out a rather large woman and keep my glass trained on her. I can see her eyes now as the wind flutters the veil she wears below them and then the stiff breeze flips it up. I see then, that, in addition to the shawl and veil, the woman wears a mustache and beard. *Yikes!*

"It's a pirate!" I shriek. "Higgins, fire the bow chaser! Aim to sweep the deck!" I launch myself down the rigging, and before my feet hit the top of the hatch, there is a *crraaack!* as Higgins fires the forward swivel gun, and it launches its load of grapeshot toward the impostors on board the pirate. We can hear cries and shouts from the enemy ship.

"Ready about, Jim, let us fly!" Although we are armed with swivel guns fore and aft and two nine-pound cannons on either side, we are no match for a full-rigged brigantine.

As we swing around, I go to the after port cannon and sight along it. Smasher McGee is at the forward one.

"Fire when she bears, Smasher," I order, sighting along my own gun.

There is a *crraack!* as McGee fires, and through the smoke I can see that he has hit the pirate on her port bow, sending splinters up in a fine cloud of destruction.

"Good shooting, McGee! That'll get his attention, by God!" I shout and then pull my own lanyard. *Crrraaack!* goes my gun.

The powder smoke drifts away, and I can see that my shot goes high, but at least it clears the decks of those supposed women in distress. I see shawls and dresses being torn off and the helm being remanned. Whoever he is, he now knows he won't take us without him getting a bloody nose as well.

"Reload, lads!" I shout, and again raise my long glass to train it on this ship that has come to bother us. The sails of our pursuer tighten and a man has leaped to the wheel and the pirate's course becomes straight—straight for us, that is, and cutting off our run to the shore. Well, we can still outrun him.

Who could it be? That rascal Captain Jack Wrenn? I thought we had parted on reasonably good terms, considering he did *not* get into my pantaloons as he so ardently... well, never mind that now...Flaco Jimenez and his band of Hispanic scoundrels? I thought we, too, had parted as friends, after we had all banded together to take the Island of— Nay, it's not either of those, I realize, as I focus my glass on a well-dressed gent who has just gained the quarterdeck. *Of course...Damn!* It ain't none of those other members of the piratical brotherhood with whom I could possibly reason; nay, it is none other than Monsieur Jean Lafitte, slaver and pirate, a man who owes me big in the way of revenge.

As the *Nancy B* swings her tail around to flee from this threat, I sense Higgins's presence beside me.

"It's that damned Lafitte, Higgins," I say, snapping my telescope shut. Our after swivel gun now comes in position to fire, and I go to it.

"Ah," says the imperturbable Higgins without comment.

I sight, dog down the gun, and pull the matchlock lanyard. *Crrraack!*

But we are too far away now, and the grapeshot merely kicks up spray in front of Lafitte's bow. The gunports open up on the sides of the pirate ship and the cannon, all twenty-four of them, are run out, and we are not too far away to feel the hot breath of those guns, should they come to bear on us. It is lucky that he cannot aim them without turning to the side and hence letting us escape, should his broadside miss us on the first pass. He must content himself with his bow chaser, which he does exercise, but not to much effect. There is a puff of smoke from his bow, and his first shot goes through the foresail, leaving a neat round hole, but does nothing else in the way of damage. 'Course, an unlucky, or lucky ball, depending on how you look at it, could bring his next shot tearing over here and take my head off, but that hasn't happened yet. Still my knees start into their usual trembling that always occurs when they realize that someone is actively trying to kill me.

*Dig it out,* Nancy, *dig it out. We've got to get away, or all is lost.*

John Thomas and Smasher McGee, both excellent seamen and seeing the way of things, leave the guns and tend to the sails, aiming to get the most possible pull out of them. The sails strain and the ropes holding them groan as the sailors bend their muscles to tighten up the winches, and the winds and good seamanship be thanked, the space between Lafitte and us grows ever more broad.

I breathe out a cautious sigh of relief—we are going to get away, and we didn't even have to dump the cargo.

"How did he know where to find us, Higgins?" I ask.

"Well," begins Higgins, musing on the question, "you did buy this boat from his boatyard, so he would know about that. And then we have made several trips, so it would not be difficult for him to pick up news of you from the various ports we have visited. He is not stupid and he does have his spies and informants, else he would not have prospered as he has. With your...uh...flamboyant ways, you leave quite a visible trail behind you. Our last visit comes to mind, in that tavern in St. Croix, when—"

"Higgins, I was just having a bit of fun with some of my mates from the old freebooting days. But I take your point."

"And, you must admit, Miss, you have tweaked his nose several times, and he owes you a few in return."

"Well, he had it comin'," says I, putting the glass back to my eye. "There's nothing I hate worse than a slaver." I see that Lafitte has been joined on his quarterdeck by his brother Pierre. He has a long glass of his own, and it is trained on me, I know. They seem to be in a jovial mood. *Well, Messieurs, don't count your Jackys till they are caught.*

"Daniel, let's load the after gun with a shot, if you please."

"Aye, Skipper," says the boy. He undogs it and points the barrel of the swivel gun skyward. He swabs it out and drops in the powder charge, then rams in the wad, followed by the ball, as he has been relentlessly trained. It's only a nine-pound ball, but it might cause a bit of trouble to our pursuer. Another wad rammed in and the lad says, "Ready, Captain."

Lafitte does, indeed, owe me a few. Not only did I steal four hundred and fifty of his prime slaves and set them free on the coast of South America—no, not just that—he also got his cheeks, both upper and lower, peppered with several whiffs of rock salt from the guns of my *Belle of the Golden West* that day on the New Orleans levee. Then, to rub even more salt into his wounds, I fleeced him the next night at cards, taking enough money from him and his brother to buy the ship on which I now stand. It was at the gaming tables at the House of the Rising Sun, the brothel and gambling den where I was so recently employed, and my success at cards was not entirely due to luck.

I crank the gun up to its highest elevation, judge the distance and angle, and then pull the lanyard.

*Crraaack!*

We watch the flight of the ball and are pleased to see it arc high in the air and then descend.

Jean and Pierre skip to the side as the ball crashes into the deck not far from their very well-shod feet. I hear Jean Lafitte bark a command and the ship begins to turn away from us.

"Ha! He's running! We scared him off!" I exult. "Look at

him fly! Go to the Devil, Jean Lafitte, you miserable bastard!" I yell, all proud and smug with fists on hips and looking aft at the fleeing pirate.

I take another look through my glass and am surprised to see the Brothers Lafitte smiling and shaking hands. *Hmmm. Why're they doing that? I've slipped away from them yet again; they should be unhappy...*

Perhaps sensing that I'm watching him, Jean sweeps off his hat and bows low to me.

"Oh, yes? Well, I'll give you a bow, you poor excuse for a buccaneer what can't even take a poor little schooner. Try this!" And I whip around and put my hands on the hem of my skirt, fully intending to bend over and pull it up and present my backside to him.

But I don't do that at all, for there, directly in front of us, is a forty-four-gun frigate, and even before I can make out the colors she flies, I recognize her instantly as a British warship.

*Damn! He's what chased off the Lafittes, not us and our puny guns! And he's edging between us and the shore! Damn!*

"Jim! Hard left," I screech. "Don't let him get between us and the shore!"

But it is no use—the Sailing Master of the frigate must be very skilled, it seems to me, as he manages to keep the larger ship leeward of us, and so I know we must make a run for the open sea.

"Prepare to jibe!" I shout, "Jibe, ho!" and the *Nancy B* swings her tail across the direction of wind and the sail booms swing over and come to on the opposite tack with a *snap!* that leans her way over on her port side.

What the hell to do? I don't know…Maybe she wants nothing to do with us? Maybe… "Dip the colors, Daniel," I order without much hope.

Daniel flies up the mast and lowers the waving Stars and Stripes six feet in salute. We watch anxiously for the return recognition.

The warship does not return our dip. Instead there is a deep *Boooommm* and smoke puffs from her bow chaser as she puts one across our bow. *Damn, damn, damn, and double damn! She means to stop and board us!*

We gain some distance, but she comes doggedly after us. She's bigger and heavier than us, but she has a greater press of sail. Still, I think we could outrun her if we weren't hauling all that damned granite. If we were headed north with our sugar, we could fairly quickly throw the kegs of molasses overboard and so lighten our load, but we can't move the stones that easily. *Damn!*

"What do you suppose she wants, Higgins? We certainly look innocent enough, don't we?"

"My thought is that she is probably looking to impress sailors," says Higgins, with his usual reserve. "Or could it be possible that…*Hmmm*…I have a bad feeling about this. Miss, please go down and change into Jacques. With your permission, I will act as Captain during this encounter, and it is to be hoped that all will end well."

Cursing myself for being inattentive to whatever else was happening on the sea while we were engaged with Lafitte, I throw myself down the hatchway and into my cabin. I'm already out of my buckskin skirt before I go through the door. Hanging on a hook on the wall is a cotton bag that I call my Jacques Sack. I open it and hurl its contents onto my bed. First, I jam my legs into the trousers, pull them up, tuck in my shirt, and tie the waistband. Then the curly black wig goes on, covering my still-short hair, and with my tanned skin and the battered straw hair I cram on my head, we have Jacques Antoine Fabierre, poor little Creole boy, not worthy of anyone's notice.

I hear another long *boooommmm.* I jam a smelly old corncob pipe twixt my teeth and run back on deck.

*Damn!* The warship is even closer! I look up into our rigging and see that we have every possible scrap of sail set.

I join Higgins on the quarterdeck, next to Jim Tanner at the wheel.

"Missy, I'm so sorry," says Jim, his face red with anger and shame. "I should have been looking forward, I should have. I was on the helm, I should have—"

"Put it out of your mind, Jim," I say. "We *all* were looking aft when this snuck up on us. The blame is all mine."

The ship looms ever closer.

"Should we even try to dump the cargo?" I ask of Higgins, who has his glass to his eye, trained on the other ship.

"I think not, Miss," he says, bringing down the scope. "It would only make us look more suspicious to them."

"Suspicious? Why, we are honest merchants, what's suspicious about that?"

"I think there is more to this than that. This ship was just too conveniently positioned."

"What do you mean, Higgins?"

"I suspect, Miss, that this is a very well-placed trap. It is all much too neat. I suspect that you have been set up."

"How so?" ask I, bewildered.

Higgins takes a deep breath, lets it out, and then explains, "Jean Lafitte, owing you for many past depredations against him and his company, has many contacts in the Caribbean world, including some of the British in their many colonies. He learns that you are wanted by Naval Intelligence so he probably contacted those people to tell them where you are likely to be found. You will recall that the agents Flashby and Moseley were dispatched out of Kingston? So, he decides to forego the pleasure of dispatching you himself so that you can be brought to bay at the hands of the British and, ultimately, hanged. He even volunteers his ship to chase you into the net."

A chill runs up my spine. "Surely all this cannot be because of me, Higgins."

"I hope I am mistaken, Miss, and no, do not put your long glass to your eye again, as they are watching us most avidly from their quarterdeck. It would be best if you would go over with Daniel and assume your role as a ship's boy, for we are sure to be boarded soon."

Realizing the wisdom of this, I put down my glass and go over to stand by Daniel Prescott, who sits next to the forward mast.

"Sit down by me, Missy, and put the pipe back in your mouth."

I slide down and put the foul thing back between my teeth and settle back to await whatever Fate has in store for me. *Damn!*

I believe I hear the rush of water off the warship's bow nearby before I hear the call, "Bring your ship under our lee!" bellowed through a megaphone from the quarterdeck of the frigate.

Jim Tanner glances over at me.

"Do it, Jim," I say, and he throws the wheel over. The sails slack and we are taken. It is naught but a few moments till I hear the sound of the grappling hooks come across the rails of my dear *Nancy B* to dig into her and drag her alongside the man-of-war.

"Strike your sails!" shouts the voice from the other quarterdeck, and John Thomas and Smasher McGee look to me. I nod, and they loose the buntlines and our sails come billowing down to lie quiet on our deck.

"Prepare to be boarded!"

We are as prepared as any ship is when it is about to be violated by another against its will. There is the sound of many feet, many boots striking our spotless decks as sailors and officers from the other ship swing down upon us. The captain of the frigate gazes down on us from his quarterdeck high over our heads.

"This is an act of war," bellows Higgins from our own quarterdeck. "You may be sure this will be reported to the highest authorities!"

"Be still, Sir," says the captain of the other vessel. "We are merely looking for English deserters as, you know, of course, is our right."

"Your right as you see it, Sir, not as we see it." Higgins is managing an acceptable American accent—he is, after all, the only male on this ship who is British and who has actually served in the Royal Navy, and it would not be good for them to find that out.

"Be that as it may," says the captain, turning to one of his officers who now stands on our deck, "Mr. Fleming! Search

20

their lower decks! Bring up anyone you find there! Examine the cargo for any contraband!"

Fleming, a young lieutenant, takes two sailors with him and heads down our hatch. While they conduct their search, the other officer addresses us.

"Who are you?" he demands of Higgins. The officer's back is to me, but still I keep my head down, the brim of my hat pulled low over my eyes.

"We, Sir," says Higgins, seemingly full of righteous indignation, "are the schooner *Nancy B. Alsop*, out of Boston and duly registered and documented in that city. I am her Captain, John Higgins, and this is James Tanner, First Mate. We carry a crew of two able-bodied seamen, John Thomas there on the right, and Finnegan McGee on the left, in addition to two ship's boys. That's all."

A man, surely the Bo'sun of the frigate since he wears the hat and jacket of one who fills that post and carries a knobby, a short, thick piece of rope, knotted at the end to use for whacking poor sailors about, confronts Smasher McGee.

"McGee, eh?" sneers the Bo'sun. "So yer Irish. Ever served on one o' 'is Majesty's ships, Mick?"

"Nay, yer honor," says McGee. "Though me sainted mither dropped me on me head when I was a wee'un and I grew up sort of thickheaded, I was never quite *that* stupid."

*Oh, be careful, McGee, you might well end up servin' under that very same Bo'sun's Mate this day!*

The Bo'sun gives McGee a slight smile as he knows he'll be gettin' even for that later, and then moves on to John Thomas.

"And what about you?" he demands, thrusting his knobby under John Thomas's bearded chin. "In what pigsty was you born, and have you ever deserted from a British ship?"

"Ah, no, Sir," replies John Thomas. "I was born and brought up on the island of Nantucket as a freeborn American. I was taught at my own mother's knee to hate three things: Mortal Sin, False-hearted Women, and the British Navy!"

*Ah, lads...*

The Bo'sun merely nods and says, "We're going to have a bit of fun with you two, ain't we?"

The search party that had gone below returns.

"Nothing, Captain," says Mr. Fleming. "Only stones as ballast. No other people."

"You checked thoroughly? You sure there are no others?" demands another voice from the quarterdeck of our captor. The voice sounds oddly familiar....

"Yes, Sir. Quite sure. Nothing but ship's stores and rocks."

"Then you will let us on our way, gentlemen," says Higgins. "We thank you for your kind help in chasing off the pirate. If you will be so kind as to ungrapple us—"

"Not so fast there," says that other voice, and from under the brim of my hat, I see that yet another officer's legs have appeared on our deck. "I will give a final inspection."

"I hope that Naval Intelligence did not pay too much for the information on the dastardly fugitive supposedly hiding on this little craft," says the Captain from above, obviously enjoying the discomfiture of what is sure to be an Intelligence Officer. This gets a laugh from the other officers, but it does not get a laugh from me. My own uneasiness increases tenfold—I am sweating bullets from under my hat, my wig, my vest, and any other part of me.

"Sir, one moment, if you please," says the newly arrived officer.

"Well, make it quick, for my lady and my children await me in London, and I would fain be off to join them!"

*Hear, hear,* says a chorus of men from the other ship.

"Yes, Mr. Bliffil, and make it very quick," adds the Captain, turning to his First Mate. "Mr. Bennett, make ready to disengage!"

*Bliffil?*

*Oh, no! Could it be?* I cautiously peer out from under the brim of my straw hat. *It is! It's him, the bully of the* Dolphin! *And how bloody perfect for a piece of dirt like him to end up in the Intelligence Branch of their Service!*

"I figure we'll take these two here," says the Bo'sun, pointing his knobby at John Thomas and Smasher. "They looks like they's *real* anxious to serve the King. And we'll take the helmsman, too. We can always use another one o' those."

I'm about to leap to my feet to protest this outrage, but Higgins beats me to it.

"Sir, you cannot! He is newly married, and his poor wife will be left alone and penniless! She will be turned out into the street!"

"Can't you just see my poor heart a-breakin', then?" The Bo'sun grins. He gestures to his men. "Take them."

"Wait," says Bliffil, who has been peering about during all this. He shoots his eyes over at Daniel and me. "Those boys—"

*Uh-oh.*

"You two! Stand up!" he orders, striding over in front of us, and Daniel and I slowly get to our feet.

He looks Daniel over and then shoves him aside to look me over much more carefully.

"What is your name, boy?" he asks, looming over me.

It's all I can do not to whip out me shiv and plunge it into the belly of the man who beat me and scarred me when I was but a little kid, but I don't do it. What I do is say, *"Je ne parle pas anglais, Monsieur,"* and duck my head.

It doesn't work. He reaches over and knocks off my hat.

"Look at me, boy!" he barks, and flicks the back of his fingers across my face, stinging my cheek. I look at him, my heart sinking as I see the smile begin to snake across his face when his eyes spot my white eyebrow. "I believe the information we gained, Captain Hudson, will turn out to be quite accurate after all."

With that he whips out his hand and yanks off my wig. *Oh my God, I am lost!*

"Well, damn me if it ain't a white boy!" says the Captain, astonished at seeing my sandy blond stubble.

"Not a boy, Sir," says Bliffil with great satisfaction, "but rather a girl, a very wicked girl we have been seeking for a long time. This is the wanted pirate and criminal Jacky Faber, and we have her at last!"

"Looks more like a child to me," says the Captain, doubtfully. "How do you know it's her?"

At that I put on the poor waif look, trying to look as big eyed, knock-kneed, and helpless as I could.

"Oh, I know her all right," says Bliffil. "I was on the *Dolphin* with her when I was a midshipman and she was a grotty little slut posing as a ship's boy." His eyes become glittering slits as he peers down at me quivering below. "She laid herself under half the crew before she was discovered. 'Tuppence a Lay' she was called, before I found her out and had her put off."

*Lies, all lies!* I cry out to myself, but I say nothing. I figure this is the time to burst out crying, and I do it.

The Captain, who I am figuring for a sympathetic sort when it comes to bawling young girls, asks, "But how can you be sure, Mr. Bliffil?"

"The wretch has a tattoo on her belly, Sir," says Bliffil. "I believe that will satisfy you as to her identity." With that he reaches out, grabs me by my shirtfront, and hauls me up before him. He puts the thumb of his other hand inside the waistband and begins to slide my trousers down.

That's when Daniel Prescott, who has been standing behind us, swings his arm back and brings his belaying pin down on the back of Bliffil's head. "You get your hands off her, you dirty bastard!" he shouts and lifts his arm to hit him again and that sets it off.

*Better to die fighting than to die on the scaffold at Newgate!*

John Thomas slams his fist into the face of the Bo'sun, who goes down, his nose spurting blood. The Bo'sun drops his knobby, which Smasher McGee picks up and uses to flail away at all those on board who do not belong to our company, and he is deadly accurate with the thing. Soon there are men strewn all about the deck holding their heads in their hands.

I take a more practical approach in this melee. Seeing Bliffil down on his knees, trying to shake off Daniel's blows,

I whip out my shiv, jump on him from behind, and wrap my legs about his middle. I take a fistful of his hair and pull back his head, laying the blade against his throat.

"You move, Bliffil, and the only reward you'll get is the one you got comin' on Judgment Day. You understand?"

A strangled gurgle is all I get from him, but it is enough.

I look over to see that John Thomas has picked up the stunned Bo'sun's Mate and lifted him up over his head. "Give my regards to Davy Jones, pig," he shouts as he pitches him over the side.

As the Bo'sun's splash is heard, the Captain shouts, "Enough of this! Boarding Party away!" and sailors and marines from the frigate swarm over the side and onto our deck. Smasher continues to flail away with the knobby and men fall, but I can see that all is lost—there are just too many of them.

"Brothers!" I shout to my crew. "Stop fighting! It is no use! Captain! Listen to me!"

My crew stops fighting, and there is a sudden silence as I address the Captain. "Let us go or I will cut his throat."

The Captain considers this and then shakes his head. "No, that cannot be. You are a wanted fugitive, and it cannot be said that Captain Hannibal Hudson let you slip away. No, if we have to fire on you and sink you, then I am sure that Lieutenant Bliffil will thank God with his dying breath that he was able to do his duty. Gunner's Mate, are all the guns primed and ready to fire?"

"Yes, Sir."

"Well, then, prepare to fire, upon my order."

We are not as high as the other ship, but we are high

enough to look squarely down the barrels of the loaded cannon. I can smell the burning of the matchlock.

"Wait," I say, not loosening my grip on Bliffil's hair nor relaxing my legs from about his waist, nor taking the blade from his neck. "Let my men and my ship go and I will give myself up."

"No, Missy, don't do it!" cries Daniel. "We'll fight them! We'll—"

A Royal Marine now has him by the scruff of his neck, and he gives the lad a vigorous shake, but still the boy struggles on.

I see the Captain, who I now am able to observe is a large man with long blond hair tied back with a blue ribbon, considering this. He thinks, and then he says, "Agreed. Now, just how shall we accomplish this transfer of female fugitive and Intelligence Officer?"

*Hmmm.* The man has a sense of humor, and I store that fact away.

"You will give me your word as an officer and gentleman that you agree to my terms," I say. "And I will release this sack of dung and then board your ship as your prisoner. Do you so give me your word?"

"I do. Now, let's get on with this. Mr. Curtis, will you see to fishing out our very damp Bo'sun's Mate? Mr. Bennett, make all preparations for getting under way again. London awaits and I think all will agree that it holds many more charms than does this desolate stretch of ocean."

*Hear, hear* is heard once again. These men are anxious to get back home.

I release Bliffil and jump back from him, so as to stay out

of his reach. He, as expected, spins around and makes a grab for me, and I dance back away from him and hold my shiv between us.

"I will be your captive when I set foot on that ship, but not before, Bliffil," I say. "Now get off my boat!"

"Ha, ha! Mr. Bliffil," crows the Captain, "it seems your little bee has a stinger! For your own safety you must come back aboard. Don't worry, our marines will see to your fearsome captive!"

There are roars of laughter from the man-of-war and Bliffil reddens and says, just loud enough for me to hear, "Oh, I will get you for this, slut, and for what you did to me back on the *Dolphin,* oh, yes, I will." And he climbs back aboard the other ship, the ship whose name I do not yet know but which will be my home for many, many days. Perhaps, even, my last home.

Two Marines come up to me and one of them takes me by the arm. "Give me the knife and come along," he says.

"Please wait a moment, Corporal. Higgins, if you would get my seabag?"

Higgins nods and goes below and returns with not only my seabag but also his.

"We are ready. Lead on, soldier," says Higgins. *Higgins, you can't...*

"Hold on there," says Bliffil, upon seeing that Higgins means to go with me. "Just the girl. Not the man. She cannot be allowed any allies on board."

"Why not?" asks the Captain.

"Sir, she has her ways of bending men of low degree to her will. She has been in command of two ships, and one of them was a British warship, the *Wolverine!*"

"*That*," says the Captain, pointing at me, "was in command of one of His Majesty's ships? Impossible, Sir!"

"The books, Sir, the stories that are told throughout the fleet," pleads Bliffil. "She is that very one!"

"I never believed those stories," snorts the Captain, "but very well. The Intelligence Branch must be served, I suppose. Bring her aboard alone."

I am shoved forward. "Sergeant, will you take my bag and see that my knife goes back in it? Thank you."

The Marine looks up to the Captain, who nods and says, "Yes, her bag, too. Maybe she has something presentable in there that she can wear on the voyage."

"Good-bye, Higgins," I say, an unbidden tear working its way down my cheek. "You have been so good to me."

"Good-bye for now, Miss," he replies, loud enough for the Captain to hear. "Rest assured there will be an army of lawyers on the dock in London when you arrive."

"Be that as it may," says the Captain, "but we are wasting this fine breeze. Get her up here and let us be gone. Is the Bo'sun back aboard? Good."

"Good-bye, lads," I say to the rest of my crew. "Do not worry about me. I have a way of getting through things like this."

They stand in a row, Jim Tanner furiously wiping his nose that's still oozing blood from the fight, John Thomas and Smasher nursing bloody knuckles, and young Daniel glaring at my captors with pure hatred in his crying eyes.

"Good-bye, Missy."

I turn my own tear-streaked face from them and climb up onto the deck of the man-of-war.

"Cast off those lines. Get back aboard, the rest of you!"

roars the Captain. "Goddammit, could you be any slower? Mr. Fleming, you have the con! Get us on our way! Christ, at this rate we'll never round Margate!"

"Topmen aloft to make sail!" shouts the Lieutenant. "Throw off those lines! Move it!"

The deck explodes with activity—orders are shouted, men race aloft to drop the sails, gangs of sailors haul on the buntlines to raise the heavy canvas, all an ordered chaos that is very familiar, and true, very dear to me. How sad that I will be here as prisoner and not as seaman, on what will very probably prove to be my last voyage on this earth. Oh, well, I'm not dead yet.

I am, however, drawn up and forced to stand before the Captain. Bliffil appears beside me and grabs me by the arm. "Tears, is it?" he rasps in my ear. "From one such as you?" He flings me back to the Sergeant of Marines. "Let's get her below and into the brig! I will search her there!"

"Hold on, Mr. Bliffil," says the Captain. He has been looking up and examining the set of sail and now, seemingly satisfied with what he sees, brings his gaze once again on me. "You will *what*?"

"You saw with your own eyes, Sir, that she had a knife up her sleeve. See, here is where she keeps it," says Bliffil, grabbing my arm and pulling back my sleeve, exposing my forearm sheath. "I must search her at once for other weapons. For the safety of everyone aboard."

"She will be searched, Mr. Bliffil," says the Captain, "but not by you." He turns to an officer standing next to him and says, "Mr. Bennett, please send for Dr. Sebastian and have him meet us down in the brig."

Mr. Bennett, who seems to be a very senior Lieutenant and who is the First Mate, says, "Aye, Captain," and nods to a young midshipman who scurries away and down a hatch to no doubt fetch the ship's surgeon.

"All right," says the Captain with a final look at the sails, "let us go below and show this...creature...to its new quarters."

As I am led across the deck to the hatchway, I steal one last glance across the sea at the *Nancy B. Alsop,* my gallant little schooner, its sails tight and its Faber Shipping, World-wide, banner snapping bravely in the breeze.

*Oh, how happy I was not an hour ago!*

# Chapter 2

We are below and I am in the brig, while the others stand outside. I note that the cage is constructed differently from the usual ones in which I've been jailed. This one has been built into the bow of the ship three levels down, such that it is a triangle, with two of its walls being the leaking hull of the ship, and the third made of thick wood with a barred door in its center. There are the usual amenities—a hard bench, a moldy blanket, a chamber pot, and that's it. The door has not yet been closed. There is a lantern hung by the hatchway, shedding its dim light on this dismal place. I seat myself on the bench and wait.

Bliffil has been going through my seabag, uttering an occasional *Aha!* The two Marines take their posts at either side of the cage door, and we are soon joined by the aforementioned Dr. Sebastian. He is a small, dark-haired, and rather sour-looking man of about thirty-five years, and he carries with him a black bag containing, I expect, medical instruments.

"You will examine this person, Doctor," says the Captain, "for proof of gender—I'm still not convinced we have not captured a wayward boy—distinguishing marks, state of health, and...er...cleanliness, and all that. When you are finished, bring her to my cabin with your report. Mr. Bliffil, if you are quite through, please leave."

"Sir, I must protest," sputters Bliffil.

"And, you, Sir, must do as you are told," says the Captain, with a cold edge to his voice, making it quite plain that he is not used to his orders being questioned. The Captain leaves, trailed by a still-sputtering and protesting Bliffil.

The Doctor turns to the Marines. "This would be better done in my surgery, as the light here is too dim. The orlop is one deck up. Bring her there." He turns and leaves.

The Sergeant reaches in and pulls me to the hatchway. "Don't try nothin', you."

I don't try nothin', knowing it would avail me little. I meekly follow the Marine up the stairs to the next level and into another space.

It is the orlop, the surgery, and the Doctor was right—it is better lighted. There are a number of lamps on the walls, and he goes around turning them up. The place gets even brighter, the light glinting off the many surgical tools hung on pegs—saws and cleavers and sharp knives that I know are for the hacking off of destroyed limbs after a battle. There is also a microscope, next to which are specimens, pieces of something or other, and next to them some crude drawings of the same. There is also a large, flat operating table.

"Please remove your garments, Miss," requests the Doctor, taking off his jacket and hanging it on a hook. "And get up on the table. Sergeant, Corporal, you will both turn around and face the wall."

33

Tears of despair begin to pour out of my eyes, as I realize the true hopelessness of my situation. Grieving for my lost future, my lost dreams, my lost life, I begin to unbutton my vest.

It is some time later and I am again clothed, this time in my Lawson Peabody black dress that the Doctor has kindly allowed me to take from my seabag after we were done with the examination. I have also donned another of my wigs—probably the most sedate one and the one that most closely matched the color of my actual hair. A little powder here and there, my black mantilla draped around my bare shoulders, and I am ready to be paraded in front of the Captain.

"Should we bind her hands, Sir?" asks one of the Marines, after he has been allowed to turn his face from the wall.

"I don't think that will be necessary, Sergeant," answers the Doctor drily, "as she is rather small, and not very intimidating."

The Marine reddens and says, "Of course, Sir. Come along, Miss. Doctor, if you will."

The four of us troop up two more ladders and gain the upper deck. The sun is setting and I look across the sea for the *Nancy B*, but I do not see her. *Ah, well, it is better that I do not, I suppose, as she is part of my past and not part of whatever short life that might lie before me.*

The Sergeant strides across the deck and addresses the Officer of the Deck. "Beg your pardon, Sir, but the Captain ordered that she be brought up to see him when she was... presentable."

*Not spread out on a table, you mean,* I snarl to myself.

Lieutenant Fleming comes down from the quarterdeck and knocks lightly on a door immediately beneath the upper deck. There is a murmur from within and Fleming says, "Sir, the girl."

More mumbles and grumbles and Mr. Fleming opens the door and Dr. Sebastian and I go in. The Marines stay outside and take positions to either side of the door.

The Captain is seated at his desk, looking through some documents. Bliffil stands next to him, and I suspect that he has supplied the Captain with those papers. I look about the cabin—its semicircle of windows facing aft, its rich woods and other appointments that so very much remind me of my own cabins on both the *Wolverine* and the *Emerald*. I heave a sigh for those lost days as I stand in front of the desk, the Lawson Peabody Look firmly in place—lips together, teeth apart, head held high as if balancing a book upon it, and eyes half hooded in a look of languid, disinterested disdain.

"So," says the Captain, continuing to peruse the sheets of paper without looking up. "Jacky Faber, Ship's Boy, HMS *Dolphin,* made Midshipman on same *Dolphin.* Discovered to be female and placed as student at the Lawson Peabody School for Young Girls in Boston, expelled, reinstated. Involved in fire that burns down a good part of that same city. Member of crew of the whaler *Pequod.* Taken on HMS *Wolverine* as Midshipman by apparently insane commanding officer. Made Acting Lieutenant J. M. Faber, by same lunatic, and becomes Master and Commander of HMS *Wolverine* upon his death and performs in that capacity for fifteen days, and takes four prizes. Evades capture for misappropriation of Crown property, to wit: one of the four prize ships. Becomes Captain of the pirate *Emerald*, eventually sunk by aforementioned *Wolverine*. Captured and escapes yet again. And finally, involved in some mischief of late on the Mississippi River in America that caused great grief to several of our fine Intelligence Agents." The Captain picks up the papers and taps them into a neat order. "Quite a résumé. How do you plead?"

He looks up at me and is visibly shocked by my change of appearance.

"Guilty, Sir," says I, my nose in the air, "of all except the piracy charge. When I sailed on the *Emerald*, I carried a Letter of Marque from Lord Henry Dundas, First Lord of the Admiralty. That my own country saw fit to betray me and brand me a pirate, well, I can't say anything to that."

He looks me up and down and says nothing for a while. Then he barks out a short laugh. "Ha! Quite remarkable, I must say. No longer the Creole urchin, eh?"

*Not Creole, but still an urchin, Sir.*

"I do not deny my origins, Sir."

"Ahem. Well, then. Doctor, your report, please."

The surgeon, who has been calmly pouring himself a glass from the Captain's bottle of brandy, takes a sip and says, "No other weapons concealed on her person. In good health, cleanly muscled, and in excellent physical condition. About sixteen years old, as she herself maintains. Small tattoo of anchor on right iliac crest. Evidence of lower ribs having been onetime broken, making her waist appear uncommonly narrow. Scar under left eyebrow, which has caused the brow hair to grow out white. Several other scars scattered about, the two most notably being one high on the left thigh that she reports to be from a sword thrust taken while escaping from the slaver *Bloodhound,* and one on left buttock from a flying splinter received during an encounter with a prize on the privateer *Emerald.* No venereal disease or body lice, and, as a matter of fact"—and here he pauses to take another sip of the brandy before continuing—"she is *virginalis intacta,* if, after all that, you can believe it, Sir."

"*Ummm,*" mutters the Captain. "Even more remarkable."

My face flares up red upon hearing this account of the examination. I don't like people poking at me and my parts if I ain't the one what invited the poking in the first place. But, even so, I must admit the Doctor was kind. He was gentle and professional, even when gently nudging my knees apart.

"Well, then, ahem," says the Captain, "I hope you will be comfortable tonight, Miss. We will discuss the terms of your confinement tomorrow."

"Thank you, Captain…" and I let it hang.

"Oh, yes," he says, slightly flustered, and rising from his chair. "Forgive me. There never is an excuse for bad manners, is there? I am Captain Hannibal Hudson, Commander of HMS *Dauntless,* at your service, Miss."

I deliver my deepest curtsy, and as I rise from it I look up from under my eyelashes and I say, "Thank you for your courtesy, Captain Hudson. I trust I may place the safety of both my self and my virtue in your protection during this voyage?"

"Captain, I must protest any kindness or courtesy you might be inclined to give to this female," blusters Bliffil. "I must point out—"

"What you must do, Mr. Bliffil, is be quiet," says the Captain. "You lied to me, Mr. Bliffil, and I do not like being lied to, even from an officer who is but a passenger and not part of my crew."

"Lied, Sir? I—"

"You said that when she was on the *Dolphin* she was the Ship's Main Pump, as it were, and physical evidence proves she was not that at all, is this not true, Mr. Bliffil?"

"But, but—," sputters Bliffil.

"You are excused, Mr. Bliffil. And, in the future, please remember who is the Captain of this ship, British Intelligence notwithstanding. And do not lie to me, ever again."

Bliffil manages a jerky bow, glares at me, and leaves the cabin.

The Captain watches him depart with an expression of deep disdain on his face and then he turns to me.

"Do not fear, Miss Faber. You will be treated civilly while you are on board the *Dauntless*, no matter what may be the nature of your crimes against the Crown. I bid you good night."

I bow my head in acknowledgment of this kindness. "Thank you, Sir. Good night."

"Doctor, please call in the Sergeant," says Captain Hudson.

He does it and the Marine comes in and I am taken back down to the dank brig. The door is opened and I am locked inside.

I lie down on the bench and pull up the rough blanket and give myself over to the deepest despair. As the tears begin again, I feel that I am lost this time for good and ever, that there is nothing but horror that waits for me, not Jaimy, not happiness, nothing but a hempen noose.

But, as sleep comes on, as it always does, even unto the condemned, I think I hear something whispered low from outside. This causes my eyes to open again and makes me lift my head to listen...*what?*...I could be mistaken. No, it's probably just the creak of the timbers, the chafing of the running gear, but, then...did I really hear it?

*Welcome back, Puss.*

# Chapter 3

Once again I wake in a cell, stiff and unhappy. *I should be used to it by now,* I think, groaning as I rise to meet the day. At least this brig, not being an open cage like the others I have been in, affords a little more privacy. 'Course it's very dark—the only light filtering through the bars of the door is that of the lantern hanging by the sentry. I have to feel around for the chamber pot.

After I have accomplished that, I peer through the bars and see the sentry, half asleep, leaning against the bulkhead. I have heard them change the guard every four hours through the night, just like the watches stood on deck. This latest guardsman looks as if he is profoundly seasick as well as tired, and it is not surprising, as we have been going through some rough seas. Since the jail is built as far forward as possible, we bear the brunt of the ship's heaving up and down and crashing into the heavy waves right outside the three-inch planks of its hull. The boards have been groaning and twisting and the seawater has been seeping in through the cracks and streaming down the brig walls, and as we are down in the depths of the ship, close to the bilges, it stinks, too. The dampness causes my undergarments to stick to me in a most uncomfortable way, and I know that if they keep me locked up in here for the entire voyage, a mortal sickness might well save the Crown the bother of hanging me. I wrap the soggy blanket around myself and sit back down on the bench, truly and completely miserable.

Then I hear footfalls on the upper hatchway, but I notice that the Marine does not. I shake off my misery. I have been in worse fixes than this, and if this proves to be my last predicament, then so be it. *Get on with it, girl.*

"Marine!" I hiss, saving him from a flogging. "Wake up! Someone's coming!"

The soldier shakes his head and snaps to, just as Bliffil comes down into the brig area.

"I am here to interrogate you," he says, and though I cannot see his face in the gloom I can hear the smile in his voice. "I have many questions."

"You go to Hell, Bliffil," I say. "I know what 'interrogation' means to an Intelligence Officer. You are here to beat me again—I remember well what you considered to be sport back on the *Dolphin*."

"Hmmm, we'll see about that, won't we? Private, open this door."

The guard, looking rather splendid in his scarlet jacket with the crossed white belts and the pipe-clay buttons, hits a brace and says, not too happily, "I'm sorry, Sir, but the Captain left strict orders that the door is to be opened only on his direct order. Sir."

Bliffil spins around and barks, "What? I am Lieutenant Bliffil and I order you to open that door right now or your back will pay for it!"

"I fear my Major and my Captain much more than I fear you, Sir, and I have my orders," answers the Marine, firmly.

*Good for you, lad.*

"Ain't so easy ordering men of real honor around, is it, Bliffil?" I sneers, getting up from the bench and putting my face to the bars. "Do the people on this ship know that you were put off the *Dolphin* for cowardice shown during an encounter with an enemy? Do they?"

*They will now, by God. If the Marine sentry does not spread the word, those others who I know are listening outside these bulkheads will do it. There are no secrets on a ship.*

Bliffil puts his own face to the bars. "You little piece of gutter trash. You have caused nothing but damage to my reputation since the moment you connived your way onto a Royal Navy ship, and I *shall* repay you. I *will* watch you hang."

I shove my face up to his. "If I do hang, Bliffil, I will leave this world knowin' I did what I could to lead a virtuous life, tryin' to do my best for my Service, my country, and my friends. What will you have to say when *your* time comes, you slimy pig?"

"Pah!" he spits and turns to leave. "We'll see about this, and we'll see about you, too, Private!"

I work up a gob of spit, myself, and launch it at his retreating back. "Go find some little boys to beat up, you cowardly bastard! I'm sure there are some ship's boys upon this vessel that will slake your thirst to hurt and shame and defile!"

The hatch door closes and we are left in silence.

After a while I ask, "Are we to have no breakfast?" Even though I am caught and probably condemned, I still get hungry.

"The watch is about to change, Miss," replies the Marine. "I'm sure they'll have something for you soon. Uh...and...umm...Miss...thank you for...you know..."

"It was nothing, Private...If I might know your name...?"

"Jonathan Morris, Miss."

"Ah, Jonathan Morris, a fine name indeed. No, we all get sleepy sometimes, especially on a boring watch such as this, and you are not to be blamed. However, if you get into any trouble over this thing with your Major..."

"Stebbins, Miss. Major Stebbins."

"Then you will refer him to me, and I will give him an exact account of what happened here. Believe me, Jonathan, you did your duty, and you shall not be whipped on account of Mr. Bliffil."

"Thank you, Miss. That eases my worry a great deal."

There is a clatter at the hatchway and a sailor, a cook's helper from the look of his dress, comes in bearing a tray.

"Under the door," says Jonathan, and the steward slides the tray through an opening under my cage door, and then leaves.

"Will you take the lantern over here so that I might be able to see what I am to eat? Thank you, Jonathan. I hope you know that your presence gives me comfort in my hour of need." A little maidenly sob and sniffle and that's it for now. *Don't overdo it.*

I stoop down to pick up the tray and sit back on the bench with it on my lap. There is a cup of steaming hot tea, and I take a sip of it and am surprised to taste the sugar that's in it. *Ummm...*it is very good, the best thing I have tasted in the last day or so. I put down the cup and turn my attention to the bowl. There is a spoon next to it, and I run it through the contents of said bowl. It is, of course, burgoo, which is oatmeal mush blended with whatever is at hand, in this case some chopped carrots and several pieces of pretty lean pork. There is even a layer of maple syrup on top and, wonder of wonders, a fresh biscuit to the side. I waste no time in getting it down, and it is very, very good. No bugs in the biscuit, either, far as I can tell.

*This is not the usual fare*, I think, putting the now licked-clean bowl, cup, spoon, and tray back under the door. Could it be that I have a friend aboard?

I see a snout poking up through a crack in the floorboards—a rat, attracted by the smell of my breakfast. I take off my right shoe and fling it at the rat and his nose disappears, but I know he will be back along with many of his friends and soon the little buggers will be feasting on *me* when I am asleep. The thought gives me shivers—between the rats, the damp, and the cold, I will not live to attend my own execution. I must get out of here. *Think, dammit!*

I lean back against the front bulkhead next to the door, the only dry wall in the cell, to do just that. *Think!*

I force myself back to yesterday, to that moment when I last saw the *Nancy B.* Despite my inner turmoil at that time, while I was watching my life falling apart before me, I remember looking over and seeing…what? Ah, the crane swinging over the hatch, that's what it was. I saw no more as I was taken away, but I now know what my crew intended—they were dumping the cargo of granite. The better to speed up north to Boston and alert Ezra Pickering, my good friend and lawyer? Nay, knowing them, it's much more likely they are shadowing this ship even now as it makes its way across the Atlantic, staying just out of sight beneath the horizon, and waiting to see when I make my break for it. *Such good friends,* I think, a tear working its way down my cheek.

I shake my head to further concentrate on my desperate situation. What else happened yesterday...? The vile Bliffil, to be sure, and then Captain Hannibal Hudson, who seems to be an honorable man, but one who knows his duty and will be honor-bound to deliver me to the Admiralty. The Doctor and his examination, what else...? What...? Yes! The Doctor! Dr. Sebastian, with his microscope and specimens! That's it!

I spring to my feet. "Jonathan! When will you be relieved?"

"At eight o'clock, Miss," answers my Marine. "About fifteen minutes from now."

"Good. Now, Jonathan, if you would, please get my seabag. It's over there. Open it up, and on the top to the right, you'll see a small, framed, miniature portrait..."

"Now, Miss, I can't..."

"You don't have to give it to me. Just take it out and put it on the top of my bag."

Anxiously watching the hatchway door, Private Morris leans his musket against the bulkhead and goes over to the bag and opens it up.

"It's not here," he says, rummaging about in amongst some of the frilly female things in there. I had not brought all of my clothes with me on what turned out to be my last journey down to the Caribbean on the *Nancy B*—none of my riding habits, nor some of my other dresses and my winter stuff, for sure, all of which I left hanging in Amy's closet back at Dovecote—but there are still plenty of things in there.

I know he's embarrassed, but I push him on. "That Blifil messed things up in there. Keep looking. It's wrapped in waxed paper. There! That's it!" I exclaim, as I see the small package emerge in Jonathan's hand. "Good! Unwrap it and lay it on the bag. Right, just like that. And when you are relieved, if you will ask Dr. Sebastian to come down to see me, I would so *very* much appreciate it, oh, yes I would, Jonathan."

Nodding, as he lays the portrait on the bag, the Marine resumes his post, at Attention, his musket again beside him at Parade Rest. Just in time, I see, as his relief, a Corporal, comes stomping down the hatchway to take his place.

"Report, Private Morris," he says, obviously a man swelled with a sense of his own importance—it is plain that he has not been a Corporal long, else he would not be quite so formal with a man only one rank below him.

"She is locked in there, Corporal Phillips," says Jonathan. "She has had her breakfast. The standing orders are that the door is not to be opened except on Captain Hudson's direct order."

"Very well," puffs Corporal Phillips. "You are relieved, Private Morris."

Jonathan salutes by bringing his arm across his chest and then leaves the room, but not before giving me a glance as I look after him through the bars. *Good boy! I just know you'll do it!*

I sit back down on the bench and wait.

———

I do not have to wait very long. In about half an hour, Dr. Sebastian, dressed in his white lab coat, comes down the hatch and into the brig area. Actually, he's wearing a once-white lab coat, one that's now covered with many stains of dubious, and generally very bloody, origin.

"So what is the problem, then?" asks the Doctor of the Marine. "Is she sick?"

"I don't know nothin' about it, Sir," replies the stolid Phillips. "You'll 'ave to ask 'er."

The Doctor strides to the door of the cage. "What is it? Hurry up. I am a busy man."

I rise to face him.

"Doctor. Please go to that bag lying over there and look at what sits upon it."

Mystified, he glances at my bag and then goes to pick up the miniature portrait of Jaimy.

"So?" he says, after looking at it for a moment.

"I did that portrait, Dr. Sebastian," I say. "At my school, the Lawson Peabody School for Young Girls, I was considered to be one of the best at Drawing and Rendering." *Time for the big eyes now, girl.*

"It is quite well done," he says, "but did you call me down here to critique your art?"

"I saw yesterday in my visit to your clinic that you are a man of Science, Doctor. I saw that you had various specimens on your laboratory table."

"Yes, the Caribbean was most rich in new species. I look forward to discussing them with my learned colleagues at the Royal Society upon our return."

Batting the eyelashes, I go on. "And next to them—forgive me, Doctor—there were some rather clumsy drawings."

47

"It is true, I do not have much of the limner's skill," he admits, stiffly. "But I needed to try, for some of my findings were quite perishable."

"Yes, but I do have that skill, Sir, and I also have my colors, brushes, and good paper right there in my seabag," I say in a rush of words. "I could do the drawings for you under your direction. You would have a fine portfolio to show your fellow naturalists and maybe even publish, and if I could get out of this pesthole for even a few hours a day to accomplish the task, oh, Sir, it would do wonders for my constitution!"

"Publish, eh?" he murmurs, fingers to chin, thinking. *That nailed him,* I'm thinking.

"Doctor, if I am kept here in this dampness and gloom for the entire voyage, you would have no fine illustrations of your work but only my poor body to dissect because I will surely take sick and die." I work up a few tears on that.

"This is, indeed, a sty. Close to what Dante envisioned as one of the lower levels of Hell." He looks about and continues to muse upon what I have offered.

"And I do have some Science, Sir, having been somewhat educated at the Lawson Peabody School for Young Girls in Boston. I know, for example, that the proper name for the black rat that was biting at my legs last night is *Rattus,* genus *Rattus,* family Muridae, order Rodentia, class Mammalia, phylum Chordata, kingdom Animalia, and I—"

"Very well, I shall talk to the Captain," says Dr. Sebastian. He turns and leaves the brig.

*Oh, thank you, Mr. Sackett, for making us dissect those dead and disgusting rats in Science class!*

———

It is not long after the changing of the Noon Watch, when the not-very-good company of Corporal Phillips has turned into the much more companionable Private William Kent, that a Marine Sergeant, a grizzled old veteran, comes into the hold. I had just discovered that Private Kent is also from Cheapside, and that we have quite a few names and places in common. I had been telling him, to his great satisfaction, of the swift end of Cornelius Muck, the Cheapside Ghoul, on board the *Wolverine*, when the Sergeant interrupts.

"'Avin' a bit of a chat wi' the bint, are ye, Billy?" growls the man to his subordinate.

"Just tryin' to bring the poor thing some cheer, Sergeant Gibbs," retorts Private Kent, once more back at Attention.

"Well, belay that and bring 'er out," says Gibbs. "Major Stebbins sez it's Captain's orders. Bind her up and let's take 'er up to 'is cabin. There's some manacles over there that'll serve."

The Private removes the cell key from his belt and thrusts it into the keyhole to open the door. I'm standing still wrapped in the blanket as I step out into the light of the lantern.

"Wait, William," I say, throwing off the blanket and pointing at my black dress that hangs on a hook on the bulkhead. I had taken it off last night and handed it out to Private Morris to keep it from the damp after I was brought back down into this pit. "Hand me my dress, if you would."

I cannot see by the dim light of the lantern, but I know he is blushing, which is silly, since I am covered in my undergarments from knee to chest, but what the hell. I pull the dress over my head and smooth it down. Then I turn my back to the young Marine. "Button me up, Billy. Sergeant, please hand me that hairpiece that hangs over there. Thanks."

I feel Billy Kent's fingers working clumsily at the buttons at the back of my neck. I can hear his breath there, too, and I smile to myself. *Oh, Billy, you silly boy, you.*

"Sergeant, my hairpiece? Thanks."

I pull the wig on my head and fluff it up with my fingers. I can feel that it, too, is damp, but I do what I can with it.

"How do I look?" I ask, and I can tell from Billy's stunned look that I look good enough. I pinch my cheeks to pink them up and then stick out my wrists for the Sergeant to clap the metal cuffs on them.

They are snapped on and I say, "Lead the way, Sergeant," and I head up the gangway between the two soldiers.

I am blinded by the sudden bright light when we emerge on deck and so grab Billy's arm to steady myself. Well, I don't really have to, but I do it anyway. In a moment my eyes get used to it, and I see that we have a beautiful day up here with a good breeze and the *Dauntless* simply tearing along, all sails perfectly set and taut as drums. It sets my heart soaring to see her rip through the waves so clean and fast. *But it shouldn't, girl,* I tell myself, *considering where this ship means to take you.*

On our way from the bow of the ship to the after part where the Captain's cabin lies, we pass sailors on deck and in the rigging attending to their tasks, and I hear, half whispered, half spoken...

*It's her! That's Jacky Faber!*

*Are you sure?*

*'Course I'm sure.*

50

*Cor, wait'll I tell me kids I saw Jacky Faber, her ownself, with me very own eyes.*

*Damn me, Puss-in-Boots, right down there.*

I reflect on the vagaries of fame as we make our way along and decide that I'd much rather be a living nobody than a hanged person of renown, rotting away on some gibbet like poor old Captain Kidd, but still, it doesn't hurt to have some possibly sympathetic souls aboard.

We reach the door to the Captain's cabin and Sergeant Gibbs knocks lightly upon it. The door is opened by a white-jacketed steward and we are ushered in.

I see that there are a number of men standing in the room—Captain Hudson, a red-coated Marine officer who I suspect is Major Stebbins, the vile Bliffil, Dr. Sebastian, and another man whose face I cannot see for he stands with his back to me, gazing out one of the windows.

It is plain that the Doctor has been speaking. "...And it is my considered medical opinion, Captain," he intones, "that if you keep the female down in that hellhole, what you will be delivering to the Admiralty will not be the desired captive but rather a corpse."

"And it is my considered opinion, Sir," says Bliffil, "that it would be foolish to grant this girl any degree of freedom, for she has shown herself very adept at the art of escape. She is a very dangerous criminal."

The Captain looks over at me—I soften the Look by opening my eyes wider and lightly rattle the chain that hangs from my wrists—"She doesn't look dangerous to me."

"Do not let her looks deceive you," retorts my once and present enemy. "By her own hand and through her cunning, she has caused the deaths of many men."

The Captain says nothing to this but only stands regarding me for a while, his hands behind his back. Finally he addresses me. "I have been informed by my Sailing Master, Mr. Jared—"

*Jared? Joseph Jared? Could it be?*

The man at the window turns, and my heart leaps to see that it is indeed he!

"Oh, Joseph," I cry, tears of happiness springing from my eyes. "Well met! Oh, so very well met!" I want to rush to him, to embrace him, but, alas, I am restrained.

He smiles that familiar and fondly remembered cocky grin at me, bows, and says, "It is good to see you, too, Jacky, but best not to interrupt the Captain."

*So I really did hear that last night!*

"Ahem," says the Captain. "If I may continue: Mr. Jared, one of my more valuable and trusted officers, informs me that in spite of the charges against your name and the wild stories about your supposed adventures that circulate throughout the fleet, you are a person of honor."

I tear my eyes off Joseph and turn to the Captain and try to restore some semblance of the Look, but not the total highborn arrogant lady Look, no, more the Joan-of-Arc-Bound-Up-in-Chains-by-Her-Cruel-Tormentors-but-Still-Holding-Up-Her-Head Look.

"I try to be good, Sir," I say.

"Oh, spare me," Bliffil mutters.

"And Dr. Sebastian tells me you might be useful to him in cataloging and rendering drawings of the specimens that he has gathered during this voyage. What do you think of that?"

"I would very much like to lend what poor skills I might have to aid the good Doctor in his scientific studies," murmur I, glancing at the Doctor and further altering the Look to that of adoring student.

"See, she's doing it again," Bliffil hisses. "Soon she'll have every stupid man on board this ship totally in love with her! That's how she works! Oh, don't you see? Can't you see?" He is wringing his hands, imploring the Captain to see the error of his ways.

The Captain ignores him.

"Do you swear, girl," says Captain Hudson, looking me square in the eye, "that if you are released from the brig and given other quarters and some light duties with Dr. Sebastian that you will not try to escape?"

I think about this for a moment—*take it! Take it, girl, and get out of that hole!*—but I do not take the offer.

"I'm sorry, Sir, but I cannot promise that," I answer, as I raise my manacled hands to my face to wipe away yet another tear.

"Oh?" asks the Captain, surprised. "But why not?"

"Because, Sir, if I were to do that, I would be sealing my own death warrant." I look down at my bound hands. "For if I fall into the clutches of the Intelligence Branch upon our return to London, they will torture me to find out what I know about a certain spy ring, and I have already told them everything I can about that and cannot tell them any more, but they will not believe me so they will hurt me more and more"—I start gasping for air—"and more, and when they are convinced that I can give them no additional information, they will kill me—either privately with a knife to the throat, or publicly with a hanging at Newgate prison. That is why not."

There are stricken looks all around the room.

"Torture?" asks the Captain, incredulous. "Surely not."

"Dr. Sebastian," I say, "in your examination of my person, did you not find several marks on my left thigh?"

The Doctor coughs and says, "Yes, there were two round wounds there, healing nicely. I assumed they were gotten from sparks from a fireplace."

"They were not, Sir," I retort. "They were put there last month on the Mississippi River by a Lieutenant Flashby, Special Agent of the Intelligence Branch. He applied the tip of his hot cigar to my bare leg while I was tied to a chair, and he was going to hurt me more when he was thwarted in that by a gallant *regular* officer, Lord Richard Allen, Captain of Cavalry. I have no reason to expect any kinder treatment when I get to the Admiralty."

"Hmm," says the Captain, "that is hard to believe, but I will take you at your word. What is to be done then? Must we put you back in the brig?"

"Yes," says Bliffil, "that is what is to be done. And I must insist that I be given a key to the cell."

I notice that Joseph Jared is no longer smiling but, rather, is glaring intently at Lieutenant Bliffil.

I lift my head and say to the Captain, "We can do this: I will give my word, my parole, as it were, that I will not try to escape until that moment when we sight land. After that, my parole will be over, and you may clap me back in chains and deliver me to Mr. Bliffil here and to whatever fate awaits me at the Admiralty." When I finish, I say, "Only if it suits you, Sir."

"Well, it doesn't suit me," says Bliffil. "This female must be put in my protective custody right now."

This is too much for me. "Protective custody? Captain,

this man Bliffil is the one who put this mark upon my brow when I was but a little girl on the *Dolphin*. He's the bully who, as Senior Midshipman, pounded my face and bloodied my mouth and kicked in two of my ribs! All for sport! Protective custody? I'd sooner consign myself to the sharks that roll by our side than be put in his so-called *protective* custody!"

"She is twisting things again!" cries Bliffil. "When that happened, she was disguised as a ship's boy, a very insolent ship's boy who was very much in need of correction, I—"

"You will be quiet, Mr. Bliffil," orders the Captain. To me he says, "Very well, I accept those terms, if you will also promise not to harm yourself in any way during this voyage, to avoid what you think is going to happen to you."

"Sir, I love life too much to ever consider that."

"Good. Then it is done," says the Captain, briskly taking care of the details. "Mr. Jared has given up his cabin for you so you will be quartered there. You will take your meals there. You will assist the Doctor in all his endeavors, and you may take the air above decks several times a day for the sake of your health. Major Stebbins, you will provide a Marine outside her door, who will accompany her wherever she goes upon this ship."

The Marine officer bows his acknowledgment of this order and the Captain continues. "And you will, Miss Faber, above all things, behave yourself, else you shall be returned to the brig for the duration of the voyage."

"Sir, I must most vigorously protest!" sputters Bliffil. "She is a convicted criminal! You cannot grant her the freedom of this ship."

"She has not been convicted of anything yet, Mr. Bliffil, as far as I can tell, and I can do anything I damn well please on my ship, including having you thrown over the side," says the Captain, fixing Bliffil with a baleful look. Bliffil turns red and tightens his lips. "And again I caution you not to raise your voice to me, Mr. Bliffil. British Intelligence does not hold much sway here, I can tell you that. I have always felt that gentlemen, be they English or be they French, should not read each other's mail."

"But, Sir..."

"You are excused, Mr. Bliffil," says Captain Hudson, turning his back on him. "Your presence here is no longer required."

"As you wish, Sir," mutters Bliffil, bowing at the Captain's back. "Good day to you then."

Bliffil fixes a glare of the purest hatred on me, and though I have the urge to smile and give him a knowing wink, I restrain myself and merely put the full-scale Look back on and regard him as if he were a toad. From his furious expression, I gather that he got the message.

When the cabin door closes behind him, I say to Joseph, "Mr. Jared, it is most kind of you to give up your quarters, but you do not have to. I have slept on many a floor, as you well know." I recall the time I spent sleeping on the floor of Captain Scroggs's cabin while his dead body lay steadily rotting in his bed.

"Oh, I can sling my hammock anywhere. And besides, the thought of you curled up in my bed will bring me joy— or at least some very interesting thoughts."

The Captain, accurately perceiving the newly rekindled heat that exists between Joseph and me, warns, "As for behaving oneself, that goes for you, too, Mr. Jared. If you think you are going to experience joyful romps with the prisoner for the remainder of this voyage while the rest of us suffer the celibate state of hair-shirted monks, you are *quite* mistaken. I think it best for both the morale of this ship and this girl's own future if she arrives in London for whatever trial might await her in the same state of…er…maidenhood… that she is in now. Do you understand me, Sir?"

Jared nods. "Yes, Sir, I do." But his cocky grin is firmly in place and his eyes do not leave mine.

There is a knock at the door, and a steward comes in, bearing a tray.

"Ah!" says the Captain. "It is my lunch. Doctor, Major Stebbins, would you be so good as to share some food and a glass of wine with me? Good. Sergeant, you will take the shackles off Miss Faber's hands and see her installed in her new berth. Remember, round-the-clock watch on her anytime she leaves that space. Mr. Jared, I believe you have duties to attend to? All right, then. I believe we are finished here."

Sergeant Gibbs inserts the key to snap open the manacles, then leads me to the door. "Thank you, Captain Hudson, for your kindness," I say, able to effect a decent curtsy, now that my hands are free.

"No thanks are necessary, Miss. Just behave yourself," says the Captain, returning my gesture with a slight bow. "Good day to you."

*Oh, I will behave myself, Captain,* I think as I leave the cabin, with a slight smile curling my lips. *I will behave myself very well…and in my usual fashion.*

I am taken one level down into the Gun Room where lie the officers' cabins. Sergeant Gibbs sends Private Kent down to the brig to fetch my seabag, while Joseph Jared, who seems to think that the duty the Captain referred to was to tend to me, opens the door to his cabin and bows low.

"Your bower, Miss. I hope you'll find it comfortable."

I enter the tiny room and look about. Yes, it is like every other one I have seen on warships—a narrow bed, a washstand with mirror above and drawers below, a small nightstand, and just enough room to stand up and dress oneself...or undress oneself, as the case may be.

"To me it looks like a perfect palace after spending last night in that awful brig, Joseph, and I thank you for it, *and* for speaking up to the Captain on my behalf." Sergeant Gibbs has taken his station outside the door, facing away.

Joseph nudges the door quietly shut with his toe and says, "You are welcome, my dear. Am I to receive any reward?"

"Still the rogue, eh, Joseph?" says I, standing on tiptoes to plant a light kiss on his cheek. "There. That's all you'll get. You heard the Captain's orders—if I don't behave myself, it's back in the foul brig for me, and I don't want that." If anything, Jared has grown more handsome in the year since we parted on the deck of the sinking *Wolverine* in the aftermath of the Battle of Trafalgar. He looks splendid in his Master's uniform, all black with gold trim and buttons. "Besides, I am promised in marriage to a certain Lieutenant James Emerson Fletcher, should I ever be allowed to see him again," I say, trying to sound properly prim.

"I am sorry to hear that. And just where is Mr. Fletcher?"

"When last I saw him he was on HMS *Mercury*, headed for China and Japan, on convoy duty."

"Good. That is a very excellent place for him to be, playing nursemaid to fat merchant ships on the other side of the world, while you and I are right here, right now."

He puts his hands around my waist. "The Doctor was right—you are very narrow there," he says, pulling me closer to him. "And what did that Latin the Doctor spoke about you mean? When he was talkin' about your condition…the scars and all…"

I work up a blush and lower my eyes. "It means I am yet a maiden."

He chuckles. "Well, you certainly do get around for a maiden. That complicates things a bit, but we'll see…"

"And how did you know about that?" ask I, puffing up a bit. "You weren't in the Captain's cabin yesterday when I was brought in."

Again the cocky grin. "I was up on the quarterdeck with my ear to the speaking tube. I, of course, recognized you right off when you were captured and felt it best to stay out of your sight till I could figure out how I could do you some good."

"Ah. And that is why I had a good breakfast this morning instead of the slops a prisoner usually gets." I put my hands on his forearms—they are still as rock hard as I remember.

He just nods his head to that.

"But we must not forget that I *am* a prisoner, to be delivered in chains to the Admiralty when we land in England. Probably to be killed."

"You will not be handed off to that Bliffil when this voyage ends, you may count on that." He does not smile when he says this.

"But Joseph, I can't allow you to—"

"We will see what you will allow, Jacky, we will see."

We hear the sound of six bells.

"Ah, yes, but it's good to see you again, Puss! Now give us

a kiss, a real kiss, to last a man through his four-hour watch that he must now go stand, and to hell with everything else!"

I lift my face and I do it. After all, even if I am promised to another, there is no reason that Jared and I cannot continue to be good friends. *Very* good friends.

After Joseph leaves and Private Kent has brought up my seabag, I spend some time putting my linen in the drawers and then there is a knock and a new Private, one named Marsten, informs me that I am expected in the Doctor's laboratory. I get out my brushes, colors, and paper and follow the Marine out and up, across the deck and down into the fo'c'sle and into the surgery where waits Dr. Sebastian, once again clad in his stained lab coat.

"Ah. Here you are, then," he says. "You may set up over there."

There is a hatch overhead and it is open to let in some welcome light. I go over to the table that is under it and place myself on the stool provided there. "Thank you, Doctor, for letting me assist you."

"Ahem. Well, yes, there is a lot for you to do," he says and picks up a small box and puts it in front of me. "Here is your first assignment."

I open the box and look in. There is a bug, a rather large bug, that is rolling around a brown ball of what my nose informs me had somewhat recently been inside a horse or cow or other large animal. I look up at the Doctor with a questioning look.

"It is a Mexican dung beetle, *Phanaeus amithaon*. I collected it when we stopped at the Yucatán Peninsula and I was permitted to go ashore to gather specimens. Is it not a marvelous thing?" asks the Doctor, something like enthusiasm coming into his voice. "It is closely related to the sacred scarab of the ancient Egyptians. Can you draw it?"

"Yes, Sir," I say. I take out a sheet of my precious paper and place it before me on the table. "I'll need a cup of water, a clean rag, and some blotting paper, if you have any."

The Doctor goes to the door. "Stritch! Come here!"

A small, rather fearful little man comes in. It is plain from his dress that he is the Doctor's assistant surgeon, the loblolly boy he is called regardless of age. "Sir?" he asks.

"Get her what she needs, and be quick about it. Water, rags, and blotting paper."

Stritch scurries away.

"Does it bite, Sir?" I ask, putting a bit of female tremble in my voice.

"No. It is quite harmless."

*All right, you. No time to be squeamish.*

I reach in and put my forefinger in front of the beetle, making it leave its dung ball and crawl up on my hand. I hold it up before my eyes and take a hard look at the creature. *This shouldn't be too hard,* I'm thinking. *At least I don't have to get an exact facial resemblance.* I reach for my pencil and begin sketching the insect's outline.

"I believe, Doctor," I say, as I peer at the bug's face, "that it would be best for me to confine my illustrations to the top half of the pages so that I can later pen in your scientific observations below."

"That would be good, Miss."

My supplies are brought and I get to work in earnest.

———

I toil on through the afternoon, drawing, inking, applying paint washes, blotting, adjusting color till my eyes cross with the effort. The Doctor is a taciturn sort and not a lot of conversation passes between us and I don't want to push it, for I must make my moves toward freedom very carefully on this ship. At least he does not hang over my shoulder as I am working.

At length I am done with this first effort. I blow on it to dry it and hand it to him.

"Excellent," he gasps. "Astounding."

I did try to get the iridescence of the beetle's carapace to really glow.

"Thank you, Sir," I simper. "Now, if you will dictate the words that are to go under, I will pen them in."

The afternoon quickly turns into evening, and our light dims so we must stop work. I am taken back down to my cabin, and I must say I am not sorry, for my eyes are beginning to cross from the effort of concentration on ovipositor, carapace, thorax, and the rest of the beetle's parts.

My dinner is brought to me on a tray and I take it and eat it and it is good. Then I slide the tray back out and undress and slide into Joseph Jared's bed as I am totally and completely exhausted.

*Dearest Jaimy, it is almost certain that I will not be there to meet you when your ship returns from the Orient, as yesterday I was well and truly caught once again, and this time it is very possible that I will not be able to wriggle my way out of it. However, on the brighter side, this day has proved much more favorable than the last, which I spent in the deepest despair. I had given up all hope, but today I have found that I have some friends aboard this ship. As I lie here, I can hear the officers out at their table having dinner and discussing the events of the day, one of which is, of course, me, and I hear some expressions of sympathy for my plight. The low murmur of their voices is lulling me to sleep, even as I think these thoughts of you.*

*I hope you are well and I pray daily for your safety. Good night, Jaimy. God be with you.*

# Chapter 4

I crack open an eyelid when I hear the hatch over the Gun Deck being lifted to let in the fresh air and light.

I rub my face to wake myself up and reflect, *Oh this is so much better than that soggy brig!* Then I push my face back in the pillow for a few more minutes of blissful ease.

There is a knock on my door and a voice calls out, "Breakfast, Miss."

I hop out of bed and throw back the latch on the door to swing it open and there stands Private Morris, bearing a steaming tray.

"Thank you, Jonathan."

"And, Miss, the Doctor sent word that he would like to get to work right after you've had breakfast and are...dressed," says the young Marine, blushing nearly as red as his coat.

I am completely covered in my nightdress and mobcap. Is it the sight of my ankles and bare feet on the floor that makes him blush and stammer so? *Men, I swear.*

"Thank you, Jonathan," I say, stepping aside. "Please put it on the nightstand there."

He does it, and I make sure he has to brush up against me on his way out.

"And if you could have the steward bring me up a pitcher of water so I could wash?" I say with a flutter of eyelashes. *Hey, I've got to make as many friends as I can. And fast, too. Every passing minute brings this ship closer to England.*

When the water is brought and the door closed, I whip off my nightclothes to do the necessaries and then wash hands, face, and parts, and dry off with the towel that hangs by the washstand. Then I sit down on the bed to eat my breakfast.

It is good—oatmeal with berries and sugar, hot tea, and a nice piece of johnnycake. As I munch away, I think about my plan. Well, it's only the start of a plan, but it's starting to come together. As usual, it involves me getting in good with the crew and then jumping overboard at the right time and swimming for it. I remember the Captain saying, "Christ, at this rate we'll never round Margate!" when I was taken. *Margate*—that means we're definitely going to London, because Margate is at the mouth of the Thames and that means, if I remember my charts and I believe I do, we shall first spot land off the Isle of Dogs, about fourteen miles away. Not an easy swim, and things are starting to get a mite chilly. Well, I'll work out that part of it as we plow along. It is not a finished plan, but it is a start and it makes me feel better. The rest will come to me later. *I hope.*

After I have eaten my breakfast, I rummage through my seabag and pull out my old Lawson Peabody serving-girl outfit to wear today—black skirt, loose shirt, and low leather weskit laced up tight under my chest, letting whatever there is of me up top swing free under the thin white cloth of the shirt. I will be in close quarters with the Doctor, as well as maybe some others, and I figure my dress exhibits a bit of poor-little-girl humility befitting my lowly stature as a captive, and yet, with its low bodice and snug waist, shows off whatever I might have in the way of female charms.

Thus attired, I throw the latch to open the door. "Take me away, Private Morris, for I am yours to command," I say grandly, as I place my arm on his and we go to the hatchway, then out and onto the deck.

Once there, I blink in the bright light and see Joseph Jared on watch up on the quarterdeck, looking down on me when he should be tending to his sails. I put my nose in the air and stride past in the safe custody of my Marine. But I turn my head just before going down into the fo'c'sle to the orlop and glance his way. Of course, his grin is in place. I pretend not to notice and toss my head higher and go down.

"Today we start with the Fringillidae *Geospiza fortis*," announces the Doctor by way of greeting. He places in front of me a dried-out and very dead little bird and explains, "It's a medium ground finch that I collected in the Galápagos."

I sigh and settle onto my stool, then pick up my pencil.

When I finish inking my drawing of the bird, he asks me to render a particularly disgusting bit of gut that has been pickled in some sort of strong-smelling liquid. After I've been bending over it for a time, concentrating on my drawing, I find my head spinning and I feel like I'm going to faint. Dr. Sebastian, noticing that his precious specimen might be ruined by my face descending onto the smelly thing, orders a halt, and I'm given a break to go get some fresh air.

"We will resume our work after lunch," he says, curtly, and takes off his lab coat. I am dismissed.

When I get out into the air, my head clears so I walk to the rail to look out across the sea. It is another fine, soaring day, and with the breeze behind her, the *Dauntless* tears right along.

"Careful, Miss. Not too close," warns my Marine.

"Oh, don't you worry, Patrick," says I, sucking in a deep chestful of the good salt air. "I'm not going to jump." *Not yet, anyway.*

I have discovered that there are four guards who have been assigned the Jacky Watch rotation: Privates Morris, Kent, Marsten, and this Patrick Keene. He's a pleasant lad from County Cork. There are, of course, many sailors about the deck, and some of them look like they'd like to have a word with the infamous Jacky Faber, but a growl and a warning look from Private Keene wards them off. I guess he has his orders.

I leave the rail to go grasp the first rung on the ratlines that lead up to the foretop.

"I'm going up on that little platform there—that way none of the sailors will bother me, and you won't have to keep 'em off. See? And I'll play you a bit of a tune to cheer you during your watch."

"But—"

Before he can do anything, I'm up the ratlines and heading for the foretop. There is a moment, just before I reach it, that I consider going up through the lubber's hole because I'm wearing a dress, but I just can't do it. I'm too much the proud salty sailor for that. No, I go to the edge, do the flip over, and land on the foretop. If anyone got a peek at my drawers, well, good for them. I hope they enjoyed it.

I pop my head over the side of the foretop platform. "You won't get in any trouble, Patrick. See? I'm right here. I can't go anywhere." *Well, I could if I really wanted to, but...*

He says nothing to that so I slide back to prop my shoulders against the foremast, then pull out my pennywhistle that I had up my sleeve and commence to play "The Glens of Killarney," which I know to be a favorite of the Irish boys, at least the ones I've encountered, anyway, and I've met quite a few. That goes well, the notes wafting away on the wind and not likely to gain the attention of the officers three hundred feet back on the quarterdeck.

Then I play "Jackaroe" and then my own "The Ship's Boy's Lament," which I had made up back on the *Dolphin* after the death in battle of my mate Benjy.

As I'm doing it, I hear footfall behind me. *Who?* I look aft and see that Joseph Jared is still on watch, so it can't be him... *what?*

"Hullo, Jack," says my visitor, who has plainly dropped down from the top.

*Davy?*

"Davy! What are you doing here?" I ask, incredulous.

"I'm in the Royal Navy, remember?" he answers, settling next to me, his own back to the mast. "And this is a Royal Navy ship. I could well ask you the same question, 'cept I already know why you're here—you've got your scrawny butt in a lot of trouble yet again and it will prolly be up to me to save it."

I squirm around to throw my arms about him and hug him tight. "Oh, it is so good to see you, Davy!" I plant a kiss on his cheek. "Have you heard anything of the others?"

"Well, Willy's still on the *Temeraire*, rated Able, and lookin' to become a Bo'sun. Tink's in London, out of the Navy and leanin' on a crutch—he was banged up pretty bad at Trafalgar, but he's getting better. They're lettin' him sleep under the bar at the Bell and Boar in return for him sweepin' up nights. Don't know where Jaimy is. Thought he was off chasin' after you."

"Poor Tink, he always was the one of us to get himself hurt," I say, remembering that time when Tink had been wounded during a fight with the pirate LeFievre. "Jaimy's on the *Mercury*, escorting a convoy to the Orient. We're going to be married when he gets back to London."

I release Davy and lean back against the mast again. "Or at least we were," I say, heaving a sigh. "Till I got caught."

"Right, I saw those wanted posters. You've been a bad girl, I reckon. I thought about running you down and turning you in myself for that fat reward."

I give him a poke in the ribs. "Not quite as bad as they say."

"Well, you always said you wanted to be famous in legend and song and I guess you got that," he says. "So you think they're gonna hang you?"

"I believe that is one of the more festive events they have planned for me, yes." I reach over and take his hand and heave out yet another heavy sigh. "Isn't this just like the old days, Davy," I say to get off the subject of my imminent death. "When we were kids back on the *Dolphin,* us lyin' around the foretop, out of sight of anyone who might want to put us to work, talkin' and dreamin' and jokin' around."

He laughs and says, "Aye, those were good days, it can't be denied." I notice that his laugh is much deeper now. Truly he has grown into a man, fully six feet tall, and in a moment I find that true in more ways than just a lower voice and a manly frame.

I crane my head around and look him full in the face because I sense something off, something not quite right.

"Where's your Brotherhood earring, brother?" I ask, looking at his vacant left earlobe and regarding him with a stern look worthy, I believe, of Mistress Pimm. "Did you lose it? Give it to some slut? Gamble it away?"

He looks at me with a sly grin. "So where's yours, Miss High-and-Mighty Nob-Come-Lately?"

I tap my breastbone. "It's right here on a chain, next to my heart. I keep it there rather than in my ear because sometimes I need to be perceived as more demure than I actually might be."

"Well, Jack-*ass,*" he says with a slight leer, "*my* golden hoop now rests on the ring finger of the left hand of one Annie Jones, formerly Ann Byrnes, which person I think you might know."

*What? Annie! How...?*

"Right-o, Jack-o, you're lookin' at a married man. Happened a week and a half ago. When we got into Boston, I explained to Mr. Curtis, who's my division officer, the way things lay twixt Annie and me, and after he told the Captain, I was granted three days' liberty whilst the ship reprovisioned, so I went up to the school, swept her up in my arms, and plighted me troth, as it were. She accepted, bless her, but then, of course, I had to ask her old man. When I told him that I was as Catholic as the Pope, he gave his grudging consent, so the next day we was married. Then we spent two whole days of, without doubt, the finest and most pure and lusty honeymoons ever down at the Pig and Whistle. Everybody said it was a right shame that you had left on your little schooner not two days before, 'cause you surely would have wanted to be there, if only to scold me into being a good husband, as I suspect you're gonna do now."

"You be good to her, you," warn I, poking my finger in his chest. "She is one of my dearest friends on this earth and if you..." My eyes well up at the thought of missing that wedding. *Oh, everybody must have been there but me...Betsey and Ephraim, Sylvie and Henry, Ezra and Amy, oh...*

"Don't you worry about her and me, Jacky. I drew out what pay I had on the books and left it with her. She's fixed all right till this war is over and I can get back. Now, let's talk about you. I know you for a conniving, devious, and cunning sort, so I know you've got a little somethin' cooked up to keep you from dancin' the Newgate jig. Am I right?"

Down below we hear eight bells being rung, signaling that it is noon and the watch will change.

"Well, I have been working on something, but I'll fill you in later," I say, squeezing his hand ever harder. "Oh, Davy, it is such a comfort to have you here, I—"

There is the thump of another pair of boots on the foretop, and I look up to see that we have been joined by Joseph Jared. It is plain that he has just gotten off watch, and it is equally plain that he is not at all pleased at what he has found here. In talking with Davy I had, without thinking, reverted to my old childish foretop posture of drawn-up knees with forearms between legs, and was not presenting a very ladylike picture.

"Well, this is awful damn cozy. What the hell are you doing here, Jones?" he demands.

I let go of his hand as Davy gets to his feet and puts his right knuckle to his brow, his face expressionless. "I was visiting an old mate, Sir," he says. I, too, get to my feet.

"Joseph," I cry, "this is none other than David Jones, my brother from the *Dolphin*, from when we were ship's boys together!"

"I know who he is, and he don't look much like a boy to me," says Jared, his voice cold. "Get yourself gone, Jones."

"Aye, Sir," says Davy. He grabs a line and goes to haul himself up into the high rigging. I catch his eye and wink, tapping my clenched fist on my right hipbone, over my tattoo, to show him I know how things stand and that the Dread Brotherhood of the *Dolphin* still exists, at least for me. Before he goes up, he does the same, showing that the same goes for him, too. *Oh, it is so good to have another friend aboard!*

"Can't leave Puss-in-Boots for a moment, can we, before our little Pussycat's snugged up with another Tom," says Jared, who had not missed that last exchange of signals.

I hit a brace. "That's not worthy of you, Joseph, and you know it," says I, suddenly angry. "He was a good friend of mine when I was a child, and he is a good friend now. I do not abandon my friends." I go to the edge of the foretop. "I believe it's time we went down for lunch."

"Ah, nobody owns Jacky Faber, is that right?" He hooks his arm around my waist.

"That is right, Mr. Jared, and don't you forget it. Nobody but me." I spin out of his grip and launch myself over the side of the foretop, grab the backstay, and go down, hand over hand.

"Please don't do that again, Miss," says Private Keene, visibly sweating under his high leather collar, plainly relieved to see me hit the main deck and to have me once more in his direct custody.

"Oh, don't worry, Patrick. I'd cover for you, and I'll be good now, I promise," says I, taking his arm. "You may lead me down to the Gun Deck."

I am escorted through the throng of officers gathering for their midday meal and put into my room. I receive my lunch and I eat it. Before I am taken back to work in the Doctor's lab, I search through my seabag and pull out an ivory disk, the kind I use for making my miniature portraits and slip it into my vest.

When I get to the lab, the Doctor is not yet there, so I take a piece of paper and begin work on the frontispiece for his folio. I've decided the nine-inch-by-twelve-inch size will be best for this thing, since that is the size of paper that seems most available here. I shall have to ask Davy to see if the Sailmaker can make us a leather folder to protect the drawings. I look about at the paintings I've done so far that have been tacked to the wall and that plainly won't do. The Doctor may have a keen scientific mind, but he certainly has no notion of order—nor any sense whatsoever of how to advance oneself in the world of Academia and Publishing. Or how to make any money from it all. I will show him.

One thing about my art—while the quality of the work I have done must be judged by others, there is one thing I know—I am fast. Having painted many pictures of fidgety children, impatient men, and flighty ladies, to say nothing of being in houses of mourning to paint funeral portraits, I have learned to be fast and accurate.

The Doctor comes back into the lab, so I slide the frontispiece out of the way, without him seeing it. I finish off the drawing of the vile gut I had been working on before, and then ink in the words the Doctor wants put under it, describing what the thing does and what poor thing it came out of, and suchlike. I now appreciate Miss Prosser's Penmanship classes back at the Lawson Peabody.

That done, I am given a butterfly, a dead one stuck on a pin.

"Ah," I say, looking at the design on its wings. "That is quite beautiful. This will be a joy to do."

"I am glad you think so," says the Doctor, "as we have many of them to do. The Lepidoptera are one of my special interests."

I turn to my work, while the Doctor turns back to his microscope, his sharp face in profile. I sketch in the shape of the butterfly's wings, then put down a wash of yellow watercolor. As I wait for that to dry so that I can paint the colorful details over it without blurring, I slip out the little disk from my vest and begin on the Doctor's portrait.

Using the pencil, I draw the outline of his face. He is sunk in his work and is completely oblivious to what I am doing. It will not be hard to get a good resemblance, I'm thinking, as he has a prominent nose with a slight hook at the bridge, thin lips, deep-set eyes, thick brows...*yes, Mr. Peet, I will keep the overall composition of the piece in mind from the start...* When you are an artist, you carry the instructions and admonitions of everyone you ever studied under right with you when you are working. It's like they're looking over your shoulder and going *tsk, tsk!* and shaking their heads sadly if you mess up. Mr. Peet at the Lawson Peabody was the one who started me on this path, and I thank him for it.

Back to the butterfly. Black now for those spots...oops, not dark enough. *There! Got it!* Let that dry and now back to the portrait of Dr. Sebastian.

And so the afternoon goes.

Later, when I am relieved of my duties in the lab, I take my painting tools with me and go down to the Gun Deck and seat myself at the long table since no officers are there yet. Private Kent takes up station behind me at the door to my room. I could go out on deck to take some air and maybe see Davy again, but I want to finish this...and I want Jared to cool his heels a bit, too.

All right, wet brush, dip in color, and get to work.

I am bent over my task as Joseph Jared comes into the room. I see him out of the corner of my eye, but I say nothing as I continue to work on the miniature. I had painted in the Doctor's basic features before, so now I'm finishing the rest from memory—his high white collar, short-cropped dark hair, pince-nez hanging from a cord pinned to his lapel, and resting on his upraised hand, his precious Lepidoptera *Danaeus plexippus.*

Jared sits down at the table across from me. He, too, says nothing. A steward comes in the room and Jared gestures to him, and soon a glass of wine is placed before him, and then another in front of me.

"If this is an apology, Mr. Jared," I say, lifting the glass, "then I accept it." But I don't yet take a sip.

He still says nothing, but just looks at me intently.

"When first I met you on the *Wolverine*, Joseph, you were standing a watch for one of your common seamen while he was ill. Do you remember that? You were Captain of the Top and I remarked on the fact that you did not have to assume the man's duty and you replied that you have to stand up for your men and for your mates. Do you expect any less from me?"

The corners of his eyes crinkle up as he smiles and taps my glass with his, our eyes still locked. "Well said, Puss." He takes a drink and so do I. "So I may consider myself forgiven?"

"Yes, you may," I say and put my eyes back on my work. I am almost done...some highlights in the hair, there...his jacket a little blacker. Now to fix that hand.

"It seems that the good Doctor is to be immortalized in paint," says Joseph, craning his neck to see. "It's very good, Jacky, I must say."

"Thank you, Joseph, but pray do not tell him of it, as I mean for it to be a surprise, to thank him for his kindness to me."

Stewards come in bearing the tablecloth and dishes so I rise to go to my room, gathering up my materials, knowing that the men must set up for the officers' dinner. Lamps are being lit and I notice that Private Kent has seen to it that my lamp is also lit.

"Till later, Mr. Jared. Thank you for your company."

He nods and stands as I turn to go into my room. On my way I pat the Marine on his red sleeve and say softly, "Thank you, Billy."

Once in there, noting once again the oh-so-dim light, I decide that I cannot spend another whole evening in this gloom—no books, not enough light to work on paintings, no company. Well, I may not be able to do anything about those first two things, but I can do something about the third.

I poke my face out the door. Joseph is still there, not having moved since I left. "Mr. Jared," I ask, "does each officer have his own place at that table?"

"No," he says, wondering at the question. "The First Mate, Mr. Bennett, sits at the head and Mr. Curtis, the Second, is at the foot. The rest of us take our seats as we find them."

"Good. Could you please see that this one is kept open?" I ask, pointing at the chair directly in front of my door.

"Sure, Puss," agrees Jared, grinning full on. "Consider that seat saved. I assume a certain bottom will rest upon it at dinner?"

I don't answer outright, but I do give him a wink and a hint of a smile as I duck back into my room. I must dress now for dinner.

I strip off my serving-girl gear and pull out my old blue dress from my seabag. Ah, the old standby dress that I had made for myself back on the dear old *Dolphin*. I had patterned it on the one worn by Mrs. Roundtree, a practitioner of the so-called world's oldest profession, whom I had met in a brothel on Palma de Majorca when I was thirteen. It was she who had clued me in on the Facts of Life, for which instruction I was, at the time, most grateful. I haven't grown much since then, but I have grown some, primarily in my upper region and a bit in the tail so the thing has gone through many alterations, and it has served me in good stead over the years since I was finally tossed off the *Dolphin* for being a girl. I wear it whenever I want to catch the attention of men.

I pull it over my head, smooth it down, and adjust the bodice—no undershirt under this dress, that's for sure. *Hmmm,* this dress buttons up the back, so I stick my head back out the door.

"Billy. Put your musket down for a second and come button me up." As I say this, I glance out and see that the room is beginning to fill with the ship's officers.

"Belay that, Private," says Jared, who obviously has been standing by to see what's going to happen here. "I'll tend to that." A plainly disappointed William Kent stands aside as Joseph enters my cabin.

I turn my back to him, awaiting the touch of his fingers along my backbone, but I don't feel that. Not yet, anyway. I do hear his foot lightly kicking the door shut and then feel his hands reach in the open back of the dress and come around to rest on my bare belly. I have to keep my hands clasped to my chest to hold the front of the dress in place or it would fall down to my waist and we can't have that, no, we can't, but what am I to do?

His hands move up over my ribs, seeking, I know, to slide under mine. Then I feel his breath on my neck and then his lips and tongue on my shoulder and I catch my breath and let out a sigh and relax my hands and then...

...then I open my eyes, which had closed, and those eyes fall on the portrait of Jaimy hung over my bed, and I force myself back to my senses.

"Belay that, Mr. Jared," I say, my breath still short. I force his hands back down by pressing his forearms down with my elbows. "Just button me, please, or else I shall raise a fuss."

He slowly draws his hands back out and begins to button up the back. "Such a waste," he murmurs. When he is done, I turn to face him. I had taken off my hairpiece to put on the dress and he reaches up to ruffle my hair. I've noticed that since my locks have been shorn, men like to do that. Maybe it reminds them of puppies they have petted. "Someday soon you will have to tell me how this happened."

"Someday I shall, Joseph," I say, "but as for now, I must finish dressing."

"All right, Puss," he says. "Till later, then." He goes to leave, then notices the portrait hung over my, formerly his, bed. "Aha. So that is our Mr. Fletcher. Well, next time we'll have to turn that to the wall, won't we?"

He leaves, passing a very flustered Private Kent, who I'm sure was conflicted in what his duties should have been in the last few minutes of his guardianship of me. *Don't worry about me as regards Mr. Jared, Billy, as I can take care of myself in that regard...I think I can, anyway.*

Back into the bag to pull out my cosmetics kit—I left many things back at Dovecote, but not that. Now for a little color to the lips, a spot of rouge to the cheeks—not too much, the image is to be a lady, after all, not a tramp—some powder all around the face and chest and shoulders... There, all done.

Another of my hairpieces is a powdered white one with a blue ribbon at the back that matches the dress. I pull it on and regard myself in the mirror. Just right, I'm thinking—very French, very Marie Antoinette, and very much just the thing for this evening. *Stand by, boys.*

I sit on my bed and wait, but I do not have to wait long. Soon there is a rap on the door and I hear, "Dinner, Miss."

I go to the door and open it to see a steward standing there holding out my dinner tray and I say, "Thank you, Simmons," and take it from him. I look past him to see that the officers have gathered at their table and food is being served. Several of them regard me curiously, and I see that the place I had asked for, three seats down from the head, is open.

Putting on the Look, I stride from my room in all my blue and white powdered splendor, advance to the open chair, and place my tray down on the table in front of it. Jared, of course, is right there and he pulls out my chair and I am seated.

"May I please join you, gentlemen?" I ask, directing my gaze at First Officer Lieutenant Bennett. "It is awfully stuffy in my room, and I am in sore need of some pleasant company." I soften the Look and gaze up at Mr. Bennett through lowered eyelashes.

"Well, I say...," he sputters, taken aback, as it were, by my sudden appearance. "But what of the conditions of your confinement? The Captain said—"

"The good Captain Hudson said, Sir," simpers I, "that I was to *take* my meals in my room. Very well, I have *taken* my dinner tray in my room just now, and then I have brought it out here. He also said that I was to have the freedom of the ship, in order to take in the fresh air so necessary to my health, always, of course, under the watchful eyes of my Marine guard. You see there, standing guard over me, Private William Kent, do you not? So all is proper, you must agree, Sir?"

*Hear, hear!* is heard from some of the younger officers, but Mr. Bennett still looks doubtful.

"After we dine, Sir, I think I might be able to bring some cheer to your gathering through the singing of songs, the recitation of poems, and the telling of stories—and believe me, Sir, I do have a *lot* of good stories."

Mr. Bennett considers, and then agrees, "Very well. Welcome to our table." He rises when he says this, and so does everybody else at the table, except for one...

"Mr. Bennett, I must protest most vigorously!" shouts Bliffil from the other end of the table. "This is a wanted criminal! She must be kept under constant guard!"

"Mr. Bliffil," says Mr. Bennett, wearily. It's obvious that he, too, has very little use for the Intelligence Officer, and I sense that feeling is shared by most of the men assembled here, they being regular, proven sailors, those who have gained their rank through rough experience and thorough testing by the Navy Board. "This is my table, and if you wish to sit at it, you will be civil to *all* who are here." It's equally plain that everyone has heard of my charges against the character of this Bliffil.

Bliffil sits down, visibly fuming. He fixes his glare upon me, but I pretend not to notice.

"Thank you, Mr. Bennett, for accepting one such as I into your fellowship," I say, lifting the glass that is set before me. "May I propose a toast?"

He nods.

"To the waves, to the foam, and to the *Dauntless*, and to all who guide her upon her watery way!"

*Hear, hear!*

I am introduced to the other officers—there are six of them and two Midshipmen, young squeakers really, who have been invited this evening. The dinner is excellent. We are not so far out from the last port that the meat is not still fresh and the vegetables have not yet turned brown. Much good wine is served and high hilarity rules.

After I pat my lips with my napkin, I rise and start reciting "When in disgrace with Fortune and men's eyes, I all alone beweep my outcast state...," the old Bard's "Sonnet Twenty-Nine," one of my standard poems, and it receives great acclaim. Then Midshipman Soule is forced to his feet to sing once again the "Jackaroe" song, which, because of the book that is about me, seems to be forever attached to my name. I pull out my pennywhistle from my sleeve to accompany the poor middie in his efforts and all turns out well. He sits down, red faced but pleased with his performance.

I hear Bliffil muttering to those near him who will listen: "There, that is how she does it, and I have it on the best authority from the Admiralty—she works her charms—and I know, I know, there is not much there, but somehow she does it. And soon every man aboard will be in love with her, or what they think her to be. But believe me, she is not that, she is instead a snake, a serpent that worms its way into the open and guileless sensibilities of simple men. Look at that so-called Marine guard—he is already a mush of unmanly emotion. Pah! Just watch and you will see! You'll see! Mark me!"

I hear it and let it go, but Joseph Jared hears it, too, and he does not let it go.

"And you mark me, Mr. Bliffil," says he, rising with a very dark look on his face. "One more word against this girl, and you shall meet me in the morning with pistols or the weapons of your choice."

"Meet *you*?" sneers Bliffil, leaning back in his chair. "Gentlemen do not fight those who are lowborn and have somehow come up through the ranks. Control yourself, *Mr. Jared*, else you might find yourself once more a common seaman."

Jared does not heed the warning. Instead he growls and goes to launch himself across the table at Bliffil and is restrained only by me wrapping my arms around his neck and by Mr. Soule, on his other side, who steps in front of him warning, "Don't do it, Joseph! He is not worth it!"

"Gentlemen, please!" orders Mr. Bennett. "You both know Captain Hudson has forbidden dueling on his ship! Save your quarrels till you step on shore. Now sit down before I call an end to this evening. An evening that, up until now, I have been enjoying very much."

Jared slowly sits back down, but everyone knows this is not over, not by a long shot.

"Ahem!" I say, to help clear the air. "If someone could put a fiddle in my hands, we might have a bit of music!"

Someone does and I do "The Bonny, Bonny Broom," and "The Quaker's Wife," then sing "Barbara Allen." Then

"Ryan's Slip Jig," and that one I end by playing and dancing at the same time.

There are roars of applause, which warms my heart, and more wine is poured and, to take a breath, I launch into a story...

"...and then Mike Fink, the King of the River, roared out his rant, 'I'M A RING-TAILED ROARER, BORN IN A CANEBRAKE, AND SUCKLED BY A MOUNTAIN LION! AND I WILL KILL THAT JACKY FABER, I WILL BREAK HER BONES AND SUCK OUT THE MARROW, I WILL...'"

...and so on, to the delight of all. Almost all—Bliffil excuses himself early on and is not missed. I then do "The Boatman's Dance," which I learned from Mike Fink, himself, and I finish with "The Parting Glass," which I have always ended with, since my days of playing with Gully MacFarland, the truly master fiddler.

*Good night, and joy be with you all.*

It was a *very* good day.

# Chapter 5

*John Higgins*
*On Board the Schooner* Nancy B. Alsop
*Somewhere in the Atlantic*
*September 10, 1806*

*Mr. Ezra Pickering, Esq.*
*Attorney at Law*
*Union Street*
*Boston, Massachusetts USA*

*My Dear Mr. Pickering,*

It is with great regret that I write to inform you that our
Miss Jacky Faber has been taken by the British Navy in an action on the high seas. From what I was able to discern from the
exchange of accusations and threats that passed between us
and HMS Dauntless, the ship that took her, she is to be taken
back to England for possible trial on a charge of piracy. Although it is cold comfort, all others on the Nancy B are well.

I am forwarding this message via a whaling ship, the Hiram
Anderson, which was bound fully loaded for New Bedford

when we managed to flag her down last week. The captain assured me he would make certain this letter is carried to you, and I believe he will be as good as his word.

Please excuse the haste in which this message is written. We are following the Dauntless across the ocean, watching for any opportunity to effect Miss Faber's rescue or to aid her in any plans she herself might have in that regard. We all know she is very resourceful in matters of self-preservation and hope for the best.

Should they manage to convey her to London, we shall contact her friends there and see what can be done.

Wishing I had better news, I remain,

Yr Most Humble and etc.

John Higgins

# Chapter 6

"If you would turn this way just a little, Sir."

Captain Hudson stands across from me, and I am sitting at his table with my colors laid out before me, painting his miniature portrait.

"That's good, Sir, right there."

I pick up the pencil and begin sketching on the ivory disk.

It has been more than a few days since I first barged into the Officers' Mess that evening, but I have so far suffered no repercussions for my cheek. I'm sure Bliffil complained, but nothing has come of it.

I have since presented Dr. Sebastian with his portrait, and he pronounced himself both amazed and pleased.

"My dear, this is wonderful!" he said, gazing at the thing. I glow under his praise—I *do* like admiration, as everyone knows. I had taken Jaimy's portrait out of its frame—*sorry, Jaimy, but your picture is still the last thing I see at night*—and popped in the one of the Doctor. "My wife will be so pleased! And thank you for including the Lepidoptera *Danaeus plexippus*! It is perfect!" These were the most words

I had ever heard come out of the mouth of the usually taciturn Dr. Sebastian. "When we get to London, you must come to my house to do my wife and daughters and…" He stumbled then, realizing the impossibility of what he had just said. "And…er…sorry…let's get back to work."

We did work for a while, and then I decided to throw a little twist into things.

"Sir, I—I know you are a member of the Royal Society…" I knew this from Stritch, the loblolly boy, a not overly bright man from whom I pump information every time the Doctor steps out of the room. "…and…and…I know that the bodies of those hanged for murder are given over for dissection to the surgeons…" It is common knowledge that the bodies of those executed for other crimes are given back to their families or else thrown whole into the common lime pit if no one claims them. I work up a girlish sob and throw aside my brush and bury my face in my hands. "…and I know they shall brand me a murderer because men did die on that ship and I will surely be blamed for it!"

The Doctor, who has seen much gore and has hacked off many a battle-torn limb, seems to be quite shocked at a young girl's distress. *Good. I have rehearsed this little scene over and over in my head as I lay in my bunk at night, and it is going exactly as I planned.*

"So, Sir, if you would be so good as to be the one to take my body down from the gallows after I am hanged, and if you would treat it with some measure of…respect when you do what you must do, I would…"

Here I collapsed into helpless tears, my shoulders shaking with chest-wracking sobs. "…oh, God, I would take it most kindly, Sir!" I wail and fall over onto him.

"There, there," he says, not quite knowing what to do with his formerly very competent girl assistant who has suddenly dissolved into a puddle of female distress on his very lap. "I would do that, but I'm sure it won't come to that, surely. Stritch, come here! Take care of this!"

But it was not Stritch. It was the Marine guard Patrick Keene who came in to calm me and I threw myself upon him.

"Oh, Patrick, I am so afraid, so very afraid!"

"Now, Miss, please be still. Please..."

And so it went. Eventually I subsided, wiped off my tears, and we got back to work.

It was not many days after that when I received the call to go to the Captain's cabin to paint his portrait, the Doctor having shown him his own portrait... and the portfolio and the frontispiece...

---

## DE RERUM
### Natura Americana

An Account of the Various Flora and Fauna
encountered and collected on a Journey
Through the Caribbean Sea on Board HMS *Dauntless*,
in the year 1806, together with appropriate
Illustrations and Comments of a biological nature.
by Dr. Stephen Sebastian, M.D., Cambridge University
Member, The Royal Society

*Illustrated by Miss J. M. Faber, Lawson Peabody s.f.y.g.*

---

I lettered those words large on the front page, sur-rounded by entwined vines and flowers, interspersed with heraldic motifs—shrimps rampant and butterflies guardant with gules—on a field of light blue. I thought it looked right nice, if I may say so. I had Davy take me down to the Sail-maker's berth and there leather was measured, cut, and sewn. The folder, when done, was soft and supple and had inside pockets to hold the illustrations. It was bound with tight twine and it gave me great pleasure to take down all my drawings from the wall, putting them in order, tucking them in the folio, and then later, presenting the whole pro-duction to the Doctor.

He said nothing, but only took it and opened it. He drew out the frontispiece, looked at it, and then turned and left the laboratory to go directly to the Captain's cabin. How do I know this? Davy's spies who lurked out-side the Captain's open window reported the following exchange:

"Look at this, Hannibal," said the Doctor, displaying the articles on the Captain's table. "They are going to hang someone capable of *this*? That would be an abomination!"

"Well, Stephen," said the Captain, who was plainly very good friends with his surgeon, "she is facing many serious charges."

"Hell, I'll adopt her or something! Bribe someone, for God's sake!"

"We shall see what we can do, Stephen, when we get to London. Meanwhile..."

It was soon after that that I found myself painting the Captain's portrait.

———

"Your wife will appreciate this very much when you are far away at sea, Sir," I venture, putting a gold touch on the hilt of the sword he holds up next to his chest.

"Ahem. That is true. Er...But, is it possible that you might do *two* pictures instead of just one?"

"Of course, Sir. Two it is."

*Aye, you dog, I know what you're about—one for your faithful wife and one for your mistress. Men. I swear.*

I work and he poses and we are silent for a while when at last he says, "About your...problem, Miss. I want you to know that I am not without influence in political circles. Although I do not trumpet it about, feeling as I do that a man should be known for his deeds and not his birth, I am a Peer of the Realm and hold a seat in the House of Lords. I shall see what I can do for you."

*Time for the waterworks again.*

"That is so good of you, Sir," I wail, turning on the tears, something I am *very* good at.

"Well, ahem, we have grown fond of you in the time we have had you with us, Miss Faber. Now calm yourself, please, and let us continue."

He assumes the pose, clutching his sword and looking nobly off into the distance, and I again wield my brush.

Silence falls between us...for a while. Then the Captain gives a small, throat-clearing cough and says, "I have heard that you have been enlivening the Officers' Mess on a nightly basis."

*Uh-oh...That last bit of dancing on the tabletop...*

"I hope I have not offended you, Sir, or disobeyed your orders."

*Simper, simper...big weepy eyes now...*

"No, not at all. And I observed how you managed to whip the seamen up to a state of high hilarity on Sunday afternoon."

On many ships, and I am glad to say that the *Dauntless* is one of those, the Captain will permit singing and dancing and playing of music by the common sailors on the fo'c'sle after Sunday services. An extra measure of grog is issued and spirits tend to run high. The past two Sabbaths I was given permission to join in with the men, and though I did not drink the rum that was offered me, I did sing and I did dance and I did fiddle away most energetically. I danced the Irish dances with the Irish lads and the Scottish dances with the Scottish laddies and I danced the hornpipe with Davy just like we did back in the old days with Liam Delaney on the fo'c'sle of the *Dolphin*. I sang and danced and played to the delight of all till the sound of the ship's bell called all to supper and put an end to the festivities. *God, how I love a good audience, and how I do love the applause!*

"I am an entertainer, Sir," I say. "And perhaps I was too enthusiastic in my performance. If so, I am sorry. I do like to give one hundred percent."

"No, no, my dear, think nothing of it. The men enjoyed it hugely and I like it when their morale is high."

Another silence. Then...

"But I say to myself, Hannibal, why should your officers and your men have all the fun, eh?"

"Sir?"

"I should like you to dine with me on Friday evening..."

*Uh-oh.*

"...as I am having my officers and midshipmen to dinner."

*Ah…for a moment there I thought I was up for yet another wrestling match with a randy male, and, though the Captain is not an unhandsome man, I am glad to find that he is an honorable one as well.*

"It is Mr. Bennett's birthday and we will be only about three days out from England and that is cause for celebration, as well."

*For you it is cause to rejoice, Captain, but not for me. While I am very glad to hear you say that you will try to help me when we get to London, I know that you will have to hand me over to the vile Bliffil as soon as we get there, and I feel your efforts, however kind and worthy, will be in vain. Nay, I shall rely upon my own efforts, as it should be. I believe I will be shortly taking yet another swim.*

"I should be honored to come to dinner, Sir. And thank you for the kindness you have shown me in so many ways."

That night I bring my knees up to my chest and curl into the ball in which I usually sleep and think fondly of Jaimy.

*Dear Jaimy, things are going as well as can be expected. I have found some friends aboard—and can you believe that our brother Davy is one of them? What a wonderful world! And I have made many others, so my future is not quite so bleak as it was a scant few weeks ago. Therefore, do not worry about me.*

*Good night, Jaimy. I hope you are enjoying many wondrous sights of strange lands and people on your journey across the seas—for, after all, isn't that why we signed on to this seafaring life?*

*Sleep well, my dear…*

# Chapter 7

James Emerson Fletcher, Lieutenant
On board HMS Mercury
off the Coast of West Africa

Miss Jacky Faber
Dovecote
Quincy, Massachusetts, USA

Dear Jacky,

  I hope this letter finds you well, safe, and happy. I know it
is too much to expect that you are back at the Lawson Peabody
School or are safely ensconced at the Trevelyne estate for the fall
and winter, as I have learned what idle wishes these might be
when I consider your wild and impetuous nature. Still, I can
hope.

  As for me, I have found the company of my fellow officers
on the Mercury most congenial. Captain Blackstone is a good
and fair man, and I would look forward to the continuance of
this cruise were it not for the fact that it separates me from you.

94

*I continually think back to the last time I saw you, when you suddenly appeared on the deck of the* Mercury, *and then just as quickly dived off the rail of our ship and disappeared into the turquoise waters of the Caribbean. The soles of your bare feet twinkling under the blue green water was the last glimpse I had of you. Well, maybe not—I did see a slight figure waving from the deck of the little schooner before it sailed out of sight.*

*We have picked up the convoy of slow, clumsy merchantmen that we are to escort to China. I know it is a duty you would find deadly dull, but still it must be done and I must admit it is good to be back in Royal Navy rig again.*

*It is rumored that the* Mercury *might be detached to deliver diplomatic pouches to operatives in Morocco. That will be a pleasant change, I believe.*

*The boat carrying the mail is about to leave, so I must be brief. Know, Jacky, that you are uppermost in my thoughts, always.*

*Your Most Obedient & etc.*

*Jaimy*

# Chapter 8

During these weeks, I have been given more and more the freedom of the ship, and with both my good Marine guardians and the very covetous Mr. Jared now used to my ways, I often visit with Davy in the foretop. We enjoy talking about the people we both know in London and in Boston—he especially delights in hearing of his new wife Annie's brave actions in helping the girls of the Lawson Peabody gain their freedom from the slaver *Bloodhound*. The weather is generally pleasant and we spend many happy midday hours there.

"The little schooner that lies just off the horizon," he says one day, "I'm reckonin' those are your friends?" We are sitting cross-legged on the foretop deck and sharing some sausage and other treats that I managed to have my steward nab for me.

"Um," I say, chewing on a particularly tasty bit. "I think so. I hope you haven't said anything to anybody about it."

"No, other than reporting it. Can't not report a sighting, else the lookout'd be whipped."

That's true. Though I have found Captain Hudson to be a decent and fair man, there have been two times in the last weeks when men have been tied to the grating and given a dozen lashes of the cat-o'-nine-tails. Both times for petty theft from the ship's stores. I was glad that I didn't have to witness the punishment as it would have brought back too sharply that time on the *Bloodhound* when I, myself, was similarly bound, stripped of my shirt, and whipped into senselessness.

"I think the officers believe that it's just a little ship makin' the crossing for its own reasons and stayin' close to us so she could run under the protection of our guns should a pirate threaten her. It's done all the time," says Davy. "So what do you plan?"

"Hand on your tattoo, Davy, and swear you won't breathe a word."

"'Course not," he says. "The Brotherhood forever and the Royal Navy be damned."

I take a breath and say, "What I plan to do is this: I have given my parole to Captain Hudson that I will not try to escape *until we sight land.* I am hoping everyone's forgotten about that part of my pledge. As soon as we do spot the coast, which I think will be somewhere around Land's End, or Plymouth, or maybe the Isle of Wight, in any case, the moment I hear 'Land, ho!' from the lookout, I will step out of my dress and fly up to the main yard and walk to the end of it. There will be a great hue and cry, but I will say, 'I'd rather die a sailor's death than be hung up like a side of mutton!' And then I will dive off."

"That's all very fine and very dramatic, as suits your show-off nature," says Davy, doubtfully, "but that would be at least a twenty-mile swim, and the water is getting cold."

"Well, I don't plan on swimming all of it. Here, try this bit of beef—it's right off the Captain's table of last night," I say and sit back against the mast. "No, what I will do is dive down and come up at the aft of the ship, under the sheer of the hull where I can't be seen, and climb up on the rudder pintle and sit up there out of sight throughout that day until nightfall, and when we get close enough to the land and I can see the lights in the windows of cottages, then I will swim for it. Those on this ship will not be able to see me and if I can get to the shore, then I will either be picked up by my little schooner, or, failing that, I shall make my way to London, and, if I can get to Cheapside, then no one will be able to catch me there."

"Lot of 'ifs' in that plan, Jack," says Davy, "but I reckon it's as good as any, considerin' your situation." He also leans back against the foremast. "Least we can do is get up an oil-skin bag with a blanket and some food in it—maybe some clothes—and tie it on top of the pintle just before you're ready to go. Me and me mates'll take care of that—cover it up with a side-painting work party."

"Thank you, Davy, that would be very good."

"Hey, Annie would never forgive me if I let you get hanged. Not that it'd bother me overmuch, but..."

"You're the best, Davy, and I mean it." I plant a sisterly kiss on his cheek and get up. "But now I must get back to the Doctor, and then I must dress for the Captain's dinner."

I think about what to wear tonight and decide to take a chance. After all, what have I got to lose?

I get out of my serving-girl rig, go to my seabag, and pull out the packet containing my uniform. First to go on is my frilly, white dress shirt, with its lacy cuffs and collar that comes up high under my chin. Around it I wrap the black cravat and tie it at my throat. Next I put on my dark blue skirt—I want to put on the white trousers, but I know I won't get away with that. Best go slow, even though time grows short—then my black boots. Lastly, I take up my splendid lieutenant's jacket, all navy blue with bright gold trim, shove my arms through the sleeves, shrug into it, and button up.

Wig? No, not tonight. I will wear my own short but no longer stubby hair, and one more thing.

I dive into the seabag again and I bring out my silver Trafalgar Medal on its loop of red ribbon and hang it about my neck. *That oughta show 'em, by God.*

Fluff up the hair, a little color on the cheeks, smooth everything down, and look in the mirror. *Smashing, I must say.*

There is a tapping on the door and Patrick says, "Miss? They are ready for you."

There is a common gasp as I come into the Captain's cabin in full naval fig—*Take that, gentlemen.* I am wearing as well my Lawson Peabody School for Young Girls "Look." I may not be a fine lady, but I certainly can act like one when I have to. Thank you, Mistress Pimm.

I hear exclamations of *My word!* and *Extraordinary!* and *Outrageous!*—the last from an outraged Bliffil—but the Captain merely beams at me and gestures to the chair next to him on his left. I do a half bow—a curtsy wouldn't be appropriate, I think—and then take Joseph Jared's proffered arm and am led to my seat. All the men stand at their places. Captain Hudson is at the head, of course, and Mr. Bennett is to his right. Mr. Curtis sits next to me.

The Captain, resplendent in his dark blue uniform with its gold lapels, picks up the glass of wine that is in front of him and says, "Miss Faber, will you give us the King?"

I reach down and pick up my own glass and lift it before me, as do all the others.

"To the health of our good King George—long may he reign—both in victory and someday, it is to be hoped, in peace."

*Hear, hear* is chorused all along the table and we are seated.

Stewards come in bearing trays of steaming food, and they begin to serve it. It seems that we shall be treated to roast beef and fish.

"You are dressed in quite a remarkable fashion, Miss Faber," says the Captain, as a platter of beef is put before him and then a tray of fish. He takes some from both. "Perhaps you will explain?"

"I was made Midshipman by Captain Locke on board HMS *Dolphin* and Acting Lieutenant by Captain Scroggs of the *Wolverine*," I say. The trays are next presented to me and I take the tongs, but take only the beef—I had quite my fill of fish on the way down the Mississippi, thank you. "And as far as I know, my commission has not been revoked."

"Ha!" barks the Captain. "Well said, well said, indeed! I see also that you wear the Trafalgar Medal. There are many here who envy you that, myself included. I was off in the South Seas at the time, curse the luck. Will you tell us how that came about?"

"I am not the only one here entitled to wear this medal," says I, looking over the rim of my glass at Joseph, who is seated opposite me. "Mr. Jared was there, too, and on the same ship. Perhaps he will tell it."

"Yes, do so, Mr. Jared," says the Captain, tucking into his dinner. "If you would."

Joseph Jared nods and says, "I believe the whole fleet has heard of how the probably demented Captain Scroggs of the *Wolverine* made Miss Faber an Acting Lieutenant after a skirmish with a French gunboat in which she distinguished herself, and then sent off all of his officers, except her, on a foolish errand for...his own reasons. He died that very same night of a poor constitution and...er...extreme exertions. Miss Faber, being the only commissioned officer aboard, then took command of the ship and commenced to take prizes. Eventually she turned command over to Captain Trumbull, and he left her name on the books as Lieutenant J. M. Faber, and thus she wears the medal. As well as the marks of the battle."

He puts his finger to his right eye and then gestures at me. Without the curls of a wig to tumble over my brow, the spray of light blue powder burns radiating from my right eye is plainly visible—my other tattoo, I like to call it. I notice that several others around the table bear similar marks, proof that they, too, have bent over a cannon to aim and fire and then felt the sharp bite of the backflash.

"Hmmm," says the Captain, taking a fishbone from between his teeth and placing it on the table. "I had heard that story and did not believe it—the very idea of a young girl commanding a Royal Navy ship, impossible! But Mr. Jared was there and so now I must believe it."

"One thing you should also believe, Sir," hisses Bliffil, far down the table, "is that Warrant Officer Jared glosses over the fact that the *Wolverine,* when under her *supposed* command, took *four* prizes and she turned only *three* of them over to the

King. She took the fourth one for herself and then set out as a pirate, and just why she sits here at this table—"

"She sits at this table at my pleasure, Mr. Bliffil," says the Captain, with a hard edge to his voice. "To lend us all some amusement and diversion. If you do not like it, you are welcome to leave our company."

Bliffil looks down at his plate, thrusts a forkful of beef in his mouth, and says nothing more this night.

A Midshipman at the end of the table, emboldened by the amount of wine he has drunk, pipes up with "Did you really spike the guns at Harwich, Miss? I am from that town and it is talked of to this day."

I look down at the squeaker, thirteen years old if he is a day, and say, "Yes, Mr. Shelton, that did happen. But how did you come to know of it?" I make it my practice whenever in a bind to learn the names of everyone involved, and so I know his name.

"Oh, Miss, the third book about your adventures had just come out when we left London. It's called *Under the Jolly Roger* and I believe it presents the case against your piracy charge most admirably."

*Good Lord, not another one!*

"...and did you really take off your..."

"I think that will be quite enough for now, Mr. Shelton," I say, blushing in spite of myself. "I do outrank you, young sir."

*Lord, Amy, did you put it all in? For a born bluenosed Boston Puritan yourself, you sure ain't shy about tellin' the world what Jacky Faber's been up to.*

Mr. Bennett takes up for Midshipman Shelton and he addresses Joseph Jared. "Did it not put you up for some ridicule in the Fleet, Mr. Jared, having served under a woman, a girl, really?" he asks. "I mean no offense, of course." The phrase *under a woman* gets some low chuckles along the table. These *are* men, after all.

"No offense taken, Sir," says Joseph. "And as to ridicule? Remember, Sir, that I came up through the ranks and as such I know how to fight, with fist, club, sword, or pistol. As a matter of fact, I received my first warrant commission from Lieutenant Faber when she was in command of the *Wolverine.* Captain Trumbull was good enough to allow me to continue in that position and here I sit today in the company of you gentlemen. And because of the prize money I earned when under her command, I now have a tidy little cottage in Hampshire. I have installed my mother and younger sisters in it and they are quite happy," he says, and then turns his eyes back to me. "And if I am ever to wed, I will have a place to put my wife." He winks his down-table eye at me and grins widely. "Sorry to have served under her? I must say nay."

You would think he would be cowed in this company comprised entirely of his social betters, but he is not. *Such a merry rogue.*

"Well, then," says the Captain later, as the main courses are taken away, "let us have some pudding and port and maybe Miss Faber will favor us with a song."

Oh, yes, I do favor them with a song, and much more than that. I have my pennywhistle and a fiddle and my dancing feet and the party roars on and on, far into the night.

# Chapter 9

The next morning, I pop up, wash, and, finding it a bit chilly, put my uniform back on, since I had left my cloak in Amy's care back at Dovecote and the dresses I have with me are too light. When I had packed for my last voyage on the *Nancy B* I thought I was going down to the sunny Caribbean, but it certainly didn't turn out that way. Guess that'll teach me to be prepared for anything.

After all, I had gotten away with wearing my uniform last night with the officers so it should go down well with the rest of the crew. I don't like the cocked hat that goes with a lieutenant's outfit because I think I look ridiculous in it, so I clap my midshipman's cap on my head and leave my room, looking for my breakfast. Strangely, I find the table in the Officers' Mess not set.

"What's up, Jonathan? Where is everyone?"

"Don't know, Miss. I think they might be sick," replies Private Morris.

*Hmmm.* I know there will be many a pounding head this morning after last night's revels—I, of course, feel fine since I don't drink spirits—but still, there should be more activity here…at least the stewards should be setting the table, even if the officers would not be up for eating any breakfast.

"Come along, Jonathan, let's go find out." And I lead the way out of the Gun Deck and head for the quarterdeck.

When I get there, I'm surprised to find Captain Hudson standing watch. Well, sort of standing. Actually he is leaning heavily against the rail, his face as white as any of his sails.

"Good morning, Sir," I say, saluting. "Whatever is the matter?"

With difficulty he brings his eyes to focus on me standing below on the main deck. "Bad…*urp*…fish…last night. Everybody sick…some worse than others." With that he turns and vomits over the side, but I'm thinking there is nothing left in his belly to throw up, so he must now contend with the dry retches, and I know from personal experience that there're few things worse.

"I am so sorry, Sir, if I can help…"

"No help for him or any of the others," says Dr. Sebastian, who has come up by my side. "Except a day or so spent horizontal. They'll be all right tomorrow." He looks me up and down. "Since you are quite vertical, I suspect that you, also, did not partake of the fish. *Um*, thought so."

"How are my officers, Stephen?" the Captain manages to wheeze.

"You are about the only one able to stand," says the Doctor. "But they'll be back on their feet soon. It's only a simple case of food poisoning. Seldom fatal. Oh, and Mr. Bliffil is not sick."

"I am so glad for *Mr.* Bliffil," growls the Captain. "Pity he is not a regular officer, else he would be standing here right now and I'd be in my bed. Oh, God..." He hangs his head over the rail again.

"I must insist, Captain, that you go below and rest."

"I cannot leave the quarterdeck without a qualified officer upon it."

"Sir," I pipes up, "I can stand the watches till the officers are well again. I am still on the books as an Acting Lieutenant. I stood watches on the whaler *Pequod* and I was in command of the *Wolverine,* the *Emerald,* the *Belle of the Golden West,* and the *Nancy B. Alsop.* Please, Sir, let me help."

"That would be highly...Sweet Jesus, my gut!...irregular," gurgles Captain Hudson, clutching his stomach. But he does not refuse outright. Instead, he looks up into the rigging. "There are several things wrong there. Come up here and tell me what they are."

I climb the short run of stairs that leads to the quarterdeck and then turn to look up, fore and aft. I decide to start off with a joke.

"Aside from not seeing the bodies of the cooks and stewards swinging from the yardarm for causing you such distress, Sir...," I begin.

"Would've flogged 'em half to death, but they're as sick as the others," he grunts, "so what would be the point?"

"...the flying jib has a bit of luff in it, and I'd trim back the t'gallant as it doesn't seem to be drawing properly, and I think we could get a bit more speed if the stuns'ls were set as the breeze seems to be lessening," I say, nodding as sagely an any old salt.

The Captain looks at me through anguished eyes, plainly considering. "Humph! Such cheek. But you are right... *urp*...and just qualified as Officer of the Deck."

I'm hoping I didn't go too far in the way of cheek, but the Captain merely turns to the Bo'sun's Mate of the Watch to bark out an order, and in a moment sailors are flying up the rigging to correct the problems.

"Very well. If Captains Locke, Scroggs, and Trumbull can play this game, so can I, and be damned to them who think otherwise. The simple fact is I must be horizontal and try to sleep until this thing leaves me. You will shout down that speaking tube at the first sign of anything irregular and before you do anything not in my standing orders. Do you hear?"

I nod. "Aye, Sir."

"Maintain present set of sails, Course 093 degrees."

"Course 093, aye, Sir."

The Captain clears his throat and announces to the Watch, "Miss...er...*Lieutenant* Faber has the con."

"This is Lieutenant Faber," I pipe, trying to suppress a grin and keep from bouncing up and down on my toes. "I have the con."

The Captain turns and staggers below to his cabin on the arm of his friend the Doctor, and I take up my old stance, one foot to each side of the centerline of the ship, so I can best feel her movement in the wind and through the water.

The ship is well maintained, as I thought it would be under the command of Captain Hannibal Hudson. The sails are tight, the course is straight, and the men on watch are well turned out and neat, which is how I like it. *They may be taking me back to hang me, but with a fine ship under my feet and a brisk wind behind me, I will enjoy this moment.*

I do enjoy it for a few moments, then I have trouble— not with the ship, but with my costume. I'm looking forward, making sure that the luff is now out of the jib, when all of a sudden a blue cloth whips across my face and I realize that it is my blue skirt blowing up over my head. The breeze ain't stiff, but it's strong enough to do that.

*Har, har! Good show, that!* All of a sudden the spars and yards are full of grinning sailors.

"Messenger, go fetch the Bo'sun," I say loud enough for all to hear. "And tell him to bring his knobby. There seem to be some slackers aboard who are not attending to their duties." The grinning faces disappear.

The bells are rung to signal the end of the Morning Watch and the start of the Forenoon Watch.

"Well, just look at this now." I look down and see Davy, looking up at me standing on the quarterdeck. "If it ain't a jumped-up ship's boy what ain't got no notion of her place, and never did."

"Be careful how you speak to me, Seaman Jones," I say, putting on my haughtiest Look, "as I am the Officer of the Deck. All the other officers are sick."

Davy cuts his eyes to the Bo'sun's Mate of the Watch, who confirms the truth of this with a quick nod and a shrug.

Then my traitorous dress flies up in my face again. *Damn! I'm tryin' to maintain some dignity here!* I try to beat the thing down with my hands, but when I succeed in bringing it down in front, it pops up in back.

"You look like you could use a little help, Lieutenant," notes Davy, unable to control his laughter.

"Yes, I could," I say, steaming. "Now go down to my cabin and get my white trousers out of my seabag. And there's a pair of short drawers in the top drawer under the sink."

Davy bounds up to the quarterdeck and surprises me by relieving the Bo'sun's Mate of the Watch. The helmsman also changes, as does the Messenger, and Private Jonathan Morris is relieved by Adam Marsten on the Jacky Watch.

"Going to fetch your knickers ain't in my job description," says Davy, just out of hearing of the others on the upper deck. "Forbush!" he barks at the Messenger, plainly a ship's boy. "You heard what she needs. Go down and get it. Private Morris will show you to her room."

The boy and the Marine leave and Davy comes up close to me.

"Do you know how hard it is for me to take orders from you, Jack-*ass*?" he asks pleasantly.

"Suck it up, Davy. If all goes well and I get back to Boston, I will give you a job with Faber Shipping, Worldwide, and then you'll be taking orders from me for the rest of your life. When the war is over, you'll want to be snugged up with Annie in Boston, won't you? Who knows, one day I might rate you Able."

"Jacky, you are so full of it." He chuckles. "But then, you always were, so why should now be any different?"

The boy comes back with my clothes and I go to the fantail, at the rear of the quarterdeck. I toe off my boots and reach up inside my skirt and pull down my long, flouncy pantaloons—they are fine under a long skirt, but will plainly not do under trim-cut trousers.

I reach for my short, cut-off drawers and am putting them on when the wind decides to lift my dress again. *Father Neptune having a bit of fun, I suppose.* I pull them all the way up and roar out, "All aboard, face forward, you dogs!"

I hear a long, drawn-out chorus of *Awwww...* but I guess they comply. Don't matter now, anyway. I pull on my trousers under the cover of my skirt, which finally has decided to be good, after the damage is done, and then unfasten the skirt to pull it down and off. *There. Boots back on and ready to do my duty, properly attired.*

"Still too damn skinny for my taste," says Davy, as I come back to the front of the quarterdeck and assume my usual stance.

"Well, that's good, Davy, 'cause you're a married man now and must not be lookin' at other girls' legs, skinny or not. 'Specially if those legs belong to your superior officer."

I pick up my folded skirt with the drawers tucked well inside and give them to the boy Forbush. "Make sure these get back to my seabag *exactly* as they are, else your bottom shall feel the rod. Do you understand me, Forbush?" He gulps and nods and carries his burden away. I do not wish to be mean, but had I not said that, I could expect my underdrawers to be flying merrily from the masthead within minutes, to the delight of all below—except me.

I check to see that the helmsman, a seaman named Bassett, is steering a properly straight course, praise him for that fact when I find that he does, and then I go over to stand next to Davy again.

"So, little man," I say, "you've come a long way to be Bo'sun's Mate of the Watch." That watch station is always held by one of the Bo'sun's more trusted men.

"Not as far as you have, Jacky, but then, I don't have the same...equipment."

"I hope you don't think that I've gotten to this position on my back, brother," I say, severely, giving him a sisterly poke in the ribs.

"Nay, I don't think nothin' about officers, Lieutenant, I'm just a common seaman what minds his own business." Saying that, he takes me by the elbow and leads me back to the fantail again. "Don't worry about Bassett, he's one of me mates."

We look over the edge of the fantail rail and see the top of the rudder sloshing through the water. "Me and a couple of the lads is putting your bag down on the pintle tonight, on the Midwatch. It'll be good if you're on watch, so it won't be quite so difficult a thing to do."

"Looks like I'm gonna be, Davy. Thanks be to the God that loves a poor sailor and gave a touch of the Bad-Fish Quick-Step to the would-be regular watch standers just in the nick of time."

"Amen to that. Well, it's a tight oilskin bag and has got a blanket and some salt pork and a jug of grog in it. 'Tain't much, but it should keep you warm enough till you're ready to swim for it. We're going to tie it to the top gudgeon right there."

I nod and touch his arm. "Davy, I know you're trying to save my life with this, at some risk to your own."

"Hey, the Brotherhood forever, right, Jack-o?"

"Right, Davy, and thanks."

We go back to the front of the quarterdeck and take up our usual positions, me with my feet again planted to either side of the centerline and my hands clasped behind me. I feel much better with the trim trousers on, knowing that I'll be able to leap up into the rigging should the occasion arise.

I look up into the set of sails to see that all is well and I'm thinking of sending down for some food, seeing that I missed breakfast, when Bliffil appears on the main deck below and regards me with utter amazement.

"Outrage piled upon outrage!" he sputters. "I cannot believe this! Get off that deck!"

He starts toward the quarterdeck stairs.

"This is Mr. Bliffil," he announces, "and I have command of this—"

"You have nothing, Mr. Bliffil, except unfortunately, your health, while many of your betters do not," I say, glaring down at him with all the contempt I can muster. "Private Marsten, you will prevent that man from coming on the quarterdeck."

Private Adam Marsten, looking very worried, steps in front of the stairs with his musket at port arms. "Do not worry, Private, he is not a regular Naval officer, merely a civilian passenger." That's not quite true, but hey, it'll work.

"I'll see that you all swing for this!"

"Bliffil, I am the Officer of the Deck, made so by the Captain, and as such I speak for that Captain in his absence. When I speak, you hear the Captain's voice. If I ask the Bo'-sun's Mate of the Watch there to throw you overboard, he will do it, would you not, Seaman Jones?"

Davy, the Bo'sun's Mate of the Watch, considers and then nods—he, too, was treated cruelly by Bliffil back on the *Dolphin,* and I know he is taking great pleasure from this scene. "Just say the word, Lieutenant."

"'Course I might have to answer for it later," I continue, "but then I already have a lot to answer for, don't I, Bliffil? And I think your taking a big gulp of the salt would be the least of them. Just another expendable Intelligence Officer who has done his duty for his King. We all want to do our duty, don't we, Bliffil?"

"Just you wait till I get you back to London, then we'll see, won't we, girl?" sneers Bliffil.

"Where did you buy your commission, Bliffil?" I spit right back at him. "A rich uncle? Some member of the Navy Board who owed your dad a favor? Just how did you get it? Everyone on this ship knows you ain't a sailor—the Captain knows that and that's why you ain't standin' watch up here right now and I am. So get yourself gone or I will ask the Bo'sun to clear the deck of trash."

"Trash? By God, I—" says Bliffil, but he does not get to finish.

"On deck there" is the call from the lookout high up on the mainmast. "It's that little schooner, again, out to the east."

I try not to smile at that. *My friends, my very good friends.*

"...and wait...More masts! Directly ahead! Two...no, four!"

*What?*

"...and three more to the south!"

I grab the long glass from its rack and loop the lanyard around my neck and race up the mizzenmast ratline and into the top to train the glass to the west. There they are... and their colors are coming into view. *Damn! They fly the Tricolor! It is the French!*

"Beat to Quarters!" I cry. "Clear for action!"

There is instant pandemonium below as the *Dauntless* prepares for battle. I hear shouts and orders and the sound of whistle and a drum. I whip my glass around to the right and look to the south...can't quite see their flags yet...

now…there…my heart sinks—they are part of the same French squadron. *We are in deep trouble…*

In the rush of the men to their stations below, I see Davy and shout, "Davy! Man the top! We're gonna turn north!" With that I plummet hand over hand back down to the deck.

"All topmen aloft to make sail!" bellows Davy on his way up the mainmast.

"What should I do, Miss?" asks Private Kent, confused as to where his duty lies. "I'm supposed to go into the top, as a marksman."

"Go to your station, Billy," I say. "The Jacky Watch is over." *And probably for good.*

The Battle-Stations Watch is now on the quarterdeck—sort of. We have the Bo'sun himself, several messengers, and a boy who had been beating on a drum waiting till the word *manned and ready* from all stations has been reported, but we have no First Mate and no Sailing Master.

I put my mouth to the speaking tube. "Captain! You must come up! We have the French on two sides of us, and they have the weather gauge! I am altering course to the north!"

I turn to the helmsman and say, "Left Full Rudder!"

The helmsman hesitates and looks to the Bo'sun. After all, I am a girl, and they have not yet seen me in this position, so I must realize that and not get mad even though I know we are in a desperate fix and they'd better hurry up.

The Bo'sun sizes up the situation—the French fleet to the west and to the south—and nods, so the helmsman puts the wheel over and the *Dauntless* turns her head, presents her tail to the enemy, and heads for Mother England.

"Steer due north, Helmsman, straight and true as if your life depends on it." *As it very well might.*

The wind is from the southeast and could not be better suited to the enemy—they are upwind of us and that spells disaster; they can maneuver freely, while we must claw into the wind; they can bring their broadside to bear on us while we only fire our bow chaser or stern gun. The ships to our south have already turned to cut off any chance of our escaping to the west. The south coast of England is north of us and I figure it would be best to try to escape in that direction—better to go north with the wind on our starboard quarter and run aground on good British rocks than to be taken by the bloody French.

There is no answer from the Captain. I shout down the tube again but again get no response.

"Bo'sun Cargill. Send a messenger down to get Dr. Sebastian. Tell him to bring Stritch and a stretcher. And gather a party of men up here right now."

The Bo'sun knuckles his brow, and two of the messengers go off. I lift the glass for another look at the enemy. Because of our turning they are, of course, much closer, only about three miles away. They know who we are, and they want us. It will be a coup for them to pluck a British frigate from within the very waters of Britannia herself. Well, we shall see about that.

The sails are set, the course is drawn, and we are running for all we are worth when the Doctor appears on the deck, as does a group of seamen, awaiting orders.

"Doctor," I say, "you must go get the Captain and bring him up here."

"Captain Hudson is sick...," says Dr. Sebastian, "...and I

have given him a dose of laudanum to ease his suffering. He cannot get up."

*Damn! Tincture of opium. So often my friend and ally, but, oh, no, not this time!*

"Listen to me, Doctor. You have been very good to me, but I know the Navy and if you do not want your friend Captain Hudson stripped of his rank or worse, you will have him brought to the quarterdeck right now! There is going to be an action and he *must* be on his own quarterdeck!"

The Doctor's face darkens, but he turns to Stritch. "Let us bring up the Captain."

Stritch lifts the stretcher and takes a sailor with him and follows the Doctor into the Captain's cabin.

"Bo'sun, send your men down into the officers' berth and bring them up. I speak for the Captain, and I give your men permission to lay their hands upon them."

"But—"

"But, nothing. I don't care if they are dead. Pick them up and place them at their stations. They will thank you for it later, if any of us survive this thing. Now go do it!"

He orders his men to do so and they go below.

From up forward, from the hatchway above the midshipmen's berth, I spy a figure emerging. It is Joseph Jared, staggering aft, his jacket on but unbuttoned, his face a very unhealthy shade of green. His cocky grin is *not* in place. He manages to gain the quarterdeck stairs, and I reach down to grab an arm and help him get up.

"I heard the drumbeat...to Quarters," he says, trying to keep his head up. He looks at me standing here in my rig. "What the hell happened...What are you doing here... What the hell is going on?"

Two men appear, carrying Mr. Bennett. They bring him onto the quarterdeck and prop him against the rail, and then leave to carry more officers to their battle stations. Little good they will do there, but there they must be.

"Everyone who ate of last night's fish is sick," I say to Jared. "The Captain made me Officer of the Deck, being the last regular officer standing. A French squadron has fallen upon us, to the west, you see them there? And to the south. You see them, too? Good. I thought it best to turn north toward England, and that is what I have done. We are on Course 000, due north."

He staggers to the rail and looks out across the water. Then he looks up at the set of sails. Then he nods. "You did well."

At that moment the Captain, lying on a stretcher, is brought to his quarterdeck.

"Sit him up," says the Doctor. "I want to give him some stimulants." He uncaps a vial under the Captain's nose, and when the Captain's eyes fly open, Dr. Sebastian puts a cup to his lips. The Captain looks about, amazed, but then his eyes roll back and he passes out again. It is no use. It is up to Joseph Jared and me.

"Joseph, if we can get to land, maybe we can slip into an inlet and yet get away," I say to Jared, who now that he's been out in the air for a while, seems to be recovering somewhat. I suspect, also, that the amount of that damned fish a man downed last night is in direct proportion to how sick he is today. I'm guessing that my Sailing Master ate very little.

"Right. I think we are probably due south of Penzance. The Isles of Scilly...or St. Mary's Isle are out there, too. If we can get in sight of any of them, the Froggies'll turn back."

"Should we lighten ship?"

He nods and so do I.

"Bo'sun," I say. "Lighten ship."

He nods and gives orders to his men. The hatches are opened and all cargo, all stores, all casks of rum, all everything is thrown overboard so as to increase our speed. The bulkheads of the officers' cabins, all the long tables, chairs, anchors, chains, chicken cages, and cows if we had 'em, *everything* goes. 'Cause it all ain't gonna mean anything if we are caught or sunk. I'm sure my seabag goes, as well as the walls of my room, my bed, my picture of Jaimy...All gone...

An hour later, the Bo'sun reappears. "We've lightened all we can. What about the guns?"

"Not yet, but have the men ready."

The *Dauntless* is a swift sailer, but several of the smaller enemy ships are even faster, so they steadily gain on us. They will soon be in range of our Long Tom stern guns. Of course that means we are in range of their guns, too, and sure enough we see a puff of smoke appear under the bowsprit of the lead pursuer, followed by a low *boooommmm* rolling across the water. The shot falls short, but not by much.

I sense Jared standing beside me. "You must think of yourself. I know you planned to jump ship when we spotted England. I heard the terms of your parole and I know you. Why don't we just put you in a boat and have you sail back to your little schooner?"

"I did plan that, Joseph," I say. "But then it would have been an escape. Now it would be desertion and I just can't do it. I can't leave my friends in this fix if I can do anything to help them. Let's just go on and see what happens."

He nods and I say, "Let's show them we still have teeth. Bring her around to starboard."

"Right Full Rudder," he says to the helmsman, and the man at the wheel puts her over. The *Dauntless* presents her broadside to the enemy and I yell, "Starboard guns, *fire!*"

There is a great rippling *Craaack!* as the mighty cannons fire. I look out with my glass and see that one of the enemy frigates has lost its foremast. *That'll slow 'em down a bit, for sure!*

"Left now, Joseph," I say, and he gives the order and the port guns come to bear.

*"Fire!"* I screech, and the port broadside roars out.

I look through the glass at the relentless enemy and, alas, see neither great damage nor a slackening of their pursuit.

I snap the telescope back together. "Rudder amidships. Steer dead north. Bo'sun, dump the guns, all except the Long Toms."

There is nothing a man-of-war hates to do more than throw its guns overboard, but there are some times when it is necessary. There are twenty-one guns along each side and each of them weighs two thousand pounds. If we can fly faster and get to safety, we can get more guns—after all, they are but dumb iron brutes and there are many forges that make them, but the ship and its crew are much more difficult to replace. There are seven enemy ships and one of us, so it is not even a contest. We must run, and run as swiftly as we can.

The gunports are opened and the cannons are tipped out to disappear under the waves. Without all that weight, the *Dauntless* leaps forward.

"Let's see them catch us now," I exult as we pull away. As

soon as this ship is safely tucked in Britannia's waters and we spot the land and my parole is over, *then* I will take Jared up on his offer of a lifeboat that will take me back to the *Nancy B.*

"On deck there!" comes the call from above. "Ship dead ahead!"

*Good God, what's this?*

Again I grab the glass and head to the top to stand next to Davy, who is looking very worried.

"I think she's Dutch," says Davy, a long glass to his own eye. "And we are in a fine mess. Give Annie my regards if you ever see her again."

"*Damn!*" I mutter, letting fly a string of curses. The Dutch are close allies of the French, and we are once again in a fine fix—now cut off to the north, as well as the east and south and with most of our guns gone. I race hand over hand back down to the quarterdeck.

"Joseph, there is a Dutchman dead ahead. I say we charge right through her. Maybe take her by surprise."

"I don't see as we've got any other choice," he says. It seems he is fully recovered, and his cocky grin is back in place even in the face of this disaster. "Full speed ahead, Puss, and the Devil take the hindmost."

"Who's on the bow chaser?"

"Hutchinson. He's good."

"Um. Well, tell him to get ready, and to fire when the Dutchman comes in range."

"He's ready, believe me," says Jared, and he sends a messenger forward with the order to fire.

"All right. Here we go." And the *Dauntless* surges forward to whatever awaits her.

Half an hour later, our bow chaser barks out its first challenge. The shot goes wide and Hutchinson and his crew quickly reload and fire again, as the Dutchman gets within a hundred yards of us. She does not respond with her own bow gun, but instead turns her head slowly, almost leisurely to the left, and then fires a full broadside right into us.

Four hundred and fifty pounds of metal tear into the *Dauntless*. Men scream and fall from the rigging as the top of the mainmast shears off and falls to the deck. From behind us, one of the Frenchmen gets off a broadside of its own and our rudder is shattered.

We are helpless.

"It's over," I say to Jared and leap back to the flagstaff. The colors wrap around me as I haul them down.

I surrender the ship.

# Chapter 10

Three days later we are in the French prison at Cherbourg, at the mouth of the Seine, the river that flows past Paris as well as past the Emperor Napoléon and his legions.

After I had struck the *Dauntless*'s colors, one of the French frigates came alongside with grapples and made us fast. French sailors and Marines swarmed aboard and began stripping our crew of their weapons and herding the men down into the main cargo hold—those who could walk, anyway. The wounded were taken to the Doctor's surgery. The dead were thrown overboard without proper ceremony. Private Marsten was one of them, and it saddened me greatly, for I had grown very attached to my Marines. *Go to God, Adam. I hope good quarters are waiting to welcome you.*

But the time for grief would have to be later, as things needed to be done.

Jared and I stood on the quarterdeck and waited for the French Commander to appear. While we waited for him, I sent for the Captain's sword to be brought up, and so it was.

I took it and laid it across his chest. I also ripped all the lieutenant's gold braid from my lapels and flung it over the side, demoting myself once more to midshipman.

Mr. Jared observed me doing this so I explained to him, "Joseph, this is serious. I must be known as Midshipman Jack…er…Kemp, as my cheeks are too downy to pass for any lieutenant. The French must *not* find out that I am female, else I am lost. They will examine me and put two and two together and figure out that I am their *Jeune Fille sans Merci,* the cruel girl pirate, and when that happens my head will soon fall into a basket. You must help me."

"Aye. I will spread that word amongst the crew when I am put down in the hatch with the rest of them, which is sure to be soon, and I'll let them know that I will kill any of them who would give you up. And that goes for the officers, too, when they recover," he said, turning to me with the old cocky grin back in place. "And I would take a kiss right now for my troubles, were it not for the fact that we are sure to be watched by that Frenchy standing right there, and it wouldn't look good for me to be bending a midshipman over and…"

"No, it would not, Joseph."

"A pity, Puss, for it will surely be the last kiss I'll ever receive from anybody for a good long while." I know the truth of this, for while captains and senior lieutenants are routinely freed in prisoner exchanges, mere warrant officers almost never are. Jared is looking at confinement till the end of the war, and that does not seem to be coming soon.

At last the French Squadron Commander bounded aboard, a short, pudgy little man who could scarcely conceal his delight. *A prize!* I knew he was thinking, *A British warship! How this shall benefit both my pocketbook and my reputation! I shall surely be made Admiral!*

As I advanced to meet him, I bowed and said, "Midshipman Jack Kemp, *à votre service, Capitaine.*"

He looked at me in wonder and said, "What is this? A mere boy?"

I swept my hand toward our recumbent Captain and continued, "*Permettez-moi à vous présenter, Capitaine Hannibal Hudson, le Commandant du HMS* Dauntless."

"*Le pauvre homme!*" said the Frenchy, seemingly concerned with our Captain's well-being. That's how it goes with these things—you try your best to murder each other when the action is ongoing, and then, when it's over, it's back to good manners again. "*J'espère que...*"

"Your hope that the expert gunnery of your ships did not bring our Captain low," I replied in French, "that is most gracious and kind. *Mais, non,* you may set your mind at ease—it was a fish."

"*Du poisson?*"

"*Oui, Monsieur, du mauvais poisson,*" said I. "The ship's officers were overcome with a sickness after having partaken of a fish that had turned against us. HMS *Dauntless,* distinguished in many a heroic battle, was brought down by a fish. Had the officers been at their best, you would have had a much harder time taking us. As you say, I am but a boy, and I did what I could, but..."

He looked me over. "You did well, young man. You have nothing to be ashamed of," he said, giving me a curt bow. "I am Captain Jules Renaud, at your service."

I returned the bow and went over to Captain Hudson to

pick up his sword to present it to Captain Renaud. He took it but shook his head and laid it back down on the Captain's chest.

"No, let the poor man keep his sword. It may give him some comfort when he awakens to find his ship and his command gone," said this Captain Renaud, who did not seem to be a bad sort. "Ha! So, a fine kettle of fish it was, as you English say. You should have carried a French cook, my lad." He laughed, shaking a pudgy finger in my face. "He would have known how to tell a good fish from a bad one!"

After the pleasantries were over, I, too, was put down into the hold.

Both the Doctor and I were by the Captain's side when he woke up deep in the darkness of his own hold. He took the bitter news a lot better than I would have, had I been in his place. He recovered quickly from his sickness, as did the other officers over the next few days.

All of us had been crammed into the hold, officers and men alike, but, as always, accommodations are made, and territories are mapped out—the Captain and the senior lieutenants aft, and the men spread out forward. I sought out Davy and found him to be safe, thank God, and rejoiced in his company during the day, but I spent the nights curled up next to Joseph Jared, his arm about my shoulders and my face upon his chest, giving me great comfort in my distress. I was *so* close to gaining my freedom, and going back to my life, and now this. *The fortunes of war* is how the Captain put it in his philosophical way, and I am forced to agree, but I have a lot more to lose than any of the rest of them if I am found out.

I woke up each morning of our journey, from seaborne captivity to a land prison, with my face buried in the nape of Joseph Jared's neck, a fact not missed by a certain member of the Intelligence Service. Bliffil was never far away, he who had hidden during the battle and had emerged only after it was over, wearing a lieutenant's jacket and hat to keep from being branded a spy. He considers me a prize, I realize, as he sits propped up against the hull of the ship, always, always watching as if he owned me. And, as it turns out later, he does.

Captain Renaud invited Captain Hudson up for dinner each night after he had recovered from his case of *mauvais poisson*, and I went with him, but not as a guest, for I am a mere midshipman—no, it was as translator, for Captain Hudson's French is not good. So, instead of sitting at the table and partaking of the wonderful spread of food out there in front of me, I stood at Attention behind my Captain's chair, and spoke only when necessary. It was exquisite torture, given my appetite, but I managed to endure.

When we reached France, however, all the pleasantries were over and we were taken, Captain, officers, and men, and stuffed down into a foul prison.

# Chapter 11

The prison at Cherbourg is built in the shape of a U, with the men being put in one wing of the jail, and the officers in another. We are, of course, not the only ones here. There are some who have been in this prison for months, even years, poor buggers.

There is a courtyard within the U, with a whipping post in the center of it. We have already been treated to the sight of prisoners being tied to the post and lashed for minor infractions of the rules. To close the top of the U, there is a great iron gate, with sharp spikes on the top, to make anyone considering escaping that way think twice.

All of us are equals now, in our confinement—the Captain, Dr. Sebastian, Mr. Bennett, and the other officers choose their sleeping spots, but one is much like any other. In our section, there are single bunks built into the stone walls, shelves like. We are given blankets and straw mattresses, and I figure it best that I sleep alone, so as not to cause discord among the officers and all. I mean, I know I ain't much, but I am a girl, and after a while here, some men's thoughts may turn to . . . well, you know. I make up my bunk right below Joseph Jared, and that first night I curl up in my customary ball, drawing my knees to my chin, say my usual prayers for Jaimy and the rest, so I figure I will get through the night all right.

But it doesn't work out that way at all.

That first night in prison, after sleep comes upon me, *they* come for me in my dream—the Newgate Hangman, the Pirate LeFievre, Captain Scroggs, Pap Beam, and all the rest, each of them hollow eyed and ghastly, like skulls, wavin' nooses at me, and then Sammy Nettles comes and gets a rope around me neck and giggles, *Now, Smart-mouth, now yer gonna get it, and get it good...* and I start thrashin' about and pleadin', *No, no, please, I'm just a poor girl what's always tried to be good and oh, God! I beg of you...*

I feel a hand across my mouth, I open my eyes and look into those of Joseph Jared whose hand it is that stifles my nightmare cries.

"You're goin' to give yourself away, Puss," he whispers in my ear. "Some of them Frenchies out there might understand a bit of English. We've got to fix this, Jacky. How are we gonna do it?"

I know right well how to fix it. To hell with discord and propriety.

"Get back in your bunk, Joseph," I breathe, my breast heaving and my breath still ragged from the horror of my dream, "and I will join you there. That will stop the nightmares. It always has."

He, clad in his drawers and scant else, it being a warm night, climbs back up into his bed, and, in a moment, I climb up, too. I get between him and the wall and he puts his arm around me and I put my head on his bare chest, take a long, slow breath, let it out, and fall into a deep, deep sleep.

I do *not* like sleeping alone.

I, of course, did sleep more soundly each night after that, and I contrived to be the first one up in the morning to conceal the fact that I had just crawled out of Joseph Jared's bed, but, really, I think I fooled no one. Still, the other officers let it go and pretended not to notice, preferring peace over discord, and I was able to sleep without waking everyone with my screams.

One night, however, I was roused by some small sound so I lifted my head to peer out over Joseph's sleeping form and thought I could make out Bliffil standing at the cage door and whispering to the guard outside. Since I was halfway between sleep and wakefulness, I could not be sure of what went on, but I thought I saw Bliffil pass something to the guard....A message? Money? I don't know...I put my head back down on Joseph's shoulder, sighed, and went back to sleep.

Other than that puzzling exchange, if, indeed, that was what I saw, things are worked out. Captain Hudson is given the possibility of parole, but he refuses, preferring to stay with his officers and men to share in their suffering. I am not sure, but I have the feeling that he also stays to protect me from Bliffil. *I have always had such good friends.*

There is an open privy in the room, and when it is my turn to use it, the others turn away and belt out "Rule Britannia" at the top of their lungs.

*Rule, Britannia,*
*Britannia rule the waves!*
*Britons never shall be slaves!*

*Thee haughty tyrants ne'er shall tame,*
*All their attempts to bend thee down*
*Will but arouse thy generous flame;*
*But work their woe, and thy renown.*

Captain Hudson lustily leads the chorus again after that fourth verse, and it gives great amusement to our guards while nicely covering up my doings.

*Rule, Britannia,*
*Britannia rule the waves!*
*Britons never, never, NEVER!... shall be slaves!*

We are there for about a week when a guard comes to the door with a French officer and he says, "Capitaine Hudson, you are being exchanged. Monsieur Bennett, also. Come with us please."

I translate and the Captain stands up to address his officers, all of whom get to their feet. "I must go, gentlemen, but rest assured I shall be tireless in attempting to secure your release."

All express their joy at the Captain's release, but he waves them off and goes up and stands before Bliffil. "Mr. Bliffil. I will be keeping an eye on what happens to our Midshipman Kemp, here. Count on that, and *know* that I *will* hold you accountable if anything untoward occurs. Do you understand me, Sir?"

Bliffil, his face dark and his lips pinched in anger, nods.

"Good," says Captain Hannibal Hudson. "Good luck to you all. God save the King. God save the Service." He shakes hands with each of his officers, including me, and embraces his friend the Doctor, saying, "We shall meet again soon, brother."

And with that, he and Mr. Bennett are gone.

Soon after the senior officers have left, Bliffil starts in with his insinuations.

"When Warrant Officer Jared there decides to finally mount her," he sneers, "will we stand back and sing 'God Save the King' to cover the sounds of their coupling?"

"You will leave off on that kind of talk, Mr. Bliffil!" warns Mr. Curtis, now the ranking officer, but Joseph Jared says much more.

He leaps forward and grabs Bliffil by the throat and slams him up against the stone wall of the prison. He thrusts his face within an inch of Bliffil's and snarls, "One more word and I'll snap your neck, you miserable piece of dung!"

"I will see you court-martialed for laying your hands upon me!" snarls Bliffil, furious.

"I don't give a good goddamn what you will do. All I know is one more word against her, and I will kill you, right here, right now," says Jared, evenly, and he begins to twist Bliffil's collar in his fist, slowly tightening it. Bliffil's face turns white, then red, then a most alarming shade of purple. He gasps for breath, but that breath does not come till Jared suddenly releases him and he falls to the floor, gasping, his hands to his throat.

After that, we resume the normal routine, one that is sure to be ours for weeks and weeks, months and months, and maybe even for years and years.

However, several days later, that routine is disrupted, especially for me.

There is a commotion at the door to our cage and another group of naval officers is thrown in. Their leader is with them, a Captain Blackstone of HMS *Mercury*. I'm wondering why he seems oddly familiar, when a litter is brought in, bearing a badly wounded young man. The stretcher bearers rudely dump him on one of the bunks and leave.

Dr. Sebastian looks at him and shouts after the departing guards, "This man needs to be in hospital!" But the guards say nothing.

I, too, can say nothing, for I am stunned beyond speech. *The wounded and unconscious young man is Jaimy Fletcher.*

# Chapter 12

I fall to my knees next to Jaimy's bunk and lay my hand on his forehead and find it hot and damp. *Oh, Jaimy, what has happened to you?*

There is an angry red groove that slashes through his dark hair on the right side of his head. Crude stitches have closed the cut, but not very well, even I can tell that. The wound still seeps and his face is covered in crusted blood. I must...I must...

"*Mr.* Kemp," says Dr. Sebastian, with a warning glance at the ever watchful guards, "you will remember your place. You must stand aside, please. I know that you feel for your friend here who is, indeed, in dire straits, but leave the medical things to me."

Dimly, I'm aware of Captain Blackstone recounting how HMS *Mercury* was taken—it had been sent off from the main convoy on a foolish errand to guard a fat, slow merchantman that wanted to put into a port in North Africa to take on a cargo of Egyptian cotton, and was surprised on the way back by a French squadron. They fought valiantly, of course—three dead officers and seventeen men, and many more wounded—but were eventually brought low and their colors were struck. "There were just too many of them," he laments sadly, shaking his head. "Just too damn many..."

The Doctor puts his fingers to Jaimy's wrist to feel the pulse, then he puts his ear to Jaimy's chest and listens. "His heart is all right, which is good."

Captain Blackstone comes to the Doctor's side. "He was hit a glancing blow from a cannonball as he stood by my side on my quarterdeck. He fell there and since then has wandered in and out of consciousness."

The Doctor nods. "Severe concussion." He, too, reaches up to feel Jaimy's forehead and then takes a whiff of the wound. "Some fever. Probably some sepsis from the wound itself. He will either live or die from that, but I worry more about the damage to his brain."

I stand aside, wringing my hands. *Oh, Jaimy, it can't come to this! It just can't end here...*

"Mr. Kemp, please tell the guard that I need my loblolly boy and my instruments. If he hesitates, remind him that I worked on both the English *and* the French wounded when first I was brought here. I'll also need more water and cloths. This man needs to be cleaned up."

I go to the door to plead for what the Doctor wants. When the guard, a French Marine, looks doubtful I say, "Please, *Corporal,* please do it. After all, we are all of us, yes, me and you, too, only poor sailors, sent out on the wild and wasteful ocean by our countries to do their will. Can you not help a fellow sailor?"

We get the stuff and the Doctor sets to work. He restitches the wound, while Stritch and I strip off Jaimy's soiled uniform and wash his body as best we can. When he is covered again with a clean sheet, the Doctor steps back and says, "I've done all that can be done."

I sit by Jaimy's side through that long day and night, putting cool compresses to his forehead.

Once during the night he becomes restless, and, by the dim light of the full moon that comes in through the high, barred window, I see that his eyes open.

"Jaimy, please lie still. It's me, Jacky."

"Jacky? No...not you," he says, his eyes wild. "The Devil...taunting me again...can't be..."

"It is, Jaimy..."

And then he drifts off, and again I put the cold rag back on his brow.

Later, in his delirium, he talks with someone named McCoy. "No, no...I killed you. Cut your throat...blood on my hands." He twists in the bed. "Beatty?...Blew your brains out. You can't come back at me, neither of you can; you're dead, both of you, you're..."

He subsides and I put the cloth back on. Then...

"Clementine? What...wait...no, don't go..."

*It doesn't matter, Jaimy, just please don't die. Please don't.*

# Chapter 13

The next morning I wake with my head on Jaimy's chest. I had intended to spend the whole night mopping his brow, but sleep overtook me and I was weak. *I'm sorry, Jaimy. I really did try.*

Jared appears at my side, buttoning up his jacket.

"How is he?"

"The same, I'm afraid. He goes in and out."

"Well, here, you must get something to eat, I'll get—"

But he gets nothing, and neither do I.

There is a rattling at the front door lock and it opens and four soldiers march in, followed by two men in civilian clothes. I see Bliffil rise and edge toward the door, his face expressionless. He points to me and the two men come forward.

*Uh-oh.*

"You will come with us, Jac-key Fay-bair," says the taller of the two, in English. "Corporal, take her out."

*I am betrayed…I am undone…*

Jared leaps from my side and grabs Bliffil by the throat before he can get out the door. "You dirty bastard. You gave her up, and I'm going to kill you for it."

Bliffil says, "No, no! You don't understand! You don't…"

But then Jared's balled-up fist smashes into his face and his nose flattens and his nostrils spurt blood all over his shirtfront, and he doesn't say anything more. Joseph is about to hit him again, but the butt of a French Marine's musket slams into the side of his head, and he goes down.

"Back! The rest of you! Back against zee wall!" shouts the tall Frenchman. Sharp bayonets force my friends back away from me. Bliffil, holding his hand to his face, rises unsteadily to his feet and staggers out the door, supported by a soldier. A barrage of curses and threats of future retribution follow him out. "Take her! Bind her hands!"

Hands are put on me and I am dragged out the door and into the hallway. I take one last look at Jaimy and then the door is closed and locked. *Good-bye, Jaimy…*

The tall cove puts his face to the grating on the door and shouts to my friends inside, "You, English! You will be treated to a spectacle! Look out into the courtyard in a few minutes!"

My hands are bound behind and I am shoved forward, down the hall, around a corner, and then into the bright light of the courtyard. The place is empty, except for the whipping post and a box with a board leaning against it. *Am I to be whipped?*

My mind reels as I am pushed relentlessly forward, but, strangely, not to the post, but rather to the box. *What is going on here?*

"English! My name is Monsieur Jardineaux! I am the Chief Prosecutor in this district!" Faces appear at the prison windows. I think I recognize Davy's face among them.

I am taken by the arms and forced to stand on the box.

"What we have here…," continues Monsieur Jardineaux, gesturing to me. He is plainly enjoying himself. "…ees the pirate Jac-key Fay-bair, sometimes known as *La Belle Jeune Fille sans Merci*. Not looking very *belle* right now, ees she?"

I don't say anything. I just try to keep a semblance of the Look on my face.

"What we also have here is an object called a bascule." He points to the board and nods to two of the soldiers. They immediately hold the thing up in front of me and I see that there are three sets of straps hanging on it. I also see dried blood on the upper end of it. I start to tremble. *Is it a device for torture? Oh, no…Please, Lord, let my end be quick.*

"And what is this bascule, you are wondering, eh? Well, it shall all be made very plain to you, yes, very plain. Strap her in," orders Jardineaux, and I am shoved chest-first up against the thick board.

The bloodstained top edge comes up only to my breastbone, and as the straps go around my shoulders, my middle, and my knees and are firmly tightened, I realize with the deepest of dread just what this board is for, and it hits me that my prayer was just answered—my end will be brutal, but it will be quick. *Thank you, Lord. Now just help me not disgrace myself and bring shame upon the Service. Head up now, girl, for the last time…Stop blubbering, stop it now!*

"What you see here is the very board that binds the condemned down on the base of *Madame La Guillotine*."

There is a roar from both galleries of English prisoners. *We'll get you, you frog-eatin' bastards! We will avenge you, Puss! We'll kill ten thousand of them for the one of you. A hundred thousand! Miserable cowards, to kill a girl! We'll hunt*

*Bliffil down to the very ends of the earth, and he will not die slow, count on that! Oh, this can't be happening! It can't—*

"Calm down, gentlemen, and *attendez-vous,*" says Jardineaux. "I regret that the guillotine could not be moved here so that you could witness for yourselves this—"

"What about a trial?" bellows someone from the officers' quarters, echoed by many a *hear! hear!* "You call yourself a lawyer!"

Jardineaux raises his thin, dark face to Captain Blackstone at the window above, for it was he who called out.

"My dear sir, there has already been a trial, in absentia, and she was found guilty, *most* guilty of Piracy and Murder and sentenced to death. Simple as that. And now that we have her, that sentence is going to be carried out in full. We shall see just how much mercy Madame Guillotine will have for Jac-key Fay-bair, the *Beautiful Young Girl Without Mercy,* as this one was called after she wickedly tortured and killed French citizens. I suspect it will be very little."

More roars and curses from above. Things—cups, bottles, pieces of chairs, anything that will fit through the bars—are thrown down, but all is in vain and all dismissed with a laugh from Jardineaux.

"If I may continue: I regret that the guillotine could not be moved from the center of town at such short notice— you see, a number of counterrevolutionaries had recently been captured and had to be accommodated."

Jardineaux leaves my side and advances to the high, strong wooden gates that guard the outside entrance to the courtyard. "Pin up her hair!" he shouts as he walks. "The High Executioner does not like to have hair in front of his blade, especially if it is female hair. He swears it dulls the edge, and we can't have that, can we? If the Queen, herself, could have had her hair pinned up on her journey to the same place, then why not this piece of trash?"

I feel hands behind my neck, taking up what little hair I have and pinning it up and out of the way.

"Open the gates," shouts Jardineaux, and the ponderous doors swing open. "Observe, English!"

Through the open gates we can plainly see down to the center of the town, and there, standing like an obscene relic from a more barbaric time, is the guillotine, its blade being once again drawn up.

"Madame has done her work for this morning, it seems, but she has one more head to take, and all of you will be able to watch. Her head will drop into the basket at noon. I shall make sure the executioner holds it up facing in this direction so that all may see. *Au revoir, Messieurs,* I hope you enjoy, or at least take a lesson to what awaits the enemies of *la République de France.*"

With that, I am picked up and thrown, bound to the bascule, into the back of a cart that has come into the yard. The driver chucks the horses, and I am taken out of the prison to my doom.

On the way to the execution place, I hear shouts of joy. "*La Belle Jeune Fille sans Merci! Stand her up that we may see her.*"

And they do stand me up, and then put me back down. I am helpless through all of it. And I am called *salope* and *chienne*, and any of the number of words they have for me.

I try to be brave, but then I never was very brave and *Oh, Lord, I commend my body to the sea and my soul to Thee and...*

...and then I am lifted up and the bascule is placed flat down on something and I am facedown again and being moved forward and something comes down wooden and heavy on my neck and I hear a young girl's voice cry out, *No, no, please, not me...please...* Is that me crying out? It must be me, but in all my terror, I don't know. I don't know anything for my mind is gone. There is only the terror... *oh, horror...* but through it all I hear a roar from the crowd. Then there is the sound of the hissing steel coming down and then an awful thunk and I feel a terrible blow to the back of my neck. I feel...nothing...all is darkness and silence.

# PART II

PART II

# Chapter 14

I awaken to find myself...I don't know where. I feel around with my fingers and find that I'm lying on my back in what seems to be a box. It is pitch-dark and my head throbs with terrible, thudding pain. I try to recover my senses, but my mind reels and spins and *Oh, God, please help me...* My hands, not tied now, lift upward and my knuckles encounter a wooden lid not three inches above my nose. Trying to quell my mounting terror, I move my fingers up to my neck and find that there is no deep and final cut there. *What, no wound at all?*

*Am I in Hell now, my head restored to my shoulders only to suffer unspeakable and eternal tortures for all of the wrongs I have done? Oh, Lord, was I really so bad as to deserve this?*

I feel the box jostled and sense myself being lifted, what...?

*What if I am still living and this is a coffin and I am being taken to be buried alive, my dying screams heard by none 'cept the waiting worms? Oh, please, God, not that!*

I give in to blind panic and try with all my might to push the horrible lid up and off me. Then I pound my feet against the bottom, but it, too, is solid and does not yield.

"Shaddup in there or I'll give ye another whack wi' me club," I hear from outside.

I stop struggling…If those are the Devil's imps I hear outside, cursing and swearing as they carry me down to Hell, they sure sound a lot like British seamen…and if this is the River Styx, I'd say that it sure feels a lot more like the waves of the open sea. Maybe…

As I lie there, it dawns on me that it was not my head that fell into the basket yesterday, no, it must have belonged to some other unfortunate soul who was forced to suffer under the blade in my place. Poor girl…I pray for her as I lie there waiting to see what is going to happen to me. I pray for Jaimy, and, yes, I pray for myself, as well. It is not something I usually do, but I have been sorely tried.

Eventually, the boat in which I have been riding bumps against some wharf and the lid is lifted from my box. Two rough-looking coves grasp my arms to lift me upright, then shove me out to stand on the swaying pier. Then I am again bound and a hood is placed over my head and I am thrown in the back of a carriage and it rumbles off. I have a good idea where it is going and I soon find out that I am not wrong.

The carriage stops, muffled orders are given, and I am again yanked out, led up a flight of stairs, and brought into what I sense is a large room. My hood is whipped off and I behold a man sitting behind a desk, looking at me with a very measured eye. I realize that I have been in this room before, and on that occasion looked out that very same window over there. Then I was in the company of Sir Henry Dundas, First Lord of the Admiralty, delivering evidence of a large spy ring. Now, I suspect that the man at the desk is the new First Lord, Thomas Grenville. My hands are tied in front of me, which I have always found to be a good thing if one is to be bound. There is a loop around each of my wrists and a six-inch length of line between. That might also be a useful thing.

Bliffil stands next to me, a bandage across his swollen nose. I reflect that this is the second time Bliffil has had his nose flattened because of me—first by Midshipman Jenkins, back on the *Dolphin,* and yesterday by Jared in the prison. I hope he enjoyed both to the fullest degree, the bastard. I sense some others behind me as well, and I turn to see two men in black garb standing against the wall.

"This is the one, then?" asks the man at the desk. "Our new spy?"

*Spy?*

"Yes, my Lord," replies the man who stands beside him and who I recognize from the last time I stood in this room—he is Mr. Peel, the Chief Intelligence Officer, a deputy of the Prime Minister himself.

"Doesn't look like much of one to me," remarks Grenville, doubtfully. He is a slight, bookish fellow who looks like he'd rather be somewhere else.

"Be careful of her, Sirs, you don't know…"

"Well, then," says this Lord Grenville, ignoring Bliffil's warning. "What do you have to say for yourself?"

I stand there in my once-proud midshipman's uniform. The jacket is filthy from the battle and from the time in prison. My white trousers are stained from the times I could not hold my water—first, on the way to the guillotine when I was sure I was to be beheaded, and then in the countless hours in that foul box on my way here.

"Say for myself?" I say, working up a ball of spit. Having accomplished that task, I launch it toward Lord Grenville's left eye, and my aim is true. He recoils in horror, the spittle dripping down his wellborn cheek. "*That's* what I have to say for myself!"

"My word!" he bleats. He pulls a handkerchief from his sleeve and wipes away furiously. "Such a thing! I never!"

"I told you so!" bleats Bliffil. "We've got to—"

But I don't let him finish.

"Say for myself?" I repeat and launch into a fury such as I have never felt before. "You degrade me and bring me to stand before you in my own stink and shame and disgrace like this and ask me what *I* have to say for myself?" I shrink back and hiss at them. "I have seen your work—in America, where your agents hired Indians to murder women and children. Is that what 'Rule Britannia' means? To kill babies and bring someone like myself to this state? Nay, Sirs, I ask *you* what do *you* have to say for your own sorry selves?"

"We do what we must to keep this island kingdom free and safe," says Mr. Peel, coming around the desk.

"Watch her, oh, please watch her, beware," advises Bliffil. "Please look at my condition..."

"Since I am *sort* of a lady I will not use the words here that I want to use, the ones I learned in the street," I say through my teeth. "I will only say, *Bless* you, Sir, and *Bless* all the lords and *Bless* all the ladies in this land and *Bless* you, too, Lord Grenville, and *Bless* the horse that brought you here, and *Bless* all the Generals and all the Admirals, yes, *Bless* them all and *Bless* them so hard that they'll never forget. Finally, oh yes, finally, *Bless the Bloody Blessed King!*"

"Miss! Calm yourself!" cries Lord Grenville, plainly distressed over the turn of events.

"I won't! I don't care! You can't do any more to me! Kill me! Hang me! Torture me! Cut off me head! I don't care!" I scream. "Do what you want to me! I can't take it anymore!"

There is a heavy paperweight on the First Lord's desk. I don't know what it is, but to my demented mind it looks like a cannonball and that is what I use it for.

I reach out with both hands and grab it and before anyone can stop me I lunge across the room and heave it through the window. With a great crash it shatters.

"Stop her, dammit, stop her!"

I remember, from the time I was here before, that, even though we are three stories up, outside that window to the left is a drainpipe and if I can get to it, I'll be able to climb down. If I can just reach Cheapside, there will be no catching me. Trouble is, the window is made up of many small panes, and my cannonball did not make enough of an opening for me to get through. *Damn! What to do...?*

They are coming at me now, Bliffil and the other two gents, but I reach over and snatch a sizable shard of glass from the window where it still hung in its lead molding—it has a sharp point and its edges are razor keen. I crouch and hold it before me like a knife blade. The two gents step back, but Bliffil does not.

"I'll get you, you conniving little—" he snarls as he charges at me. His face, what I can see of it behind the bandage, is bright red with rage.

I take a sidestep, put my weight on my left leg, and bring my booted right toe deep up into Bliffil's crotch.

He goes *Oooff!*, staggers, and is about to go down when I pivot and leap up on his back. Throwing my hands over his head, I bring the six-inch piece of cord between my wrists up against his neck and pull back *hard*. He gives a most satisfying gurgle, and then I put the shard of glass to his throat, right next to his jugular vein. *Thank you, Professor Tilden, Mr. Sackett, and Dr. Sebastian for your excellent Anatomy lessons.* I jab it in just far enough to draw a little blood, a thin stream of which runs down across the glass and over my thumb to fall on the floor.

"You there," I shout to the taller of the two so-far silent men. "Open the window or I will cut his throat and you will be less one miserable agent. Do it now."

But the man looks over at Mr. Peel for orders, and Mr. Peel shakes his head sadly and says, "No, Mr. Carr, do not do that. Mr. Bliffil, though he has done well in this matter, is expendable, as we all are expendable, as it were, in this battle against Napoléon and his minions."

Mr. Peel comes up in front of me, as Bliffil and I do our deadly little dance, and says, "Give it up, Jacky Faber, for there are grander things for you to do than that. Things that your country might someday thank you for."

"My country? My country?" I ask all incredulous. "My country has done nothing but abandon me to the streets, deceive me, denounce me, hound me, and finally run me down like a dog. My country? What country is that?"

"You may say that, Miss, but we know that you have performed admirably in defense of that very same country in at least three actions. You cannot put all that up to your sense of adventure and innate greed. Now lay down your blade and let poor Mr. Bliffil go. He looks the worse for wear in his late encounters with you. Please. Do it now."

I know there is no way out, so I relax my grip to let the shard fall and reluctantly remove my garrote from Bliffil's neck and let him fall to the floor.

"That is good," says Mr. Peel. "Mr. Bliffil? Ah, Mr. Bliffil, as soon as you are recovered, you may be excused. You have done admirable work in bringing her here, and you may expect promotion and monetary reward."

He nods to the other two gentlemen who lift Bliffil under his arms and carry him to the door to put him out.

"Whatever are you thinking, Sir?" asks First Lord Grenville, completely mystified by what has gone on here.

"I am thinking, my Lord, that she is *just* the thing," says Mr. Peel, beaming at me.

# Chapter 15

The First Lord excuses himself and leaves the room a few minutes later, pronouncing what has gone before to be extremely distasteful to him, and lets Mr. Peel take over the proceedings.

I am immediately put into a chair and tied to it by Mr. Carr and his partner, and the proceedings begin in earnest.

"You must forgive the First Lord. He is more interested in his books, his library, and his studies than in these rather distressing affairs of state. There have been three First Lords since you met with Lord Dundas, but I remain constant, I am always here. It would be well for you to remember that, Miss."

"Ah, so Lord Grenville does not have the stomach for watching you hurt an innocent young girl?" I say, trying to keep my head up, which is hard, for my arms are pulled around the back of the chair and my wrists are tied tight. "He does not want the joy of watching you torture me? How odd. I thought it would be one of the benefits of his job."

"What makes you think we are going to torture you?"

"Your men have done it to me before."

"Oh?"

"Yes, your Mr. Flashby put his hot cigar tip to my bare leg this past summer on the Mississippi River. I can expect nothing less from the likes of you. You are cruel and heartless and evil. So just do it. I have no secrets nor information I can tell you to prevent it. You will hurt me and I will cry and then you will have me taken out and killed and that will be that."

"Ah. Flashby. Well, he does have his methods. But his techniques are not mine. And I have been informed that you paid him back in full. By the way, we haven't heard back from his associate Agent Moseley for quite some time. Do you have any idea what became of him?"

"The last I saw of that particular tub of rancid lard was when I had him stripped down to his drawers, put the fear of God in him, and then threw him over the side of my riverboat. He walked the plank, as it were, and if he has not yet crawled back to you, then he was either scalped by a hostile Indian or eaten by ally-gators. If the former, I wish the Indian the joy of his scalp, and if the latter, I hope the reptile did not suffer indigestion."

Mr. Peel laughs. "Oh, you are a pistol, no doubt."

"And as for torture, what do you call what you did to me yesterday if not the cruelest of torture? Making me think I was going to be beheaded, then keeping me in that box all that time."

"We want the French to think that *La Belle Jeune Fille sans Merci* is dead, so they would no longer look for you." He pauses. "And we wanted to show what we are capable of."

"That poor girl..."

"A common prostitute and thief. She had already been condemned and was...convenient for our little charade.

You are surprised we were able to pull off something like that? You see, we have operatives everywhere, and they are very adept at subterfuge, very skilled indeed. And, of course, money talks, and it speaks both English and French, most fluently. We paid a lot of money for you, my dear."

"So what do you want from me then, in return for your blessed money?"

"Now you are being disingenuous. You heard the First Lord say the word 'spy'?"

"I did, and I was not pleased. I don't like spies and spying. It all speaks of treachery and betrayal to me. I know some of both."

"I'm sure you do, but that is beside the point. I will be direct: We want to place you in Paris, as a member of a dancing troupe, a *corps de ballet,* as the French call it, to gather information for us."

"That is all very good, but I don't know how to dance like that."

"You will be taught, and we know you to be a very quick study."

"But what kind of information could I get as a mere dancer?"

"None. But the gentlemen of Paris—some of them men of business and commerce, but also some of them Colonels and Generals and even Marshals in the military—take great delight in escorting these dancers about in the nightlife of the city, as these girls are known for their beauty, their willingness to prance about in scant costumes, and their somewhat questionable morals."

"Ah. So you would have me prostitute myself, then?"

"You will do whatever is necessary for King and Country."

"Do you realize that I am scarce sixteen years old and yet a—?"

"Ah, yes. Dr. Sebastian's report. Bliffil told me about that. Remarkable...but it holds very little weight with me. Every girl sells her maidenhead for a price when it comes down to it—a secure future, a warm home, a man to protect her, food for her children..."

"But never for love, I suppose."

"Not in my experience, no."

"Then I pity you. Shall we get on with this? My wrists and hands are going numb."

"Mr. Boyd, will you loosen her bonds a bit?" I feel the fingers of the other gent fiddling with the rope that binds my wrists. It is slackened and blood once more flows into my hands.

"And if I refuse to do any of this?" I ask.

"You don't really have a choice, as I see it. We could throw you into Newgate, and you would be hanged this coming Monday. Let's see, that's only four days from now. Will that give you time enough to get right with the Lord?"

"So do it. I don't care. I made my peace with God yesterday at the foot of the guillotine. You can't frighten me anymore. So go bless yourself."

"Very colorfully put. Consider me blessed. However, we have other things for you to think about. For instance, there is the matter of a Mr. James Emerson Fletcher, lying grievously wounded in a French prison...as well as the London Home for Little Wanderers. A worthy enterprise and one that reflects very favorably on your charitable nature—however, there is the question of proper licensing for such an orphanage...fees, you know...and back taxes...Oh, I am sure the Home would win in the end, as it has some powerful friends, but till then, the poor children would be put back out on the streets. And there is your grandfather to think of...and the staff."

"So you would hurt my friends to make me do what you want?"

"'Hurt' is such a harsh word, Miss Faber, but—"

"Why me? Why am I seen to be so valuable?"

"Do you not know that most females being brought into this room would have simply swooned away and not thrown Lord Grenville's priceless Egyptian sculpture through his window and then tried to strangle one of his men? No, Miss, you are a rare find—a girl raised as a feral beast in the slums of London and then educated and turned into one who can pass for the grandest of ladies. You speak French fluently, with just a touch of an American accent. You are a girl who is as comfortable wearing silken stockings as she is concealing a wicked knife in a sheath up her sleeve. A girl who, though quite small, has a talent—may I call it a knack?—for bending men three times her height and weight to her will. A girl who has been in command of three ships—"

"Four ships."

"I stand corrected. *Four* ships, and who has exhibited very credible survival skills. There are many male intelligence operatives—'spies' is such an ugly word—abroad in the world, but there are virtually no female ones. Since no one will suspect a female spy, especially one as diminutive and charming as yourself, you should be able to worm your way into the confidence of any male whose acquaintance you might make."

"Ah. Back to my becoming a whore again."

"Another ugly word, Miss. I'm sure you could come up with a better term—'adventuress,' perhaps?…maybe, 'woman of the world'?…'courtesan'?…'femme fatale'? All much prettier titles, you will agree."

I seethe, I fume, but I know there is nothing for me to do except to agree. "All right, I will do it, but if you want me to enter into this thing with any sort of spirit, I must insist that you order the following. I want Lieutenant James Fletcher exchanged and brought back to London to be placed in the care of his family. His attending physician, Dr. Stephen Sebastian, must accompany him as he is the one most acquainted with Mr. Fletcher's case. And a warrant officer, Joseph Jared, as well as a Seaman David Jones, confined in the same prison, must also be released. And I shall want to see Mr. Fletcher when he arrives here. I'll need new clothes and fine ones at that. And money—*lots* of money if I am to go into enemy territory. If you do all that, then I will do my best for you, without reluctance. I will do my duty."

Mr. Peel nods. "Well, certainly money is no object—we have plenty of that. There is an exchange coming up and Lieutenant James Fletcher, if he is still alive, will be exchanged. Perhaps Mr. Jared as well. As for Dr. Sebastian… He is, ah, shall we say, known to us. We'll do what we can for Seaman Jones. We are agreed then?"

"Fine, but one other thing."

"Yes?"

"I want a bath. And I want it right now."

# Chapter 16

I lie in my bath, ah, yes, my good hot bath, which feels... *ahhhh*... oh, so fine. They had delivered on this lovely bath, which I knew would not be easy for them—finding the tub, then hauling the pails of hot water—but they did it and I am glad. It is the first real bath I've had since Dovecote, and I am enjoying it to the fullest. That and still being alive to enjoy it.

I sink down farther into the tub and think back to Dovecote, the estate of Family Trevelyne. I had taken to staying there with my dear friend Amy Trevelyne between voyages on the *Nancy B,* so as to avoid being nabbed by British agents in Boston—a lot of good it did me in the end, though, as here I am, very well and completely nabbed. The end of summer was lovely at Dovecote, but, sadly, I was denied the company of Randall Trevelyne, which I would have much enjoyed. He had a ferocious argument with his father and stormed out of the house and has not been seen or heard from since. Amy is very worried about him, and I, too, hope he is all right, as he is a rash and a roving blade, and not at all temperate in his ways.

*Oh, Randall, I…* I hear the door open and I cross my arms on my chest as a woman comes into the room. She did not bother to knock, but I suppose I must get used to the fact that I am the Admiralty's property now, body and soul, to use as they see fit.

"Stand up, girl," she orders. She's a small, very tightly wound woman of some age, dressed all in black, which seems to be the color of choice around here. She has an accent of some kind, which I can't quite place, along with an authoritative air of someone who is not used to having her orders disobeyed. Oh, well, I was about done with the bath, anyway.

I stand up.

She regards me with an appraising eye as I step out dripping and reach for a towel to dry myself. *What is this, then?*

The clothes I was wearing when I had been brought here were sent out for cleaning, and I pity the poor washerwoman who's got that job. In the meantime, a nightshirt has been scrounged up for me to wear until tomorrow when I shall go shopping for new, very fashionable clothes. And believe me, I do not intend to spare the expense. If I'm to be a courtesan, then I intend to be a fine one. The fact that King George's treasury is paying for it makes it ever so much better.

Somewhat dry, I reach for the nightshirt, but she says, "No. Do not put that on. Walk over there. I must examine the muscles, the tone." Mystified, I do it. I mean, everybody knows that I've never been particularly shy in that regard, especially when it's only in front of an old woman, so what the hell.

"Put the arms over the head. Now out to the side. Turn around. Make an effort to be graceful. Um…They tell me you are accomplished in country dances?"

"I have been told that," I say through my teeth, growing a bit resentful. If she asks me to demonstrate, I shan't do it. I mean, in my present state of undress, my dignity and all.

"Um. That might help. Stand on your tiptoes. Now extend the right leg back. Um. Now the left. All right, girl, you may put on your clothing." And with that she goes over to rap on the door. I pull on my nightshirt just in time, as the door opens and Mr. Peel comes into the room.

"Well?"

"I vill do it," says this woman. "She is fit and trim. Give me two weeks and she vill be suitable for the back rank of the *corps de ballet,* nothing more, but she vill not be a disgrace. Four hundred pounds sterling. Have her in my studio Monday morning at eight. With the money. Goot evening."

And with that she sweeps out.

Mr. Peel nods with obvious satisfaction. "Madame Petrova has agreed to take you on as a student. That is good."

"May I pronounce myself less than overjoyed?" I ask.

Two workmen come in to lift up the tub and take it to the window and pour it out. I hear curses from some unfortunate passersby below. Then the men carry out the tub and leave me alone with Mr. Peel. I perch on the edge of what will prove to be my bed for the next several weeks.

"You may pronounce yourself anything you want. However, you will go there and you will do your best."

"I have always tried to do my best, Sir, in any kind of performance. You will find that to be true."

"That is all very well. Now here is my cloak. Wrap yourself in it, as we are going to meet with the First Lord again."

I wrap the thing about my shoulders and pad out of the room and into the hall in my bare feet. The team of Carr and Boyd are there, of course, and soon I discover that they will always be there. Almost always.

Down the hall we go, then it's into the office.

The First Lord of the Admiralty is back at his desk, looking over some papers.

"Ah, Miss Faber. I assume you have refreshed yourself?"

"Yes, my Lord. I am now quite fresh." I seat my newly refreshed bottom in his chair before him without being asked. It has been a long day, and I do not give a tinker's damn about the propriety.

"Well. We must go over some of the conditions of your...employment. I take it we will see no more exhibitions of violent behavior from you?"

"No, Sir, I have given my word in this matter, and I always keep my word," I say, "as opposed to others I have met in this room." I glance over at Mr. Peel.

He comes over and asks, "And just what is that supposed to mean?"

"It was in this very room that I was given a Letter of Marque, I thought, in good faith. It proved not so. Why should I believe anything you say now?"

"That was a different set of circumstances. And you must admit you contravened the terms of that agreement by your taking of the *Emerald* without any permission whatsoever."

"Well, that is all water under the bridge, and since you

are holding all the cards, I will sit back and listen." I fold my hands on my lap and look attentive as any schoolgirl.

"*Harummph*...You are to take lessons in the French form of dancing from Madame Petrova. You will receive further instructions from Mr. Peel on how you are to conduct yourself when you get to Paris. He is expert in such matters. Messrs. Carr and Boyd will accompany you wherever you go in the city. You have a strict six o'clock curfew. If you are in public, you will wear a veil—it is a common thing with some of the finer ladies here and will not cause undue comment."

I nod in understanding of the unspoken reasons for the veil.

"When you get on French soil, there will be a gentleman there who will be your contact. He will make himself known to you and will direct you in your actions and you shall communicate to him the information you have gathered."

"And that information will be...?"

"We must know what Boney is up to. When he begins to form up and to move his army. We must know where they are going and what they intend to do. Do you understand that?"

"Yes, Sir, I do."

"Do you further understand what you must do, what we all must do, is *anything* to keep Napoléon Bonaparte from *ever* setting his foot on this island we call England? *Anything.*"

Heavy sigh. "Ah, yes. *This blessed plot, this earth, this realm, this England.* Yes, I get it."

That little speech raises a lordly eyebrow. He gives a small cough and continues. "Good. Now as to the conditions. You will be conducted to Madame Petrova's studio each day except Sunday, when you may attend—"

"May I meet with my grandfather, the Reverend Alsop, and others at my Home for Little Wanderers and take part in services there?" I already know the answer.

Lord Grenville looks to Mr. Peel and, even though I can't see him behind me, I know he shakes his head.

"No, I'm afraid not," says the First Lord. "Secrecy and all, you know."

"Then it would be my greatest hope to worship at Saint Paul's Cathedral. That was the church of my youth and it would give me great comfort to go there again, considering the danger into which I am very shortly going to be put."

"Well, I'm sure that can be arranged under proper supervision," says Lord Grenville. I'm certain he again looks to Mr. Peel for confirmation. Whether he gets it or not, I cannot see, for he is behind me.

*Ha! Church of my youth, right! Saint Paul's, which wouldn't let the likes of my filthy street-urchin self in the front door on any kind of bet. No, the only way I ever got into that place was in the winter with Rooster Charlie and our gang burrowing in through the catacombs to gain a bit of warmth—and maybe a shot at what might be in the poor box, which wasn't much, the cheap buggers...*

"Well, maybe, under proper supervision," says Mr. Peel, coming around to face me. "But be warned..."

"I know the deal. I know what happens. If I escape, you will hurt the ones I love, so therefore I will not escape. Besides, as I have said, I have given my word and I know the terms of the agreement."

"All right then. Tomorrow you will be taken out and new clothing will be bought for you."

"And tomorrow, if it please you, Sirs, I would like to

inform Mr. James Fletcher's family of his impending repatriation and arrival, as it would give them a measure of joy. You did say you would let me see him before I go off to France."

The First Lord again looks to Mr. Peel, and the younger man puts his hand to his chin to ponder this for a while. Then he answers, "Very well. But you must go veiled and not tell them who you are. When Mr. Fletcher arrives, if he is still alive, then as a Royal Navy Officer, he can be sworn to secrecy and can be expected to swear his family to the same, but not till then will you reveal yourself to the family. Understood?"

"I understand and I thank you," I say with a slight bow of my head. Then I look to Sir Grenville and put on the big eyes. "My Lord, the six o'clock curfew will confine me to many long hours in my room alone, and if I might have some books and some pens and paper, it would give me great comfort." Just a little flutter of the eyelashes, not too much.

He is interested, as I knew he would be, from what Mr. Peel had said of him earlier, about his being more involved with his library than in torturing prisoners.

"Why, yes," he says. "What would you like?"

"Well, I have not yet been able to obtain a copy of Izaak Walton's *The Compleat Angler*, and I do desire to read that, for both its practical advice on the science of fishing, as well as for its philosophical asides. Boswell's *Life of Johnson* has also eluded me since I've been away from my country for so long. And Mr. Pope's poetry..." Here I manage a blush. "I hear it is *quite* scandalous. I don't know if I dare, Sir..."

"Why, my dear, I have all those titles! Have you read Swift's *Gulliver's Travels*?"

I reply that I have not, even though I have. "I hope to name you my literary guide, my Lord, during these last weeks that I will spend here in my native land."

"Well! I do have some books near at hand, and I will get them for you." With that Sir Thomas Grenville, First Lord of the Admiralty, and Leader of the British Royal Navy, a man who has the ear of King George, Himself, rushes from the room to get Jacky Faber some books.

When the door closes behind him, Mr. Peel looks at me, again with a very appraising eye. "You are a piece of work, aren't you?"

"Well," I shrug, all innocent, "we all ride our little hobby-horses, don't we, Mr. Peel?"


When at last in bed, curled up, knees to chest, in my usual ball of anxiety, fear, and doubt, I reflect that at least this bed is more comfortable than that coffin in which I spent last night, and for that I am glad. I am also glad to still be alive. I do miss having Joseph Jared at my side to calm me when I start screaming at the phantoms that come to visit me in the night, though. Oh, I know they will come tonight, too, but only the guard outside my door will hear as I thrash about and shriek out my terrors.

Before I fall asleep and surrender to the night dreads, I think of my mates still back in that prison, and I fear for them. I cannot imagine what they must have felt when that executioner, next to the guillotine, held up a head for them to behold...a head they had to believe was mine.

*Davy...Joseph...I hope you didn't do anything rash, I hope...Oh, God, I am so very hard on my friends...*

# Chapter 17

The next day, which is Saturday, I am taken out, wrapped in Mr. Peel's cloak, and put in a coach. We rattle off to Regent Street in the fashionable part of London and I am bought new clothes, clothing appropriate to wear in Paris. I am fitted in the new Empire style, long pleated dresses gathered up under the low bodice, with short, puffy sleeves. I am given several of those, in white and pink and mauve. Dressy hats are bought, along with a number of fine scarves and shawls. New hairpieces, neat shoes, and silk stockings, too, in addition to delicate underclothing and frilly garters. And cosmetics—oh yes, cosmetics and perfumes, definitely. The tailors and shop mistresses are plainly overjoyed with my visits, and I wish them all the joy of their unexpected windfall.

I must confess that I do not find this at all unpleasant, being fussed over and measured and fitted with the finest of attire.

Oh, and a riding habit, of course, I must have one of those—the jacket deep blue this time, with matching bonnet and skirt. I must confess I have a certain affection for this style of rig—I like the tight clutch of the jacket about my ribs and the feel of the soft white lace about my throat and wrists. I wanted to get a jacket made of red cloth, but I am going to France, after all, and they tend to view wearers of that color with some suspicion just as the Americans do when they see the scarlet coats of the British. *It's funny, ain't it*, I muse, as I pick out half a dozen fancy embroidered handkerchiefs to the extreme delight of the shop owner, *that these three countries, Britain, France, and America— sometimes friends but most often enemies—all use red, white, and blue for their colors? Funny, that. Ironic, even.*

The skirt of the riding habit is cut in such as way as to give the legs of the wearer some freedom to move—I mean sometimes you have to get on a horse and all—and that is good, because tomorrow I intend to do some moving… some quick moving…as in running.

I wear my spanking new riding habit out of the last shop, my veil now attached to my bonnet, only my eyes showing above it, making me look, I think, quite the lady of the manor. I grandly say to Carr and Boyd, "Brattle Lane, please. The offices of H. M. Fletcher & Sons, Wine Merchants. It is close to Saint Paul's Wharf."

"We know where it is, Miss," says a weary Carr, uttering a rare complete sentence as he pushes aside the mountain of packages that now occupy the carriage in order to sit across from me. Boyd issues instructions to the coachman, and then he, too, crams himself inside. I know that both clearly wish they had other duties—like maybe picking lice off nasty monkeys at the London Zoological Institute. Some men just do not like to shop.

I have been guarded in the past, generally against my will, by any number of soldiers and Marines, and I've always been able to use whatever charms I may have to gain at least their sympathy if not their affection. But not these two, oh, no. All my little ventures into their histories, or accounts of their wives or sweethearts, have been met with stony silence. Never a glimmer of humor, nor even a response except for a terse "yes" or "no" or a grunt. *Well, we shall see, lads...*

As we rattle along, I reflect on how close Jaimy might have been to me during that time I was growing up and running with the Rooster Charlie Gang and living under Blackfriars Bridge. I mean, the warehouses of H. M. Fletcher & Sons were not half a mile from our kip, in fact, there they are right over there, and I'm sure he must have been there sometimes. Oh, I know he'd have been in school most of the time, while I was in the streets, but then, we might have met. Who knows?

I jerk myself back into the present. *Back to business, girl.* The carriage pulls up in front of the offices of H. M. Fletcher & Sons, Brattle Lane, London. I get out and walk in, followed very closely by Carr and Boyd.

There is a young man sitting behind a desk who looks up as I enter.

"Yes, Miss?"

"I wish to see Mr. H. M. Fletcher," I say, from behind my veil, as I glance about the room. The young man looks so much like Jaimy that I must assume that he is his brother George.

"In what regard?" the young man asks, rising. *So much like Jaimy! Calm, now, you!*

"I...I have information concerning a certain James

Emerson Fletcher, with whom I believe you are acquainted. I have seen him recently."

The young man's eyes go wide. "James? You have seen him. What...?"

"Please get your father, Sir, and I will go on."

He leaves the room and I hear *Dad! Dad! Come here! News of Jimmy!* In an outer office.

An older man comes into the front office. He is the same man I saw four years ago standing on the dock as the *Dolphin* prepared to get under way and he sent Jaimy off to be a ship's boy with the likes of me. He and his family have certainly paid for *that* move. He has aged a bit, but not by much, and he looks at me with expectation and not a little suspicion upon seeing me behind my veil.

"You have seen my son, James?" he demands. "We have not heard anything of him since he stepped off the dock last spring. Who are you? What...?"

"Father," says young George, "I think we both know who this is."

"Oh. Oh, yes, of course. That's Ja—"

"If you do think you know my name, Sirs," says I, looking back at Carr and Boyd, "please do not speak it, as it will not go well for any of us." I put as much warning into my eyes as I can. "Before I begin, let me say that I saw Jaimy a week ago, and though he was severely wounded, he was alive, and I have arranged that he will be delivered to your house within a fortnight."

"Thank God he yet lives!" cries Mr. Fletcher, grabbing the back of a chair for support. "How badly is he wounded? Where is he? How do you know about it?"

"He received a head wound during a fight at sea that left him with a severe concussion. He goes in and out of his senses, but is otherwise healthy, although right now he *is* in a French prison. That is where I left him, under the care of an excellent doctor. Both Jaimy and Dr. Sebastian will be exchanged next week, and he will be brought here to recover, which is, of course, my fondest hope."

"We should send for your mother, George, she will want to hear this!" says Mr. Fletcher. "Go get her..."

George shakes his head and looks at me. "I don't think it would be wise right now, Dad..."

*Ah, so the old witch still hates me... Good to know.*

"Let's hear the story and we'll tell it to Mother later," suggests the very wise George.

I give a sniff and put on the Lawson Peabody Look, even though they can't see enough of it to fully appreciate its grandeur, and say, "I am glad to tell you that the head wound was not disfiguring, not that I would allow that to in any way diminish my great affection for your son. I have been given permission..." Here I dart my eyes to Carr and Boyd, "...by my, ah... *associates*... to visit with Jaimy when he arrives, if you could see it in your heart to allow me into your house, Sir. I would greatly appreciate it. I know I am not welcome here, so I will now bid you *adieu*. Rest assured I will be praying both night and day for Jaimy's full recovery. Good-bye."

I do not have to dramatically rise, for I have not yet been invited to even sit down. *Bleedin' nobs, after all I've done!* I sweep toward the door, a bit steamed. *But what sort of love did I expect from them? Did I not steal many cases of fine wine from this family, when I sailed and raided on the open sea with both the* Wolverine *and the* Emerald? *As well as gaining the devotion of their youngest son? Hey, I'd throw me out, too.*

"No! Wait! Stop! Nonsense! Who told you you were not welcome here?" says Father Fletcher. "Please, sit down and tell us more of what you know of James."

A chair is brought and I place the oft-despised Faber bottom in it. Mr. Carr looks at his watch and says, "Curfew in fifteen," and then leans his back against the wall and waits, a look of extreme boredom upon his face.

I tell the story.

"You know your son, and brother, took ship from London in the spring of this year, following a certain person to Boston with thoughts of matrimony. When he got there, he did not find this person, she being abducted by a vile slaver, whereupon he initiated efforts to gain her release. When this person was, indeed, restored to freedom, she was promptly arrested on board HMS *Juno* for supposed crimes against the Crown. Managing to escape that confinement, she headed off into the frontier of America, not knowing she was being closely followed by James Emerson Fletcher, her former shipmate and own true love. He did never catch up with that person...*oh, yes he did, but I ain't gonna tell 'em about that little encounter, me bein' starkers with Lord Richard Allen at the time and...well, never mind...*but he did have many adventures with Red Indians, bandits, and various other scalawags...*him being in a Pittsburgh jail, breakin' rocks for two weeks with Mike Fink, comes to mind...*on his way down the Ohio and Mississippi rivers. Upon reaching New Orleans, he booked passage for Kingston, having given up, for various reasons, any more thought of an amorous alliance with the person he formerly had been seeking. There, at the British Station, he managed to outfit himself once again in Naval uniform and to regain his commission and was taken on as Third Mate of HMS *Mercury*. While aboard this ship, the person he once had been seeking did arrange to meet him, their differences were resolved, and they once more plighted their troths to each other, each promising to meet here in London upon his return. Whereupon that person did take leave of Mr. Fletcher...*Aye, she did, diving over the side of the* Mercury *in simple shirt and Indian buckskin skirt*...he and his ship being bound for the Orient as escort to a merchant convoy, and she saw him no more until he was brought into the same French prison that she was held in."

I take a breath and continue. "I was...removed...from that prison and brought back to England. Negotiations with a certain branch of our government resulted in the imminent release of your son. And here we are. End of story."

There is a bit of silence and then George says, smiling at me, "Father, I think you did me a disservice, sending James off to sea instead of me."

I put some heat into my eyes, the only part of my face visible above the veil, and say to him, "A life of adventure is ofttimes better in the telling of, rather than in the living through. Your brother James has seen some very hard times, I can tell you."

"Curfew," says Carr with a pronounced finality, and I rise.

"I must hurry to my wife with this news," says Mr. Fletcher, somewhat breathless. "I assure you, Miss, that you will be afforded the utmost courtesy from both Mrs. Fletcher and the rest of my household when James arrives. Good day to you, and thank you."

I am hurried back into the coach and returned to the Admiralty. When we get there, all my packages, as well as my own self, are put back in my room. I am informed that the First Lord has some more books for me and, surprise of all surprises, he will take his dinner with me this evening, his wife being away at their country estate.

I doff my riding habit to get ready for dinner. I get into one of my new Empire dresses. The drawers I have on are all right, but I'll wear no undershirt under this thing, that's for sure. I tuck myself into the gown and tug it down into place. Do I miss Higgins's helping hands at times like this? Oh, yes, I do, but I soldier on and manage to get everything right.

The top rounded curves of my chest peek perkily out. I do not want to encourage anything, but I have felt Sir Grenville to be a gentle soul, plus the fact that Mr. Peel will also be there makes me feel more at ease. Powder all around, some here, some there, some perfume, and off to dinner.

There is a *hummm* of appreciation as I enter the room, and I like that, but the talk is all about books and that is all right with me. The dinner is excellent and the conversation is bright. Sir Grenville is most knowledgeable in the way of Literature and I sparkle as best I can. It is, all in all, an excellent evening.

Later, back in my room and clad in my nightshirt, I begin to mull over my day and thinking of Jaimy and all, as I wonder, *Why do nations bother to trade prisoners?* Then I recall that I had once asked that of my sea dad Liam Delaney, a seaman wise beyond both his years and his rank, when we were both on the *Dolphin*. "It's because, Jacky, they don't want to feed 'em is why. Better to trade a prisoner who just lies around all day complainin' of his lot for one of your own captured seamen who can be brought back and made to work and fight. Plus you don't want to waste your soldiers as guards for the irritable and often dangerous gang o' louts. Nay, trade 'em, and get rid of 'em quickly." Liam's logic was clear and indisputable.

Thinking of Liam brings a tear to my eye, but I brush it away. *Dear Liam, the last I saw of you was when you were led off the* Wolverine *to be pressed onto another warship, and your young son Padraic with you as well. I know you are still in this fight and I pray for the health and safety of both of you.*

One thing that has been troubling me is that all my friends, both in England and in America, will think me dead and I can't have that. The French newspapers will carry accounts of the girl pirate Jacky Faber's final journey to the guillotine and copies will make their way over the Channel and then to America. And in the case of my dearest friend, Amy Trevelyne, that bit of news might be deadly. She loves me as I do her, and if she falls into a deep melancholy, she could waste away and die. A pistol is quicker, but deep, aching, and abiding sadness can do the job just as well, and that is exactly what could afflict Miss Amy.

I had been counting on Davy's spreading the word when he got out, but he ain't gonna be sprung right away. What to do? But then I recall something Davy had told me back on the *Dauntless*, so now I have a plan on how to go about it.

I had asked for paper and pen and they had given it to me—they probably think I'm writing out my Last Will and

Testament, as I certainly wouldn't be allowed to send mail to anybody, but I am not—no, my actual will rests in Lawyer Ezra Pickering's safe in Boston. This will be something different.

I take up the pen and begin to write.

# Chapter 18

The service at Saint Paul's Cathedral was lovely, and I thoroughly enjoyed singing the hymns. Even the sermon was not too boring, for it taught a good lesson on the Sin of Pride, which I took to heart and resolved to be better in that regard. I'm dressed in my riding habit and look splendid, I think, drawing more than a few interested stares from some gentlemen along with some glares from their wives.

I take much pleasure in gazing about the magnificent interior of this pile of stone upon stone—the rows of great high windows and the massive vaulted dome high above. It brings a smile to my veiled face to think that the last time I was in here, I was dressed as an altar boy and had baby Jesus with me. At least today I got to come in the front door of the place for the first time ever.

But that's all over now and I am back outside with Carr and Boyd on either side of me as we walk up Ludgate Street on our way to our coach, me girlishly chattering away, and those two mugs as silent as tombs. We are parked on Creed Street, just off Ludgate, the crush of carriages about the entrances to the cathedral being too much to put up with, as I knew it would be.

I am *very* familiar with this part of the city, for as soon as I set foot on Ludgate, I am back in Cheapside, and on the turf of the old Rooster Charlie Gang, of which I was once a proud and, I think, useful member. We are not more than a five-minute run to our old kip under Blackfriars Bridge.

"...And then, lads, at this one shop I saw this perfectly divine little baby blue frock with tiny pink bows that ran all along the bodice, just like that, don't you know..." The eyes of both Carr and Boyd roll back in their heads. I'm sure that they're asking whatever gods of espionage there be just why they were assigned to guard this silly little twit.

*Cheer up, lads, things are about to get very exciting.*

When we reach our carriage, Boyd hands me up and I charge through and straight out the other door, having made sure, when we drove here, that the inner latch was not engaged. I hit the ground running.

"Stop!" I hear shouted behind me, but I don't even pause. Oh, no, I pound on for all I'm worth, right down Creed and take a sharp right at Shoemaker. I hear them behind me, but I know there's an alley up ahead so I duck into it and run to the end, where there used to be a low shed. *Yes!* It's still there! I clamber up on it, then over the fence behind it, and find myself, as I knew I would, on Water Street. I hear no more sounds of pursuit, and farther up, at the corner of Water and Broad, squats the Bell and Boar Tavern, certainly not the finest establishment in the city, not even close actually, but it is my destination. I yank the veil aside so I can take some deep breaths and charge on.

I burst through the front door and look around the dim interior—it smells of spilled beer and lost hopes, like all these places, and there are a few working girls over in the corner giggling over a pickled old gent and undoubtedly picking his pocket. But I don't see what I'm looking for.

"'Ere, 'ere, you!" shouts the landlord at his bar. "You can't come bustin' in 'ere loike that. This 'ere's a respectable inn!"

"I can see that, Sir," says I, frosting him with the Look and glancing at the old bawds working over the drunk. "I came here looking for someone. John Tinker. Where is he?"

"And who wants t'know?" smirks this landlord. "Ye look like a foine lady, but I gots a suspicion in me 'ead that yer just a high-class hoor, bein' that yer down 'ere in Cheapside wi' no gent wi' ye. What do you girls think...Bessie? Mildred?"

I ain't got time for this. I march to the bar where several unwashed tankards rest, left over from the last customers. I pick up one and slam it into the side of the landlord's head. It is a good, heavy tankard, with lots of weight at the bottom to fool the customers into thinking they're getting honest measure, and he goes down behind his bar like a poleaxed steer, squalling out his anguish.

"Know this, ladies," I warn, "I was raised up in this gutter, just like you, so don't let the clothes fool you. I can fight as dirty as any of yiz. Get me John Tinker!"

I pick up another tankard and fling it at the two slatterns. It hits the wall above their heads and drools a bit of leftover foam down the wall, which brings their mark back to his senses.

"Wot?" he asks, gazing blearily about.

"Blimey, Bessie, she means to do us all! Go git the boy, 'fore we lose us Mr. Burrows 'ere!"

Mildred gets up and runs off while Bessie pats Mr. Burrows's brow and says, "Now, now, sweetie, you go back to sleep now. No more trouble, you'll see..."

In a minute, John Tinker, my fellow ship's boy from my days on the *Dolphin*, hobbles on a crutch into the main room, his left leg dragging slightly behind his right one.

"What? Who?" he asks, wondering at me standing there in all my finery.

I go to him and say, "Tink. It's me, Jacky. Davy told me you were here."

"Jacky? Jack Faber? No, it cannot be. How...," he says, bewildered.

"Later, Tink, let's get out of here," I reply, and with my arm around his waist, we leave the Bell and Boar to go out into the street where we lean against a wall.

"Jacky. I can't believe this...," he says, gazing wonderingly at me. "Last time I saw Davy he said that you was all growed up. I didn't believe him then, but he sure was right. You're some fine lady."

"You ain't so bad yourself, Tink. Still the same thick black curls and ruddy complexion. 'Course you've grown some. But never mind that now. We'll lift a pint together in the future and catch up on things." I look to the right and left to make sure that Carr and Boyd have not come upon us unawares. They have not. "Right now you've got to take this letter and deliver it to my grandfather, the Reverend Alsop, at the London Home for Little Wanderers on Brideshead Street. Can you do that?"

"Aye. It is not that far from here. I'll go there now." He stuffs the letter into his shirtfront.

"Good. They'll give you some money and employment if you want it. Do you want to go back to sea, John Tinker?"

"It is my fondest wish, Jacky," he answers sadly, looking down at his leg, "but..."

"But nothing. There's always room for an able seaman at Faber Shipping, Worldwide, one-legged or two-. You'll see. Just deliver the letter. Now I must go, as they are after me. Remember, if anyone asks, you haven't seen me."

"Faber Shipping?" He laughs. "You always did go on about that."

"Yeah, it ain't so big right now, just one schooner and two fishing boats, but it does exist, so there."

"Well, I'll be damned. What of the others?"

"Willy's still on the *Temeraire*, last I heard. Davy's newly married to a friend of mine back in Boston, but now he's in a French prison. Jaimy's wounded but still alive, and you are there, and I am here. Benjy's still up in Heaven watchin' over all of us, and laughing at all our trials. The Brotherhood forever!"

With that we each put our fists on our Brotherhood tattoos and I grasp his hand and give him a kiss on his forehead and then run off down the street and he heads, not as swiftly but just as determinedly, in the other direction.

I spot a familiar drainpipe and shinny up it to a low rooftop, then climb onto a higher one, and then an even higher one. I spent a good deal of my youth clambering over these roofs so I know them quite well. When I reach a height that gives me a good view of what is going on down below, sure enough, I spot Carr and Boyd feverishly searching Broad Street, so I cross over a few more rooftops and then drop down onto Paternoster Street. Then I cut down Creed and hop back into our carriage, none the worse for wear. Up above, the driver is deep in slumber, his whip across his knees. The job is done.

I sink against the cushions, chuckling over Messrs. Carr and Boyd, who by this time must be planning new careers for themselves, knowing that surely they will be sacked from the Intelligence Branch, if not taken out and shot, for the misplacement of one small female.

I draw the veil back over my face and I manage to drift off into some sweet slumber, only to be awakened when Mr. Carr jumps into the coach and plops down on my left side with Mr. Boyd on my right.

"Gentlemen," I ask, yawning and rubbing at my eyes, "wherever did you get off to? I was fearing for your safety, as this is a very rough neighborhood."

They say absolutely nothing, just stare stonily forward. The driver clucks at the horses and we are off, returning to the Admiralty, and, hopefully, to a good dinner with Sir Grenville.

"Don't worry, lads," I say as I snuggle down between them, "I shan't peach on you to Mr. Peel." I lift the veil for a moment to plant a kiss on each of their impassive cheeks as we ride back in silence.

The letter I gave to Tink? Oh, yes, here it is:

*Unknown Person in Some Degree of Peril*
*London, September 1806*

*To Whom It May Concern:*

*I will keep this letter short and anonymous for reasons that should be obvious. Suffice to say that a Certain Person Who I Hope Is Dear To You did not die under the guillotine recently, no matter what the reports from France of her demise might indicate.*

*Please send word to certain Persons in the United States, especially to Mr. Ezra Pickering and to John Higgins, that I am not yet dead, even though I may well deserve to be so. However, it would be best if this information is kept secret for a while.*

*Please give the bearer of this letter money for passage to America and provide him with a Letter of Reference from me to Mr. James Tanner that begs him to employ this same messenger in some sort of seagoing fashion, as he is a thoroughgoing seaman in spite of his infirmity.*

*Please give my love and regards to the children and to Mairead and Ian as well.*

*I will not be able to correspond for a while, but do not worry about me.*

*All my love,*

*J.*

# Chapter 19

The next morning I am again off in the carriage, this time to Madame Petrova's dance studio. Carr's and Boyd's unusually flinty gaze adds little joy to the ride. This time they make certain that both entrances to the carriage are firmly latched.

Madame's studio consists of a number of large rooms with polished wooden floors and absolutely no furniture or decoration. A metal barre runs around three sides of the room, the other side being a bank of windows. I know she has classes, too, with other girls, as I hear them out there going through their routines, but I am not allowed to mingle with them. No, I take my instruction alone, just me and the Witch Petrova.

On that first day, I am given a sort of body stocking to wear along with a pair of blunt-toed shoes that lace with ribbon about my ankles and then the instruction begins.

"Place your left hand upon the barre. We will now learn the Positions of the Feet, and how to move between them. Then the Positions of the Arms. Now First Position is..."

I'm given lessons in just how the poor feet should be twisted and the soon-exhausted arms lifted and held out just so, and then told to practice these things till noon, whereupon she sweeps out of the room to attend to her real students. *Three hours of this! I shall die!*

But I don't die, I just do it.

After a lunch of hard bread, cheese, and cold tea, we go back at it again. Madame is *not* pleased with my progress and is quite free with her cane.

At five o'clock I'm brought back to my room, aching in every muscle and bone. I flop facedown on my bed and do not move until I am called to dinner. I'm afraid I'm not very good company.

I suffer days and days of this treatment, progressing from the security of the barre to dancing in the center of the room. Beginning with the *bourrée,* a simple series of gliding steps on my tiptoes, I advance to *grands jetés,* big leaps in the air, then she pronounces me ready to learn the *rond de jambe en l'air et l'arabesque.* When she gives that command, I must lift my arms into the air and then slowly lower them in a sweeping circular motion until my turned-in fingers touch the tops of my thighs, at the same time letting my knees bend slightly, turning my legs into coiled springs. I hold that a split second and then, throwing my arms back up again, I leap to my toes in Second Position, my legs stiff as any mainmast backstay. Then I come off *pointe,* allowing my knees to lower my body slightly. Then I leap out of the crouch, smoothly landing *en pointe* on my left foot, my right leg in the air. I hold this, steady as any rock, feeling the instep of my left foot bulge with the strain.

*So far, so good…*

Then slowly, slowly, I begin moving my right leg, bent at the knee through the arc of a circle to my right and then bring it up behind me, at the same time letting my torso move forward and down, my back arched, my chin up. My left hand gracefully coils upward as I again bring my airborne leg up behind me, toes level with shoulder, completing the *arabesque.*

*Ha!* exults I to myself. *How's that, you old crone?* I release myself from the *arabesque,* returning to Fifth Position, my arms slowly floating down to my sides.

"Pathetic," says Madame Petrova. "Do it several hundred more times, then I will be back to see if there is any improvement."

*Grrrrr…*


After a week and a half of this torture, I once again take my dinner with Sir Grenville and again we are joined by Mr. Peel.

After all pleasantries are exchanged and the dinner is served, we engage in a spirited discussion concerning Dr. Sebastian and the drawings I had done for him—one of the reasons I had the Doctor sprung was that I wanted my drawings to be published. Sin of Pride, I know, but I put a lot of work into those things. At dinner, I described Dr. Sebastian coming off the *Dauntless* after the battle was done and we were taken, him clutching the leather portfolio to his chest as we were led down into the hold.

"A true scientist, through and through!" proclaims Lord Grenville. "Oh, it shall be so good to see him again!" It is then that I realize that Dr. Sebastian did not need my help in getting released, oh, no, he did not. "An excellent story, Miss. Another glass of wine with you?"

*Of course, Sir.*

The good Sir Grenville has been supplying me with books during this time, as well as paints and brushes, so I can more profitably spend my evening and weekend times. I have done a portrait of the First Lord and he pronounces himself enormously pleased. I hope his wife likes it. Once during this time at the Admiralty, Mr. Peel came to my room, flipped a book down on my bed, gave me a significant look, and then left. It was a potboiler named *Under the Jolly Roger, Being an Account of the Further Nautical Adventures of Jacky Faber, as told to Miss Amy Trevelyne,* the book mentioned by Midshipman Shelton back on the *Dauntless.*

Heavy sigh. When I had gotten ready for bed that evening, I had picked it up and spent a good part of the night reading it by flickering lamplight. *And, no, Amy, dear sister, you didn't leave anything out.*

As I closed the book on the last page, I recalled recent times back at Dovecote, after I had just returned from my Mississippi run. Amy and I had spent many happy hours lying back in the grass, me telling her of the events on the slaver *Bloodhound.* Another heavy sigh. I guess there will be yet another book, and I am sure she will have interviewed the other girls who lived through that adventure and *nothing* will be left out of that story, either. Oh, well, I am what I am, and those who don't like me can leave me alone.

"Actually," Mr. Peel had observed when he was dropping

the book on my bed, before leaving me to my evening ablutions and prayers, "it presents your case rather well."

But at this particular dinner, Mr. Peel gets down to business.

"You will be placed in a small dancing troupe that plays at some of the more, well, less-artistic venues. You'll be performing before audiences at private parties, if you catch my drift. The men at these events will not be in pursuit of high art, but rather will be more interested in the dancers themselves when they come out the stage door at the end of the night. Do you understand?"

"Yes, I do, Sir," I say. Lord Grenville looks away, seemingly more distressed than I. Not true, but I can act a part.

"Madame Petrova has been given the choreography of the dances the troupe performs, so that you will know them when you get there. Do not worry. She has said you are up to the task. After all, as she so derisively sniffed, it is not exactly the Paris Opera."

Again I nod and lower my head. Shame blushes my cheeks.

"Please, dear," says Sir Grenville, "perhaps it won't be so bad."

Mr. Peel leans back in his chair and says, "You might find this bit of information interesting: We have learned that the story of your death under the guillotine has spread throughout the fleet..."

*Spread by you, no doubt.*

"...and it is reported that men are lining up at tattoo parlors to have a certain design put on their flesh: It is of a kitten, a plainly female kitten, wearing boots and hat, sword in hand, with the word *Vengeance* underneath. What do you think of that?"

"Almost makes me wish I did perish," I say. "For the sake of the Fleet's fighting spirit."

"Well said, even if it is a lie," says Mr. Peel. "We know your instinct for self-preservation to be quite strong, and we will all be counting on that when your mission begins, which will be very soon."

At that I put down my fork. "Soon, Sir? But…"

"The prisoner exchange has been effected. Your Mr. Fletcher still lives and will arrive in London within days. You will see him, so then our part of that particular bargain will have been kept. You will leave on your mission at dawn of the following day."

My sleep that night was ruined.

# Chapter 20

I got the call two days later, in the early afternoon, at Madame Petrova's. I had been doing exercises at the barre, which I have come, against all odds, to enjoy. I had placed my left foot about three feet from the base of the wall and hooked the heel of my right foot on the barre itself, which is slightly below my shoulder height. I'd begun bobbing my upper body toward my outstretched leg, getting closer with each bob. The muscles of my legs and back flexing and loosening with the exercise gave me a certain feeling of pleasure. After a bit of this, I'd brought my torso down to recline full length on my leg, my chin resting on my shin just below my knee.

Then I reversed the positions of my legs and had run through the exercise again, and then...

...and then it was all over. Madame Petrova came into the room and ordered, "Get dressed. They have come for you."

I think I know what has happened and my heart starts to pound. *Jaimy is back!*

Madame pivots on her heel and strides to the door. I assume she is going to walk out of my life without another word, but, no, she stops with her hand on the doorknob and turns to me. "I know you tried your hardest," she says. "You could have been a dancer." With that, she leaves the room and I see her no more.

*Thank you, Madame, for your instruction.*

I'm halfway back into my riding habit, just cinching my skirt and buttoning my jacket, as it were, when Carr and Boyd burst into the room.

"Blimey, lads, a little privacy for a poor girl!"

"Right, right, just get it on, and let's go."

Two of the hardest caramels I've ever tried to chew, and I didn't get 'em softened even a bit. *A good lesson to you, girl, that your charms do not always work wonders.*

I am taken directly to Number 9 Brattle Lane. The carriage door opens and I jump out to rush up the stairs, followed closely by Carr and Boyd. Carr lifts the knocker on the door and raps for me. In a moment a girl, a servant by her dress, opens the door to admit us.

"You are expected, Miss, upstairs."

I have been in this house before and at that time I was, without ceremony, thrown out into the street by Jaimy's mother. I do not know what to expect this time, but I do not care. I *will* see Jaimy.

On the second-floor landing Jaimy's father, brother George, and Dr. Sebastian are gathered deep in conversation.

"Yes, it was a severe concussion, but he seems to be coming out of it," says the Doctor. "He drifts in and out of consciousness, but he is lucid for longer periods of time now than he was a week ago. I think it bodes well for his future recovery, but one never can tell with these things. We only hope for the best. I will be at your disposal to render what help I can. The primary thing is to have him rest, put cold compresses to his head, and above all, keep him still—let him not rattle his brains, as that could prove disastrous... and what is this, now?"

Dr. Sebastian says this upon seeing my veiled self come marching up the stairs.

"Good day, Mr. Fletcher...George," I say as I come into their midst. I pull my veil to the side. "Dr. Sebastian, it is so good to see you. May I see James Fletcher now?"

Dr. Sebastian's mouth falls open. "But...but...I saw you taken away...I saw the blade rise...and fall...I..."

"No, Doctor, that was not me, but if your scientific mind ever permits prayer, please offer up something for that poor girl who did die under the hissing steel that day, as I have prayed for her soul many times myself." I go up to him and put my lips to his ear and whisper, *It was a ruse, Doctor. We have a very creative Intelligence Service, as you well know. Now let us get on with this.*

"In here, Miss," says Mr. Fletcher, opening a door. "He has been unaware of his surroundings since he was brought from the ship this morning."

Dr. Sebastian, recovering himself from his encounter with the supposedly dead me, explains, "I gave him a sedative to keep him still on the journey. He should be coming out of it soon." He pauses and takes a deep breath. "So good to see you again, Miss."

I give the Doctor a pat on his arm as I enter, and there is Jaimy, lying still on a bed, clean sheets pulled up to his chin.

*Oh, Jaimy, please wake up, please...*

I go to kneel by his bedside, take his hand in mine, and

look into his face while tears stream down my face and I hear as if at a distance...

"No, not her. Anyone but her! Not here. Put her out! She has turned my son against me."

"Mother, *she* is the reason he is here now and not in some filthy French prison. Do you not know that?" I hear Brother George say.

"I don't care. I'd rather he be lying there than have my blood mixed with hers. I will not have it! Do you hear?"

I tear my eyes from Jaimy's face and through my film of tears look into the face of his mother and the old rage rises in me again. She is sitting on the opposite side of the bed, holding his other hand as she glares at me with the purest hatred.

I look right back at her and say defiantly, "I love your son and he loves me, and I don't think there's too much you can do about that, Mrs. Fletcher. It's true that I grew up as a beggar on the streets of London and I still have what you might consider to be rough ways. But I have made my way from there to here, and I believe I deserve some respect for that." I pause and look back at Jaimy again, but see no change— he continues to sleep. "Blood? My blood mixed with yours? I learned in the past couple of years that my people were from the north of England, and my grandfather was a vicar in a church. My blood's as good as yours, but that is all by the board—I don't believe in blood, or bloodlines, or any of that nonsense. Some of the best people I have met in this life have come from the basest of origins, and some of the worst from the highest birth." I turn back to Jaimy, who is much more important to me than some bitter old biddy.

Jaimy stirs and rolls his head from side to side, and then his eyes open and all else in the room fades into insignificance.

He recognizes his old room and an expression of joy crosses his face when he realizes it might not be a dream. He sees his mother, his father, his brother...and then he looks at me. His eyes widen in total and complete surprise and the name he says first is...

"Jacky...I dreamed I saw you...back where? A prison? I don't know...where...?"

"Just hush, Jaimy, and lie back, you must rest," I say and squeeze his hand. "Oh, Jaimy, I'm so glad. I was so afraid."

"James," says his mother, "do you not know me? Please tell me you do."

"Dad? George?" he says, looking wildly about till his eyes light on Carr and Boyd with arms crossed, leaning against the wall. "Who are those men? What are they doing here?" asks Jaimy, looking from Carr to Boyd with great suspicion. He might be foggy, but he is not totally stupid.

"They are members of the Intelligence Branch of our Service, Jaimy. They are my personal escort," I explain with a rueful smile. "Do not worry. They are decent men."

"But why?" asks Jaimy, his mind not yet completely clear, I can tell. It takes a while for the tincture of opium to take leave of your brain. *Poor Jaimy, soon you shall be happy to be back with your family again. I give you permission to forgive your mother.*

"I must go away, Jaimy. I have made a deal."

He cuts his eyes to mine, and I know his mind is now absolutely clear. "They took you...and you made a deal...for me. That's why I'm home."

"Not only for you, Jaimy. There are other reasons, other people."

"I won't have it, I won't…" He tries to get up.

"Please be calm, James," begs his mother. "You must rest or you will harm yourself."

I place my hand on his chest to hold him down. "They finally caught me, Jaimy, they did, and I have many things to answer for, and now I must go where they send me."

"But where are you going?"

"Ahem!" warns Mr. Carr, behind me.

"I can't say, Jaimy. I am going away, but I will return to you, I promise, and you must vow to do your best to get well." I put on a smile, but the tears again are beginning to trail down my cheeks. "Just let me sit by your side for a bit and hold your hand."

"Ten minutes, Miss," says Carr, pulling out his pocket watch and gazing at it. "Curfew." He nods to Mr. Boyd and they both turn their backs and face the wall.

Jaimy's father comes and takes his wife by the arm. "Come, Adelaide, we must give them ten minutes alone."

"I will *never*! I will—" protests Mrs. Fletcher.

"Oh, yes, you will," says Mr. Fletcher. "George, escort your mother out, if you please." And he does, and Mr. Fletcher follows them out of the room with a slight bow to me.

I return a nod of thanks and turn back to Jaimy.

It looks like he might pass out again, but he does not. He struggles to speak once more, but I say, "Jaimy, please be still. All I want to do is sit here by your side while I can." I put a kiss upon his cheek. "No, no, lie quiet, it is what you must do now. You have to get well."

He lies back on the pillow and looks at me.

"Do you remember that time on the *Dolphin* after I was beaten and you took care of me? Do you recall that, Jaimy?"

"Yes," he says, recollecting that day. "I hated what happened to you."

I pat his hand and say, "It's all right. I got over it, and so will you."

"Jacky, I..."

"Hush now. Don't say anything more, Jaimy," I beg, tears pouring out of my eyes and onto his sheet. "Just know that I will love you forever, no matter what happens."

And with that I place a kiss upon his lips and Mr. Carr says, "Time, Miss."

# PART III

# Chapter 21

They brought me ashore by rowboat with muffled oars at Boulogne-sur-Mer, and, after a quick run up some dark, desolate, and lonely beach, they loaded me into a coach with drawn curtains and I'm taken down to Calais, and then on to Amiens.

There my escort left me, with my baggage, a letter of introduction to a Madame Pelletier, and some rather forlorn hopes as to my future. Another man gets in the coach, and we push on for Paris. I feel certain that he is another agent, assigned to keep an eye on their prize pigeon.

Upon my arrival in Paris, I have been ordered to establish myself in my apartment at 127, rue de Londres, to take a day to acquaint myself with my surroundings, and the next day to present myself to Madame Pelletier at her place on rue de Clichy, which is supposedly right around the corner. *How very convenient for the gentlemen admirers who might want to escort a girl home,* I'm thinking. Her troupe is called *Les Petites Gamines de Paris,* and I am to become part of that company. My contact, or my *control,* as the Intelligence Service likes to put it, will make himself known to me some time shortly. I don't like the word, but I guess I'll have to put up with it.

As we rattle on and on through the night and the next day, I have plenty of time to think back to my last night on British soil.

After I had been dragged from Jaimy's side and returned to the Admiralty, I was told to pack my things. I was given a trunk, so I folded up my fancy new clothes and put them in neatly. During the previous week or so I had made some small demand for additional articles of clothing—black stockings and gloves, black corset, and a white bustier, as well as other garments that appeal to men who like such frilly things. Mr. Peel, when informed of these purchases, was happy to pay, pleased that I was seemingly getting into the spirit of the thing, as it were. We shall see.

In the middle of the frilly things I stowed the two tightly corked and wrapped bottles of my old friend, Jacky's Little Helper, also known as paregoric or camphorated tincture of opium, that I had requested from Dr. Sebastian, with the proviso that he tell no one, and which he promptly supplied, asking no questions. Probably thought I was going to use it on myself to ease my coming troubles—he's part of this gang and he knows where I'm going and exactly what I'm expected to do.

When he delivered the bottles, he had something else with him, wrapped in a bundle of leather, and he handed it to me. I opened it up and was delighted to see my old shiv in my leather forearm sheath.

"Doctor!" I gasped. "This is something very dear to me, and I thought it lost forever!"

"Bit of a strange thing for a young girl to hold dear, but there it is. I took it off you when you were first brought to me for examination back on the *Dauntless*. I told the French it was one of my surgical instruments, even though a rather colorful one. I thought it might hold you in good stead now."

"Bless you, Doctor," I cry, clapping my arm around the dear little man and planting a good one square on his lips. "You have been so good to me."

"Ahem...well, none of that, please," says the Doctor. "I just wish we could have worked together a bit longer."

I take him by the shoulders and hold him out at arm's length. "Maybe we will labor together again someday. A trip to the South Seas? Would that not be splendid? I do have a small ship, you know, perfect for a scientific expedition."

His eyes light up at that. "The South Seas, oh, my, yes... if it weren't for this wretched war."

That night we have a last dinner together, the First Lord, Mr. Peel, and I, and we are joined by Dr. Sebastian. I have collected myself, stifled any tears that might want to pop out, and I tell myself that I will make an effort to be gay—never let it be said that Jacky Faber ever ruined a party. I wear one of the Empire dresses, and I think my fellow diners are quite taken with it.

Before the dinner is served, we take some sherry while the Doctor displays his *De Rerum Natura Americana* to great acclaim. When I am complimented on my skill, I blush and say it is really nothing, anyone could do it, but I know that is not true. Sir Grenville pronounces the work a great success and is sure that it will be the talk of the upcoming session of the Royal Society.

"I have so many more specimens for her to render," says Dr. Sebastian. "Are you quite sure we can't send someone else on this mission?"

"No, Doctor, if we keep her, we'll have to hang her. I'm afraid the King would insist." This gets a round of laughter in which I force myself to join.

"I still cannot believe that she sits in front of me, with her head still on her shoulders," remarks Dr. Sebastian, observing me in wonder that the very good wine is sliding down my throat and that same throat is not on some French dissection table. The French have the same rules about the disposal of the bodies of executed murderers as do the English.

"Yes, our man there, he is one of the best. He has worked wonders," says Sir Grenville, turning to me. "You will recognize him when he contacts you. He will be your *control*."

*I will? Who…?*

I guess the question is plain upon my face, for the First Lord looks to Mr. Peel, who looks to me and says, "You knew him as Monsieur Jardineaux."

*Jardineaux! The man who had me dragged out into the prison courtyard and tied to that hateful bascule!*

"You must be joking, Sir," I gasp when I recover the power of speech. "That man—"

Mr. Peel holds up his hand to silence me, and after I've snapped my mouth shut, he says, "I have grown fond of you—you do bring out the protective nature that is a part of many men and the lustful nature of many others. It is one of your unique talents, I know, and one of the reasons we value you so highly. But I'd rather lose a hundred of you than one of him, so you must be very, very careful. I don't want to lecture you at this late date, but information you provide for us through him may save many thousands of British lives. You do want that, don't you?"

I lower my head in submission. "I do, Sir," I say. "Now let us be merry. Shall we have a song? Ah, here's our dinner."

When the food is eaten, and all the wine drunk, and the songs sung, Mr. Peel gets to his feet and says, "Come, Miss, you must retire. Morning comes early."

I rise and Sir Grenville asks, "Will you give us a last toast, dear?"

I look at the dregs in my glass and then lift it up. "Rule, Britannia," I say and then drink it down, as do the others. No more is said, and it comes to me that those might well be some of the last words I will say in my native tongue for a long, long time. Maybe my last English words ever.

That night, on what could be my last night ever on British soil, and after I had donned my nightshirt and got up from my knees after praying for Jaimy's recovery, I strapped on my arm sheath so it would be ready for the morning. I pulled out my shiv and looked again at the cock's head I had carved into the handle several years ago.

*Don't you wink at me again, Charlie, I don't know as if I could take it right now.*

I am shaken back into the present as the coach begins its journey into the center of Paris. I see that there are dozens of cafés, taverns, and bistros that at one time I would have been delighted to be playing in, but no, now I must go to one place and consort with men who must be pumped for information while they pump me in other ways.

Heavy sigh. I'll hold out as long as I can.

It is early evening and I would be able to see the wonders of the French capital, the City of Light, as it is called, if I weren't so dead tired, my sleeping head bouncing against the side of the coach. I come back to my senses only when the coach stops and I find we are parked on a quiet side street in what seems to be a pretty respectable-looking neighborhood.

"Get out," growls my latest escort. "Go to that door and see the concierge. She will show you to your room. You will be contacted. And you will be watched."

"Thank you for your company, Sir," I reply, as I climb out of the coach. The sod has not said a single word during the entire journey from Amiens to here. He grunts and goes to get my trunk, which is shoved in the doorway of 127, rue de Londres. Along with me.

A surly man presents himself to take up the chest, and a woman of considerable girth appears on the stairs.

"*Je m'appelle* Mademoiselle Jacqueline Ophelia Bouvier," I announce as I put on the Look. "I am an American and I will be joining Madame Pelletier's *Les Petites Gamines*."

"I know who you are," she says, her eyes cold as two bits of black ice buried in the pasty white flesh of her face. "And I know *what* you are. I am Madame Gris, the concierge, and I am in charge of this house. Here are the rules: You will get your key from me anytime you enter, and leave it with me anytime you leave. No one enters after midnight or before seven in the morning. There will be no riotous behavior in the halls or foyer. For each man who comes to your room, you will give me two francs when next you leave off your key. Do you understand all that?"

"Yes, Madame."

"I trust that you do. Your room is at the top of the stairs. Number seven. Third door to the right. Behave yourself and you will get along. If not, beware."

She roughly thrusts a key in my hand and sits herself down in a chair behind a desk. Behind her, rows of keys hang on hooks. It appears most of the inhabitants of this house are out.

I turn away from Madame Gris and climb the stairs, pass two doors, and enter the third. My trunk is shoved in behind me, and as soon as the churlish porter leaves, I lock the door.

While the room is very plain, it does have a window, a washstand, a dressing screen, and a chamber pot slid under a straight-backed chair. The most prominent thing in the room is the bed, and I certainly can guess why. I turn back the sheets and see that they are not stained, or not much, anyway. I sit down on the edge of that bed and feel very alone, and very, very afraid.

I think back to that little girl in Cheapside, standing in her rags, listening to the sailors sing at the Admiral Benbow Inn, and wishing for a life of adventure. *Well, you sure got it now, girl, so stop your complainin'.*

Now there is the sound of female laughter out in the hall as well as some raucous revelry coming from the street. I go to the window and see that lamps are being lit across the city and below me are men and women, some arm in arm, some single, and some walking toward the entrance of 127, rue de Londres, my new home. I nip into my trunk to take out the wooden wedges I had made last week and jam them under the door as I do not trust the lock. Thank God the door opens inward. Then I go behind the screen to undress, pull on my nightdress, and crawl into bed.

*Good night, Jaimy, I hope you are feeling better and take joy in being back in the bedroom of your youth. It gives me comfort to think of you there.*

*I...I may not come back in any fit condition for you to marry, Jaimy, and once again I release you from your vow of marriage. Be well.*

# Chapter 22

The next day I'm feeling a bit more cheery. We all feel better in the morning, don't we? The dreads that come in the night are generally chased away by the rising sun, and, by and large, we get on with things the next day, come what may.

I get up, stretch, and look out the window at the new and strange city laid out before me, just now emerging from the mists of the morning. Imagine that, little orphan Mary of Cheapside, Boston, the Caribbean Sea, and late of the American frontier, now in Paris, the City of Light. I reflect that God does work in some mysterious ways, and also start to think that this job might have some side benefits, as it looks to be a wondrous city.

I raise the window and am pleased to see that it does, indeed, open. I stick my head out and look up and down the street. It is not a bad neighborhood, really—it doesn't stink too much, there is no open sewage running in the gutters, and there appear to be several interesting shops lining the curbs.

*And* there is a drainpipe right next to me, coming down

from the roof and going all the way down to the street. I reach out and shake it and it seems strong and well fixed. I might find it useful someday. *Hmmmm.* Could it be that they trust me, or is it that they don't know me as well as they think they do, to give me such a room? I'm sure Carr and Boyd did not report that they had lost track of me that day back in London for fear of losing their jobs, or worse. I'd certainly never heard any mention of it. So maybe the ever-so-efficient Intelligence Service overlooked something and is not yet aware of my willingness to work in, well, high places—as in leaping about on rooftops. *Hmmm,* we shall see.

Certain that I am being watched, I give my hair a bit of a ruffle, then with a great big smile I greet the City of Paris and anyone who might be watching. Then I turn away to get ready. There are some things I need to do today.

First, I remove the wedges, then I unlock the door to look out into the hallway. Sure enough, there is a pitcher of water next to each door, as even girls of low morals do wash themselves. This is a high-class house, I now realize. And for all Madame Gris's cold greediness and the goings-on around my room last night, I also know that this is not a true brothel into which I have been put. Rather it is a place where no questions are asked if one of the local girls happens to entertain a gent for the night, and if a man shows up asking to call on a particular girl, he is not re-fused admittance. I am grateful for this, as it gives me some room to work my plots and plans.

I grab my own pitcher, pull it in, and relock the door. My door had been tried several times last night, but no one managed to get by my wedges. Still, I slept with my shiv in my hand.

I do the necessaries, then I wash up and empty the dirty water into the chamber pot, which I place along with the empty pitcher outside the door. I note that others have done the same. Ah, it is good to know that I'm right in figuring out how things are done around here.

I put on one of my everyday dresses—not everything I bought in London was high fashion—then throw my cloak around my shoulders, clap my hat on my head, grab my purse, and go out, the Lawson Peabody Look firmly in place. I have my shiv up my sleeve in case someone in this house would be of a mind to have me for nothing. One thing for sure, I will not go cheap. But it is much too early for the inhabitants of this place to be stirring, so I am undisturbed.

Madame Gris is seated next to the door and I fear for the health of the chair. It creaks as she shifts her bulk to stretch out her palm. She says nothing in the way of greeting and neither do I.

I slap the key in her fat fist, sweep out the door, and hurry down to the street. I look right and left. Which way to go? Ah, there is a café—the *Café des Deux Chats*—first some food and then it's down to business.

Following an excellent breakfast of coffee, omelet, and some cunning little rolls, and while reflecting yet again that the French sure can cook, I stroll up the street, looking all about me at the bustle of the city and feeling its quickening pulse—the shouts of vendors, the clatter of carriages, the snorting of horses, and the stink of their manure—yes, I am a city girl at heart, that is for sure.

At least I'm shed of Carr and Boyd, and it is good to be free—sort of free, anyway. I had asked my waiter at the café if there was a clothing store close by and was told by him that there was, indeed, one right up the street. Now it's time to see if I can spot who's been assigned to tail me.

I stop to look in the window of a *boulangerie*. All of the different loaves of bread and pastries look so very good, but I must watch myself. I have been given enough money to buy whatever I want, and the former urchin in me, the greedy little thing, wants much, but I must stay trim and so I must suppress her urges as well as my own.

As I peer in the window, I cut my eyes to the left, not moving my head, and notice a young man who has taken a similar interest in another shop window—one I know to be a women's hat shop. I move on.

Again, I pretend interest in a store, cut the eyes, and, ah yes, there he is, doing the same. I am sure he is the one. He is young and quite good-looking, but he is plainly not very good at this. And I thought Jardineaux's organization was supposed to be a crack outfit. *Hmmm.* Maybe they don't care if I know I am being followed. Maybe they want it that way. Well, let's see how they feel about that when I go missing.

Shall we make a game of it then, young man? Very well. You shall be the cat and I will be the mouse.

I spot a clothing shop across the street so I saunter over, and as I enter the shop, I see that he, too, has crossed over. I buy several yards of black cloth, some soft leather, a buckle, black thread, and a card of needles. Oh yes, and a tight black sweater. The packet of my purchases under my arm, I head back out. It is all I can do not to wave merrily at him and give out with a big *yoo-hoo!*

But I don't. What I do is nip into the *marché des vins*, which is right next door, where I buy three bottles of brandy—*cognac*, as the French would have it—two fine glasses...no, get three in case one should break...and some nice napkins. Several bottles of good wine, a corkscrew, and...*playing cards? You have them, too?* Bon! *Such a fine store that has so many things for sale. You shall have all my commerce!*

That should do it. I ask that my purchases be delivered to 127, rue de Londres, room number seven. The proprietress, who has been beaming at me during all this, now gives a bit of a sniff and a look when she hears my address, but I suppose I must get used to that. At any rate, she lets her son make the delivery. Money still talks.

Now, back to the game.

He is out there, sitting on a bench, pretending to read a newspaper. On my part, I pretend not to see him peeking out over the top of it. I march on to the end of the street where rue de Londres meets up with rue de Clichy. It is a busy intersection and I find several coaches there, waiting for fares.

I go up to the first one in line. It is a cabriolet, a carriage that has a top that can be raised or lowered, sort of like an umbrella. The top is up now as I approach the driver and hand him several francs.

"Monsieur. Take this. I will get into your cab and go out

the other door. If you will drive around the block, then come back and pick me up again, there will be more money for you. Do you understand?"

He nods but looks at me with that Gallic raised eyebrow, questioning just what is up.

"It is a joke. On a friend. You will see."

"Ah. *Mais oui.* Young love and all that?"

"Just so, Monsieur."

"Well, get in and play your trick."

I jump in the carriage, go to the other side, release the catch to the far door, and jump down, hidden from the young man who I know is on the other side of the street. There is an alley there and I duck into it, signaling for the driver to go on. He slaps his reins on the haunches of his horse and the cab moves away.

The young man comes running across the street, plainly perplexed. He signals for the next cab in line and says to the driver, "Follow that carriage!"

"What carriage, Monsieur? I see none."

"The one that just went around the corner, damn you!"

"You may damn me, Sir, but that cab could have gone in any of three directions, rue de Clichy, rue Saint-Lazare, or rue de Châteaudun."

The young man stands on the sidewalk, his head down. He knows he's going to catch it when he reports back to Jardineaux, and catch it good.

I tiptoe up behind him and take his arm. "Have you lost something, M'sieur?" I purr. He looks down at me and I give him the Big-Eyes-with-Three-Flutters-of-the-Lashes salute.

He takes a deep breath and stares straight forward. "This is not how it was supposed to go."

"Yes, M'sieur, but this is the way it went. Ah, here is our carriage," I say, as my faithful charioteer brings his cab around once again. "Please put the top down, driver, as it is a most pleasant day," I order grandly. The cabbie does it, and I pile into the seat and beckon the young man to join me. "Come on. You will now show me the charms of your most beautiful city, as I am a stranger here, and am in need of your kind guidance. Come on, I will not bite you." *Not yet, anyway.*

He shrugs and climbs up into the seat next to me.

*You will show me the charms of your fine city, lad... and I will show you some of mine...*

"First let us go up rue de Clichy so I can see where Madame Pelletier's studio is..."

He snorts at the word "studio," so I know what he thinks of *that* establishment.

"...so I will know where to go in the morning. Ah, there it is. Now, let us be off to the river, the Seine, of which I have heard so much. And Notre Dame, is it possible we can see that?"

It is possible. We clatter over the cobblestones, and it is not long before I have him laughing, having gotten to my feet in the coach time after time to point at some especially grand fountain with Neptune surrounded by nymphs and mermaids spouting streams of water from their mouths, or monstrous gargoyles hanging off the roofs above us. It is *such* a wondrous city.

After one such outburst, I flop back onto the seat. "Your name, Sir?" I ask. "You have me at a disadvantage—you know mine, but I do not know yours." He seems to be a nice young man and just what he is doing in this nasty business, I don't yet know. But I am sure I will find out.

They had asked me to pick a new name for myself, as I certainly couldn't waltz into France under the name Jacky Faber, *La Belle,* and so on. So I picked Jacqueline Ophelia Bouvier. I thought it had a certain romantic dash, plus it hints at a possible French ancestry, which I might find handy someday.

"I am Jean-Paul de Valdon, Mademoiselle Bouvier. *À votre service.*"

"And why are you here?" I ask, looking at him closely. He has brown hair, more light than dark, a narrow nose, and a high, I might even say noble, forehead. The nobility of that forehead is softened somewhat by the curls that spill over it. His mouth is framed by a small brown mustache. He is very well dressed in a dark suit of what I suspect is the finest fabric. Not cut from the Carr and Boyd cloth, I know that.

He considers my question and replies, "I am a Royalist. I hate Napoléon and all he stands for."

"And why is that?"

"I lost my grandfather, many uncles, aunts, and cousins to the guillotine, all for the supposed crime of being aristocrats. Most of our lands were seized and our family was left disgraced and almost penniless."

"Ah. Too bad," says I, but having been penniless for a good part of my life, I really can't muster too much pity for the surviving members of his family. I do feel sorry, of course, for those who died under that monstrous chopping block. My dreams have already been invaded by memories of the day that I believed that my own head was going to fall into the guillotine's basket.

"But Napoléon didn't have anything to do with that," I say. "That was much earlier."

"It is all the same. The guillotine is still kept busy."

"I, too, have a nodding acquaintance with that same guillotine, but let us talk of happier things. What is that over there?" I ask, pointing at a large park.

"That is the *Jardin des Tuileries*. It is a beautiful spot. It has seen its share of bloodshed, but now Napoléon uses it for ceremonies and festivals. Would you like to walk there?"

"I would like it very much, Jean-Paul," I say, "if you will lend me your arm."

Though it is early autumn, there are still many beautiful blooms to enjoy, and after our walk, we have an equally lovely lunch at an open café right next to the Seine. As usual, I eat too much and too lustily, but he seems mildly amused by it.

"When are you to be relieved of your Jacqueline Watch?" I ask, wiping the grease from my lips. At least I manage not to burp.

"At four," he says, trying not to smile.

"Well, we shall make sure you are back on your corner, keeping a sharp eye on the very slippery American girl, so do not worry. Now, you must show me the rest of your city, Monsieur Jean-Paul de Valdon."

———

Later, when I get back to my room, I find my packages have been delivered and sure enough, one of the bottles of cognac is missing. The concierge tax, I suppose. Well, I must say I expected that, which is why I bought three.

I flip off my hat and cloak and set up my bar on my washstand. I take one of the bottles, uncork it, and empty about a quarter of the brandy out into the chamber pot. Then I refill it with tincture of opium from my stock of the same, shake it up, and recork the bottle. With a dab of my rouge I make a little red mark on the top of that one, which I dub the Loosen-Up-Their-Tongues Potion, or Mixture Number One. With the other one, I pour out a good half, again refilling the bottle with Jacky's Little Helper, and give it a quick shake. That one shall be called the Knock-'em-Clean-Out Bottle, or Mixture Number Two. I put the sparkling new glasses next to the bottles and step back to survey the work. Looks good, I think, feeling rather like a spider who has spun her web and has only to be patient and wait for the fly.

Satisfied with that, I work with the playing cards a bit, lengthening the odds considerably in my favor, should I find a game and be able to use these now-altered cards. Then, pulling out my needle and thread and black cloth, I begin to stitch up a black hood, complete with eyeholes, which will be my burglar's outfit. I wouldn't feel comfortable not having that at hand.

Time for Jacky to get another seabag, oh, yes.

Much later, as darkness falls, and following a fine dinner of bouillabaisse, the best fish stew I ever tasted, it's back to my room. With the wedges shoved under the door, I go behind the screen, strip off my clothes, get into the nightdress, climb into bed, and reflect that it was not a bad day, not a bad day at all. And that Jean-Paul, he...

*Enough of that, you. Good night, Jaimy.*

# Chapter 23

Once again, I had breakfast at *Deux Chats,* and I ate it alone.

Seeing Jean-Paul at his station back on the corner, I had gone up to him, hooked my arm in his, and said, "Come, Monsieur de Valdon, and break the fast with me. At *Deux Chats.* It is a nice little spot. Very clean, with good food. My treat."

He took my hand from his arm and dropped it, looking straight forward, unsmiling. "No, it is not professional. You kidnapped me yesterday, but I have come back to my senses now."

I looked down at my spurned hand, my face flushing pink.

"Ah," I said, narrowing my eyes and deciding to throw a bit of a snit. "It is clear to me now. You, a young royal, cannot be seen in public with one such as me. That is it. You are afraid someone will see." Seemingly well steamed now, I poked a finger in his chest and glared up at him. "And I showed you such a good time yesterday, you foolish boy!"

He looked pained. "No, that is not it at all, it is…"

"Well, here, a last kiss for you, silly puppy, for you shall receive no others from me." I stretched my neck upward and kissed him on the cheek as I did yesterday when we left the carriage after our day in Paris. "There, Jean-Paul de Valdon, Aristocrat of France. Now run along home and tell your *maman* that you were kissed by a bad girl and she will wash your face for you, with strong soap, so you will be clean again! And maybe she'll wipe your bum for you, too! Baby!"

I shoved him away and strode down the street to *Café des Deux Chats*, leaving Jean-Paul de Valdon behind me. The food was, again, very good, but I didn't enjoy it as much. *Stupid boy...*

When I arrive at the front door of Madame Pelletier's studio on rue de Clichy, my knock is answered by an old man with white hair and whiskers, dressed in what I suppose is a French butler's rig. He is very courtly and escorts me in to meet Madame Pelletier.

On my way in I notice that Madame Pelletier's establishment is more than a mere studio—it is actually a small theater. There is an entrance hall, a foyer that contains what appears to be a bar, and beyond that, a large open room with seating for perhaps a hundred patrons of the art of dance. The walls are lined with elegantly framed paintings, most of them, to my eye, very fine.

I can see that there is a stage raised about three feet above the level of the floor, with room in the front to seat a small orchestra. I assume the dressing rooms are in back.

Madame, herself, a small, trim woman, is seated at the bar, sipping a cup of tea and reading a newspaper. She looks up, I dip down in a medium curtsy and say, "*Bonjour, Madame.* I am Mademoiselle Jacqueline Ophelia Bouvier. I believe I am expected?"

I hand her my letter of introduction supplied to me by British Intelligence. She takes it and opens it.

As she reads it, the other girls of her troupe come straggling in, singly or in pairs, yawning and whining about the earliness of the hour and the wretchedness of their lives, and asking why do they have to practice anyway when they already know the routines.

"Ah, yes. You are our American girl. Good. Welcome, Jacqueline. I just lost a girl to a Polish general who took her as his mistress last week and I need a replacement. I like to have an even dozen in my *corps de ballet,* and I was assured you were qualified." Madame takes another sip of her tea, puts down the cup, and raises her voice to call, "Blanche, come here!"

A harried-looking older woman with pins held in her thin lips emerges from a side door, looks me up and down, and raises her eyebrows in question to Madame Pelletier.

"*Oui?*"

"This is the new girl. Her name is Jacqueline. Take her back and fit her out in costume. Then we will have practice."

The woman named Blanche looks at me and points to the door of the room from which she had just come. I bow slightly to Madame Pelletier. "Thank you for receiving me so graciously, Madame."

Madame nods and goes back to her newspaper as I follow Blanche into what I find are the dressing rooms...or rather, dressing *room.*

The other girls are already there, getting into their costumes, calling out to one another, making jokes, and laughing uproariously. There are two long benches on either side of the room, two lines of lockers, and two large windows at the rear of the room to let in some light and air.

They quiet down a bit upon seeing me enter.

"And what is this?" asks a tall girl who is seated on the bench, pulling up her stocking.

"I am Jacqueline Ophelia Bouvier from America, here to join your company," I say.

"That is your locker there," says the taciturn Blanche, very little interested in who I am and where I came from. "Take off your clothes, and then stand on that box there."

"But why are you here?" asks the same tall girl. I sense that she is the leader of the pack, and I find I am not wrong.

"I am here to dance," I say. I slip off my shoes and hang my hat on a hook in my locker.

"There is no dance in America, that you have to come all the way over here?"

"There is not much," I say. "Have you not heard of the Puritans? They do not like dancing." I shrug off my cloak and hang it on yet another hook.

"I think she comes to dance *le jig-jig* at 127, rue de Londres," giggles another girl, and this is met with great gales of laughter from the others.

"You know my name, but I do not know yours," I say to the girl who has just made the joke.

"I am Giselle," she replies, rising to put on her skirt. "And this is Zoé," nodding to the tall girl. "And that is Béatrice, Yolande, Georgette, Yvonne, Isadora, Francette, Héloïse, Véronique, and Sacha."

"I am most pleased to make your acquaintance," I say, with a deep curtsy. "Thank you for making me welcome."

It is then that I unloosen the fastenings on my dress and pull it over my head, exposing my shiv held in its sheath on my left forearm. The room goes dead silent. If I had known this was going to happen, I would not have worn it, but I did. And maybe it's good that they see it and know I am not a helpless waif. Even though, at the moment, I am feeling exactly like one.

I take off the sheath and stuff it on the upper shelf in the locker. I quickly pull off my stockings and under-clothes and then bounce up on the box to await Blanche's fitting.

"*Ooh là là...,*" whispers Giselle, looking about at her sisters in wonderment. "She looks like a baby, but she has a sharp tooth."

"And a tattoo," says Zoé, walking about me as I stand there. "And what looks like a whip scar. What do we have here? *Une petite tigresse?*"

"Just a simple American girl," I say, grinning. "And how about this?" I reach up and pull off my wig, revealing my short-cropped hair.

*That* gets more gasps than anything. I think I may have won over this audience.

The tape measure goes around my waist, and I am fitted for my costume. It consists of a tight white sleeveless chemise top with narrow shoulder straps, white stockings that reach only the midthigh and are held up by pink garters, and very short drawers with ruffles that run across the rump. A gauzy white skirt that barely comes to the knees completes the thing. *Ooh là là,* indeed.

Then we have rehearsal.

Madame conducts it herself. The old man at the door picks up a fiddle and saws out some music for us to dance to. It's Luigi Boccherini, I think, Concerto in D Major or something or other. The choreography is quite simple, and, since I have been provided with instruction on the dances she stages, I get along quite well. It is mostly step, kick, step, kick, side step, slide back, and kick. There are lots of high kicks and flashings of ruffled tail. If I stumble, the other girls help me out, and soon I have everything down pat. They really are a pretty good bunch.

Lunch is brought in and we have a great time eating and telling stories. I regale them with tales of Boston and my journey down the Mississippi and New Orleans—they can't get enough of New Orleans, being French and all—and then we go back to practice.

After two more hours of rehearsal, Madame calls a halt, we get dressed again, and she warns everyone to be back at six o'clock for tonight's show at seven.

Before I put my hat on to leave, Madame calls me aside for a bit of a talk.

"Ahem," she begins. "As for the men who will come here... You will not be forced to go with any of them, but we expect you to be friendly—mix with them in the intermission, flirt with them. If you leave with one of them, what you do then is your own business. But we like to keep them happy, so they will keep coming back to *Les Petites Gamines*. Do you understand? Some rich and powerful men come here, and more than a few of my girls have made very profitable liaisons. *Comprenez-vous?*"

"Yes, Madame, I do."

"Good. You did well today. And your accent, *Américaine*, is it? I'm sure some will find it very charming. Good day."

I go back to rue de Londres, take a nap, get up, freshen myself, and go out for a bite before returning to *Les Petites Gamines de Paris*.

I'm sitting at *Café des Deux Chats*, polishing off an excellent plate of snails, when the chair across from me is pulled out and my blood runs cold. It is Monsieur Jardineaux, my would-be executioner and now my promised *control*.

"A glass of wine with you, Sir?" I manage to offer through clenched teeth.

"Shut up, girl. Listen to me and heed me well. We are too exposed here and will not meet like this again." He looks about him to make sure we are not observed.

"What could be better cover?" I ask, recovering myself a bit. "A man sitting at a table talking to a known denizen of the demimonde. What is more ordinary in Paris, the City of Light?"

"We'll see. Now, here are some rules. When we want to talk to you, we will put a light in the window directly across from your room. You will then go down to the corner to await further instructions. If you want to talk to us, hang this yellow handkerchief out your window and we will contact you. Do you have that?"

"I am not stupid, Sir," I say, taking the yellow rag from him and stuffing it up my sleeve.

"I know you are not that. You have been here for only three days and already you have turned one of my valued operatives into a babbling idiot. Monsieur de Valdon is quite unsettled. One more slip on his part and he will be sent back to the provinces for retraining."

"I shall try to be good, and I will bother the confused Monsieur de Valdon no more."

"That is good. Now…At the performance tonight there will be many men, and you must mix with them all, but I want you to focus in on one in particular, Marshal Hilaire de Groote. He is a General of the Imperial Guard, Napoléon's finest regiment. We need to know when and to where Napoléon is going to move the Grand Army. He had massed it at Dunkerque to move across into Britain, but his fleet was destroyed at Trafalgar."

"I know that, Sir, as I was there."

He greets that statement with a cold laugh.

"That may be so, but what you don't know is where he plans to move that army. General de Groote does know, and it is up to you to find out.

"The General is a tall, heavy man with a large mustache who will be wearing the Imperial Guard uniform—dark blue coat with long tails and red turnbacks, red epaulets, and white lapels. He will probably be wearing his medals, too, as he is not a modest man. It shouldn't be difficult for you to recognize him."

"I am sure I will be able to pick him out," I say. "But why do you think I will be able to get close to him? There are many girls there, and they are all very pretty."

He gets up and looks down at me.

"One thing that is known about Marshal de Groote—he likes his girls little and he likes them young."

"Ah" is all I say.

"Do your duty, girl," he says. "Report to me tomorrow morning. *Adieu.*"

He leaves just in time, as Giselle and Zoé waltz into the place and I wave them over for a final aperitif before we head off to our work.

The place fills up quickly. I peek out through the curtain, excited. Though both myself and my virtue may be in deep trouble, still I do love a show, I do love to perform. There are both men and women in the crowd and all are very finely dressed. There are also many men in uniform, and splendid uniforms they are—Grenadiers, Lancers, Hussars, Light Cavalry, Dragoons, Cuirassiers—all plumes and cockades and tight trousers and boots and epaulets and bright turnbacks and snowy lapels...and that is just the men, the women are—

"Come back from there, Jacqui," orders Zoé, taking me by the shoulder and pulling me back from the curtain. "Time for mixing with them later. Tell us another story of America, while we wait for the opening number." It hadn't taken them long to figure out that my English name is the same as the French so they shorten it almost immediately to Jacqui. They pronounce it "Jacky" so it sounds right familiar to me.

There is an orchestra out there, too, and they are tuning up. They have two fiddles, a viola, cello, oboe, trumpet, and bassoon. I have never worked with such an ensemble! Joy!

I go back into the dressing room. We are all in costume and ready to go. The orchestra runs through the squeaks and squawks of tuning up and getting ready. I'm in the middle of telling the girls about the House of the Rising Sun in New Orleans while they interrupt with questions, when everybody falls silent.

"All right, girls, places!" announces Madame Pelletier. And we all hit our marks. The curtain rises and the music swells.

The first number is a thing where we all pretend to be fluttering swans on a lake, all on tippy toes and moving our arms like softly flapping wings, and Isadora, dressed as a hunter, lifts her crossbow and shoots Zoé, the head swan, in the breast and she falls fluttering to the ground and the rest of us swans gather around her and mourn her death. Actually, given the caliber of this troupe, she doesn't do a bad job in dying. I could do better, but, hey, let it go.

Curtain down, applause, the orchestra cuts into a new piece, Haydn, I think, and we get a slight break. I do love the applause.

Again the curtain rises and this time we are elves in a forest cavorting about most scandalously. Toads and frogs are involved. Hopping about, I get to the front rank in this one and I spot him, and he is looking directly at me, no question, and his look does not waver. It is, without doubt, Marshal Hilaire de Groote, in full military rig, and with lust in his eye. He is, however, seated next to a very stern-looking woman. *Hmmm...*

The number ends, the elf queen is restored to her throne, and the curtain falls. It is intermission and we get to take a bow, lining up, hand in hand across the stage.

The crowd gets up from their seats and heads to the bar for refreshment, and we girls, throwing silken shawls about our shoulders for modesty, go there to join them.

We receive attention from all the young men, of course— drinks are thrust into our hands, and compliments given on our performance. And not just the young men, either— plenty of older gents who should know better come sniffing around, too. *Old hounds...* But I laugh and giggle and simper and am pleasant to all, and then I feel a large hand on my shoulder, and all the other men look down and fall away.

"You are new here," he says, removing his hand and bowing slightly. "I enjoyed your performance."

"I am pleased that you did, Sir," I reply with a slight curtsy. "But you have the better of me, as I do not know your name." I damn well do, of course.

"I am Field Marshal Hilaire de Groote, of the Imperial Guard," he says, lifting my hand and kissing the back of it. "*Et vous?*"

Deep curtsy this time. "I am Miss Jacqueline Ophelia Bouvier, late of Boston in the United States."

"Ah. The Americans. Our sometime allies."

"The French are never far from our hearts, Sir. We remember Lafayette."

"Well said. *Hmmm.* I find you a well-spoken young woman and I would like to spend a bit of time with you... discussing America and all. Unfortunately, I am here tonight with my wife, who is somewhat of a jealous sort and does not understand simple…conversation between people of like minds." For an old rogue, he is certainly smooth.

"Perhaps tomorrow, Sir?" I say, trying to conceal the dread I feel. "I would very much like to have some…conversation with you."

"Alas," he says, shaking his big head, "I am unfortunately called out on military affairs till Tuesday." He straightens up and intones, "The Emperor calls and I must obey."

"Of course, *mon Général*. Tuesday night, then, Sir," I say, lowering the eyelashes. "After the performance. 127, rue de Londres, room number seven?"

"It is done, my dear. I shall be there, and you shan't regret our meeting, I assure you," he answers, with a slightly furtive cut of the eyes to make sure his wife is not watching this exchange. She, occupied in polite conversation elsewhere, apparently is not.

There is a bell to signal the end of the intermission, and all us girls flee to the dressing room, where Giselle immediately collars me.

"You watch out for that one, Jacqui," she advises, all serious. "He is known to be brutal and rough. Ask Sacha there."

I look to Sacha, a small, quiet, and very young-looking girl. She nods and points to a bruise on her temple. "We call de Groote 'the Goat' for good reason, *chérie*. If you go into a room with him, make sure you have a way out."

I take that advice to heart.

The music comes up again, as does the curtain, and we are on.

The rest of the program is similar to the first—lots of silly plots and plenty of high kicking and flashing of legs. At the finale we are all in a line, and after some especially high kicks, we turn our backs, bend over, and flip up our skirts.

As I look down at my ankles with my tail in the air and shake the ruffles on my drawers, I think, *Oh, if Amy Trevelyne and my sisters at the Lawson Peabody could only see me now!*

# Chapter 24

I hang the yellow signal handkerchief in the window while I'm washing up and dressing. Then I take it down, shove it under the mattress, and go down the stairs.

"I trust you enjoyed the cognac," I say to Madame Gris, as I flip her the key on my way out without looking to see whether or not she catches it. All I hear from her is a snort. *We'll see, you old cow.*

A closed carriage pulls up in front of me, the door swings open, and I climb in. Jean-Paul de Valdon sits in the opposite seat.

"*Bonjour,*" I say by way of greeting. "I see they have sent the boy instead of the man."

"Monsieur Jardineaux was called away this morning on an affair of great importance," he says.

"I'm sure," I murmur, as I settle myself. "Anyway, here is my report: I met Marshal de Groote last night, and he seemed quite taken with me. Things would have come to a head, so to speak, right then, but, unfortunately, his wife was with him, so I was unable to strip down and get under him right then, as I assume that even in Paris there are rules about such things—Madame Pelletier's theater being a public place and all."

"You are not being funny."

"*Non?* I thought I was just giving you my report. Anyway, he will come to my room Tuesday night. I will get the information. First, I want to see where he lives."

"What ever for?"

"I should explain to you? Am I not a member of this organization, too? Have I not a mind?" I say, fixing him with the Look. "Very well, I shall tell you. When I am...entertaining him, I will want to compliment him on his fine house, his high station in life—that's how girls like us inflate the male soul and make him tell us even more of himself. Do you understand now?"

"All right." He leans his head out the window. "Driver. Rue Saint-Lazare." To me he says, "It is not far. Only two blocks."

*Good. Then I shall not have far to run tonight.*

We clatter through the streets down rue de Londres, turn left onto a large boulevard, and then left onto a quieter street, lined with fine houses.

"Armand. Drive slowly but do not stop."

"*Oui,* Monsieur." It's plain that the hack belongs to this bunch. Its driver, too.

Presently we arrive at what is probably the finest residence on the street. It is a two-story house, a mansion, really, set back about twenty yards from the road, and it's surrounded by a wrought-iron fence approximately eight feet high, each upright topped with a halyard spike. Still, not too bad—better than stone with broken glass imbedded in the top. There are two uniformed guards at the gate. There are no guards at the entrance to the mansion itself, but I suspect the Marshal is well protected inside as well. Well, it is not him I want.

I notice a delivery being made to a side door—must be the servants' entrance. A girl in maid's clothing receives the groceries. Wonder if de Groote gets on the help...probably does. *Hmmm*...There is an attic window at the peak of the roof...probably the servants' quarters. I hear a dog bark... maybe two.

"Well, that's enough, boy," I say and give him a kick in the shin. "Now take me to Notre Dame Cathedral. It is Sunday and my day off."

"We were there just the other day. Why go again?" He looks at me in anger, and maybe, with just a little hurt in his eyes.

"Because I wish to pray for my friends, of which you are not one."

"For the Mass? I did not know you were Catholic."

"I am anything I want to be. I have many Catholic friends in the States and I have been to church with them. You will show me the proper time to kneel down and when to get up and when to—"

"But why should I cart you about like this while you insult me and call me a baby?"

"Because I am going to perform a very great service for you and your people. A service, I might add, I am going to find *extremely* distasteful. No matter what you might think of me."

"All right," he says, and gives instructions to Armand. We rattle forward and sit in silence for a while.

At length he clears his throat and says, "Mademoiselle

Bouvier. Yesterday, when I spurned your hand...It was not for the reason you said—that I had no respect for you. No, it was because I caught the wrath of hell from Monsieur Jardineaux for letting you slip away the previous day. I don't even know how he found out, but he did." He flushes. "I was almost sent away in disgrace."

I decide I have tormented him enough, and as I need this boy on my side, I pop over to seat myself beside him.

"That makes me feel much better, Jean-Paul. Thank you." Arm back in arm, with a bit of a snuggle. "Do you think lightning will strike the steeple of Notre Dame for one such as I being in it? Will the gargoyles stand up to roar in anger?"

"No, I do not think so, Mademoiselle Bouvier. It is all about sin and divine grace and forgiveness, is it not?"

"All us working girls certainly hope so." A bit more of a wiggle and a snuggle on that. "And you must call me Jacqui. Everybody does, you know," I say to him as I watch the city roll by while we head down to the great cathedral.

We go in the front door of the *Cathédrale Notre-Dame de Paris* and Jean-Paul dips his hand in a little stone basin next to the door and puts his hand to his forehead and does that Sign of the Cross thing. I am amazed at the interior of the place—if I considered Saint Paul's in my old neighborhood impressive, it was a minor wonder compared to this. I stand gaping in awe at the rosette window high above me, a great round stained-glass piece of artwork, with the sunlight streaming through. Below it are nine long, double-wide stained-glass windows depicting Biblical scenes. A Mass is going on at one of the altars, but Jean-Paul takes me by the arm and leads me over to a nearby dimly lit alcove where many candles are burning, some freshly lit, some guttering out.

"I think this is really where you want to be."

He gives a coin to a woman clad in black who sits quietly to the side, and she hands me a candle.

"You kneel on that low bench and light the candle from one that is already burning and then put it there in line with the others. I'll be outside." And he leaves me alone.

I put my knees on the padded bench and stick the wick of my candle into the flame of a candle that is about to wink out, and it catches. Then I put it in line with the others.

*I am kneeling in a Catholic church, Jaimy, and I know that it would drive your family quite mad to know this, but it is all that I have available to me to pray for your recovery. Actually, it is a very nice place and I think you would like it and I hope to visit it again sometime with you by my side.*

"That was very nice, Jean-Paul," I say, as I come back out into the light of the plaza in front of the cathedral. He waits by the carriage.

"Will Armand tell on you? Or us?" I ask, as I climb in.

"He would if he thought it a serious breach on my part. But he won't for this. He is from my village in Normandy. He knows my family, and I know his," he says. "And as for you, Jacqui, everybody is finding it very hard to dislike you."

"Ha. You'll find eventually that a little of me goes a long way." I laugh. "But now, we must have some lunch."

———

As I polish off the last of yet another staggeringly good meal at a cozy little restaurant near the Seine, we return to the carriage and after he hands me up, Jean-Paul gives some instructions to the driver. He climbs in next to me and Armand chucks at the horse and we are off again.

"Where are we going now?" I ask, fearing that he just might be taking me off to my room...or his, for a bit of a tumble in the sheets. After all, from what he thinks he knows of me, all he would have to do is put twenty francs on my dresser top to pay for my services and on to the romp. But my fears are unfounded. Probably thinks he might catch something from me. A wise boy.

"I have read your dossier. You like to paint? Make drawings and such? Fine. I shall take you to the Louvre," he says.

"And that is?"

"A former palace of the King. It is now full of paintings looted from the royal treasures. It was set up for the education of the...people."

"You want to say the rabble, don't you, Jean-Paul?"

"No, I am for the people of France, above all things."

"That is good of you," I say, pressing my lips together firmly. "In your dossier on me, did it also say that I grew up on the streets of London, a penniless orphan, just like those urchins begging over there? Hmmm? Tell Armand to go slowly by them. I will throw them some money."

He does it and I dig in my purse for some coins and then lean out the window. "Here, *mes petites,* have something good to eat tonight." The centimes hit the cobblestones and the kids shout in delight and scramble for the coins.

"You see that girl there?" I ask, pointing to a very skinny

girl, about ten years old, clad in a dirty rag, who holds up her prize coin and waves her thanks. "That was me."

"I am sorry."

"Don't be. I made many friends there. Lifelong friends. There is more to the rabble than you might think."

I have never before been in an art museum, or any other kind of museum, for that matter. I am overwhelmed by it all. Jean-Paul points out huge paintings of battles, of gods and goddesses flinging thunderbolts, naked fat ladies being hauled off to certain ruin by soldiers and Minotaurs, small, jewel-like portraits of fine Venetian ladies, stern Dutch burghers, crucifixions both of Jesus and others, martyred saints, and beautiful children.

"I may never paint another picture again, Jean-Paul," I say, my head down. "Never have I been so humbled, and to think I counted myself an artist."

"I have heard that you are quite good, Jacqui," he says, patting my hand that rests on his arm.

"Then maybe someday soon I shall paint your portrait in miniature. Would you like that? I brought supplies with me from England. You could give it to your sweetheart, and she would treasure it in your absence."

"I have no amorous alliances," he sniffs. "I have no time nor inclination for that sort of thing."

"A handsome young man like you? I cannot believe it."

"But it is true, nonetheless."

"Jean-Paul, do you have this evening's Jacqui Bouvier Watch in the window across from mine?"

"Yes, I do. I have virtually all of the 'Jacqui Watches,' as you call them. Armand takes over sometimes when I need to get some sleep." Here his face tightens. "Tuesday night, when you…accommodate de Groote, Jardineaux will be in attendance as well. Why do you ask?"

"I am quite dazzled, and I think my eyes cannot take in even one more pink cherub, one more beautiful stained-glass window," I say, with the back of my hand to my forehead. "So why do we not go back to my place, and I will paint a miniature portrait of you. You can give it to your sweetheart when you decide to get one, and she will treasure it."

"But I don't know…"

"Oh, poof! What better way to watch me than to be in the same room with me? I know you cannot be with me in the usual man-woman way, but we can still enjoy each other's company, n'est-ce pas?"

"I suppose it would be all right," he agrees, doubtfully. "But before we go, I want to show you something."

"Oh?" I ask, a bit mystified.

He takes me by the arm and leads me over to stand before another painting. It shows a beautiful young woman with long, flowing chestnut locks. She is seated in an elegant room and is dressed in the finest of clothing.

"So?"

"Look at the placard beside it."

I do and it says, *The Traitor Charlotte Corday, Murderer of Jean Marat, Patriot.*

"Who was she, then?"

"My cousin. She was guillotined on July 17, 1793."

"Her crime?"

"She murdered a murderer—the Revolutionary Jean Marat, who was responsible for butchering thousands of people during the Terror, many of whom were members of my family."

"Oh," I whisper.

"I remember her. She was beautiful and was very kind to me as a child. I loved her. This picture was painted just before she was executed. It is said she gave the artist a lock of her hair so he would get the color just right. She died bravely." Jean-Paul turns to look in my eyes. His face is grim. "Perhaps this tells you something of me, and of what I do."

*It does, Jean-Paul. It does, indeed.*

And so we go back to 127, rue de Londres, get a knowing look from Madame Gris as we enter—*and yes, you old witch, you shall get your two francs*—collect the key, and go up into my room. I shuck off my cloak, get out my paints and brushes, and pose Jean-Paul in the chair by the window.

"There. Lift your chin a little... That's it. Now turn your head and look at me. You have very beautiful eyes, Jean-Paul, did you know that? No? Well, you do know now. Yes. Hold it right there."

We spend a very pleasant afternoon... and evening. The portrait went well, and, as the light begins to fade, we send out for food and wine. We sit by my window and look out on the glowing lights of the city and have a fine dinner by candlelight.

When we are done, we rise and I give him a kiss—a real one—for being a good model and an honorable man, and he leaves to take up his post.

And, oh yes, before he left, I did pour him an aperitif— from Mixture Number One. I mean, rue de Londres is not very well lit at night, but still I can take no chances as there might be a moon out tonight.

I lean out the window to make sure he makes it across the street. He does, if a trifle unsteadily.

Then I get into my burglar's outfit and wait.

After about an hour, I open my window and climb out.

# Chapter 25

"Tell us more of Monsieur le Fink, Jacqui," begs Véronique. We are dressing for the night's performance, and the girls again press me for stories about America. I'm a bit tired, because I had been out a good deal of last night, but being the natural show-off that I am, I draw in a breath and give it to them.

"Oh, my friends, what a piece of work was Mike Fink! Big as a house and covered with enough hair to stuff all the mattresses in Paris! And that time when I first saw him, he bellowed..."

*WEEEEEE... OOOOOP! LOOK AT ME! I'M A RING-TAILED ROARER! I'M THE ORIGINAL IRON-JAWED, BRASS-MOUNTED, COPPER-BELLIED CORPSE MAKER FROM THE WILDS OF ARKANSAS! I'M HALF HORSE AND HALF ALLIGATOR! I WAS BORN IN A CANE-BRAKE AND SUCK-LED BY A MOUNTAIN LION! CAST YOUR EYES ON ME, AND LAY LOW AND HOLD YOUR BREATH FOR I'M ABOUT TO TURN MYSELF LOOSE. WEEEEE... OOOOP! WEEEE... OOOOP!* 'Course, it was somewhat difficult for me to translate all that into standard French. The French, unlike us British, have an Academy that keeps an eye on how French should be spoken, and so you don't have all the dialects, accents, slang, and thus everybody speaks sort of the same. Ain't no Cockneys here, *par Dieu*— but with many loose gestures, pantomimes, and Fink-like grimaces and scowls, I think they get the flavor, and a taste, admittedly strong, of Mike Fink, *Le Roi de la Rivière.*

I finish that story and hear raucous laughter all through it and am happy for it. I do like to tell a good story...and why not take it further?

I see that Georgette is now fully dressed. "Georgette," I say, "will you go to see if Monsieur Percheron will lend me his fiddle for a bit?" Monsieur Percheron is not the lead violin in the orchestra, he's the butler and the old man who grinds out the melodies for us when we practice.

"*Mais oui,*" she says, ducking out through the curtain. I take this time to finish dressing, the garters being the last to go on with a snap on each upper thigh. In a moment she is back, and I take the instrument from her and walk to the middle of the dressing room. It is not a fine fiddle, but it will do.

"This is a song taught to me by that same Monsieur Fink. It is called 'The Boatman's Dance.'" And to their utter astonishment I rip into it with both fiddle and feet.

"Out here, out here," the newly arrived orchestra calls upon hearing the fiddle tune, and I nod toward the opening in the curtain and the girls follow me through it and out onto the stage. They line up on either side of me.

I keep the fiddle going and say, "See, these are the steps. They are very simple. Step, step, hop, and step. Got it?" They do. "Then here we go."

*Dance the Boatman's Dance,*
*Oh, dance the Boatman's Dance,*
*Dance all night till the broad daylight,*
*And go home with the girls in the morning!*

Their feet, clad only in the soft ballet slippers, cannot
make the hard rapping sound of booted boatmen feet, but
still it is a pleasing thing. I sing a few more verses, then notice the doors being opened to admit the night's guests so I
end it with

*Hi, ho, the boatmen row, floatin' down the river on the*
    *Ohio!*
*Hi, ho, the boatmen row, up and down the Ohio!*

Even though we have not done it before, we all end together, to a round of applause from the band, and from
Madame Pelletier as well, who casts an appraising eye on
me as she claps.

"*Bravo! Bravo! Encore!*" comes from the orchestra, but it
is not to be, as our public begins to come in and we all flee
behind the curtain again.

"*Brava, bien sûr,* Jacqui," says Béatrice, as we all col-
lapse laughing onto the bench to await the opening of the
show.

"But what about this House of the Rising Sun in New
Orleans that you talk about, Jacqui?" asks Véronique. "It is a
good place to work? The Madame is kind? I always wanted
to see America."

Madame Babineau kind? Well, if you brought a dollar

into her house coffers, she was kind enough. If not, you were out on the street.

I take a breath and say, "I recommend you stay here with Madame Pelletier. Here you get to pick and choose your men. At the House of the Rising Sun you do not. You must take what comes in the front door." I don't tell them that when I worked at the Rising Sun, I was employed as musician and card dealer, not as working girl, but I get the message across. Véronique nods, taking my meaning, as do many of the others.

There is a silence from outside the curtain as the musicians, done with their tuning, await the tap of the conductor's baton. It comes, and the music swells. We also get up and wait for the curtain to rise, and as I wait, I think back to my work last night.

Last night, after I saw Jean-Paul back to his post and when I was sure that he was deep in slumber, I donned my burglar's gear, threw my small bag over my shoulder, slipped out the window, and climbed down to the street. Once there, I whipped off my hood, becoming just another street urchin and not worthy of notice, and started running through the dark night for rue Saint-Lazare. It took me about twenty minutes to get to de Groote's house, and, after pausing to catch my breath, I put my hood back on and leaped up and over the fence. I crouched on the other side behind a low bush and waited. Nothing. I waited for another minute and then started across the lawn to the house. That's when I heard the long, low rumbling growl. I froze.

Then I reached into my bag and pulled out the hunks of meat I had bought that morning for just this possibility, hoping I could get them out in time before the jaws closed on my throat, and tossed them in the direction of the growl. "Nice doggy," I whispered. "Nice doggy."

It seemed there were two of them. I heard them sniff at the meat, and then settle down to eat. I let out my breath as the sounds of chewing and gnashing of teeth on bone was the only sound heard, and then I continued on to the house.

It was all dark now, except for one dim light in the attic window. *Perfect.* It would be that of a servant who could not go to her bed until all the cleanup of the day was done. I grabbed a drainpipe and began climbing and soon gained the roof, where I leaned over to look into the room. Sure enough, a young girl was preparing for bed, and the window was open. I pulled out my shiv.

I watched, and after doffing her clothes and washing, and pulling her nightshirt over her head so that she could not see, I crept into the room and came up behind her. When her head popped out of the collar of the shirt, I reached out and clasped my gloved hand over her mouth and put the blade to her throat. She stiffened, not believing this, and I don't blame her.

"Listen to me," I hissed into her ear. "You are a very lucky girl. You are about to make two hundred francs. Would you like that?"

Her eyes, wild, looked over at my hooded eyes. I felt her head try to nod.

"Good. Now, do you like your mistress?" Another nod.

"What about Marshal de Groote?" No nod on that one. *Good.*

"Now, all I want you to do is to deliver a letter to your mistress. Today is Sunday. Make sure she sees it on Tuesday morning. No earlier. If you do it, there will be two hundred francs waiting for you in an envelope at *Café des Deux Chats* on rue de Londres Wednesday morning. Do you understand?"

Another nod.

"Very well. I am going to let you go now. If you scream, then I shall be out of this room in a moment and gone into the night and you will have nothing. *Comprenez-vous?*"

Another nod, and I let her go. She did not scream. I put my shiv back up my sleeve and pulled the letter from my bag.

"To your mistress. No one else. I will know if you do not do it, and you will not get your money. What is your name?"

"Yvette."

"All right, Yvette. Here is the letter. Good-bye." And I was back out the window and gone. I hoped that she would do it, but I was somehow sure that she would. She was a pretty little thing and de Groote is not called the Goat for nothing.

I dropped down to the ground, past the snoring forms of the dogs—of course I had marinated the meat in some of my paregoric—and went back over the fence. Once again out on the streets, I reflected that it would be a shame to waste such a lovely evening, but since I was dressed for nothing other than running across rooftops, I hurried back to my room and went to bed.

The letter? It was a simple thing and not overly wordy:

*My Dear Madame de Groote,*

*If you wish to catch your husband with a prostitute, then go to 127, rue de Londres, Room #7, at midnight tonight.*

*A Friend*

That was all, but I think it will be enough.

This night, at intermission I go to the foyer and mix with a number of the young men I find there. A glass of champagne is pressed into my hand, and I laugh, I flirt, I giggle, I make jokes. In short, I sparkle, for I must choose one of these men to take home with me tonight.

I did not see Jean-Paul this morning. Instead, I was summoned by Armand to see Jardineaux and he made it very plain that he wanted me to start bringing officers back to my room, starting tonight. *You've been here long enough, girl. Get on with it!* was what he said. *Or I will report you to London.* God, how I hate him.

I settle on a handsome artillery captain named Hercule Belmonte. This is to be his last night in the city, and he begs to be allowed to spend it with me.

To the great disappointment of the other young men who have been vying for my favor, I lower my eyes and give him my hand and say yes, he may meet me at the stage door after the performance. Groans of envy come from his friends, but I pretend not to notice.

He leans over my hand and kisses the back of it, and he tells me that I have made him very happy. His eyes fairly shine with triumph and anticipation.

The bell tinkles and intermission is over.

I pull my shawl around my shoulders against the chill of the evening and step out the door to find a group of young men looking to go off with a dancer. A very eager Captain Belmonte claims me and I smile at him and take his arm.

As we go up the alley to rue de Clichy and are about to turn left, I spot Jean-Paul standing by the front entrance of the theater. I give no sign of recognition and neither does he, but I can feel his gaze burning into my back as I lean in to Captain Belmonte and we walk toward 127, rue de Londres, room number seven.

# Chapter 26

Next morning the yellow kerchief again dangles from my window, and then very shortly Armand pulls his carriage up out front. Dressed in my sporty riding habit, jaunty bonnet on head, I trip merrily down the hall, deposit my key and two francs in Madame Gris' outstretched hand, and then skip out the front door. It is a lovely day in the City of Light and I look forward to enjoying it.

Armand stands by the door of the coach and I give him one of my best smiles as he hands me up and in. I am pleased that it is Jean-Paul whom I find seated within and not Jardineaux. He sits stony faced, staring straight ahead, as I slip in beside him and plant a good wet kiss on his cheek.

"*Bonjour,* Jean-Paul," I chirp. "I hope you are well." The coach begins to move forward.

He nods. "Good morning, Mademoiselle," he says, not looking at me or, for that matter, at all well. Something is preying on his mind and I know exactly what it is.

"Good. I, myself, had a *most* successful evening last night." Folding my hands in my lap, I put on a look of absolute schoolgirl innocence.

"So I gather. I saw him come out an hour ago," says Jean-Paul, tightly. "He was…smiling."

"Ha!" I exult. "And well he should—after all, he spent the evening with an enchanting young woman."

"More than just the evening…"

I give him my elbow in the ribs. "Come on, Jean-Paul, be a big boy now. You know why I was brought here and you were complicit in it."

He takes a breath, holds it, and then slowly releases it. "Yes, I know."

"Very well, then, Agent Valdon," I lift my hand to my hat in mock salute and say, in an officious way, "Agent Bouvier, having returned from the field, reporting." I clear my throat. "Ahem. Aforementioned Agent entertained a certain Captain Hercule Belmonte in her quarters last night and gained the following information: He is an Artillery Officer, attached to the Second Battalion of Marshal Soult's IV Corps, and has been recalled to his unit. Because of that summons to duty, Hercule believes the Grand Army of the Republic will march soon. Probably toward Germany. His men are in a high state of readiness and morale is excellent. End of report." I give him another nudge. "I hope you found it valuable, you."

In speaking French, I have begun using the familiar *tu* for *you* when addressing Jean-Paul, rather than the more formal *vous*, which he continues to use in reference to me, however. *We shall see, lad.*

I intentionally used the artillery captain's first name in a familiar way to give Jean-Paul a bit of a jab. Yes, it is evil of me to do so, but I do enjoy it so. While I know he is attracted to me, at the same time he is repulsed by what I have been doing. What he *thinks* I have been doing, that is. *Poor Jean-Paul. Poor boy...*

Last night, as soon as Captain Hercule Belmonte and I had gotten to my room and began shedding clothes, I poured him a goblet of Mixture Number Two, knowing I had already gotten all the information I would get out of him. It wasn't much, I was thinking, but maybe it'll show Jardineaux that I am doing what I have been told to do. It wasn't hard pumping Belmonte for all he knew, for he had plainly drunk quite a bit at the theater bar and was quite willing to babble on about what a fine fellow he was.

After I got down to my underclothing and he was completely out of his, he lay down on my bed, raised his arms to me, and then his eyes rolled back in his head and he passed completely out.

I pulled the covers up to his neck and tucked him in so he would not get cold, cleaned up the place a bit, put on my cloak and wrapped it about me, and plopped into bed with my back to him. I slept till the morning light crept in my window and then got up, washed and dressed, with him snoring blissfully away. Then I sat down next to him and nudged him into wakefulness.

"Come, my fine Captain, you must be up and away for the sun is high in the sky, and you must be off to your regiment."

He blinked and sense came back into his eyes. He shook his head and reached up for me.

"Jacqui...come..."

"*Non, mon cher soldat brave,* no, not now. Never in the daytime. It is silly of me, but I fear that God might see me in the light and doom my poor soul to perdition for my naughtiness." I placed my fingertips on his lips to silence his protests. "Up with you now, my brave soldier."

I hand him his linen and fuss about getting him dressed.

"There are your trousers…Here, let me help you with your shirt. There. Good. Hurry, now, your friends will be waiting for your account of your night of love with *la petite gamine Américaine*. Let me tie your tie…There. What a fine young man you are, I do hate to see you go."

*Yes, I am sure there will be many stories you will tell of your last glorious night here in Paris with a petite gamine, none of which, alas, will be true, but, ah well, of such stuff are personal legends made.*

"But I was…," he protests, as I smooth out his coat.

"But, nothing…you were truly magnificent! A veritable stallion!" I exclaim, batting the eyelashes and letting a blush rise in the cheeks. "I shall never forget it. *Quel amour! Quelle passion!* But now I must be off to Mass to atone for my sins." I tapped the top of my dresser and gave him the big eyes. "A little something for the collection plate, Hercule, *hmmm*?"

He nodded and fumbled for his billfold and soon a twenty-franc note appeared on my bureau.

I thanked him for it and got his confused self out my door in very little time after that. At the threshold I gave him a big kiss on his cheek, a quick pat on his rump, and sent him happily, I think, on his way. I am pleased, for I do like to keep my customers satisfied.

As the coach rumbles on, Jean-Paul takes a small notebook from his pocket and pencils in a few words concerning what I have told him about Captain Belmonte.

"A useless little bit of information, no?" I ask, peering at what he has written.

"No, all information is useful."

"So I have done my job, then?"

He sets his jaw. "Yes, you have done your...job."

"Good," I say. "I have served my country *and* I made a tidy twenty francs last night as well."

He says nothing to this, but a knot of muscle begins working in his cheek. Although I like to play this cat-and-mouse game with him, I find it...well...touching that he cares for me. I know that, for my part, I like him very much. Very much, indeed.

"Come now, my lad, you must cheer up. It is a lovely day and I intend to enjoy it," I say, turning to him and slipping my hand beneath the lapel of his jacket till I can feel his ribs under my fingertips. "Are you ticklish, Jean-Paul? Let's see. Coochie-coo."

I give him a bit of a tickle and he, shocked, grabs my wrist. "Stop that!"

"I'll stop when I see a smile on the face of the stern secret agent Jean-Paul de Valdon." I purse my lips and blow a puff of my breath into his ear, and, in spite of himself, he smiles.

"That's much better," I say, and withdraw my hand from his chest. "Now tell me what we are going to do today. After lunch, of course. I want it to be something exciting."

He thinks for a moment and then says, "Do you like horse racing? They are running this afternoon at the Hippodrome. Would you like to go?"

I let out a whoop and commence bouncing up and down. "Oh, that would be just the thing! Yes, oh, yes, Jean-Paul, by all means, let us go!"

He leans his head out the window and to the coachman, "Armand. *L'hippodrome de Longchamp.*"

"*Oui,* M'sieur," says Armand and turns the carriage at the next intersection.

*A racetrack! And I've got twenty francs burning a hole in my pocket! Hooray!*

# Chapter 27

Yes, I lost all my twenty francs at the track, but it was worth it, for I had a glorious time. The Hippodrome de Longchamp was all green and beautiful and it seemed the entire *beau monde* of Paris was there in all their fine carriages and fine clothes and fine women and fine men. I spent each race at the rail screaming at the poor horse I had bet on, progressing from French—*Allez, allez, Numéro Trois!*—to Standard English—*Oh, do hurry up, Number Three!*—before lapsing totally back into the Cockney of my youth—*Move yer arse, ye lazy bugger!*

My cheering of the unfortunate Number Three resulted in nothing more than his finishing dead last, but Number Nine in the fifth race did win for me and when he crossed the finish line victorious, I leaped on Jean-Paul, threw my arms around his neck, and peppered his face with kisses. *I won, Jean-Paul! I won!* Some of the Quality standing nearby raised their cultured eyebrows at my behavior, but Jean-Paul lifted his own brows and gave them the Gallic shrug and announced that *elle est Américaine* and all around us nodded in silent understanding. *Ah, une sauvage.* But I did notice with some pleasure that his arm was tight about my waist.

The races after that chipped steadily away at my winnings, but still it was a wonderful time. There was wine and snacks and pageantry and spectacle—all the things I thrive on. Yes, all in all, I conclude, a fine, fine day.

On the carriage ride back, I fell asleep against Jean-Paul's shoulder, which I counted as good, if not very elegant—I do hope my mouth did not fall open as I slept, but it probably did, and in that case I further hope that I didn't drool on him. But yes, to the good, for I need my rest to gather every bit of strength I can muster. Because tonight, Marshal Hilaire de Groote, General of the Imperial Guard, comes to collect me.

The crowd is seated, the limelights are lit, the music swells, the curtain rises, and *Les Petites Gamines de Paris* dash out to whoops of laughter and applause and launch into the first routine of the evening.

The curtain comes down and it is intermission. A little powder and rouge here and there and we go out to the bar area.

De Groote is on me in an instant. He grabs my hand and kisses it. "The wolf will prowl tonight," he says, with a low chuckle. "And he is in fine form. At what time should he scratch at Little Red Riding Hood's door?"

"At eleven, Monsieur le Loup," I whisper and put my hand on his.

"Will you have something to drink, my dear?"

"Champagne, Monsieur, *s'il vous plaît*," I simper.

"*Garçon!*" he barks out. "*Du champagne pour la belle jeune fille.* The best!"

That *la belle jeune fille* remark makes my blood run cold for a moment, but no one here makes the connection and I relax.

"*Bien.*" He picks up my hand and kisses the back of it. "You will not regret this, *ma petite pêche.*"

*The little peach dearly hopes the same.*

There are other men, quite good-looking young men who look like they'd like to talk to me, but a glare from the old Goat that clearly says *This one's mine* sends them off to other girls.

He gives me a slight, very slight, bow and says, "Till tonight, then."

I give a modest curtsy, and he turns away to join some men clustered about the bar. He says something I cannot hear, and there are gales of laughter and glances my way.

I take a sip of my very excellent champagne and look about the room and am mildly surprised and pleased to see that Monsieur Jean-Paul de Valdon is in the room tonight.

I go up to him and take him out to the foyer, out of de Groote's sight.

"You have honored us with your presence tonight, Jean-Paul," I say. "Why?"

"Just keeping an eye on you is all," he says. I notice that he glances in de Groote's direction with a certain amount of ill-concealed loathing. He should watch that, I'm thinking. He is a good boy, but he is really not a very good spy.

"Everything is going as planned. He will arrive at my room at eleven o'clock tonight," I say, giving his arm a squeeze. "I will let him in and I shall get the information. But tell me—why does he fear his wife so?"

"He has the rank, but her family has the money. He gambles and is deep in debt."

"Ah. That is good to know. Here, have a sip of my champagne. It is very good, Jean-Paul."

He does not take the glass. He reddens and says, "How can you do what you are about to do?"

I hold up a finger and shake my head. "Forbidden subject, Jean-Paul. I do what I must to help my friends and my country. I'm sure you would do nothing less."

At that his face goes rigid and he says, "*Non.* I am a traitor to my own country."

"No, you are not. You are against Napoléon, not France herself. Keep that in your mind. Know that I would not keep company with a base traitor, one who sells out his country for money or position. Know that, Jean-Paul." I give him the big moist eyes and his arm an extra-hard squeeze on that one.

He says nothing for a moment and then…"For all that you are, I think you are a finer person than I."

I don't get to respond to that, for the music is starting up again. I take his face with a hand on either side and put a kiss upon his lips. "Do not forget that you are a good man, Jean-Paul de Valdon. *Adieu.*"

With that, I bound back to the stage, back to the dressing room, and we ready ourselves for the second set.

At the end of the evening, when we all bend over and flip up the skirts, I give my tail feathers an extra wiggle. *That is for you, Jean-Paul. I hope you enjoy it.*

———

The performance ends, the costumes are shed, good nights are said, and I am back in my room, making preparations.

First, I take off my clothes and get into the white bustier I had bought back in London. It looks like a frilly piece of female undergarment with much lace and tiny ribbon bows and such, but I see it also as a quite formidable piece of female armor. Although it only covers from the top of my chest—well, middle of my chest, actually—down to my crotch, it is made of good, strong cloth and laces securely up the front. It will take a very determined male to peel this thing off.

Then I put my outer clothes back on. And wait.

A little after eleven, there is a scratching at the door. I open it and there stands a large man in the uniform of the Imperial Guard, wearing a bearskin hat and a wolf's mask.

It is not uncommon for men to wear masks at night in Paris, or Berlin, or London, or any city in Europe—to hide identity, keep off noxious odors, fend off airborne diseases—but still it is a shock to see him thus, towering over me like some monster in all his overpowering maleness.

"Come in, Sir," I quaver. "And make yourself comfortable."

He strides in and whips off his cloak, then his mask, and throws them both on the bed. His face is already red from much drink, and I count that as good. I close the door behind him, but I do not lock it, nor do I put in my wedges.

He wastes no time in getting down to business, putting an arm about my waist and burying his face in the nape of my neck, his lips working their way around my throat and toward my face.

"Please, Sir," I say, wriggling out of his grasp. "The night is long, life is short, let us enjoy our time together, slowly and with the deepest passion. Let us share some cognac and then I shall undress and we will be as one."

He lets me go and I pour out two glasses from Bottle Number One. I do need the information he has to give—his tongue must be loosened, but not deadened. Not yet, anyway.

He drinks deep and I pretend to take a sip. Then I nip behind the dressing screen. I judge the time, waste a few minutes in pretending to mess with my clothes, and then strip down to my bustier. I throw my cloak about myself and then step out from behind the screen.

"I hope you will like me, Sir," I say, as I slowly take off the cloak.

"Exquisite!" he gasps, his hands in front of him as if in prayer of thanks for a great gift. *"Comme une petite poupée!"*

Like a little doll? The little doll does not feel particularly exquisite, especially since she is sweating like a little pig, but we must get on with this.

"Please sit, Sir, in the chair. It would give me great pleasure to sit in your lap and be gently petted."

He throws himself into the chair and opens his arms, his face radiant. I refill his glass and give it to him. He drinks, and then I put myself in his lap. I take off my hairpiece and I know that without it I look all of twelve. It seems to please him.

He immediately hugs me to him and claps his lips on mine. I try not to be too rigid, but it is hard. I liked the feel of Jean-Paul's little mustache this evening when I kissed him good-bye. It was soft and tickled my upper lip in a pleasant way. I do not like the feel of de Groote's massive whiskers. They are rough, and I swear I can smell the soup he had tonight still in them. I must not show my disgust. *Steady now, girl.*

"You are the finest thing I have ever seen! I shall keep you forever!"

I pull my face from his and say, "You pronounce yourself my great protector, but I do not know where you will be tomorrow or the next day. When the Grand Army moves, you will go with it, and I will be left alone, friendless, without my good Marshal de Groote to care for me."

"Ah, do not worry, little one. The Army does not begin to move until next week. We have plenty of time! Be a good girl and let us get you out of this thing." He begins to unlace the top of my bustier, and I let him do it.

"But where will you go, my dear *Général,* will it be far from me? I could not bear it to be too far," I simper. He has gotten the lacings about halfway undone.

"What?" he says, his voice now thick with both drink and opium. "Oh. We go to Germany to kick the shit out of those cabbage-eating Prussians. After we cross the Rhine, we're going to head for the western plateau of the Saale River. We've got to kill them before they get us. Enough of that. Let's talk about you. Ah, you are so beautiful…you…"

There is a commotion outside my door. It flies open and a very angry Madame de Groote stands there with two pistols in her hands.

*Pistols! Mon Dieu!* I thought this would be the usual pointed fingers and accusations! I guess I don't know French women very well.

I roll out of de Groote's lap as she fires. The bullet plows into the wall right next to her husband's astounded head.

"You pig!" she screams. "Consorting with whores! Divorce! Yes, divorce, right after I kill you!"

She fires again, but I don't wait around to see if her bullet finds its mark. I leap to my window and am out of it, clinging to the drainpipe for my own dear life.

There is much noise above as I crawl down that pipe, run across the street, and climb up the one that will take me to the window where Jardineaux's men watch me each night.

When I get there, I rap on the window and yell, "Open up, damn it! Let me in!"

The window opens and I slide in.

"What the hell?" Both Jardineaux and Jean-Paul are there, and I don't know which one said that, but I suspect it was the big man.

He is at the window. "Look at that! The police are coming! Damn! You've blown this whole setup completely apart! Damn!"

I hear whistles and shouts outside and go to the window where I see the police pour into 127, rue de Londres. After a while, Madame Gris is taken out screeching, with her hands bound, and is put in a police wagon. A smile works its way across my face. *Good for you, you old sow.*

In a little while, two men come out bearing a large man on a stretcher. It is entirely possible that Marshal de Groote will not be joining the march north.

I cross my arms across my chest and start to shiver. "I did not do this. Madame de Groote did it. I was an innocent bystander. Here is the information: The Grand Army will begin moving next week. They will leave Boulogne, and after they cross the Rhine, they'll head for the high plain west of the Saale River."

Jardineaux brings his gaze upon me. "Right" is all he says, and then he is out the door, probably to try to repair the damage to his network.

I turn from the window.

"Jean-Paul. I do not have much on and I am cold. I am very, very tired, and I wish desperately to go to sleep. There is a bed there, and I am going to lie in it." I go over to the bed, yank back the covers, and crawl in. *Ahhhh...*

Jean-Paul watches me get in but stays at the window, looking out. There is a long silence, but after a while he says, "You do not know this, Jacqui, but I hold a commission as a lieutenant in the Fourteenth Division of Light Cavalry in Marshal Murat's Corps. From the information we have gotten by your efforts, and from others, we know that Napoléon's Grand Army is preparing to move. I will move with them. A system of couriers, riders, will be set up to carry what intelligence I might gather back to Jardineaux and the Royalist forces in ... London."

I am now wide awake. I know how hard it is for him to say the name of that city he has been taught from birth to hate, and that in naming it he is branded a traitor to his own country. I remain silent and he goes on.

"I will leave the day after tomorrow to go to the Army. I will join my unit." He pauses. "It all seems so silly, sometimes. We all know that Bonaparte will march north to meet the Prussians because they would not accede to his demands. What more is to be learned? Tell me."

"I don't know," I say. "I hate being a spy, too."

He comes to the bedside to stand over me, looking down at my eyes peeking above the cover and I think I know what is going through his mind:

*I am a young man in the prime of my youth and I am about to go off to war. I know that I might very well be killed when the battle rages. I also know that there is a girl, a girl I like very much, lying half clothed in that warm bed next to me.*

What could that girl expect, except that the young man should take off his jacket and lay it over a chair and then loosen his tie and take off his shirt? That he should sit in that chair and remove his shoes and socks and then stand and reach for the top button of his trousers.

*Oh, Jean-Paul, I like you so very, very much, but...*

But I know that things are going to change between us and I decide to tell him just how things lie. "Jean-Paul, I'm going to tell you something that's going to tie your mind in a tight little knot."

"And what is that, Jacqui?"

"*Je suis une vierge,*" I whisper. "Whether you want to believe that or not is up to you, *mon cher.*"

His eyes go wide. "What? You? *Non!* It is not possible!"

"It is true, however." I wiggle deeper into the bed. "And I am promised in marriage to a Lieutenant James Fletcher, a British Naval officer who may, or may not, be still alive, and who might not even want me when I come back to him."

"But the artillery captain...? The others...? How...?"

I am getting very drowsy, but I manage to say, "There were no others. And as for him, do you remember the other night, after I painted your portrait? How you came back to this room and then fell fast asleep? Hmmm?"

He thinks on that for a moment and then says, incredulous, "You...you *drugged* me!"

"Just a little," I say.

"But why?"

"I did not want to think of you awake all night watching my window when I was up to nothing wrong."

*Almost nothing...*

He stands there, his fingers still on his top trouser button. In the gloom, I hear him sigh and I think he hangs his head. "I am no good at any of this...to be gulled by a simple girl...I don't know. I just don't know..."

"I don't know anything, either, Jean-Paul. All I know is that the night is growing chill and if you were to get in here beside me, it would give me great comfort."

I feel the covers being drawn away as he slips in beside me. I can tell that his pants remain on.

"Thank you, Jean-Paul," I murmur as I turn over and snuggle into him and lay my head on his chest. "You are a very good man and I am very fond of you."

*G'night, luv...*

# Chapter 28

I am still wrapped up in the covers as the dawn breaks and Jardineaux returns to the flat. Jean-Paul had wisely gotten up before and put his shirt, tie, and jacket back on.

"This situation is no longer going to be productive for us, now that *la Grande Armée* is going to move. We've got to find another way to use her."

*Use* me?

"Use her, Sir?" asks Jean-Paul, now burdened with new things on his mind.

I lower the covers such that my eyes peer out at Jardineaux.

"I am convinced she had something to do with that debacle last night." I put on the innocent look, and he gazes at me, not believing it for a minute. Then he looks away and nods. "...but her information was good, very good, I will give her that. I would keep her next to de Groote, but he is suffering a bullet wound to his lower groin area and will not be leading any part of the Imperial Guard in Napoléon's new campaign...nor will he be needing a mistress."

"I am sorry for Marshal de Groote's pain," I say, pulling my knees to my chest, enjoying this last little bit of bedtime. "He was *such* a nice man."

Another glare from Jardineaux. "Be that as it may, girl, but we must have more information on this coming conflict. Lord Wellesley will demand it."

*Lord Wellesley? Hmmm... First time I've heard that name.*

He puts his hands behind his back and paces back and forth. "I believe I shall place her with a certain group of camp followers...laundresses by day and companions for the men at night. It might prove useful. Monsieur de Valdon here holds a commission with the Light Cavalry so he will be on the march with *la Grande Armée*. He will be your contact. It is all very simple."

"Sir, I must protest," sputters Jean-Paul, but I beat him to it in the way of protestation.

I leap out of the bed, still clad only in my bustier, and point my finger in Jardineaux's face. "What? You must be mad! I am to be a laundress and scrub clothes all day and then let myself be covered by privates and sergeants by night? What use is that?"

Jardineaux curves his lips into a cold smile. "The lower ranks sometimes know more than the generals—morale, state of readiness, and all that."

I'm thinkin' hard and fast. *How can I get out of this?* Then I remember what Jean-Paul said last night about the line of couriers.... *That's it!*

I take a deep breath. "You may think me a common trollop, but I am not and I will prove it to you. But for now, you'll just have to take my word for it."

I jump to the window and fling it open. "I will see you both on the corner at six o'clock this evening, and then we'll see what we shall see!"

With that, I am out the window and down the pipe, and across the street. It is still just dawning and the sight of a young girl dashing to the opposite side of the road in her underclothing would not be a rare sight around here. And then it's up another drainpipe and into my room.

Gaining it, I survey the damage. The place is in disarray. The bed is askew and my chest is open with its contents scattered about. There are also a couple of men, policemen, I believe, asleep on the floor. I check their pockets for money— it is the Rooster Charlie Gang urchin in me, I know—and find a considerable amount, which is good. The two are, of course, lying right next to my now half-empty bottles of cognac. *Come into my parlor, said the spider to the fly...*

I take a pillowcase and begin stuffing things inside it—a few dresses, some underclothing, handkerchiefs, my burglar gear, a bonnet or two, one of the blankets from the bed, the remaining laced cognac poured into one bottle and tightly corked, and that's it—except for...I crawl under the bed to retrieve the packet of money that I had shoved up under the mattress. That, and my shiv and sheath, which had been hidden in the same place.

All that done, I take leave of my room. A pity, really, because I had come to like it, and the street, and the neighborhood and Paris and all that. But it's over. Time to move on.

Taking two hundred francs from my stash, I wrap the bills in a piece of paper and then go out the door, down the stairs, my bag over my shoulder. Madame Gris is not yet out of the slammer—probably she's been charged with running a house of prostitution. I hope she enjoys her stay. At least I don't have to toss her my room key, nor two francs for my last visitor, the unfortunate General de Groote.

I go out the door of 127, rue de Londres for the last time and head down to *Café des Deux Chats*. I am ravenous and tuck into breakfast with a certain passion—croissants, pastries, coffee, it all goes down the neck.

As I linger over the second bowl of café au lait, I am gratified to see a young girl, whom I know on slight acquaintance, enter the café. I note that she, like me, has a bag packed. Before she can inquire at the cashier, I call, "Yvette," and wave her over to me. She sits at my table, and I signal for café au lait and rolls to be brought to her. When it comes, I hand her the envelope.

"What will you do with it?" I ask.

"Get as far away from here and *Chez de Groote* as I can," she answers. "I will go back to my village, and now I will have a good dowry with me. For that I thank you. There is a young man there named Philippe...We have plans for a shop."

"Good. I wish you the joy of it," I say as we finish our breakfast. "Now, if you could do one last thing for me?"

"*Oui,* Mademoiselle...?"

"Take my cloak here, put it on and my bonnet as well, and when you leave, cover your face and go to the right down rue de Londres. That is all you have to do. And you may keep the cloak and bonnet."

"Of course, I shall be happy to do it. It was a lucky night when you came into my room. *Au revoir.*"

I pay for the breakfast, and the girl, now dressed in my gear, leaves. Peeking out, I notice that poor Armand is in hot pursuit of the decoy. I am glad it is not Jean-Paul who will get in trouble this time. I head out to the left, my bag over my shoulder.

I know I am too young and too green to wear the uniform of the holy Imperial Guard, so I shall settle for something entirely different. Perhaps something that approximates the uniform of the Massachusetts militia, in honor of one Randall Trevelyne? I mean, how are these Frenchies gonna know what that looks like? Feeling free in the way of military fashion, I go for the blue Hussar's jacket with the thick gold braid across the front, good for both protecting against a sword slash as well as for concealing a female chest that might lie beneath.

Telling the shopkeeper that I am buying this uniform as a birthday present for my little brother who is the same size as me—*Oh, won't Maman and Papa be so proud to see little Gaston dressed all fine as a little Grand Army soldier!*—I continue fitting myself out.

For headwear I have the choice of the common bicorne, a front-to-back thing that, to my eye, lacks elegance, or the helmet of a Cuirassier, which I find too heavy, even though I do like the long horse-tail plume that trails down the back. I could look quite dashing in that, but no, I settle on the bearskin shako of the Grenadiers, a high hat with braided festoon, metal shield, top patch, and plume. Yes, I think that will do quite nicely.

Then on to tight blue breeches that have a lining strip of leather that runs up inside the thighs from one knee across the crotch and down to the other leg to the opposite knee. This is to prevent chafing from being in the saddle for too long on an extended march. It will also serve to conceal my lack of male equipment. A pair of fine, knee-high boots, and I am well fitted out. Yes, Madame, I will wear it out.

A rolled overcoat to go behind me on the saddle, two pistols, an ammunition pouch, a small tent, military cloak, bedroll and knapsack, and the smallest cavalry saber, belt, and sheath complete my gear, and I am back on the street and off to the stables.

"How much for that one?" I ask, pointing to a likely looking gelding.

"Six hundred francs."

"For someone who is about to ride out and fight for the honor of France, you would ask that?"

The Gallic shrug yet again.

"Yes, the honor of France, and all that, but still my family must eat, *non*? Now, here is a spirited little mare, her size just right for one such as you. Her name is Mathilde."

I put my hand on her muzzle and she whinnies softly and tosses her head and I fall in love.

"How much?"

"Four hundred francs."

"I don't know..."

"With saddle."

"Done."

At six o'clock Mathilde and I walk slowly up rue de Londres. When I see Jardineaux and Jean-Paul standing on the corner of rue de Clichy, I put my heels to her and bring her up to a trot.

They both look up as I approach. Jean-Paul, who knows me better, catches on first.

"Oh, my God," he says, shaking his head.

"Is this not better?" I ask of Jardineaux. "A galloper, a messenger who will carry orders back and forth between the battalions, privy to all that goes on, rather than just a common laundress?"

He looks up at me. "Amazing."

"You will have a system of couriers ready to carry back any useful information I might gather and give to M'sieur de Valdon. Is this not better than what you had planned?"

Jardineaux nods, and what passes for a smile crosses his face. "Yes. It is much better."

I look to Jean-Paul and lift my hand in salute. "I will see you on the march to war, Lieutenant de Valdon. *Adieu.*"

With that I turn and go up the street, heading north out of Paris, France.

*I am Jacky Faber, Midshipman and Acting Lieutenant in His Royal Majesty's Navy, and I am going north to join the French Army. What a crazy world this is.*

# PART IV

PART IV

# Chapter 29

*When Boney commanded his army to stand,*
*He leveled his cannons all over the land.*
*He leveled his cannons, his victory to gain,*
*And slew my Light Horseman on his way coming home.*

I'm humming that cheerful little ditty as we clop along, heading for Boulogne where the Grand Army is massing before marching east across Flanders and then into the Rhineland.

It is good to be back in harness again, feeling fit and tight in my new gear and astride my fine horse on yet another superb day. I give her an affectionate pat on the back of her neck as we press on. She really is a good-looking bay filly, with white boots on each leg and a white blaze down the center of her forehead. Her mane is darker, almost black, and I don't think I could have found a finer mount.

One thing I regret is not getting more money out of Jardineaux before I left. I had spent most of my coin cache in outfitting myself, and in my haste to get out of Paris and escape the fate of being made laundress or worse, I had neglected to ask for more. I do have the money I got out of the pockets of those hapless policemen, but that is running out fast. Oh, well, I'll be seeing Jean-Paul sometime and I'll get more from him. After all, I do have to buy oats for Mathilde.

My last extravagance was the purchase of a fiddle and bow, and oilcloth to protect them against the weather. I, of course, have my pennywhistle, and should worse come to worse, I can always get back into female clothes and work a few taverns, of which there are plenty about—this is *not* the American wilderness. To save what money I have left, and to toughen myself up for what is to come, I sleep out in the open most nights. The weather has been generally kind and I do not often have to put up my tent or stay at an inn.

Last night I slept under some trees in an orchard. I gave Mathilde her oats in her nose bag, ate some bread with meat and cheese myself, and even had a little celebration with a small bottle of wine, for it was the second of October, eighteen hundred and six—my birthday, as it were. For the most part of my life, I had not known exactly when I was born, for it was part of the memories erased after the deaths of my parents and sister on That Black Day. I found out later from my grandfather, Reverend Alsop, when we met last year. He was astounded that I did not know that I was born in the small village of St. Edmund Standing-in-the-Moor in North Allerton, in the north of England, in the year 1790.... *It was entered into the parish book, child, so I know. I was there...*

I am now officially sixteen years old. Funny, I had always assumed that I was born in London. I take out my pennywhistle, play my "Ship's Boy's Lament," then curl up in a ball, offer up some prayers for various people, then go to sleep, with Mathilde standing quietly beside me.

———

As I get closer and closer to the grand encampment or bivouac, as the French would have it, I see more and more troops marching from all directions—Infantry, Fusiliers, Hussars, Grenadiers, Dragoons, Cuirassiers, Light Cavalry—there are soldiers everywhere, many pushing, pulling, or dragging what seems to be miles and miles of caissons bearing Napoléon's famous artillery. There are also supply wagons and camp followers and wagons full of laughing girls, and herds of cattle and sheep, and crates of chickens, ducks, and geese. And, I hate to say it, but there is a feeling of high excitement in the air, and it affects me, too.

I rise in the stirrups as I come over the last hill on the approach to Boulogne and see the encampment laid out before me and am astounded. There are hundreds, thousands, of little white tents laid out in neat rows. Soldiers parade, far away, shouted orders are heard, and trumpets are blown.

In the center of it all is a group of larger tents, and it is to that cluster of tents that I go.

There are some guards at the perimeter of this cluster of tents, but they do not hinder my passage. I spy a man at a table, an officer of the Guards, by the look of him, so I hop off Mathilde, and trailing her reins behind me, I walk up to him.

He wears small spectacles and is writing furiously in some journal.

"*Pardon*, Monsieur," I say, as I walk up to him and salute, my hand to the brim of my shako. "But I am Cadet Jacques Bouvier, American, of the Massachusetts Militia, Third Brigade, here to volunteer as a galloper, Sir." I had thought about giving myself the stripes of a corporal or even a private because of my very obvious youth, but then I could not have gotten into the Officers' Mess and that's where the valuable information will be found.

His weary eyes look up at me from over the top of his glasses. "American, eh? An' what in hell are you doing here?"

"I am here to help repay the debt that the United States owes to France, Sir! *Vive Lafayette! Vive l'Empereur! Vive la France!*"

"You have papers, boy?"

"Yes, Sir." I pass them over. I did stay one rainy day at a cozy inn for the express purpose of making up these forgeries at a convenient dry table. With my pen and brushes and colors and sealing wax I worked up an account of my time at the West Point Military Academy—I earned High Honors, of course—as well as a letter of introduction from a Colonel Randall Trevelyne, Third Militia. I think he would be pleased with the promotion. The whole thing is not as good as Higgins would have done, but it gets by.

"You come all the way here to fight for France?"

"There is little chance for military advancement in America right now, and that is what I seek. That and glory."

He looks at me doubtfully. "Have you had your first shave yet, Cadet?" There are several other scribes by his side, and this gets a laugh from them.

I decide to bristle at that. "I did not come here to be insulted, Sir. If you will give me the satisfaction of…"

"Oh, be quiet, boy," he grumbles, shuffling through some papers. "Yes, the Sixteenth Fusiliers could use a messenger. Theirs fell off his horse last week and broke his damned neck. You shall be attached to them. Report to General Charpentier. You will find him over there—the big tent at the end of that row. Now go away."

I give a short bow and say, "Thank you, Suh!" putting a bit of American Virginia accent into it. I mean, why not lay it on, for what do they know about America?

I get back on Mathilde, for I know I will want to make a show of horsemanship before my new commanding officer. I trot down to the designated tent, where several officers are standing about, talking and smoking cigars.

I ride up, wheel Mathilde around, and dismount, bowing low to the one I perceive to be the most senior officer. It occurs to me then that perhaps I was a bit hasty in arriving like that, as the dust from Mathilde's hooves settles over all who stand there.

Well, too late now, I figure, as I salute and report, "Cadet Jacques Bouvier, Massachusetts Militia, Third Brigade, newly assigned to your unit, Sir, as messenger!"

"I commend you for your promised service, boy," says General Charpentier, brushing at the sleeves of his deep blue coat. "But I do not thank you for the dust." He is a portly man, with whiskers, but his eye is sharp and keen, and it is trained on me.

"I am sorry, Sir, but—"

"Do not be sorry, Cadet," he says. "After all, it is war. We must all get dirty." He puts his hands behind him and walks around me. "So. We have been blessed with an American Cadet, then? We do not even have such a rank in the *Grande Armée de la République*. What shall you be, then? A private? A corporal? Surely not a sergeant, for your cheeks are too downy, like the soft belly of a goose."

I feel my cheeks flaming. "I will be whatever you want me to be, General Charpentier."

He considers me and then glances off to his right and

says, "We shall see what you shall be. A messenger, for sure, but right this moment we have not the need for such. Look over there. Do you see that?"

I look over and see what seems to be a confused bunch of men and young boys. It is a squad of sorts, about a dozen men, and it looks like they have just been issued their uniforms, as they are ill fitted and look a mess.

"Yes, Sir, I see," I say.

"Do you know how to drill, Cadet Bouvier of the United States Militia?" asks the General. He flicks the ash off the end of his cigar such that it lands on my boot. "Do you know your right flank from your left? Forward March from Advance Columns to the Right? Do you know how to load and fire a musket? Do you?"

Again I answer, "I did not come here to be insulted, Sir!"

"Very well," replies General Charpentier. He points the wet and well-chewed end of his cigar at the group of men. "They are a gaggle of farm boys and shopkeepers newly arrived to fight for the glory of France. They are nothing but cannon fodder, and they are yours, Cadet Jacques Bouvier. Do what you can with them, and then we will see what you will be in this Army."

I take Mathilde over to a watering trough and let her drink her fill, tie her to a hitching post, and walk over to what I know, for better or worse, will be my men. Time to get started.

"Who is in charge here?" I ask, as I come upon them. Some of them sit on the ground, some wrestle with their gear, and some just stand there, looking around in awe at what is happening all about them.

A little round man, half bald with large round pop eyes, says, "I am Sergeant Gaston Boule. I raised this gallant band of warriors from our province of Burgundy to fight for Napoléon and for France!"

I notice that his uniform does not have any sergeant's stripes upon it.

"And I am Cadet Bouvier, and I am your new commanding officer. From now on, when I arrive in your presence, you will leap to your feet and stand at Attention. Is that understood?"

"But it is just a boy," says a tall young man with lanky brown hair hanging about his shoulders. "How—"

"Get to your feet now!" I shout, and whip out my sword and with its point, draw a line in the dirt. "Line up on that, you ignorant pack of yokels!"

The shambling pack manages to do it, but just barely.

"All of you are a disgrace. You there, trade jackets with that one. You! Do your shoes fit? *Non?* Then how the hell do you expect to march two hundred miles? Do you think we shall stop to massage your poor feet? No, what we will do is put you up against a tree and shoot your sorry ass for malingering, that's what we will do, count on it!"

I pause for breath. "What a pathetic gang of clowns...To think I came all the way from America to command such rabble as this. Maggots! Scum! You, trade shakos with him! Don't you think it might be good if you actually could see to fire at the enemy rather than looking at the inside of your hat? The Prussian will certainly be able to see your stupid head in his sights! You, lace up your gaiters; you, pull up your goddamned pants! Try to look like a soldier! Try to look like a man! Damn it!"

They start trading parts of their uniforms and in a while they look halfway presentable. But just halfway. Night is about to fall and we'll get on with the rest of it tomorrow.

"Who's the youngest one here?"

"I am, Sir," pipes up a small voice belonging to a very tiny boy. "My name is Denis Dufour. I was going to be the drummer. See, I have a drum."

"Well, at least one of you came prepared," I growl. "Denis, you shall be my orderly. Unsaddle my horse, brush her down, and see that she is fed and cared for. Set up my tent right there, and the rest of you pitch your tents in a line in that direction. A *straight* line if you can manage it, and all facing the same way, for the love of God! Now get to it. Tomorrow we shall drill till you drop!"

"Uh, Sir," says my Sergeant Boule with a slight cough. "We do not have any tents."

*Oh, Lord!*

# Chapter 30

The next morning, my eyes pop open to the sound of reveille blown on a hundred bugles and behold the whiteness of my tent above me. One moment to groan out the universal soldier's groan at having to get up at that ungodly hour of the day, and then I fling myself out of my bedroll and onto my feet. As I struggle into my uniform, I call out to my orderly, who had slept outside my tent as I had ordered. "Get me some wash water, Dufour."

"But, Sir…"

"Find it, boy! You are no longer a goatherd. You are a soldier in the Grand Army of the Republic on the march! You must learn how to do things. How to get things. You are on campaign. Do you think your mother is here with a glass of warm milk? I tell you she's not, unless she's one of those bawds back in that wagon that is painted red!"

I hear him scurrying off.

On with the stockings, then trousers, then boots. Damn close in here, no room to move around at all. All right, now on with the jacket, fasten up the frogs, and step outside into the bright light of the morning.

As I come out, I see Denis Dufour struggling toward me

with a bucket of water, sloshing most of it over his feet, which I now note are quite bare. Judging from his voice, size, and clumsiness, I'd say that he's about ten years old. I also see the rest of my squad, groggily getting to their feet, having slept tentless in a small ravine out of the wind.

"You men of the Sixteenth! Go to the latrine and then come back and form up on the line I drew yesterday. Sergeant Boule!"

"*Oui,* M'sieur," says he, buttoning his pants. I am sure he has already availed himself of the bushes. I am equally certain that it was my men who had been set to digging the latrine before I arrived, so the rest of them are sure to know exactly where it is. And because of their assigned duty, I can figure out exactly how they are regarded by the others.

"Line up the men by height, shortest to tallest. Do you think you can manage that?"

"I will try, M'sieur," he says, putting his fingertips to his brow. I'll wager he wishes he were back in his village right now, and I don't blame him. I imagine that many of the men feel the same.

I have Denis place the pail behind my tent. I already have in my hand a piece of soap and the towel from my knapsack. Putting my towel on the ground, I kneel upon it so as not to get grass stains on my knees. I plunge my head into the bucket, run the soap over my head, scrub at it, then dunk my head again and run my fingers through my hair to rinse it. Afterward I wash my face, ears, and neck, then pick up the towel and stand to dry myself off.

"Here," I say, throwing the damp towel to him. "You may use the water to wash yourself, and I suggest that you do it, as you are filthy."

*Poor lad, ain't even got a uniform yet, 'cause of his size. Well, we'll see…*

"Then wash out the towel and hang it on the tent pole there to dry."

Grabbing a smaller wet rag, I head off into the bushes myself. Accomplishing that duty and donning my shako, I toss the rag into the bucket. "Wash that, too."

I go back to my squad and find them lined up as ordered.

Sergeant Boule pulls out his sword and puts the hilt to his mouth in some sort of semblance of presenting arms. I notice the sword is rusty and dull. Probably picked it up at a secondhand store. I return the salute with a flick of my hand to my shako's brim and look up the line. They are still barely presentable.

From what I hear, Gaston Boule, baker in the village of Pommard in the province of Burgundy, inspired by the might of the French Empire as personified by the Emperor Napoléon Bonaparte, decided to raise a company of boys and men from his little town and then march off to glory. Bored with country life, they chose to follow him. Fools. And here they are—tentless, bootless, and absolutely clueless—and all for me to take care of.

I go to the first man in line, the tallest. "Call off your names as I pass you," I order.

"Laurent," says the tall man with long lanky hair.

"Keep your eyes cased, looking straight forward when addressed by an officer. Do you understand, Laurent? Do you all understand?"

"*Oui*, M'sieur."

"Good. Remember it. And you?"

I take another step and come up before the next man.

"Simon," he says. He is a large, broad man. Probably an ox driver back in his village.

Next is Vedel, then Gobin, then Bouchard, all unremarkable, except for their lack of military bearing. Lambert, Bertrand, Michaud, Pannetier call out next, followed by Dubois, Chaisson, and finally Guerrette. That makes twelve in the ranks, and with Sergeant Boule and the drummer boy, fourteen in all.

"Very well. Now we shall do some very basic maneuvers. The first is the state of Attention. Put your heels together like this and stand up straight—straight, I said, goddammit!—shoulders back, thumbs on the seams of your trousers!"

I walk the line, scanning them, poking a belly here, pushing back a shoulder there.

"All right. Now I—"

"Your pardon, Sir, but when are we going to eat?" asks Chaisson, a stout man who looks like he has not gone for very long without a meal.

I go up before him. "You shall get your breakfast, Chaisson, we shall *all* get our breakfasts, when we are able to march to the mess tent like soldiers and not like a shambling gang of convicts. Understand?"

He gulps and nods, his Adam's apple working up and down.

"Understand also that you are not to speak to an officer unless he speaks to you first," I say coldly.

I had noticed the mess tent for the Sixteenth Fusiliers down below, its stoves working and sending out great clouds of steam and very good smells. My own traitorous stomach growls, a sound that I am sure is not missed by the idiots who stand before me now.

"Good. Now the next position will be Parade Rest. When I say the word 'Rest' you will put your left foot thirty-one centimeters to the left and will clasp your hands behind your back, your right hand in the palm of your left. Are you ready? Very well...Parade...Rest!"

Feet shuffle out to the side and hands go to the back. Hmmm. That was not bad. So far, so good.

"Very well. We will now do a Right Face. Come back to Attention. Good. You will watch my feet. When I say Right *Face!*, you will pivot on your heels like this"—and I demonstrate—"and then bring those same heels back to the Attention position. Are you ready? *Bon.* Sixteenth Fusiliers, Bouvier Squad, Right *Face!*"

Half of the silly buggers turn left and half turn right. It is then that I realize we are being observed by the officers and men of some of the crack divisions quartered nearby, and they are laughing at us. My face burns. I hear for the first time *Farm boys! Look at the farm boys! Clodhoppers!* and I don't like it one bit.

But I decide to use it.

"You hear it? Clodhoppers? You see how they laugh at you?" I say in disgust. "Re-form yourselves and come to Attention. Good. Now hold out your hands. Put your right hand now above your head." The hands go up, some of them right, some left, but eventually they all get it right. "That is your right hand and below it is your right foot. Do you have that?"

There are nods all around.

"Now remember this. That is the hand you write with, or if you cannot write, the hand you make your *X* with."

More nods.

"Do you think you can keep them straight now?"

They sheepishly nod.

"Very well. Let us try it again. Clodhoppers, Right *Face!*"

This time they all get it right.

"Good enough," I say. "Now we will march to breakfast. When I say Forward March, you will step out on your *left* foot...you do remember which one that is, don't you? All right, ready now...Forward *March!*"

And they start out pretty much in step and march down the hill to the mess tent. At least they had been issued mess kits with their uniforms and so will be able to eat. There are men standing in a long line and my Clodhoppers go and get behind them.

Leaving them there, I go to present myself to General Charpentier. He is again at his table outside his tent as the day is warm. He is having his breakfast with another senior officer and it looks and smells awfully good. His aide-de-camp looks at me in question when I come up.

"Begging your pardon, Sir, but my men need some supplies. Where shall I get them?"

The officer looks to his General, who beckons me over to stand before him.

I salute and say, "Good morning, Sir."

"Um," he says, making a gesture with his hand that passes for a return salute. "What do you need?"

"My men do not have tents. Some of the men's uniforms do not fit. Others need proper shoes. The drummer boy needs a uniform."

He nods to his secretary, who sits at a small table nearby,

and the scribe begins writing out the requisition. He is a civilian.

"…and muskets, Sir. My men do not have guns and they are supposed to be Fusiliers. We'll need cartridges, too, of course."

"We were afraid to give them guns, afraid they would blow their own fool heads off and save the Prussians the bother," says the Colonel, and the others laugh. "Maybe with *le Grand Cadet Bouvier*, the Scourge of Two Continents, now in charge, they can be trusted." More chuckles. I have always noticed how ready subordinates are to laugh at the jokes of their superiors. I do not smile, but merely stand there waiting.

General Charpentier again nods to the man scribbling away. "But just give them the muskets, not the powder."

Turning back to me, he says, "Show me they can do close-order drill, and the basic maneuvers, then we will see about the powder. We really do not want them killing any of our own, now, do we?"

"How many?" the secretary asks of me. I note the absence of the word *Sir. Hmmmm.*

"Thirteen men, one boy," I reply. No "Sir," only a frosty Look. After all, he is not a soldier. "And we need a drummer's uniform for the boy."

"We do, now?" The General's eyebrows have risen.

"I'm sure you want the Sixteenth Fusiliers to look its best, Sir, as, otherwise, it will reflect on you, *mon Général.*"

"You do have something of a mouth on you, Cadet Bouvier."

"*Je suis désolé, Monsieur.* I am sorry if I offended you, Sir."

"Ummm," he says, and turns to the civilian. "Will the Quartermaster have all he needs, Monsieur Dupont?"

"All except the tents, General," briskly answers Monsieur Dupont. "The supplier did not come in with them in time." He stops and gives a bit of a cough. "I happen to know some are for sale from the…uh…merchants who follow the camp."

*Damned thieves, you mean. The supplier probably sold them to the highest bidder, contract with the* Grande Armée *or no contract. Entretiens d'argent*—Money talks, in every language.

"Well, there you have it, Cadet. Let us see how you provide for your troops. Go now and do it."

I salute, do an about-face, and leave, steaming.

Going down to the Quartermaster's huge tent, I see my men still standing in line. *What is this, then?*

I go up to them and ask, "Why have you not yet been fed?"

"*Pardon*, Sir," says Sergeant Boule, sheepishly, "but others have been cutting in front of us. They say it is their right. We don't know what to do." I notice burning looks in the eyes of some of my plowboys.

My steam increases. "Their right, eh? Now what would you do if you were in your village and marauding soldiers came in to take your women, your girls? Eh? What would you do?" I hear some growls from the ranks. I want to go up to the first of the sneering bastards who cut in front, a Corporal of Grenadiers, and stick my shiv up his nostril and ask him how his mistress would like him if he comes back from this war with two noses, neither of them very pretty. But I don't. Not yet.

"Steady, boys, your time will come. Stay here, be patient, and you will be fed. But your time will come. Count on it," I say, calming myself, and, I hope, them. "Sergeant, after the men have eaten, meet me at the Quartermaster's tent over there, and we will see them more properly fitted out. Try to assemble them in some order."

"Yes, Sir."

I stride over in the direction of that Quartermaster's tent, signed requisition form in hand, to see what can be done in that regard, when I hear some laughter, derisive guffaws, coming from a table set up in front of a large tent. There are four officers seated there, and I turn to see that they are all Grenadiers, Elite Infantry—a major, a captain, and two lieutenants. They were playing at cards and now they are all looking at me, and yes, they are laughing. I turn to face them.

The Major reclines back in his chair, a cigar clamped in his mouth. I note that, in spite of various blockades and embargoes, nobody around here seems to lack a supply of that vile weed.

"Can you smell manure, Montrose?" asks the Major.

"Indeed I can, Major Levesque," replies one of the lieutenants. "It seems to be coming from that pack of farmers over there."

I know my men can hear this. A glance back shows their heads drooping in shame. This is not what they had signed up for.

I also know that General Charpentier is listening as well. This is it, then.

I hit a brace, put on the Look, and ask, "You have a problem with my men and myself, Major?"

"Only with the stench, boy," answers this Major Levesque, grinning around his cigar smoke. "It looks like you've got some manure on your boots as well."

"Very well," I say. "I cannot bear that insult. I will meet you, Sir, tomorrow morning at dawn. You will name your Second, and your choice of weapons. *Adieu.* My Second will meet yours shortly to make the arrangements."

"What?" exclaims Major Levesque, shooting to his feet. "You are calling me out, you insolent pup?"

"Yes, Sir, I am," I say, as calm as I can manage. "If you are not afraid. If you are afraid, you will keep your damned mouth shut as regards me and my men!"

He considers this and then throws his head back and laughs till tears trickle from his eyes. Recovering himself, he flings his cigar off to the side and then lunges forward, grabbing me by the neck, catching me by surprise before I can jump back out of reach.

"We in the Guard do not fight boys!" he snarls, bringing my face up to his so I can smell the tobacco and the herring he had for breakfast on his breath. "Just what do we do with insolent boys in the Guards, Lieutenant Depardieu?"

"I don't know, Sir?" asks the lieutenant. "Shoot them?"

"No, Sir, what we do is *spank* them!"

With that the brute sits back down in his chair, bends me across his knee, lifts his open hand, and then brings it down hard on my rump.

*Yeeeooow!*

I start to wriggle and struggle, but I know it will do no good. What I do is tighten my buttocks so I don't present too girlish a tail and I grit my teeth and I take it. I do not cry out. I just endure it.

After he gives me twelve, he throws me over into the dust. He holds his arms up to his friends and accepts their applause and reaches for another cigar and calls for a drink.

"Hot work, that! Let's have a drink, men!"

*Spanked! In front of everybody! Spanked like a child! This cannot stand, else I am lost!*

He almost makes it back to his chair before I am up with my sword drawn with the point at his throat.

"If you will not meet me on the Field of Honor, coward, then you will fight me right now. *En garde!*"

"What? You speak to me thus?" He gets to his feet and goes for his sword. "You go to Hell, boy!"

"I will probably go to Hell, Sir, but not just yet, and I do not think it will be you who puts me there, since you can't seem to even get your sorry sword out of its scabbard!"

Major Levesque roars out something unintelligible and his sword flies out, goes over his head, and sweeps down at me.

I manage to just parry it and skip back out of the way, my sword held in Fourth Position, waiting for his next attack.

"Stop!" shouts General Charpentier from his table. He is convulsed with laughter. "Stop it, I say. Good sport all around, but I order you to stop. Gentlemen, this is our fiery new messenger from the United States, Cadet Jacques Bouvier. They must grow them very fierce over there, *n'est-ce pas?*"

"He is lucky he is not a dead cadet," mutters Major Levesque.

I lift my sword again and put the point on a level between our eyes.

"I told you to stop it, Cadet," warns General Charpentier, no longer laughing. "You will now apologize to Major Levesque."

I really had no intention of actually fighting him, as I know he would have killed me in another instant. But it worked out. They saw it, everybody saw it, and my men saw it. And it was good.

I lift the hilt on my sword to my mouth in salute to the General, and then to Major Levesque.

"I am sorry if I gave offense, Sir."

"Humph!" says Major Levesque, slamming his sword back into its sheath and sitting down at his table again. "Deal," he says, to the others, and turns away to again play at cards, ignoring me.

I do an about-face and go back to my men, my face still reddened with the humiliation of the beating. One of them, Laurent, seeing my burning face, speaks out of turn.

"Do not worry about it, Sir. You stood up for us. We saw that. Everybody saw that."

I hear someone come up behind me. It is the Captain who had sat at Levesque's table. He claps me on the back. "Well done, Sir. I am Captain Bardot. Come take some breakfast with me. The Officers' Mess is right over there. I hope you will be able to...ahem...to sit down and tell us something of America."

And so the job was done. I am now a member of the officer corps.

The men are better turned out now—uniforms fit, boots are on and shined, and each man has a musket on his shoulder. Sergeant Boule has them back in line.

The breakfast was excellent and Captain Bardot's company proved most kind. I was introduced to the other officers of the Sixteenth and, I believe, well received. Now we shall have a bit of Inspection and then on to the drill.

Each of the men wears a heavy felt white shako for head covering, as well as white pants with knee-high black gaiters, and a blue coat with white lapels and tails trimmed in red worn over a white vest. Over it all are two crossed white belts that hold a rucksack to house the soldier's personal gear, if he has any. On top of that sits his bedroll wrapped up in his blue gray greatcoat, and below it hangs his bayonet on a hook, as well as a cartridge pouch. This, on each of my Clodhoppers, hangs empty.

I walk up to each of them, do a left face, look the man over, say nothing, do a right face, step to the next man, do the same thing again, and so on down the line, till I come to my drummer, Denis Dufour. He is now in a uniform similar to the others, except that his coat is orange. Drummers and other unarmed men wear different colored uniforms so that enemy soldiers, if they are inclined to show mercy, will not intentionally shoot those without weapons. The English do the same. Sometimes it works.

"Well, Drummer Dufour, you are smartly turned out," I remark. "If your girl back home were to be here now, you would not lack for kisses."

He has his drum strapped to his waist and holds his drumsticks in his hands. He blushes mightily at what I say, but he is pleased, I think.

I step out in front of the others.

"The next time I hold Inspection, I will have something to say to each of you. For now, I will only say that you all look…acceptable. But I will expect better. Tomorrow I'm ordering all of you to shave before breakfast. You may grow your mustaches, if you wish, as it is said the Emperor likes them on his men. I require you to be clean and your gear in good order. Is that clear? Good. Now we shall drill."

I walk back and forth in front of them, my hands clasped behind my back, and intone, as a teacher would, "As Fusiliers, there will be various formations you will be told to get yourselves into. You are now standing in the formation that is called the Line. Simple enough, isn't it? All you have to do is remember the man to the right and to the left of you, and you will form up correctly. This formation is effective when you are facing skirmishers, or attacking a line of artillery. I tell you this in passing so you will know, but your officers will order you into these various formations as suits the conditions of battle. You do not have to think about it, you just do it."

Another pause, as I collect my thoughts, then, "We will now form the Square. Clodhoppers…ready…*About-Face!*"

The thing is accomplished, though Michaud's musket barrel knocks off Pannetier's shako as they turn about, but he recovers quickly.

"Three steps Forward *March!*"

They manage to do that without further disaster.

"About-*Face!*" Again it is done and they are facing me again.

"First Rank, Guerrette, Chaisson, Dubois, and Pannetier. Move up to the line." The line I drew yesterday is still faintly visible, and the men go up and put their toes upon it. Good. "Now Michaud, Bertrand, Lambert, and Bouchard, line up behind them, and the rest of you behind them.

"You see the wisdom of it? The shorter men are up front and the taller behind. When it comes to a battle, you will be shooting over each other's heads, do you see? This formation is very effective against cavalry, and remember, good infantry *always* beats good cavalry. Hannibal knew it, Caesar knew it, and the Emperor knows it, too."

They haven't got the foggiest idea of what I am talking about, so I stop talking history. "*Bien.* We will now drill in this formation. Sixteenth Fusiliers, Bouvier's Own, Forward...*March!*"

And we drill and we drill. *By the Left Flank, March! By the Right Flank, March! Company, Halt! Right Face! Forward March!*

We drill and we march over hill and down dale. I take them far away from the main encampment so they are not further laughed at. Hours and hours of it, till I know they hate me to their very marrow. We drill all morning and well into the afternoon.

Since I'm a sailor, no one would expect me to know very much about land maneuvers, but they'd be mistaken. While it's a fact that I was not specifically trained in military movement, I did manage to pick up most of my knowledge of land tactics from watching Randall Trevelyne drill his militia troops back in Quincy. Of course, it's also true that most of the time I was there, I delighted in making raucous fun of him as he marched his tangle-footed troops about. Sometimes I even hoisted a broomstick over my own shoulder and marched right along with them. I did soak up a lot, though, certainly enough to get along here. And I do know how to load and fire a gun, but I did not learn that on land—I was drilled in that by my very able Master-at-Arms,

Peter Drake, back when I commanded the *Wolverine*. And as for the rest of it, did I not see our Royal Marines drill every day when I was aboard a King's ship? I certainly did.

At noon, we march back into the encampment in good order to see if we can get something to eat and maybe get some powder.

Once again, I am back in front of General Charpentier, heels together, chin up, shako held under my left arm.

"I believe they are ready to fire their muskets, Sir."

The General looks at me closely. "I did see you up on that hill marching them about." There is a long glass next to him on his table. I thought this morning that I might have caught sight of a reflected glint from something like a long glass. "You think they will not hurt themselves? We can keep them digging latrines and graves, you know."

"No, Sir, they will acquit themselves well as soldiers. That is what they came here for," I say, "and it is said that we ship out...er...march out in three days, so I do not have much time with them."

"Your information is good, Cadet. Very well, Monsieur Dupont, issue the cartridges."

"Here is the Musket Drill," I say, holding up a white paper cartridge in front of my Clodhoppers, their bellies full and newly marched back out onto a far field. "This is called a cartridge. You each have one in your hand. If you feel it, you will discover that it has a hard, round thing at one end. That thing is called a bullet. Watch me now."

I have taken Sergeant Boule's musket and hold it up. "Open the pan, and bite the bullet out of the cartridge and hold it in your mouth. Like this." I put the corner of the thing between my teeth and rip out the bullet and tongue the lead off to the side of my mouth so I can still talk.

"Put the hammer on half cock. Now prime the pan." I tap some powder into the little pan next to the hammer that holds the flint. "Close the pan, pour the rest of the powder down the barrel, then spit the bullet down in after it. Take your ramrod and jam it down. Remove the rod, full cock the hammer, present arms, and aim, then wait for the order to fire."

I do all that and put the musket to my shoulder. "On the order, you will fire." I aim at a tree not far off and fire, tearing a bit of bark off the tree's trunk.

"Good shooting, Sir!" enthuses Denis. I cast him a gimlet eye—I do not need a critique on my marksmanship from my drummer boy. He looks properly abashed. "Sorry, Sir."

"All right, musketeers! Have you got it? Half Cock, Prime, Close, Pour, Spit, Ram, Full Cock, Present Arms. You have it? Good, let's do it. On my order. Load and Present!"

I have them arranged in the Line for this, not wanting any of them to shoot any of their comrades in the back of the head, as might happen if they are formed in the Square.

It is a disaster. *Non! Michaud, do not look down the barrel! Dubois, you've spilled your powder! Damn! Gobin, take out the ramrod, take out the ramrod! Sweet Jesus! You are to shoot the Huns, not spear them!*

Eventually, they get it all done. They stand there, their muskets pointed at the tree.

"Very well," I say, glaring at them. "Aim...and...Fire!"

There is a blast of musketry and a piece of bark flies off the tree. At least one of them hit it.

"Good. Reload. Same drill—Half Cock, Prime, Close, Pour, Spit, Ram, Full Cock, and Present. Fire on my order." They fuss with their muskets again. "A real soldier can load and fire three times inside of a minute. Before we march out of this camp, you must be able to do it at least two times a minute, or else you will be back to digging latrines. Ready? Present...Aim...Fire!"

This time much more bark is ripped off the luckless tree, and a cheer goes up from the men.

"Good. Give yourselves a real cheer, and let's do it again."

Laurent lifts his fist and shouts, "Bravo, Clodhoppers!" And the rest of them follow suit. "Clodhoppers! Clodhoppers! Clodhoppers!"

Well, good. Now let's get back at it.

We do it over and over again, and when we are finished, we begin our march back to the camp for supper. I look with some worry at the clouds, as my men still do not have tents. I had been able to scrounge up a few large tarpaulins, generally used to cover cannon, and they will have to crowd under those should it rain. Before we leave the far fields, I spot a small, cozy inn tucked down in a little village below. *Hmmm...*

My little drummer has been tapping out the time for our marching feet, and I have a thought. I am English, posing as American, and have no notion of French marching songs, so I say, "Drummer boy. Have you a song for us to march to?"

He, being a child, begins to sing a child's song.

*Na-po-léon avait cinq cent sol-dats!*
*Na-po-léon avait cinq cent sol-dats!*
*Na-po-léon avait cinq cent sol-dats!*
*Mar-chant du même pas!*

The men, with the exception of their older Sergeant Boule, of course, all know the song from their schoolyard days, and it turns out to be just the thing to march to—*Napoléon had five hundred soldiers, marching all in time,* it roughly translates. Here, Napoléon has but fourteen, marching sort of in time. Fifteen, counting me.

When we get back, I see the men settled as best I can. Laurent, whom I am finding to be one of my cleverest men, has managed to stretch the tarps over some nearby cannons for the men to sleep under. He has also scrounged up some wood to make a campfire so they can gather about it and take some comfort in each other's company. They go to get their dinners, then return to the fire to eat. I hear a song raised as I head for the Officers' Mess.

Lieutenant Depardieu waves me over and I take a chair next to him. A glass of wine is put in front of me and then food is brought—good food—and I tuck in. There are several others about whom I had met before, and we have a fine dinner. They, too, wish to be regaled with stories about America, and I give 'em what they want.

As the tables are cleared and the wine mellows the company, they turn to singing songs, and demand one of me.

"Alas, Messieurs, I have no voice…"

"I think the reason is, the *man's* voice is changing," says one of the wags to some laughter, but I choose not to take offense.

"...but, if you will excuse me for a moment, I might be able to provide you with some music." I rise, bow, and stride through the tent. I notice, on my way out, that a card game has been set up, and Major Levesque sits at the head of it. I do not meet his eyes.

In a moment I am back at the Officers' Mess, with my fiddle under my arm...and one of my decks of cards in my pocket. My men *will* have proper tents.


"Messieurs! Some American tunes for your pleasure!" I put the bow to the fiddle and tear into a medley of fiddle tunes starting with "Cumberland Gap" and ending with "Hop High Ladies," which I top off with a bit of a dance. When I finish, I lift bow and fiddle and give a deep nod to an excellent round of applause.

"Bravo, encore!" shouts one of them, but just then bugles blow outside for Lights Out, and my fiddle must fall silent.

Officers, of course, do not have to turn in at this time and the place stays brightly lit.

I walk from table to table, sharing wine and conversation with some of my new acquaintances. Eventually, as if by chance, I end up close to Levesque's table.

He looks up at me. "You again."

"I trust that things are now well between us, Sir?"

"That depends. Do you have any money, boy?" There is a big stack of coins and bills in front of him. One of the officers, plainly cleaned out, gets up and leaves.

"Very little, Sir. But I do have some."

"Good. Sit down."

I sit down. "But I do not know how to play at cards, Sir."

He chuckles and looks knowingly at his friends. "We will teach you, young Sir."

I pull my few remaining coins out and put them on the table in front of me.

Levesque deals out the cards, two to each of us—one down, one up. "The game is called *vingt-et-un*. Place your bets, gentlemen."

*The game, Major Levesque, as taught to me by Mr. Yancy Beauregard Cantrell on the Mississippi River, is also known as blackjack or twenty-one, and Mr. Cantrell taught me very, very well.*

In the game of blackjack, at least as it is played here, the odds are in favor of the dealer, as he is the house against which everyone else bets. Yes, he does have to cover all bets *but* he wins all ties, and therein lies the advantage. The object is for each player, by asking for additional cards, or hits, in New Orleans parlance, to get as close to twenty-one without going over. Aces count either one or eleven, depending on the rest of your hand; all face cards count ten. If you go over, whether dealer or player, you lose. If you stop at, say, nineteen—a four, a six, and a nine—while the dealer shows two tens, alas, you lose again. It is very good to be the dealer, but…and here is the good thing…the deal passes to the next player to get blackjack—an ace with any face card on the first two cards dealt to you.

Having not much money, I bet very cautiously, waiting for my chance to deal. Levesque deals several rounds and rakes in even more money. He deals again and one of the lieutenants at the table scores blackjack, and, though irritated, Levesque passes the deal to him. I notice that he, too, bets carefully when the deal is not his, waiting for it to get back to him. *Hélas, M'sieur,* I think it will never come to you again, not this night.

The young officer deals for a while—I lose a bit, then win some back, aboveboard and all, and then I see my chance. I am dealt a four down, and a queen up. The other two players go bust and I see the cards they flip over. I palm the four and, under the table, pull out an ace of spades from my sleeve and replace the four with the ace, hoping desperately that Levesque does not have the legitimate ace as his hole card.

"*Vingt-et-un,*" I say, flipping over my ace. The others throw their cards in, and I am not discovered. The deal is mine.

As if on cue, Captain Bardot saunters over to check on my fortunes. He carries a glass of cognac and places it before me.

"Here, Bouvier, this will fortify you in the face of these formidable adversaries."

He puts his hand on my shoulder and grins impudently at Levesque, who growls back at him, "So, Bardot, have you adopted this puppy? It seems you could occupy yourself with grander things than with … underage messenger boys."

Bardot's smile disappears from his face. I know the implied insinuation will not go unanswered if I don't do something. *Damn!*

I quickly take the glass of cognac and toss some of it back in my mouth and then make a great show of gasping and coughing, as if it were the first spirits I had ever tasted.

"*Mon Dieu*, how that burns! Oh, how can you stand to drink that stuff? Oh, God, that's ghastly!"

There is laughter all around the table at my boyish inexperience, but, thankfully, it defuses the potentially explosive situation and Bardot walks off.

*It also gave me a chance to switch the decks of cards beneath the table.*

I return the ace of spades back to my own deck and commence to deal, and I do not give up the deal for the rest of the night, to Levesque's absolute frustration and disgust. I intentionally lose some, but I win most and steadily thin down the pile of money that used to rest before him. The other players are soon wiped out and it comes down to Levesque and me. I especially delight in giving him close hands—totals of nineteen when I come up with twenty, or tantalizing him by dealing him a king and a deuce, and when he asks for a hit, busting him with a queen. *Spank me, will you?*

Others are now grouped around the table, watching the cardplay. As the night is winding down, I deal him his two cards, and me mine. He shows an ace of clubs up, and I show a six of diamonds. He looks at his hole card and exults, "Ha! Double down on aces!" and he flips over his other card. It is, indeed, the ace of spades.

In double down, when a player is dealt a pair in his first two cards, he may play each card separately and he may increase his bet to whatever he wishes. Double down in aces is a very good thing, for all you have to do is draw a face card on each and you have a double *vingt-et-un*.

*Formidable…*

Levesque divides his remaining money, which is still

considerable, and puts a stack next to each of his aces. Then he smiles and says, "Deal, boy."

I place a nine of clubs on his first ace, making that add up to twenty, and he looks at my six of diamonds and nods. "I'll stay with that. Hit me on the other one."

On his other ace I deal out a three of hearts. That gives him fourteen and he does not smile on that one. "Another," he says.

I turn the next card and it is the deuce of clubs. He now has a total of sixteen.

I see him looking at my six of diamonds showing. I know he is thinking I probably have a face card down, and, if I did, he would lose on that half of the double down. He must take another card. "Hit me," he says.

I deal him another card and it is the five of hearts. *He has twenty-one.*

He leans back, smiling, and lights up another cigar. His friends gather about and clap him on the back. Bardot again comes up to stand behind me.

"So what have you got, boy?" asks Levesque, grinning through the smoke.

I flip over my hole card. It is a five of spades, giving me a total of eleven. A hush falls over the watching crowd. Levesque has lost his smile.

"I will take a hit, M'sieur," says I, turning over the next card in the deck and dealing myself, as I knew I would, the lovely queen of hearts.

"*Vingt-et-un,* Monsieur, I believe I win," I say, rising. "Pardon me, but I must go now and see to my men. Thank you for your kind instruction. *Bonsoir.*"

I hear a low chuckle from Bardot behind me. "Messenger boy, indeed, eh, Major?"

Major Levesque stands in a cloud of cigar smoke and fixes me with a glare of the purest dislike. He turns and leaves the table, giving me ample time to, unobserved, switch back the decks of cards. I scoop up the money and leave.

*Thank you, Yancy, once again.*

# Chapter 31

*James Fletcher*
*Brattle Lane*
*London*

*Dear Jacky,*

*I came out of my dream yesterday, for good and ever, I hope. It was as if a breeze had come up and blown the clouds out of my mind, leaving it free and clear.*

The next day I was able to dress and to stand up with little dizziness and was both shocked and amazed to see your Mr. Higgins come to call upon me. After graciously inquiring after my health, he told me of how he and the loyal crew on your schooner followed you across the ocean, till the *Dauntless* was taken. Seeing there was nothing more to be done, he directed the *Nancy B* to London, to see what might be done there.

Upon his arrival he made discreet inquiries into your whereabouts and was greatly alarmed to hear rumors of your grisly death, and then was just as greatly relieved to learn that those reports were not true. This he learned when he visited your orphanage and found out from the Reverend Alsop that, while your location is unknown, you are still among the living.

Higgins renewed his efforts on your behalf, and that is a great comfort to me, for I do not know of a more competent man.

Later on that same day, I received yet another visitor.

"Joseph!" I exclaim upon seeing a very grim Mr. Jared enter the drawing room where I sat writing this very letter. "How very good to see you! Come, have a glass of wine and something to eat."

"Got anything stronger, Mr. Fletcher?" he growls, looking over at the crystal decanters resting on the sideboard.

"Certainly," I say and pour out two generous libations of some rather nice Scotch whisky. I hand one to him and lift my own glass. "To the poor old *Wolverine*! We've both seen a lot of water under our various keels since then, eh?"

He gives me an appraising look, clinks his glass to mine, and then tosses back his whisky, neat.

"You seem pretty cheerful, Mr. Fletcher, considering..."

*Considering what?...and then it comes to me...Oh, my God, he does not know! What the poor man must have been going through...*

*Of course he would not know, for who would have told him? Not British Intelligence, not Dr. Sebastian, a member of the same organization, not anybody.*

I think about what promises I have made to others in this regard....I vaguely remember being sworn to silence when I was groggy with my wound. Does that count? I decide it does not count. To hell with it—this man cannot live with what he thinks he has seen.

"Sit down in that chair, Mr. Jared, and I will tell you something," I say as I take his glass to refill it and hand it back to him. I have taken only the merest sip of mine. As he seats himself, I cross the room to pick up a Bible that I know rests on a shelf. "Put your right hand on that book and swear on your honor as an officer and a gentleman that you will never divulge to another soul what I am about to say."

He transfers his glass to his left hand and places the other on the Bible. "I do so swear," he says, seemingly disinterested in anything I might have to say, and is about to bring the glass to his lips again. *You are so very hard on your friends, Jacky.*

"I know that you have witnessed a horror that is very hard for you to bear, Joseph Jared, so I tell you this: *She is not yet dead.*"

He puts down his glass and gapes at me in wonder.

"What?"

"The execution was an elaborate sham, designed to get her out of France so that she could be forced to work for British Intelligence."

"But I saw..."

"What you saw was another girl, similar to her in size and description, being beheaded in her place."

His hand shakes as he puts his glass on the table next to him, and then a smile works its way across Joseph Jared's rugged features. "She yet lives..."

"I assure you it is true. She sat by my bedside not a fortnight ago, very much alive."

He puts the glass once more to his lips, this time much more relaxed. He takes a sip and then looks off into the distance. "Ah, Puss...maybe you do have nine lives."

"I am glad I was unconscious at the time," I say, to interrupt what I assume is his fond reverie. "For I'm sure I would have gone quite mad when that atrocious deed was done and the poor girl's head was lifted and shown to the disbelieving eyes of the prisoners. I cannot imagine what you went through when you beheld the severed head and thought it was hers."

He is silent and I know he is savoring the glad news I have just given him. At length he brings his eyes back on me and says, "Quite simply, I went insane. I knocked down two guards, swore I would kill every living Frenchman I could lay my hands on, then I was beaten senseless and hauled out to the whipping post and given twenty lashes. All of which stopped my rash actions, you may be sure, but did not calm my raging mind."

He pauses, and then goes on. "The sailors in the other wing of the jail also rioted, tearing apart their section of the prison and very nearly overwhelming the guards. When the uprising was quelled, ten sailors, who were pointed out as ringleaders, were taken out and given fifty lashes each. I regret to say that Jacky's friend Jones was one of them. To his credit, he took it well. However, I am glad to report, that he, too, for some reason, was also exchanged when I was. Rare for a common seaman to be treated such. I reckon the French prison warden was glad to get rid of both of us."

"It was not the French, Mr. Jared, who accomplished that. It was Miss Faber—the repatriation of all of us was part of the bargain she made with people I do not know and could not tell you about even if I did know."

"Ah. So very like Puss to watch out for her friends," he says without further comment.

*Yes. I am trying to control myself in talking to this man who, I believe, has had much closer contact with you than I ever had. Steady, boy, steady. I realize that others have claims upon your affections, Jacky, and I must get used to that.*

"You know, Mr. Fletcher, that I have been assigned to HMS *Lorelei,* and we sail tomorrow…"

*Good. Be gone with you.*

"…and Seaman Jones has also been billeted on that ship. May I break the vow that I just made and hint to him that she still lives? Apparently they are dear friends, and I know he took her supposed death very hard. For his fifty lashes and all…"

*Ah, Davy, for all your spittin' and scrapping with Jacky there in the* Dolphin's *foretop—"If you two don't stop yer goddam fightin' we'll throw both of yiz over the side, we will"— still you love her, too.*

"Yes, you may," I say and smile. "Have him swear on his tattoo, and he will not break that promise."

I put my fist on my own Brotherhood mark. "We all grew up together as ship's boys on the *Dolphin,* and share the same mark upon our skin."

"I knew about her and Jones, but not about you."

"'Tis true. I have the same tattoo right here on my hip. The same as the one she wears and which, perhaps, you have seen?"

"I might have glimpsed it, in passing," he says, his eyes hooded. He rises and picks up his hat.

*I want to kill him.*

"She says she is promised to you, Fletcher," he says, looking me directly in the eye. "In marriage and all. Is that true?"

"I have been so honored," I reply, with a slight bow. "But

who knows? Her mind might change...the fortunes of war, and all..."

"Who knows, indeed, but then, all is fair in love and war, is it not?" says he, going to the door. "You have given me the greatest of news, and I thank you for that, but now I must report to my ship."

"I wish you great good luck in your new post, Joseph," I say, as I let him out.

"And you, too, James. And if you should see our Puss-in-Boots again, please tender my *best* regards."

He puts on his Master's hat and salutes, and I bow in return.

*But deep down in my throat rumbles a low feral grrrrrowl.*

*Attempting to be civil, I am,*
*Yr Most Obedient, and etc....*

*Jaimy*

# Chapter 32

"Is this not better, Laurent?" I ask, surveying our new line of tents, smartly pitched and lined up in a neat row. I do like things neat.

"Yes, Sir, it is. We feel much better for it."

I look up at him. He stands easy, with his hand on his musket. As each day passes, I feel more and more that this man should be the sergeant rather than Boule. Not that Boule is not a good man, he is, but he is also a bit of a bumbler. The men call him Papa Boule to his face, but out of affection, not malice. I find myself doing the same.

"When we first shot at that tree, one of you hit it. I suspect it was you."

He nods, his long hair swaying under his shako.

"How did you learn to shoot?"

He smiles. "Poaching, Sir. On Major Levesque's estate."

*Hmmm. A rascal after my own heart.* "We will be on the march soon, Laurent. I am going to ask the Colonel to make you Corporal."

"Thank you, Sir."

"I shall go see him now. Help Papa Boule form up the men for morning drill."

"*Oui,* M'sieur."

General Charpentier is dictating some orders to Monsieur Dupont when the General notices me approaching and remarks, "You did well with those men."

"Thank you, *mon Général.*"

He leans toward his secretary. "What shall we make him then? We have no rank of 'Cadet.'"

"*Sous-Lieutenant* is our lowest officer rank, Sir."

"Very well. Make him that," replies General Charpentier to Monsieur Dupont. To me he says, "You shall draw your pay as a Second Lieutenant."

"Again, my thanks, Sir. And one more thing, if I might. My squad lacks a corporal and I have a man, Private Laurent, in mind. He has proven himself steady and able."

"Very well, do that. If he is not up to the task, that stripe will come off fast enough. We reward those who—"

He does not finish. A galloper charges through the camp and pulls up in front of us.

"*L'Empereur!* He is coming now! *L'Empereur!*" he shouts, and then rides off to spread the word further.

*Napoléon Bonaparte himself…Mon Dieu!*

The place explodes into frenzied activity. I salute and turn away to prepare my boys, but no one notices me in the uproar.

I pound back to my squad.

"Clodhoppers! Form the Line! The Emperor is coming!"

They jump to and I walk the Line to see that all is right, the proper spacing between, the uniforms neat, the shakos on square.

"Sergeant Boule. You will be at this end. Corporal Laurent at the far end…yes, you have been made Corporal, by

General Charpentier himself. Get your stripes from the Quartermaster later and sew them on. Shall we have a cheer for Corporal Laurent, lads?"

They do it with all their might, and when they are done, I step out in front of them. They stand at Attention, their muskets on their right shoulders.

"Bouvier's Own Clodhoppers...Parade...*Rest!*"

The heels go twelve inches apart and the gun butts thud into the ground next to their right feet.

"Good. Now, when, and if, the Emperor's carriage goes by here, I will say 'Order Arms' and you will come to Attention and bring your musket up before you like this"—and I take Papa Boule's musket from him and hold it rigidly in front of me, two inches from my nose, the barrel pointed straight up, the butt against my belly. "Do you have that? Answer."

"Yes, Sir!"

"Good. Let's try it. Bouvier's Own Clodhoppers... Order...*Arms!*"

And they do it reasonably well. It ain't the Royal English Horse Guards, but it will do.

I get out, front and center. "Dufour, you will stand by me, with your sticks at the ready, but you will not use them unless I tell you to. Right?"

He nods and comes to my side. I turn to face my squad.

"Now that the Emperor is here, you know that we will be marching very soon. I shall march with you till then, but when it comes to the actual battle, I will not be there." I feel my drummer boy stiffen at this news. "*Non.* I am assigned as a galloper, a messenger on horseback, conveying orders back and forth between the commanders. Your officer will be Captain Bardot. I have met him, and taken bread with him. He is a good man and will do his best by you. Follow the lead of Sergeant Boule and Corporal Laurent and you will be well led. That is all. Now we wait." I turn my back on them and face the road in front and go to Parade Rest myself, my hands clasped behind me, my sword still in its scabbard.

We do not wait too awfully long. Soon there is a great tumult down below us to the south. I see a cloud of dust, and I know he will come right by us.

"Steady, boys," I say, as I see the cloud approach. Soon a platoon of Cuirassiers march by, with their brass breastplates and high helmets with the mares' tails hanging down behind. Then a troop of the Light Cavalry, splendid in their red, green, and gold Hussar uniforms, with...oh, my God, there's Jean-Paul among them! I lift my sword in salute and he sees me and our eyes lock, but we give no other sign of recognition. *Later, Jean-Paul,* I think to myself, and I am sure he thinks the same. He is looking *very* fine.

Then come the Lancers, then the Horse Grenadiers, then the Old Imperial Guard, itself, the Supreme Elite, the *crème de la crème,* the best soldiers in the entire world, wearing their tall bearskin hats decorated with a gold plate, red plumes, and white cords. The best in the world and they know it. The best in the world...so far.

And then it comes. A single white carriage drawn by two horses. It draws up close to us and I say, "Clodhoppers... Order *Arms!*"

The muskets come up, the eyes are cased, and the carriage draws up abreast of us and I see the acanthus wreath circling the letter *N* and above it the Imperial Eagle.

I whip out my sword and put the hilt to my face and then bring the blade down sharply to point next to my right foot.

The man in the carriage looks out the window and catches my eye and nods, two of his fingers to his forehead in a salute.

*It is him. Without doubt.*

The carriage moves on and, unaccountably, tears begin to pour out of my eyes. I look to Denis and see his face is equally covered with tears.

Tearing myself away, I turn back to my troops and try to collect myself, but it is so hard....*Little Mary, Orphan of the streets of London, member in good standing of Rooster Charlie's Gang of Urchins, has just traded salutes with Napoléon Bonaparte, Emperor of France, and Ruler of much of the world.*

As I look down my ranks, I see that my own is not the only wet eye here. I know that they love him, no question, and I know why. He has raised up worthy soldiers from the ranks and made them generals. He has set up schools for all children, rich or poor, all across his land—I have found that all of my men, well, at least the young ones born after the Revolution, can read and write. He has built roads and visited factories and shaken hands with common workers. I have heard that he has stopped the practice of flogging on his ships, and I have certainly seen no soldier whipped since I have been here, which I would have in any British unit or British ship. I do not know what to think about any of this. I know that he has been responsible for hundreds of thousands of deaths in his march to conquest, but still, I don't know. As I so often come to realize, I don't know nothin' about nothin'.

Shaking off these thoughts, I again address my squad.

"The excitement is over. Let us go back to the drill. Today we march here, and tomorrow we march to Germany. Corporal Laurent, form the men and let us go over that hill and far away from all this ceremony. This is now for the Marshals and the Generals. Ready? Good. Forward March!"

*Dear Jaimy, I hope you are well and quite recovered from your wound. I, myself, am in good condition, curled up in my bedroll and under my neat little tent, and am officially a Second Lieutenant in the French Army. How about that for the world turned upside down? 'Course if I am found out, I shall certainly be stood up and shot—while Boney doesn't flog his men much, he certainly doesn't hesitate to shoot them should they disobey their officers or desert their units.*

*I have a small squad of Infantry under my command— farm boys, really, who now proudly call themselves Jack Bouvier's Own Clodhoppers—and this afternoon, after we had drilled enough, I slipped them out of the camp and down to a little tavern I had spotted before and stood them to a treat for all their hard work. With muskets lined up against the wall, we had cakes and ale and sang some songs and had a very good time. Maybe the last one we shall have for a long time. On the way back to our tents, Private Gobin, perhaps having had a bit too much for his young self to drink, threw his arm around my neck in a most unmilitary way, and said, "I would follow you into Hell itself, Sir!" As the other men pried him off me, I replied, "That is good, Private Harve Gobin, for that is exactly where we might very well be marching to tomorrow."*

*I had gotten the money to pay for that treat from playing at cards with a certain Major Levesque, actually Chef de Bataillon August Levesque, as the French Military would have it. I* wonder at what you would think of me cheating at cards, Jaimy, you being so upright and noble? Ah, well, I consider my skill in that regard as just another arrow in my quiver. Besides, Major Levesque had it coming. I will never tell you this to your face, for it would enrage you, but he spanked me in front of all the troops. Yes, spanked! He had it coming, for sure.

And then there is the matter of Jean-Paul de Valdon. I think you would like him, Jaimy, if you two were ever to meet. He is my contact out here on the field, and is, therefore, a traitor to his country, yet he is going to march out with us as a lieutenant in the Light Cavalry and risk his life for Napoléon. 'Course he doesn't see it that way. He sees it as fighting for France, not for Boney. He is still a loyal Frenchman and will fight for his country, no matter what. Don't expect me to work all this out... male honor and all that, which I have never really understood.

I do know I am training troops that might someday fight and kill British boys. I don't know what to think about that. I just take it day by day. At night I tell myself that I should not care how my pack of farm boys acquit themselves when it comes down to it... but I do... oh, yes, I do.

And y'know, Jaimy, they are just boys, and just like ours... It is such a pity.

Good night, Jaimy. I hope I will dream of you tonight. Now I will go to sleep.

# PART V

# Chapter 33

"An army moves on its stomach." That is one of the Emperor's more often quoted sayings, and it is true, at least of this army—it moves across the land like an enormous slug, sucking up everything in its path. Yes, there are endless supply wagons that trail behind us, but woe be to any chicken or pig we happen to encounter. I find that my Clodhoppers, for all their lack of military skills, prove to be very good poachers, and we have dined very well on the fruits of their efforts. Several very succulent geese that paid the ultimate price of being delicious come to mind—and I would advise any farmer who had daughters to keep them well under lock and key.

I ride alongside Bouvier's Own Clodhoppers as we march merrily along, across Flanders and the Rhine into High Germany itself. Napoléon's *Pontonniers,* engineers adept at getting the *Grande Armée* across rivers and such, have constructed bridges so Mathilde and I do not even have to get our feet wet. Well, I generally ride alongside— Dubois had developed a blister on his heel, and after I'd poured pure alcohol on it and bandaged it up, I let him, bearing the hoots of derision from his comrades, ride Mathilde till it got better, while I marched along with the others. It is good for me, I think. I would not like to believe I am getting soft.

Though I pitch my tent with my men and see that they are taken care of, I now spend most of my time as a member of General Charpentier's staff, running messages back and forth between the generals and field marshals. It often turns out that I am given a message—rolled, sealed, and put into the leather pouch that hangs over my shoulders—and Mathilde and I pound off to deliver it, only to be told to wait while another correspondence is prepared, and then I am given that to deliver to yet another high officer. When not occupied doing that, I hie back to the Sixteenth Fusiliers to rest and to await further orders. That rest is hard to come by, as Bonaparte has ordered many forced marches on this trek to battle. While a normal army counts itself lucky to move fifteen miles in a day, the French Army, when ordered to, can do twenty or even twenty-five. It is a great advantage when armies are jockeying for position, which is exactly what we are doing now. But it is hard on my men, and I hate to see them suffer.

"Asleep, lad?" asks Captain Bardot. I jerk up my head, which had nodded and finally had fallen onto Mathilde's soft mane. I see, to my shame, that Captain Bardot has pulled his own horse up next to mine, and I realize that sometime a while back Corporal Laurent must have noticed my fallen reins and had taken them up to walk alongside and lead me along as I slept.

"Sorry, Sir. Afraid so," I say, rubbing my eyes and setting my shako straight. I had been awake most of last night, galloping between lit-up tents that held the senior staffs of the three columns, many of them miles and miles apart. But that's no excuse, and I know it.

"That's all right, Bouvier. Get all the rest you can. I've got a strong suspicion that we'll see *l'Empereur* steal a march on these Germans before we finally meet," says Captain Bardot, pulling back on the reins to his horse, so that its pace will match that of my Mathilde.

*Stealing a march! That means marching all one day, then marching all night and into the next day! Mon Dieu!*

I rub the sleep out of my eyes and take the reins back from Laurent, thanking him for his trouble and giving Matti a chuck to bring her up to speed. *Poor baby, you certainly got no nap.* I pat her neck and hope it gives her some comfort. We round the top of a hill and look out over the *Grande Armée de la République.*

Bonaparte has one hundred and sixty thousand soldiers in this army, almost all battle-hardened veterans, and on this march he has divided them into three parallel columns: The left column is led by the V Corps, commanded by Marshal Lannes; the center one led by I Corps, with Marshal Bernadotte at the head; and the right column headed by IV Corps under Marshal Soult. The other three Corps commanded by Marshals Davout, Ney, Augereau formed up behind. The front of the Army is about thirty-eight miles wide, and its length is about the same. Prince Murat's Cavalry Reserve, seventeen thousand strong, fans out across the front of the Army as a protective screen. I learned all this from Captain Bardot, who is turning out to be an excellent source of information.

"You see, Bouvier," Captain Pierre Bardot says, pointing out over the multitude, "this formation, being essentially a square, gives the Emperor the ability to attack in any direction, merely by ordering simple flanking maneuvers." Bardot trots by my side, pointing out things he finds are of military interest. He has taken a bit of a shine to me, it seems, and I have become his protégé. This is good for me, since, under his unofficial protection, I do not have to endure insults and issue any more ridiculous challenges to duels—duels I would most surely lose if it came down to it. "And, since the length and the depth of the Army is only a two-day march, the Emperor will be able to bring down the full force of his attack on any point in only forty-eight hours. Brilliant, *n'est-ce pas*? It is not for nothing that he has been called the 'God of War.'"

I have to nod in agreement. At times, when we top yet another hill and I can look out over everything and see that mass of disciplined men spread before me, I think that I would not want to face it. Again, I ponder what would have happened had Nelson and the British Navy not won at Trafalgar.

"When do you think we shall meet the Prussians, Sir?" I ask.

He rolls his ever-present cigar to the other side of his mouth and considers. "Well, today is the tenth. We begin to cross the River Saale tomorrow, which means we'll probably meet them on the thirteenth or fourteenth. I gather from General Charpentier that the Emperor's overall plan is to get between the Prussian Army and Berlin, thereby forcing them to fight where he wants them to fight—in the open, on the plateau around Jena." He chuckles and claps me on the back. "Whatever, lad, it's sure to be hot work and glory enough to go around."

*Well. That is some information I must get to Jean-Paul. Don't know what good it will do, since it seems to be general knowledge if a mere captain knows of the plan, but it's some-thing...and I don't really know if I want it to do any good... or any bad. As usual, I don't know nothin'.*

"Well, we all want that, don't we, Sir? Honor and glory and all?"

He snorts and pitches away the stub of his cigar. "But of course. Honor and glory, to be sure," he says, and I look into his eyes and I know that he is thinking of what he has seen in the way of war—the mud, the filth, the hunger, the burning towns, the ravaged women, the murdered children, the battles where men fall rank upon rank before the merci-less cannons like wheat before a scythe, and, finally, after it's all over and the butcher's bill is added up, the sickening sweet stink of the honored dead as their bodies lie rotting on the battlefield. "*Mais oui*," he says with a certain weari-ness, as he pulls out yet another cigar and clamps it in his jaw. "Thank God we French invented matches, eh, Bou-vier?" he says, striking one on the pommel of his saddle and firing up his cheroot. "Proves we're good for more than just making war, *non*?"

I like him. We have visited a few taverns together on our way to this place, and I found his company welcome. He fancies himself quite the hand with the ladies and has gone off with more than one on this journey. He even offered to buy me a girl once, in a tavern two days back, but I begged off, citing my youth and shyness. He reminds me a bit of a certain Captain Lord Richard Allen, of recent acquaintance—'cept he's about five years older, dark where Allen was fair, and is about half a foot taller and twenty pounds heavier, and much more cynical. Maybe it's those awful cigars...no, I think it's all in his attitude toward the military, his superior officers, and life in general that brings Richard Allen to mind.

*And where are you now, my bold Captain Allen? Hmmm? Well, wherever it is, I'm glad you're well out of this one, 'cause I know it ain't gonna be pretty.*

"By the way, Jacques," Bardot says, offhandedly, "do you know you are not the only American volunteer here? *Non?* Yes, there are several others. Most from the South of your country, but one other from the North. I met him at a staff meeting yesterday, but I cannot recall his name."

*Damn! Just what I need! Some other American to blow my cover!*

"...and he did not know your name when I mentioned it."

"It is a big country, M'sieur," I say with a certain amount of dread.

"Ah, yes. But no matter. Here comes Depardieu with something obviously on his mind."

Lieutenant Depardieu comes pounding down the road and pulls up next to us.

"Bouvier! The General wants you! Right now!"

"Aye, Sir!" I say, glad that he did not see me sleeping earlier. I put the heels to Mathilde, wave good-bye to Pierre, and gallop off.

———

"Lieutenant Bouvier. You are to ride forward to see how the *pontonniers* are proceeding with the bridge over the Saale. Take their report and then deliver it to the Emperor's camp," orders General Charpentier.

My jaw drops open.

*L'Empereur!*

"Yes, Bouvier, the Emperor. Things are heating up, messengers become scarce, and it is possible you will not return to us for a while." The General hands me my detachment orders, and I tuck them in my pouch. Without them I could be shot as a deserter if found away from my unit. "Take some Fusiliers with you for protection, as you will be exposed, out in front of the army. Watch for skirmishers, as there are always plenty of rascals who lurk at the edge of an army looking for easy prey."

"Thank you, Sir. I shall be careful. Thank you for your concern and thank you for your kindness to me. I will take four of my unit with me. Laurent, Michaud, Guerrette, and Vedel." All former poachers, long of leg, and excellent marksmen.

The General nods to his aide-de-camp, who writes out the detachment chits for my men and then regards me with an appraising eye. "In the short time you have been here, Bouvier, you have made something of a reputation for yourself. You are a swift messenger, but there are swifter. You are a good officer, but there are better. I don't know what it is, but there is something about you that makes you very easy to like." He shakes these thoughts out of his head and looks away. "Good luck to you. That is all."

I salute and then go to collect my men. My drummer

boy, Dufour, gives me the big eyes and begs to be taken along, so I let him come. After all, he is my orderly; he knows his duty. He is also a boy who seeks adventure, and I can understand that. Within a half hour we are off, me on Mathilde, and the five of them loping easily alongside, the poachers' muskets at Trail Arms, and all eyes alert to danger.

And danger there proves to be.

# Chapter 34

Yancy Beauregard Cantrell, River Gambler Extraordinaire, once told me as we floated down the Mississippi, "Miss Faber, if you ever want to lose your money, attend a twenty-five-mile race where a man on foot is pitted against a good horse, and bet on the horse. The man, if he is a runner in good condition, will win every time."

When I expressed disbelief at this, he said, "No, it's true—I've seen it done. The man won by a mile. You see, the horse is good for short bursts of speed, but the man has the endurance. Plus, the horse has to carry his rider, while the man has only himself to propel along. The man will win a twenty-five-*yard* race as well, for he is quicker off the line. As always, Jacky, you beware of betting on what looks like a sure thing."

I have always tried to take that advice to heart, but sometimes I fail.

My long-legged poachers, two on each side of me, keep up the quick-march pace as we close the distance to the river, and at last we see the Saale gleaming down below us. It's been a brisk twelve-mile hike and Mathilde is puffing like a bellows, and my Clodhoppers are a bit winded as well.

"There it is, lads," I say, pointing to the encampment below. The place is abuzz with activity—wagons are bringing in loads of fresh-cut logs, and men are in the water placing them upright and lashing them down to form $X$'s on which to place the planks that will support the heavy cavalry and troops and even heavier artillery cannons. They seem to be about halfway across. There is a large tent set up in the middle of it all, and that is sure to be the command post of Colonel Maurais, Chief of Engineers.

As we go down into the river valley, I turn to Laurent. "That looks like a mess tent. Go there and see that you all get something to eat. Make sure you get a plate for Dufour, too. Dufour, stay by me." My orderly and sometime drummer boy looks up at me. "When I dismount, take my mare and walk her till she cools, and then get her to a trough for some water. Not too much, though…"

"I know horses, M'sieur," asserts Denis Dufour. "I'm a Clodhopper, a farm boy, remember?"

"Good. Then get her some oats if you can find some, and afterward rejoin your comrades for some food of your own."

In a few minutes we reach the camp, where we are challenged, so I give today's password, which is *Victoire,* so we are allowed through the lines and I dismount in front of the big tent and hand the reins to my boy. "Have her back here as soon as you can." My Special Poachers Division of Bouvier's Own Clodhoppers has already gone off toward the steaming mess tent, and I don't blame them, as my own belly is setting up a fierce growl. As Denis leads Mathilde away, I give her a pat on her flank, then I go up to the tent to present myself.

The guard outside the tent looks me over and lets me in. I take off my shako, tuck it under my arm, and duck down under the flap and look about. There is yet another table with men about it, but instead of studying maps, they are looking at drawings of bridges, fortifications, and other structures. Many have mud on their boots, and one officer is wet to his waist. These men are Napoléon's fabled engineers, men who have made it possible for him to get his army where he wanted it to go.

A grizzled old man in the uniform of a colonel looks up as I enter, and I bow to him. "Who are you and what do you want, boy?" he asks, irritation plain in his voice.

"I . . . I am Lieutenant Jacques Bouvier, Messenger of the Sixteenth Fusiliers. Compliments of General Charpentier, Sir," I manage to get out without too much stumbling. "He wanted me to convey a report of your progress to *l'Empereur* . . . Sir."

"He did, did he?" grumbles the Colonel. "Huh! Well, we'll see." He looks me up and down. "You certainly look the part of a damned jockey. Skinny enough, for sure. Take yourself off and come back in half an hour and we will have dispatches for you."

He turns back to his assistants so I bow again and exit the tent, fuming. *Skinny, am I? If you only knew, Sir.*

I go in the direction of the mess tent and notice my orderly emerging with two mess kits in his hand. Mathilde is tethered nearby in a little grassy meadow, contentedly munching on some grass. My men are sitting there about her, cross-legged on the ground, their guns across their laps, eating their own food with great gusto.

"Here, Sir," says Dufour, "I brought you a plate."

"Thank you, Denis, you are a good boy," I say. "Sit down and have yours. I'll be right back."

My throat is dry, but I had noticed a wagon nearby that was selling wine and spirits, so I stride over to it. *Camp followers do prosper in a war,* I'm thinkin' as I dig in my pocket and pay twice the going price for three bottles of cheap country wine.

I take them back and sit down amongst my men. I uncork a bottle and lift it to my lips. *Ahhh...* Then I pass it to Guerrette, who sits on my right.

"Bless you, Sir," says he, taking the bottle and drinking from it.

"Bless us all, Guerrette," I say, uncorking the next bottle and handing it to Laurent on my left.

We sit in a companionable circle on the green grass, chewing our bread and sausage and cheese as we pass the bottles around. The sun is not out and there is a heavy mist from the river, but still it is warm and we feel, for the moment, content, and that is all a poor soldier can ever hope for.

After a while, a man comes out of the Colonel's tent and signals to me. I get up.

"Get ready, lads, I think we're moving out." They groan and rise and shoulder their muskets and stand ready while I go down to see the Chief of Engineers.

"All right, Bouvier," says Colonel Maurais upon my entrance into his tent. His adjunct, a lieutenant splattered with mud, hands me two folded letters, one sealed with red wax, one sealed with blue. I take them and put them in my pouch.

"The blue one goes to the Emperor, with my compliments. And, since you will be riding through Marshal Murat's Cavalry Line on your way back, it will be no trouble for you to deliver the red one to him. I am sure he will be glad to know that we will be ready since he will be the first one over my bridge in the morning. Ride hard, young man."

I hit a brace, click my heels, bow, and leave.

We push on back toward our lines, hoping to reach them before dark. Things are going well—the men, rested and fed, are moving along at a steady pace, as is Mathilde. Denis did manage to find her some oats. I look forward to getting in my tent and going to sleep.

On our way we cross a field, and then come upon a road. The traveling there is easier, and I welcome it, but Laurent has other thoughts.

"We are too exposed here, Sir," he says, his eyes darting about, peering at the thick forest that lines either side of the road. "We could be ambushed. I don't like it. It's the poacher in me, Sir. Never let yourself be taken in the open, *non*."

I think on that but decide to stay on the road. "We will be back all the quicker, Corporal Laurent, and we have seen no sign of Prussians on our journey so far. I think they have all retreated north to get ready for the big battle. It will be all right, you'll see."

Laurent grunts in assent, but he does not look convinced. He directs Guerrette, Michaud, and Vedel to patrol out close to the encroaching woods.

As I ride along, my thoughts turn to Jaimy, and I pray once again for his recovery. *Did it go well, Jaimy? Are you back on your feet again? Did you—*

That's as far as I get on that line of thought.

*"ANGRIFF! ERGREIFT SIE!"*

A patrol of Prussian heavy cavalry bursts from the cover of the woods, helmets gleaming, sabers drawn and raised.

*"Run, boys! Run!"* I scream, as I wheel Mathilde about and try to flee. I draw my pistol to aim at the man charging at me, not ten yards away. I cock and fire, but Mathilde, startled by the sudden attack, rears back and my shot goes wide, merely nicking him on the side of his metal breast-plate. *Damn!* I hear shots from my men, and from the edge of my vision, I think I see one of the Prussians slump forward in his saddle.

The man comes relentlessly on. I can see his clenched teeth, and I know he means to kill me and to smile as he does it. In terror, I drop the pistol and reach for my sword, but I have my hand only on its hilt as he raises his saber and starts the swing of the killing slash. Just then his leader riding by his side points his sword at me and shouts, *"Halt, Günther! Den Offizier nehmen wir lebendig!"*

The one named Günther changes his swing in midair, and instead of cutting my throat, slams down the heavy hilt of his sword on the side of my head. As my shako falls into the dirt and I slump forward against Mathilde's neck, my one thought is that they mean to take me alive. Dimly, I hear my men still shooting, and then the Prussian leader shouting, *"Verschwinden wir! Schnell! Schnell!"*

Then I don't know nothin' for a while.

———

When my senses return, I find my hands are bound behind my back and my head is throbbing like someone had slammed it with a sledgehammer. Indeed, someone had—that Günther has an arm powerful as the leg of an ox. I sit up on Mathilde, shake my head, and look about. There are only about eight of them—a small band of skirmishers out to make trouble on the flanks of the Grand Army...and pick up what intelligence they can, *and, oh they have picked up some here, no doubt,* I think with growing dread, knowing what is in my messenger's pouch.

We pull up before a farmhouse where all dismount and I am pushed off Mathilde. I land on my back on the ground below and my breath is knocked out of me. I groan and try not to cry out in my pain and misery, but it is hard, *so hard.*

I am picked up and shoved in the doorway, where I trip over the sill and end up sprawled on the floor. I am quickly taken up by Günther and plunked in a chair that sits in front of a table. The officer in charge of the patrol stands at rigid attention next to me. On the table are spread maps, with words and arrows and numbers scribbled on them. An officer, with shaved head and gold on his shoulders, is seated there, and behind him is hung a flag—white with a black double-headed eagle on it, its talons clutching a brace of lightning bolts.

The man, who wears what I take to be the insignia of a major, glances up from the desk and looks at the officer with raised eyebrow.

"*Ein Französischer Kurrier, Major Papen. Er hat Papiere bei sich!*" the junior officer announces, putting my pouch on the table before his superior.

"*Gute Arbeit, Leutnant Grasser,*" acknowledges the higher

officer, plainly complimenting the junior man on his catch. He cracks open the letters and reads their contents.

"So," he asks me in French. "The bridge across the Saale is almost done, eh? Well, it is possible we might be able to concentrate some forces there to prevent the crossing of the Grand Army. What do you think of that?"

"I am only a poor messenger, M'sieur," I say. "They give me letters and I deliver them. That is all I do. I do not think of anything else. And I do not know of anything else." I hang my head at this, and try to look contrite.

Major Papen tosses the letters back on the table and says, *"Leutnant Grasser. Schaffen Sie ihn raus hier. Erschiessen Sie de Mann."* Günther, upon hearing this, puts his hand under my arm and lifts me up.

I don't understand the lingo, but to my horror, I think I get the gist of what he has just said—*Dear God, that sounds an awful lot like—*

"Take me out and shoot me, Sir? But you cannot. *Je suis un soldat,* a soldier, just like you, and I must be treated as such! I am not a spy! You cannot—"

"You have here in your pouch letters concerning dispositions of bridgework across one of the rivers of the Fatherland. How could you not be more of a spy? No, you shall be shot," he says, getting to his feet, pulling a pistol from his belt and cocking it. "And I shall personally administer the *coup de grâce.*"

He nods to Günther and I am dragged out into the farmyard and stood up in the center of it.

The firing squad forms—four of them, standing in a line in front of me, preparing their muskets.

*Oh, Lord, not here, not now…*

Major Papen comes out of the farmhouse, his cocked pistol by his side.

"*Soldaten! Anwesende waffen!*" He shouts the order and four muskets are raised and pointed at my chest.

*The Look. Mistress would expect me to put on the Look. I'll try, Mistress, I'll try...* I lift my chin and bring my eyelids down to half-mast, lips together, teeth apart. *Jaimy, I...*

"*Abfeuern!*" barks Papen.

*CRRAACCKK!*

Four muskets fire and I pitch forward into the dust. As I taste the dirt, a part of my numb mind wonders why I wasn't thrown back by the blast of the bullets, instead of forward. I look up and see that it was not my own breast that was shattered by that volley, but Major Papen's own head. He falls, half his face gone, his pistol by his side.

*CLODHOPPERS!* is the shout. Günther goes down along with several others. Then Lieutenant Grasser, clutching his neck where a bullet has penetrated his throat, kneels there choking on his own blood. Laurent lopes through the barnyard, and with his bayonet puts an end to Grasser's troubles.

I feel something at my wrists and they quickly fall free and I put my hands on the earth and push myself to my knees.

"Your shako, Sir." It is Denis Dufour, holding it out to me. Seeing me still confused, he puts a hand under my arm and pulls me to my feet. Still addled, I shove the hat on my head and yank the strap under my chin. "How could you have been so brave, Sir? Standing there like that with your head up and that look on your face..."

*Brave? What...*

"We've got to get out of here, M'sieur, they might be back at any time!" shouts Laurent, reloading.

My head clears. "My letters. I must get my letters. Dufour, see if you can find my horse. Corporal, keep a sharp watch. Vedel, Guerrette, see if that officer has any papers on him... money, too. Check the others, also. Michaud, come with me." Stooping, I pick up the pistol that lies by Papen's dead hand and look down at his body—*so you would put a bullet in my brain with this?* Michaud and I go into the farmhouse.

A quick check shows no one in the room—I suspect the family that lives in this place is cowering upstairs—and I go over to pick up my dispatches and thrust them back in my pouch. "Michaud. Take that flag." I scoop up the maps and other papers from Papen's desk and shove them in there as well. They might prove of interest to the Emperor's staff.

Michaud grabs the flag by its pole, and we go back outside, where I'm glad to see Denis standing there holding Mathilde's reins. "M'sieur! There are other horses in back! Most of them saddled!"

Must have been the mounts of the party that ambushed us. "Good. Each of you men go back and get one," I say, as I take the reins and mount up. This is *very* good, I'm thinking, as I know my men must be exhausted.

Vedel hands me up several purses of coins and some papers, and I stuff all in my pouch and tie it shut.

Within a minute we all ride out of the farmyard and thunder down the road.

We ride the horses hard and encounter Prince Murat's outriders within two hours. We are challenged so I give the password, and we are quickly escorted to Murat's headquarters. The Grand Army has been ordered to stop its advance and is making camp, though nightfall is still a few hours off. I suspect that Napoléon doesn't want his army sitting exposed on the banks of the Saale, waiting for the bridge to be finished. I also surmise that he will be very glad to receive my dispatch from Colonel Maurais. We shall see.

"The seal on this has been broken, Lieutenant!" says Murat's aide-de-camp severely. "I trust you have an explanation?"

"Yes, Sir," I answer, standing stiffly at Attention under his angry gaze. "We were ambushed by a Prussian Cavalry patrol on our way here. I was taken prisoner. The dispatches from Colonel Maurais were discovered in my pouch and read by their officer, a Major Papen."

"That is *not* a good thing, messenger," he growls, reading the letter. "Now the enemy knows where and when we will cross the Saale."

As I am being dressed down, I notice out of the corner of my eye that my poachers, who are standing next to their puffing horses, are excitedly telling the tale of the day's events to others of their rank. They often point at me in the reporting of it.

"Major Papen lies dead, Sir. My men rescued me and I retrieved our papers. I am positive that no one else has read them, and...if I may, M'sieur..." I reach back for my pouch, then pull it open to show the charts and such that Major Papen had both on his person and lying about his desk. "I got his papers as well."

"Hmmm," he says, considering this. Then he points to the entrance of the biggest tent. "All right. Inside, boy."

I take off my shako and walk into the tent, followed by the aide-de-camp. There are several men standing around a table, staring down at a map. The man in the middle looks up and asks, "What is this then, Paradis?"

"This messenger has a dispatch from Colonel Maurais of the Engineer Corps. The bridge will be ready tomorrow…"

"That is welcome news, indeed," replies the man, smiling broadly. He turns to the others. "We will cross tomorrow!"

"…and he has other things as well. He will explain, Marshal Murat."

I suck in my breath. So it is the man himself—Marshal Joachim Murat—Napoléon's trusted brother-in-law and comrade-in-arms since Bonaparte first grabbed power back in the last century. Marshal Murat, famous throughout Europe for his bravery, dash, and military skill. I bow and tell it. Then I spread Papen's papers out on the table, and they pounce on them. There are gasps of astonishment.

*Look! Prince Ludwig has concentrated his forces at Schleiz!*

*And Brunswick has withdrawn to the west! He means to outflank us!*

As they go over the maps, I gaze at Murat. He is a very good-looking man—slim, with curly hair falling to his shoulders, good straight nose, strong chin, gold braid all over his uniform. And, as his subordinates continue to exclaim over my find, he comes up to me and says, "You have a strange accent, messenger."

"I am an American volunteer, Your Excellency," I manage to stammer out.

"Hmmm," he says. "Interesting. I, too, have an American on my staff. He has proved very valuable."

"We Americans owe a great debt to France, Sir. Some of us mean to repay that debt."

"Well said," replies Marshal Murat, turning back again to his staff. "Gentlemen! We are but simple cavalry. These papers must go to the Emperor for his study."

"I do have a letter that I must deliver to him," I say, holding up the letter with the broken blue seal on it.

Murat laughs. "Put the maps back in his pouch and let him be on his way, and let us prepare to cross the Saale tomorrow."

My leather shoulder bag is handed back to me and I take it, bow, and go to leave.

"We will, of course, provide you with an escort, to ensure your safe passage. The Emperor has brought up his Old Guard and is encamped immediately behind Bernadotte's I Corps. It will not take you long to get there."

"I thank you, Sir. I'll be off now."


"Mount up, boys," I say to my fine poachers, and they climb on their horses. I get on the long-suffering Mathilde and pat her neck—*be patient, baby, soon you shall have fresh oats and sweet rest*—and to Michaud I say, "Give the Prussian flag to Dufour. Let our brave drummer boy carry it." Michaud has been carrying it wrapped up under his arm.

Denis takes the flag, unfurls it, then proudly plants the base of the pole on the pommel of his saddle.

"Let's go."

And so, with the captured double-eagle flapping above us, the Clodhoppers gallop through the ranks of wondering soldiers, bound for the headquarters of Napoléon Bonaparte, Emperor of France.

# Chapter 35

We pull up at the edge of the Emperor's heavily guarded encampment.

All along our gallop from Murat's headquarters to here, there have been looks of astonishment at the sight of four common musketeers mounted on heavy horses, one rather small officer clad in a Hussar's uniform, all led by a drummer boy carrying a Prussian battle flag.

*It does not speak well for me, but I do like a good show, especially when I am in the center of it.*

An Imperial Guard officer, a lieutenant, flanked by several flinty-eyed members of the same elite corps, comes out to confront us.

"Who are you and what do you want, *garçon*?" he asks, with great contempt in his voice.

I decide to ignore the insult, for the moment at least. I put on the Look and reply, "I am *Sous-Lieutenant* Bouvier, Messenger of the Sixteenth Fusiliers, and I bear a dispatch from Colonel Maurais, Chief Engineer of the *Pontonniers*...concerning the progress of the bridge across the Saale."

The officer thrusts out his hand to grab the letter. I decide to meet insult with insult.

"The message is for *l'Empereur,* M'sieur, not for one such as you."

"What! You insolent puppy!" snarls the officer, astounded. He and the other Guardsmen reach for their swords, but then again, my poachers reach for theirs, too. *Good boys.*

This rattle of sabers is noted by an officer of a much higher rank who has just stepped out of the big tent. *"Qu'est-ce que c'est?"* he asks, striding up before me.

He seems to be a colonel, and I figure this is as far up the chain of command as I am going to get. It turns out that I am wrong in that assumption.

Again I say that I have a message for *l'Empereur* and I dismount, salute, say the password, and hand the dispatch to him.

He takes it but does not open it. Instead he looks up at Dufour, sitting there dazzled by the realization of exactly where he is. "That is a Hapsburg flag, boy. Where did you get it?" demands the Colonel.

Denis is unable to speak. I clear my throat and give a quick account of the day's events and hand him my leather pouch.

"Here are the papers we took from the Prussians. Marshal Murat is of the opinion that *l'Empereur* would like to see them."

He takes the bag, nods, and says, "Wait here." He turns and goes back to the tent.

"Dismount, boys," I say to my men, and they slip off their horses. "Stand easy."

As I wait for what I think will be yet another message to deliver, I gaze about me. The Army stretches to the horizon in all directions—thousands of just-pitched tents in neat rows, the smoke of hundreds of cooking fires rising into the sky, rank upon rank of cannons. The camp followers, too, have worked their way into the center of the Army, and I hear the lilt of female laughter as well. No, an army does not travel only on its stomach.

The tent that the general had entered has two guards standing at attention on either side of the entrance, and each holds a staff on which is mounted a shining brass eagle—Napoléon's battle standard—the Imperial Eagle.

*Hmmm.* The Emperor of France is in that tent, I figure. As I'm getting used to that idea, thinking on that old saying that "a cat may look at a king," a man in a blue coat with a golden sash across his chest comes out, followed by two other men. *Oh, my God, it is him.* He looks at the flag and walks slowly toward us, his hands clasped behind his back. My knees commence to shake, and beside me I hear Dufour gasp.

"Dufour! Down on one knee! You will present the flag to the Emperor!" I whisper. I whip off my shako and put my own knee to the ground, bowing my head. In a moment I'm starin' at Napoléon Bonaparte's gleaming black boots, twelve inches from my nose.

Napoléon stands before us and says, "Get up, both of you. There is no need for that sort of thing on the battle-field. After all, we are all fellow soldiers, *non*?"

I struggle to my feet, unable to reply.

"So you have captured a Hapsburg battle flag?" he asks. "You have the honor of having taken the first prize in this campaign," he goes on. "You have done well, Lieutenant."

"*N-N-Non,* Your Excellency, I have not," I stammer. "My men took the flag, not me. I was but a helpless captive at the time."

He looks at me, and I uncase my eyes and sneak a look at him. He is not the small man the British press would have us believe, no, he is of medium height, and a good head taller than me. His dark hair is cut short and an errant curl falls over his forehead. For the ruler of much of Europe, he is very young-looking. Many thoughts are rushing through my head, but the chief one is *Here is Little Mary, member of the Rooster Charlie Gang of Street Urchins, and just what the hell is she doing here?*

He nods and says, "Well and modestly spoken, Messenger Bouvier. However, I have found the papers you captured most interesting, and I suspect that *you* were the one who realized their value. You are to be commended."

Well, I can't argue with *that.*

"Thank you, Excellency," I manage to say. "Our drummer Dufour here would like to present you with the flag, if you will accept it."

Napoléon nods and turns to the boy. Denis, his eyes wide, hands the flagstaff to his leader, who takes it and hands it back to one of the men behind him.

"Thank you, Dufour. That flag shall stand in the center of all the battle flags we shall take in the coming days when we march victorious back into Paris."

Denis Dufour weaves on his feet, his eyes go back in his head, and then he topples over in a dead faint.

The Emperor chuckles, looking down at the boy. "See to your drummer, Lieutenant. It seems the events of the day have overwhelmed him. Then wait here. I will have a message for Marshal Murat for you to deliver. *Bonsoir.*"

With that, Napoléon Bonaparte turns, clasps his hands behind him again, and returns to his command tent.

"Guerrette, Michaud," I say, turning to my men, who stand dumbfounded behind me. "Pick him up and see if you can revive him. Does anyone have any water?"

It turns out that they have. There were canteens attached to the Prussian saddles, and after they carry Dufour off a little distance, they apply a flask to his lips.

He awakes sputtering, looks about, and then starts crying. "I disgraced myself!" he wails. "In front of the Emperor! I shall die of shame! Oh, God!"

"No, you did not, Denis Dufour. You distinguished yourself today, and the Emperor knows it," I say, looking deep into his teary eyes. "You were exhausted. After all, you had run on your own feet for fifteen miles then rode back the same distance in the same day. Who would not keel over after that?" I take him by his thin shoulders and give him a gentle shake. "You delivered an Austrian battle flag into Napoléon Bonaparte's very hand today. Count on it, you will tell that story to your children, and their children will tell it to theirs down through the ages, generation after generation. Now hush. There is work to do. Laurent, take the men back to the Sixteenth Fusiliers and pitch your tents. Get something to eat. Dufour, set up our tent and make sure there is a bucket of clean water for me when I get back...no, *two* buckets of water. Do you have that? Good. I will be back later, after I deliver the message to Murat. Do not worry, I am in no danger here in the middle of the Army."

They get back on their horses.

"And, men," I go on, looking up at Laurent and trying not to choke up, "I cannot thank you enough. You saved my very life today and I shall never forget it. Know that. Now go."

And they are off.

I wait by Mathilde, stroking her neck, and reflect that I really could use a bath. *And yes, baby, I know you could use some good oats and a bit of rest, too, but just wait and we shall both get what we need.*

Presently an officer comes out of the command tent and hands me a sealed message. "For Marshal Murat."

I take it, salute, and I am off.

We pound into Murat's encampment and I leap off Mathilde and stride to the front of the tent. I salute the guard, say the password, and am admitted to the headquarters of the Reserve Cavalry.

"Ah," acknowledges Marshal Murat, looking up from his charts. "It is our bold messenger back from *l'Empereur.*"

"*Oui, mon Général,*" I answer, holding out the message. "With his compliments."

Murat takes the letter, breaks the seal, and reads it, then turns to the other men in the tent. "It is as I thought it would be. We cross the Saale tomorrow, and we shall be the first to go!"

There is a cheer from the others as Murat goes on. "Based on the Prussian plans taken today, the Emperor is considering dividing the army in two, one half to draw out and strike the main Prussian force on the open plateau above the Saale, near the town of Jena, the other at a place called Auerstädt. We are to start moving before dawn tomorrow. You will have your men ready."

There is much clicking of heels and reports that yes, they will be ready and they can't wait to go, and then they go back to poring over their plans. Murat turns to me, smiling.

"We plan and we plot, but who knows upon whom Fortune will shine, eh, *Sous-Lieutenant* Bouvier?" he says. "We have heard how you stood up before the firing squad today. I only hope that when my time comes, I will be as brave."

I bow my head and say, "I was not brave at all, Sir. I was too terrified to have any thought of bravery in my mind at all."

"Well, you acquitted yourself well today, whatever your state of mind," responds Murat. "I am preparing a message for your General Charpentier concerning our deployment tomorrow. Right now, please refresh yourself at our table, and, oh yes, you might acquaint yourself with your fellow American who is attached to my staff. He is right over there."

"Thank you, Sir," I say, and I look over to the table laden with bottles of wine and plates of bread and cheeses and choice meats, and my belly growls and both belly and I say *oh, yes!* and to hell with any fellow American, whoever and whatever he may be. Murat turns back to his men, and I go to the table, where I quickly gobble down some sausage and cheese.

There is a man standing there, facing away from me. He turns, and I am amazed to look into the equally astounded eyes of Lieutenant Randall Trevelyne. I break out into a real sweat and my jaw drops, but I have enough presence of mind to say, very quietly, "Good to see you, Lieutenant

Trevelyne. If you say anything about this, you will have killed me. If you want that, do it."

He shakes his head and laughs a quiet laugh. "So. Here you are. And already you are a hero. How can I possibly keep up with you, Jacky?"

"Pour me a glass of wine, Randall, and we shall see."

He grabs a wine bottle by the neck and a wineglass by its stem and fills it up and hands it to me. I lift it to my lips and drink. *Oh, Lord, that is good!*

"So this is where you went, Randall, after you left Dovecote," I say as I lower my glass. "You know everybody back in Boston is very worried about you? How did you get here?"

"Lissette's father, the Comte de Lise, got me the commission. I had to do something when my father kicked me out of the house after I was expelled from Harvard for a second time for being drunk in chapel. So let them worry. I don't care. Besides, everybody back in Boston is worried about you, too."

I know it had always rankled Randall that even though he was a Lieutenant in the militia and I was just a stupid girl, he had never seen a real fight, whereas I had been in lots. Me, who never wanted to be in any fight at all and would have happily lived out my life in peaceful pursuits, 'cept it didn't work out that way.

"I came over here to test myself in fire and what do I find? The renowned Jacky Faber already a goddamned hero and the battle hasn't even started yet!"

"You're a fool, Randall. I'm no hero and never was. Everything's been accident or luck. You don't know what it's gonna be like when it comes down to it. You don't know what's gonna happen in a few days."

"Well, I'll find out, won't I?"

I put my glass back down on the table as one of Marshal Murat's aides comes up to us. "Lieutenant Bouvier," he says, handing me a letter. "For General Charpentier."

I nod, let my eyes bore into Randall's, and say, "*Bonsoir,* M'sieur Trevelyne. I suspect we shall meet again on this march. Till then, *au revoir.*" I bow, click my heels, and exit the tent.

*Well, I'll be damned... What a world!*

I get back on Mathilde and head back to the Sixteenth Fusiliers, and I am glad, for I am very weary, but, tired as I am, I find my day is not yet done. As I trot along, my head nodding, I find I am joined by Jean-Paul de Valdon, another Lieutenant of Cavalry.

"Ah," I say. "My Bonny Light Horseman. And how are you, Jean-Paul? Well, I hope." I reach over to take his hand. It seems that it is my day for meeting up with handsome young cavalrymen. Dropping his hand, I say, "You are here for a report. Very well, here it is: The Army begins to cross the river Saale at dawn tomorrow. Murat will lead. Napoléon will divide his forces as soon as all are across— one half to face the Prussians near a town called Jena, the other to fight them at Auerstädt."

"And just where did you get that information?"

"I delivered a message from the Emperor to Marshal Murat, and I was in the Marshal's command tent when he opened it and gave orders to his officers."

"From Napoléon, himself?" he asks, aghast.

"Yes. I met him today," I say, yawning. "Gave him a message from Colonel Maurais of the bridge builders."

Jean-Paul is struck dumb. After a moment, he says, "A

month on the job and already you meet the Emperor of France. You have certainly wasted no time getting into the tents of the mighty. I can barely gain entry to my own commanding officer's tent."

"I am but a simple messenger," I say, and kick poor Mathilde up a little faster. We do have to deliver the message to General Charpentier, after all. "So tell me—have I done well at this spying? You know I hate it, don't you? Well, I do—I hate being a sneak—and I now ask of you, 'Is it enough? Have I done my job?'"

"Yes, you have, but—"

"You know you could cross the river and go give that information to the Prussians. They would find it very valuable." I watch his face. "If you wanted to do that."

"I do not wish to do that. My quarrel is with Napoléon, not with French soldiers. I will send that information back to Jardineaux and he may do with it what he wishes, but it will get to him too late for him to do any harm to this army."

"I don't care. In fact, I am glad of that, Jean-Paul. I would not like to think I did anything to hurt my friends."

He smiles at that. "Your friends? Just who are you working for, Jacqui?"

"I don't know. I am just a simple girl who tries to do her job, whatever it might be, and I leave the politics to others."

"Um. A simple girl? Right. At any rate, this will be my last dispatch because my line of couriers will be broken when we cross that river. Napoléon is sure to take up a section of the span after we're over, to prevent the Prussians from using it. But that is not what is important to me right now."

"Oh? And what is?"

He clears his throat and then says, "Jacqui. I must… see you."

"See me? Here, you are looking right at me, *non*? Here I am, *mon cher*, all of *Sous-Lieutenant* Jacky Bouvier—tired, dirty, stinky, and very much in need of a bath."

"*Non.* I do not mean that. As man and woman, I must see you. Ever since I first met you on that day in Paris, when you tricked me with the carriage, I…" He pauses. "…I have not been able to get you out of my head."

*Hmmm…*

"Ah, Paris. I do miss her so. And it's only been a few weeks," I sigh, wistfully. "We did have some fun there, didn't we, Jean-Paul?"

"*Oui, ma chérie,* and some of the finer moments of my life," he replies. He reaches over and takes my hand.

I give his a gentle squeeze and then take mine back. Full night has not quite fallen.

"Two very junior officers should not be seen holding hands, Lieutenant Valdon. I'm sure the French Army is a little more forgiving of that sort of thing than is the British Navy, but still…"

We ride along in silence for a while, then he speaks again.

"I…heard something of what had happened to you today. I am sorry. I cannot imagine how you endured it, but I am most thankful that you survived."

"Me, too, Jean-Paul, believe me on that. I am not ready to leave this world just yet, however glorious are the promised charms of Heaven above," I say. "But let's put that out of our minds."

And I fall silent, then say, "I have thought upon what you said, and yes, we shall meet again as boy and girl, but it will be when we get to the other side of the river. I have a way. All right?"

He looks at me and nods as we come to a bend in the road and we are out of the view of the Army for a moment. I bring Mathilde to a halt.

"One kiss is all that can be risked, Jean-Paul," I say. I remove my shako and lean over to press my mouth to his. I feel both the puff of his hot breath on my cheek and the feel of his hand on the back of my head as he holds my face to his. *Oh, yes...*

After a few moments, I raise my hand to his chest and push him away.

"No more, Jean-Paul. Not now. In a few days," I tell him, my breath a bit ragged. "You will know me when you see me, count on it. Now go."

I put my heels to Mathilde, and we are off, leaving a very confused Lieutenant Jean-Paul de Valdon behind us.

After I deliver the message from Murat to General Charpentier—and yes, there is much shouting of orders of how we leave in the morning and what everyone is to do to prepare for it, but I am so tired that I don't take much notice of it. As soon as I am dismissed, I turn toward my lovely tent for some blissful sleep.

But it is not to be, for my poachers have plainly been spreading the word.

"Bouvier! By God, you're back! Bravo!" says Captain Bardot upon seeing me emerge from Charpentier's tent. He claps his hand on my back and pushes me toward the Officers' Mess and in through the door flap.

"Please, Captain, I am not fit, I am filthy..."

"What? Who cares about that? We all get dirty in a campaign. It's to be expected. No, you must go in! I order you, *Sous-Lieutenant,* so you have no choice!"

I reckon I don't, so I go in.

"Behold, comrades!" bellows Bardot to the assembled officers, who turn astounded faces to us. "I present our *beau sabreur* Jacques Bouvier, who has faced the enemy today and captured the first enemy standard and delivered it into the very hand of the Emperor himself! Stand up, all of you!"

And they do it with a roar. *Bouvier! Bouvier! Bouvier! The pride of the Sixteenth Fusiliers!*

I protest that it was not my doing, but they will have none of it, and glasses of wine are pressed upon me and toasts are proposed and soon my head is spinning with it all.

I am seated at a table next to Bardot and food is placed in front of me. I eat it and I am glad of it. But soon my head drifts down toward my plate so that eventually Bardot picks me up and takes me out to deliver me to my tent where my Clodhoppers take me from him.

"Dufour," I say to my orderly, who had, commendably, gotten the two buckets of water I had asked for and had placed them in my tent, "thank you."

After Bardot left me off, I had revived myself by plunging my head into one of the buckets, and then I sent Denis out. I stripped down and spent the next half hour washing both myself and my small clothes, all of which really needed the washing after the events of the day. After I laid them out to dry, I put on my nightshirt, crawled into my sleeping bag, and then called him back in.

"You shall put your bedroll over there on the other side of the tent and sleep there. If you hear me scream in the night, you will take that rag and dip it in the water and then lay it over my face until I stop and come out of the nightmare. Do you understand? Very well. Good night, Dufour. Sleep soundly. You acquitted yourself well today."

I, myself, am asleep before my head hits my rolled-up uniform jacket that I use for a pillow every night.

# Chapter 36

*James Fletcher*
*Snoggins Pier, Margate, England*

*Jacky Faber*
*Somewhere in France*

*Dearest Jacky,*

*Yes, Jacky, we now know where you are, or, at least, where you were when you were last seen, thanks to the invaluable Higgins.*

Figuring logically that the Admiralty would have more use for you alive than dead, Higgins began to worm his way into the Navy's Intelligence Branch. Armed with impeccable references from the very influential and powerful Hollingsworth family, he managed to gain an interview with First Lord Grenville, and immediately established a rapport with that gentleman. Meetings with a Mr. Peel followed, and then conferences with a Dr. Sebastian, with whom I believe you are acquainted. Higgins, or should I say *Agent* Higgins, is now well established in the Intelligence Branch.

I shudder to think what danger you might be in, dear girl, but then I know you to be extremely resourceful and hope for the best. Yes, I know you have been sent to spy upon the French, and fear not, none of this is actually being written down. It is only my random thoughts while I think upon you as I look out over the bay.

Believe it or not, as I'm pondering all of this, I am standing at the rail of your own beautiful little schooner, moored here in Margate. I have once again left my family's home on Brattle Lane in London, as I found it stifling there, and have taken up my quarters on your *Nancy B. Alsop*. Mr. John Higgins, as the senior corporate officer here at Faber Shipping, Worldwide, has seen fit to appoint me Captain in your absence, and I thank him for it. Being here has chased many shadows from my mind.

Now that I'm fully recovered, I have gone out to the Home for Little Wanderers, where I have acquainted myself with your grandfather, Reverend Alsop, as well as the delightful Mairead. She and her new husband, Ian McConnaughey, send their love and wishes for your safe return, as do all of us. In addition, I have met up with John Tinker—yes, Tink, our old shipmate and charter member of the Brotherhood. He is now on board the *Nancy B* as Second Mate and seems to revel in his new position. Like the rest of us, he wants to be off to sea, but we must wait to see what develops. Jim Tanner, as First Mate, has come a long way since last I saw him. He, too, is anxious to be off to reunite with his new wife, Clementine, and for that I cannot blame him. But I try not to think too much upon that.

Young Daniel Prescott is coming along well as a seaman, and I mean to rate him Able soon. He is quite a contrast to John Thomas and Smasher McGee, who have spent most of their time in jail during their stay here, for fighting in taverns. I have had to bail them out several times, as well as call on my brother George for his legal services to keep them from being transported to Botany Bay. At this moment they are belowdecks and confined to quarters. I hope they will stay there.

We have taken out the *Nancy B* several times for short runs, and oh, yes, she is a sweet sailer. She reminds me so much of you, Jacky. Quick, responsive, playful, and spirited as a new colt as she cuts through the waves. Were it not for my worry about you, I should be supremely happy.

I sleep in your cabin, in your bed, even, and I gaze about at the things you have in here—mementos of your travels in the Caribbean, North Africa, and other far places. I notice sculptures of bears and seals carved from parts of whalebone, and other pieces scrimshawed with pictures of the taking of whales and sightings of mermaids. Is that an actual shrunken head? No, it cannot be. There's a guitar leaning against the bulkhead...and there are rugs from Persia on the deck, and boldly decorated cloth from Africa hanging on the wall, and I cannot imagine what *that* is...and I shan't ask.

But the thing that warms my heart the most is your portrait of me that hangs on the wall next to the head of your bed. You have made me far too handsome and noble-looking, but still it gladdens me to see it there. *Ah, yes...*

Higgins cautions us to be ready, as he perceives things are happening quickly in France. He is not at liberty to say what exactly, but he has contacts there now and is convinced that he knows, and that gives me great comfort. That, and the fact that what you are doing is for the greater good of England, our homeland.

*We wait, Jacky, for news of you.*

*Your Most Humble & etc.*

*Jaimy*

# Chapter 37

"Come, Bouvier, let us go a-whoring!"

I have been spending a lot of time with Bardot—he is excellent company, and after the work of the day, we have been hitting some of the makeshift taverns that the camp followers have set up to cater to junior officers. We were one of the first ones over the river, so we have some time to kill while the rest of the Army catches up. I bring my fiddle to add some joy to the proceedings, and we have a good time. Bardot has embellished the firing-squad story so that not only am I shown as having stood up bravely, head held high before the guns, but also, supposedly, I had delivered a speech proclaiming my joy at the privilege of giving up my life for the glory of France.

"He stood up before the firing squad, threw back his head, and cried out, 'Shoot, if you will, you lousy Kraut bastards, but the last words upon my lips shall be *Vive la France!* and damn the whole sorry lot of you Prussian pigs straight to Hell!'"

I protest that it was not that way at all, but now it seems

that I am given even more credit for modestly disavowing Bardot's tale. Ah, well, I seldom have to buy my own drink.

When it comes right down to actually going off with one of the girls, I manage to make myself scarce so that it appears as if I've already followed one into her tent should Bardot look for me. In fact, I'm lurking outside, waiting for enough time to elapse so I can go back in and wink lewdly at Captain Bardot if he sits again at our table.

"Come on! Before they're all taken!"

But this time I have other plans so I beg off, saying I have a last message to deliver.

"Too bad for you. I hear they've got a new crop of fillies down at Madame Augustine's, and it's a fine evening for a gallop, my boy!"

I tell him I'll try to come along later and he leaves.

When I am sure that he is out of sight, I duck into my tent and dive into my knapsack. I pull out several items of clothing and stuff them into my leather message pouch. They just barely fit.

"Don't wait up for me, Dufour. I can roll out my own sleeping bag. Just set out the bucket of water, as usual."

*"Oui, M'sieur."*

I leave without my shako, but as I often go without it when off duty, nobody notices. The Clodhoppers are too tired to lift their heads to look at me anyway, the poor fellows having been assigned road-repair duty today, where they worked like mules—Artillery Corps does like its roads smooth.

I head down to where the taverns and brothels are set up,

then skip quickly past Madame Augustine's, where I hear Bardot's hearty laugh from within, then take myself toward an establishment that I know is strictly an inn because I have checked it out. Well, sort of strictly an inn—it's set up as a tavern inside with tents pitched outside for rent by the hour, for whoever might want to use them. It is not always har-lots—no, sometimes the love-struck wives and girlfriends of young officers follow their men into the field, and when they have the opportunity to meet, they need their privacy, and Velour's Traveling Inn provides just that.

I go into Velour's and plunk down several coins for a couple of hours' rental of a tent.

"Thank you, Lieutenant. The third tent to the left," says the clerk. "Fresh linens in there for you; yes, Sir, I do hope you enjoy your stay."

I give him a wink and go out and into my rented tent.

I take off my boots, stockings, trousers, jacket, and shirt, and put on the one dress I had brought with me, and then I pull on my wig. It's the brunette one, and the hair comes down to about my shoulder blades. When I had packed it, I figured that it would be a good contrast to my regular hair color; plus its ringlets come in close around my face, hiding my white eyebrow. The dress is the Empire style, coming down fairly low on my chest, being gathered up underneath that same chest, then falling in pleats down to my ankles. It is low on my back as well, and my dark tresses brush my bare shoulders. I think he will like it.

*Why are you doing this?* I ask myself, and indeed, it is a question that needs to be asked. It is risky because I could be discovered, and I'd have a *very* hard time explaining certain things away. Very well, self, here are my reasons: It is because

I have been playing a boy for the last three weeks or so, and I'm a bit tired of it, so I look forward to an evening of being a girl again. Also, I'm sure I can get away with it—remember, people see what they expect to see. And the last reason is...I really like Jean-Paul de Valdon. And that's reason enough for me.

I wrap one of my silk scarves around my head and stick my head out of the tent to look about. Good. Nobody around. I step out and head up the path to Velour's front flap, which is where I had told Jean-Paul that I would meet him this evening.

And there he is, looking fine in his best uniform—blue jacket, white turnouts, gray lapels, white pants, black boots, gold sword, and blue bicorne hat.

*Yum...*

He looks at me and recognition comes over his face. And the look on that face is worth all the risk. It glows, and I'm sure mine does, too. We move toward each other...but someone gets in the way.

*Damn!* It is a Sergeant of the Guards, plainly drunk, who lurches between us.

"Ha. Look what we have here. Come, *ma petite*," he slurs. "We have some business to get done." He throws his arm across my shoulders.

"Pardon, M'sieur, but I am for someone else. Not you. Now, please go away."

"I'll not. There. Get in the bushes, girl. Move it." He grabs me by the neck and pushes me roughly toward a hedge that lines the path. *Damn! He's big and he's strong, and I—*

"Back away, man," orders Jean-Paul, his sword drawn and pointed at the man's throat.

The Sergeant releases his hand from my neck, looks up at Jean-Paul, and sneers, "Officer's meat, eh? I should have known. Much too clean for the likes of us real soldiers."

"Off with you, before I have you shot for disobeying an officer's order," says Jean-Paul.

"Right, *Sir*," the man mutters scornfully as he stumbles away. "Damned cavalry *pouf*."

"No, Jean-Paul," I say, putting a restraining hand on his sword arm. "Let him go. We haven't time for that. Come with me. Let us go in and have some fun."

We enter Velour's and sit at a corner table. There are several couples at other tables nearby. Wine is brought along with some plates of food.

"So you see, Jean-Paul, we are now out as boy and girl, just as you wanted," I say, putting my hand on his and giving myself a little bounce. "It is nice, *n'est-ce pas*?"

"You could not be more lovely," he says, ignoring the food and bringing his hot gaze full upon me. "I can't stand it."

"Yes, you can, *mon cher*," I answer. "Look here, Jean-Paul. We do not have all that much time together in this place, at this moment. Let us not waste it." I select a choice piece of pastry and put it to his lips. "And now a glass of wine with you. Please, Jean-Paul. Relax. Enjoy this."

He takes his wineglass and drinks from it, all the while not taking his eyes from mine. "All right," he says.

There is no music in this place and it is too bad. I'd really like to dance with him, but...

"Shall I sing you a song, Jean-Paul? Would you like me to do that?"

He nods and I stand to face him. Then I begin to sing.

*Plaisir d'amour*
*Ne dure qu'un moment.*
*Chagrin d'amour*
*Dure toute la vie.*

It is the same song I sang at the House of the Rising Sun in New Orleans, and one of the few love songs I know in French, although, thanks to Bardot, I now know plenty of really risqué ones. I'm about to give Jean-Paul the second verse when I'm shocked to see Bardot, himself, and two of his cronies come into the place, and he's looking right at me.

*Damn!*

I plunk myself back down in my chair real quick and nuzzle into Jean-Paul's side.

"Bravo," shouts Bardot, clapping his hands. "That was nicely sung, girl."

*Right now this girl is very glad she made that decision never to sing while being Jacques Bouvier, else he might have recognized my voice!*

I nod my thanks, shaking my wig's tresses even more into my face, but I needn't have worried—it ain't my face he's lookin' at.

"New girl, eh?" he says, his eyes fixed on my bodice. He sways slightly, plainly already a bit drunk. He looks at the other couples in the place, then sticks his hand in his pocket and pulls out some coins. "I'll give you ten francs for her. What do you say, boy?"

"Sir! I must protest!" cries Jean-Paul, jumping to his feet.

"She is my fiancée, Sir, who has come to be with me here. She is a good girl from a good family, and I resent your insinuation!"

"That true?" asks Bardot of me, not looking particularly frightened by Jean-Paul. I nod with the big waif eyes and try to look very small.

"Damn me. Young love, of all things, here in this place," sighs Bardot, bowing to Jean-Paul. "I compliment you, M'sieur. She is a neat piece, and she must love you very much to come all this way. Well, enjoy her, boy. May your tent reverberate with her squeals of ecstasy. *Adieu.*"

Bardot turns from us and looks about the place again and plainly does not find it to his liking.

"It's too quiet in here," he growls. "We need a tune, by God. Where the hell is Bouvier? We need his fiddle. Hmmm…Maybe he's back at Augustine's by now." Bardot is quite well into his cups, it seems.

"I believe he carries messages to Murat concerning—" begins one of his comrades.

"To hell with all that. I need a song and I need a girl and I need them now and it's plain I'll get neither one here. Let's go, *mes amis.* Back to Augustine's."

*That was a close one…* I'm thinkin', slowly letting out my breath…*can't afford any more like that.*

In the silence that follows I put my hand on Jean-Paul's. "Come, *mon cher,* let us take up our bottle and go. I still have some time left on my tent rental."

We have already paid for our food and drink, so we do not have to tarry on our way out. We cross the path, and I take his hand to lead him into my tent.

———

Somewhat later, there is a scratching on the outside of the tent and a voice says, "Time, M'sieur."

Our lips part and I catch my breath and say, "You must go, Jean-Paul. I must change and go back."

"I do not want to leave you, Jacqui, not now, not ever, no, I—"

"You must, my dear. We will be missed."

In the dim light, I watch him stand and slowly put on his jacket and rebuckle his sword about his waist. When he is fully dressed he says, "I must have some token...something of you, Jacqui, to carry with me into the fight."

I laugh, laying my head back against the pillow. "Like the knights of old, eh, Sir Jean of the Silken Mustache?"

*How sweet.*

"Very well, my bold chevalier, you shall have my silk scarf as your favor. Here." I stand and scoop it up off the floor where it fell soon after we entered the tent.

He takes it and presses it to his face. From the look in his eyes, I gather there is still some lingering perfume. *I hope you enjoy it, Jean-Paul.*

"One last kiss...*ummmm...oh, yes*...now off with you. We'll meet again, my very good friend, and soon."

He takes a deep breath, lets it out, and stuffs my scarf behind the lapel of his jacket. Then he takes my hand and kisses the back of it, bows, and is gone.

I heave my own great sigh and climb back into my uniform, stuff my dress and wig back in my pouch, then I, too, am out of the tent and making my way back through the bars and brothels from which come much raucous laughter and voices raised in song.

I think about going into Augustine's and meeting up

with Bardot again, but I decide against it and hurry past. I've had enough excitement for one day. *And don't stretch your luck, girl...*

I find that I have already extended it and stretched it very thin, indeed.

I see the tents of my Clodhoppers up ahead, beyond a small stand of trees, and am heading for my own sweet shelter when a hand reaches out from the shadows to grab me by the neck and drag me back into the trees. I see with horror that once again it is the drunken Guards' Sergeant who had tried to force himself upon me a couple of hours before.

He pulls my face up to his and I can smell the cheap rotgut brandy on his breath.

"You dare to touch an officer, man? You will be shot for that!" I bleat.

He grunts and presses his slobbery, whiskery mouth on mine. I jerk back, astounded.

"Officer, huh?" he asks, grinning widely. "I don't see no officer here, *non*. Hee, hee. What I see is a stupid girl. You know why? Because I sat and watched, I did, after your little *pouf* boy stuck his puny sword in my face and you went off with him. Oh, yes, I did, because I've got patience, I do, and I can wait for what I want. And then what did I see? I saw a boy and a girl go into that tent, and yes, I know it was a girl 'cause I seen her *tétons* about to pop out of her dress before. And then, later, the boy comes out. And then, what do you know? I bet you know, don't you? Right. Another *boy* comes out. Hee, hee... Only, it's not a boy, it's *you* that comes out, dearie. What's a poor old Sergeant to think?" He runs his other hand over my tail and squeezes. "What's a poor old Sergeant to do? *Hmmm?*"

*Oh, God!*

"Oh, that's nice, oh yes, it is. Now what you are going to do is get behind that bush and drop your drawers, girl, all the way off, or else I'm gonna tell just about everybody what I know about a certain young officer, and you'll be dead. Think about it. Now get 'em off!"

He reaches for the buttons on his own britches and pushes me farther back into the bushes.

I fall down, then get to my knees and reach for my shiv...but *oh, no,* it is not there. I had decided that there would be no need for it tonight, plus it would interfere with my getting into my female gear, so I left it wrapped up in its sheath in my knapsack.

*Damn! Stupid!*

I think to run so I stumble to my feet, but even if I managed to escape, he would tell, and I would be undone. I see no way out...except to call out...

"*Clodhoppers! To me!*" I cry out, loud enough for my men to hear but not so loud as to alert the other encampments nearby.

"Now what the hell are you going on about, *putain?*" sneers the Sergeant. "You call for help and I'll just let everybody know about you. And they'll join in the fun, too. Now let us get on with it." He takes his hand from his belt and his trousers drop to the top of his gaiters. He shoves me to the ground, then puts his hand on the waist of my pants and tugs and then...

...then there is a dull *thump!* as the butt end of Corporal Laurent's musket hits the back of the Sergeant's head and he pitches forward, out cold as a dead cod.

I struggle away from him and manage to get back to my

feet, as Laurent gives the fallen man's head another solid whack, just to make sure he's out.

"*Tas de merde*," sneers Laurent, sending a gob of spit in the Sergeant's direction.

"Laurent," I ask, regaining my breath and pulling my pants back up, but still despairing of the situation. "What did you hear him say?"

"Hear him say what…M'sieur?" asks Laurent, looking at me with a sly smile. The moonlight glints off the white of his teeth. "*Non*. I heard nothing. Just that drunk *cochon* going on about some…girl or other. Was that it, Lieutenant? Did you take his girl and he did not like it?"

"Um…" is all I can come up with. I have come to know that Laurent is sharp, very sharp indeed. I also know that now…he *knows*…and so do the others. He then gives a low whistle and the other poachers—Guerrette, Vedel, and Michaud—appear from the bushes, their muskets at Trail Arms, and they gather around me.

"Ah, well…Still, he shouldn't have messed with an officer," says Laurent. "He could be shot for that, or, at the very least, brought up on charges."

But we look at each other and both know that cannot happen. If the Sergeant is arrested, he will tell, and then it will be me who is shot, not him.

"What to do, Laurent?" I ask, realizing that my life is now in his hands, and in the hands of my men.

"Do not worry, Lieutenant. If it pleases you, go to your tent. We will take care of this."

"Why would you do this for me, lads," I ask, suddenly very weary, "knowing what you know?"

"Who else would we want to lead us? Something like that?" says Laurent, kicking the leg of the man who lies in the dirt at our feet. "*Non.* We will stick with you, Lieutenant, till the end."

"Thank you, all of you," I say, and turn away. What must be done will be done, I know that; but I don't really want to know what is going to happen to the Sergeant. Not now, anyway.

I look down and notice that my drummer boy orderly is here, too, and that he has missed nothing. *Christ!* I heave a great sigh and throw my arm around his thin shoulders and say, "Let us go to our beds, Denis Dufour. It has been a long, *long* day."

*Uh...hullo, Jaimy...I hope you are getting well and would not be too disappointed in me and how I have been behaving. Y'see, we go into battle soon, and who knows what's gonna happen? Both Jean-Paul and my own poor self could be lyin' dead on some German field tomorrow. So, a glass of wine in a dismal bar, and just a few kisses here...and, well, there, too... what does it hurt? It ain't like I gave myself totally to him, no, Jaimy, not that. I'm still your lass till you tell me differently. But there are other games of love that two people who like each other a lot can play...really, just a little of me and my usual messing around...you know...oh, never mind. But...I gotta say this about Jean-Paul de Valdon—never have I been handled more gently, never have I been touched with more tenderness and love.*

*G'night, Jaimy. I pray daily for your recovery. And I have been good...well, mostly.*

# Chapter 38

It took us three days to get our Grand Army across the river, but, at last, we did it. It is the twelfth of October, and I realize with a shiver that the battle is getting closer.

Bardot, nursing what seems is a hangover of heroic proportions, rides by my side for a while as we drive into Germany.

"Damn, Bouvier, where were you last night?" he grumps.

"Otherwise occupied, in *affaires d'amour, mon Capitaine,*" I say, not entirely lying, for once.

"Well, good. I hope she was sweet. Damn! My head feels like it's going to explode!"

I reach back into my knapsack and pull out a bottle, draw the cork, and hand it to him.

"Here, my good Captain Bardot. One good swig and no more, else you shall fall out of your saddle and be shamed."

"What is it?"

"A simple palliative. You will see. One swallow, then hand it back. On your honor."

"Um. Like candy," he says, after taking a healthy slug and handing back the bottle.

"Others have said that," I say, stuffing it back in my sack.

It was a mixture of Bottle Number One and Number Two from my room back at 127, rue de Londres in Paris. The two policemen did not drink it all, so before I left I combined the contents of the two bottles to take with me.

"Matter of love, eh?" asks the rapidly improving Captain Bardot. "Say, you wouldn't happen to have a sister, would you?"

"A sister, M'sieur?" *Uh, oh* ... I give a slight cough and say, "Yes, actually my twin. Her name is Amy. But she is far away, back in America."

A puzzled look comes over his face, as if he were trying to remember something. "I wouldn't be quite so sure of that, Bouvier."

Just then General Charpentier's aide-de-camp rides up and hands me a message. "For *l'Empereur*. And hurry." I take it and am off at a brisk canter, grateful for the interruption of *that* conversation.

On my order, my squad of Clodhoppers has kept the five horses we took from the Prussian cavalry, and the poachers, my elite corps, has, well ... acquired ... a wagon from somewhere and we have hitched two of the horses to it to carry all our tents and gear. Now my men do not have to carry heavy bundles on their backs, and for that they are most grateful. Happy, too, is Papa Boule, who gets to ride in the wagon as well—he was having trouble keeping up with the march, and I know it distressed him to know that he was slowing us down.

Of the other horses, Laurent claims one for himself, and that is as it should be, because he is the corporal. The other two horses are passed about among the men, so that each can ride at least part of the time.

Denis Dufour drives the wagon, and I know he takes great pride in it. Part of that job is finding grain and suitable grazing for the horses at night, and he has managed to do it.

None of them has yet said a word about that night with the Guards' Sergeant, but I notice that the poachers pitch their tents very close to mine now and Dufour has gotten himself a pistol and he sleeps with it close by his side. Before I climb into my own bedroll for the night, I make sure his weapon is on half cock so he doesn't hurt himself with it.

Today, I call Laurent to my side and we ride along together for a bit. Then I ask him straight out. "What did you do with the Sergeant? I do have to know."

He grins, his long, straight brown hair blowing about his face. "Well…M'sieur…you know we were right close to the river at that camp. So what we did was pick him up, throw him across a horse, and take him down there to get rid of him."

I stiffen. *Have I caused yet another death? Is this one more mark against my soul?*

It turns out it is not.

"The bridge builders had a lot of rafts down there, but since they were done with their job, we figured they didn't need them anymore and they surely wouldn't miss just one, so we loaded the Sergeant on a small one, cut it loose, and sent him off down the river."

"Was he alive when you did that?"

"*Oui.* He started to come to, so we whacked him again,

and then took some rope and tied him spread-eagle on the logs. He's probably about twenty miles downstream by now."

I begin to relax a bit. "Very crafty, Laurent," I say, smiling in appreciation of his cleverness.

He chuckles. "Right. When he gets off that raft, he'll be deep in German territory, wearing a French uniform. How he will explain that, I do not know. Nor care."

Now that we are close to the day of battle, almost all of my duty consists of carrying messages to Napoléon, and orders from him to his commanders, as he is, without question, the center of command. When I ride up to the column he is in, I see other messengers coming in from all directions, and I know they bear intelligence reports on the situation as it develops. Based on the intelligence that is being gathered, the Emperor has divided his force, sending Marshals Davout and Bernadotte, with their III Corps and I Corps, north toward a place called Auerstädt, while the rest of the force, including me and my Clodhoppers, drive toward a town called Jena, with Marshal Lannes's V Corps in the lead. I know all this because I was there as the orders were given.

Today, as Mathilde and I clatter up with the message from General Charpentier, I can see the Emperor riding at the head of his Imperial Guard. I get in as close as I can and wave the message over my head, and I am called forward to place the sealed letter in an officer's hand. Then I pull Mathilde over to the side to trot along and await further orders. I see the officer reading the message, whereupon he kicks up his horse and falls in next to Napoléon. He speaks to him and the Emperor nods, and then, incredibly, looks over at me and motions me to approach.

"Our bold young American," he says, as I draw close. "I remember you."

"Th-thank you, Excellency," I stammer.

"I do not want to stop to have a message written out. You are known to me now. Simply ride to Murat and inform him that we have received word that Marshal Lannes is about to take the town of Jena, and that he is to have his cavalry ready to move on my order. Do you have that, Lieutenant?"

"Aye, Sir...er...Yes, Your Excellency."

"Good. Then go."

I wheel Mathilde around and gallop off, gasping for breath.

Within an hour I am in Marshal Murat's camp. He is far enough ahead of the others to be able to stop and bivouac.

"I have a message from the Emperor for Marshal Murat," I announce to his aide-de-camp.

"Then hand it over."

"I cannot. It is verbal. The Emperor was busy and could not stop to have a message written out."

The officer raises his eyebrows. "You have come a long way on this campaign, Lieutenant, to be trusted so," he says, and then waves me into Murat's tent. I take off my shako and go in.

The Marshal sits at his table, having dinner with several of his officers. He looks up and says, "Ah. Our very small messenger. Bouvier, is it? Well, what news, Lieutenant?"

"My compliments, Sir, and the Emperor has directed me to tell you that Marshal Lannes is about to take the town of

Jena, and he requests that you have your fine cavalry ready to move on his order."

"Ha!" says Murat, striking the table with his fist. "That is very good news! We are about to be in it now, for sure! Gentlemen, stand to your glasses. Steward, a glass for our young Mercury!"

A glass of wine is quickly put in my hand.

"To victory," cries Murat, raising his glass.

"To victory," we all echo, and drain our glasses.

I am dismissed and told to return to my unit, as Murat has no further messages to send this day.

I get back on my long-suffering Mathilde, pat her neck, and promise her rest and oats very shortly. I start back to the Sixteenth Fusiliers at an easy trot. I'm thinking about getting something to eat myself and just what I would give for a good hot bath, when another rider comes up and falls in beside me on my left.

I look at him and say, "Jean-Paul. It is so good to see you, but be careful. We are out in the open here."

"I know," he says. "I just want to ride here beside you for a while." I notice that he wears my silk scarf about his neck. "And I want to tell you that yesterday was the greatest day of my life, and that I love you and I will—"

"You will what, Frenchy?"

*Uh-oh.*

Another rider has joined us, pulling up on my right, and speaking in English. I see Jean-Paul's eyes flash in anger as he reaches for his sword.

"No, Jean-Paul, don't. He…he is an old friend, from back in the States." *Damn! Just what I need!*

"An 'old friend'? Is that all I am to you, Jacky?" asks Randall Trevelyne. "I am wounded to the core."

I sigh and say, "Lieutenant Jean-Paul de Valdon, may I present Lieutenant Randall Trevelyne. Randall, Jean-Paul."

"Not necessary, Jacky, my dear. You see, we know each other, as we are in the same division, same Officer's Mess. Pity. We were actually becoming friends. Until this."

It is plain that Jean-Paul does not like this intrusion, and it is equally obvious that Randall knows that full well.

"So, Valdon, what mischief has she been up to this time? You been getting any of this?" says Randall, hooking his thumb in my direction. "Hmmm?"

Jean-Paul, while not entirely fluent in English, gets the sense of what Randall has just said. Randall caps his little speech by reaching over and putting his hand on my upper thigh.

"Get your filthy hand off her!" cries Jean-Paul, enraged. His sword comes all the way out now, as does Randall's. They wheel their horses about to face each other, swords raised.

"What, Froggy?" taunts Randall. "You think your hand is the only one that has been there?"

"Randall," I hiss. "You are going to ruin everything! You are going to get me killed! Please! Back off, both of you! Jean-Paul, please, I beg you!" I bury my face in my hands and start bawling. *Oh, God! Two of my dearest friends in all this world are going to destroy me!* I cry out in despair.

Their swords cross, but my tears drain the fight right out of them. They stick the swords back in their sheaths and just sit in their saddles, glaring at each other.

I snort back my tears and plead, "Please, Randall…Jean-Paul…please go back to your division. Please be friends. Please. For me."

With that, I kick up Mathilde and gallop back to the Sixteenth Fusiliers, the Clodhoppers, and my tent, leaving my two young men behind me, their heads down. I need a drink, some food, and a good dose of Bardot's cheerful company.

# Chapter 39

This morning, as I crawl out of my tent and stretch, I look about and see nothing but mist, a deep gray fog, all around me. Dufour strikes the tent, rolls it up, and stows it in the wagon with the others.

After we all eat, I say, "All right. Let's go, boys," and we move out with the rest of the Grand Army of France.

"Looks like we'll be in it soon, Bouvier," says Captain Bardot. We both hear the distant rumble of artillery to the north.

"It does, indeed, Sir." My usual cowardly butterflies begin their fluttering in my belly. I reassure myself that, as a messenger, I will not be on the front line of battle, but, rather, back at command posts, and so, pretty safe.

Once again, we are approached by a rider. *Here I go again...*

"You, Bouvier. Report to the Emperor's staff. He is much in need of messengers. Don't expect to come back till the battle is over. Go now."

"*Oui*, M'sieur," I say, as the rider pulls his horse's head over and is off.

Bardot chuckles as he pulls out yet another long thin cigar from inside his jacket and lights it—he seems to have an inexhaustible supply of the vile things. "Looks like things are going to get hot, Bouvier. Very hot, indeed."

I nod and say to him, "My men will be attached to your unit. Please look out for them as best you can."

"Of course. No evil, hard-nosed Sergeant for Bouvier's Own, by God! I will assign them to my best man." He grins around his cigar and sticks out his hand and I take it. "Good luck, Jacques. You are a good lad."

"And you have been just the best of company, Sir," I say, giving his hand what I hope is a manly squeeze, my own small hand feeling puny in his grasp. *"Bonne chance. Adieu, Capitaine Bardot."*

I turn Mathilde around and return to my Clodhoppers, who struggle along the uneven road. Laurent looks at me expectantly as I come upon them.

I pull up next to him and lean over so that only he can hear what I have to say. "Laurent. I am being sent off. You are the leader now, so be a good one and watch out for your men. Place your poachers where they will do the most good. And especially take care of the boy. For me, you will do this?"

Laurent looks me in the eye. *"Oui,* I will do that, yes." He sits up straight on his mount and looks back over his troops, then he turns his gaze to me. "You, too...M'sieur... be careful of yourself. You are small, yet a bullet could still find you. And men are not the only ones who die in war."

I look at him for a while, sizing up the man. *Ah, Laurent, you are a sly one. In another place and time, perhaps when on my ship the* Emerald, *one such as you would have made the very finest Captain of my Marines, but no, we are not there, and we never will be. We are here.* I shake those thoughts out of my head and just smile and say, "Thank you, Laurent. I will address the lads now."

I pull Mathilde to the center of the squad and I say, "Men, I have been detached to the Emperor's staff until the war is over. You are assigned to Captain Bardot's company—he's up ahead. See, that is him right there. Follow him and he will tell you where to go and what to do. I will try to get back to you after the fighting is done. Dufour, my knapsack and bedroll, please. Thank you, lad. And please, Denis, don't look so downhearted."

I ruffle the boy's hair as he ties my gear to the back of my saddle. He is not happy with this, I know.

"*Au revoir,* you pack of ignorant plowboys. I could not have found better men to serve with!" I say in parting, "We shall meet again, I just know it! *Vive les Clodhoppers! Vive la France!*"

I pull my shako down low over my eyes and leave then so they won't see the tears about to spill.

As I ride away, I hear their cheer of *Vive la France! Vive Lieutenant Bouvier!*

Reporting to Napoléon's staff, I am assigned to a pool of messengers. All of them are like me—young and small and quick. We ride alongside the moving column in a group, and when our names are called, we ride forward to take our orders and then are off at the gallop. There are six of us here now—others are off on their missions. We talk among ourselves as we wait to get news from the riders as they return.

*I hear Lannes has moved the V Corps...*

*Yes, but where's Bernadotte and the I Corps? I hear the Emperor is furious!*

*They say the Prussians have over a hundred thousand men!*

*Who cares? We have ninety thousand right here in Jena! And one of ours is worth two of them!*

*Wish this damned fog would lift. Can't see a thing!*

We try to outguess the generals and marshals to impress each other with our military expertise and personal bravado, but I know it is all for nothing—it is all rumor, all the fog of war. Me, I just sit astride Mathilde and wait. I have the feeling it is going to be a very long day, and an even longer night.

One who is not impressed with any of us is a certain Colonel Dupré, Napoléon's communications officer. He has a short temper and a very sharp bark, and he is in charge of us messengers. He is coming up to us now.

"Genet, take this to Marshal Ney at VI Corps. Wait for his reply," orders Dupré, handing the letter to the lad next to me and then turning to another. "Beaulac, deliver this to Marshal Murat. Both of you get back as fast as you can. Move it!"

The two shoot off like scared rabbits.

*Too bad... I would like to have been chosen to go on the Murat errand—I might have been able to see Jean-Paul for a bit. And maybe Randall, too... Ah, well, it's probably for the best.*

Napoléon's carriage is right over there. Messages are passed into the windows and written orders are handed out and taken up by the designated messengers to be delivered.

The dust has barely settled after their departure when another rider, this one from the north, pounds up to the carriage and submits a letter. Then he comes to join us.

"Marshal Lannes has encountered the Prussians and bloodied their noses, by God! He has occupied the town of Jena and awaits further orders from *l'Empereur*!" the messenger shouts, panting from the excitement and the exertions of his travel. His horse is clearly exhausted.

A minute later Colonel Dupré is handed a message from the carriage and cries out, "Bouvier!"

I give Mathilde a nudge and hurry over.

"To Marshal Lannes! In Jena, about ten miles ahead. It is of the utmost importance! While you are there, take your instructions from the Marshal's staff! Go!" he shouts, giving me the letter. I put it in my pouch, salute, and charge off.

It takes me over an hour to reach the headquarters of V Corps. There was dense fog all of the way, and I was glad of the cover—I would hate to be picked off by a Prussian skirmisher. I was well ahead of the Army and in open country, having passed through Murat's screening cavalry on my way. I looked for Jean-Paul but did not see him. I did, however, catch a glimpse of Randall in Murat's camp and waved to him as I thundered through. He recognized me and waved back, shaking his head over the unlikelihood of seeing Jacky Faber, Soldier, Sailor, Beggar, Spy, galloping through a French army camp in Germany. *Yes, Randall, it is, indeed, a bewildering world.*

I deliver the communication to an officer on Lannes's staff, and I am told to stand by for further orders. After looking over the message, he calls for his horse and is gone. Apparently the Marshal is off somewhere else.

Well, good. I didn't want to be sent right back, for Mathilde's sake. I take advantage of the wait to rest the poor girl and to find her some food. Looking about, I see a stable nearby so I take her there, where I manage to hustle up a good drink of water and some oats for her. Then I look around for something to eat myself.

It is strange being in a town again, I'm thinking, as I cast my eyes about.

Lannes has taken over an inn as his headquarters and I'm thinking, *what the hell,* and wander in. Amazingly, I am not stopped and thrown out but instead find a table loaded with food and drink. There are not many people around, most of the staff probably being at Lannes's side, wherever that is, so I help myself.

I'm halfway through my third sausage, first loaf of bread, and second glass of some really excellent Rhine wine when there's a great clatter outside.

*Uh, oh . . .* My Street-Urchin Alarm goes off, so I proceed to cram the remainder of the provisions into my mouth, chewing and swallowing as quickly as I can without choking.

A man, who, by the grandness of his uniform and the dignity of his bearing, must be Marshal Lannes himself, strides in, followed by his staff. "The fog has lifted! We can see them!" he announces to those of us in the room, and there is a cheer. "We must inform *l'Empereur*! Quick, Lucerne, get out your ink and pen and write!"

"Where's that damned messenger?" grumbles the officer I had seen before.

"Right here, Sir," I mumble, my cheeks full of cheese. I make a sort of bow.

"Well, good. Put down that glass and go get your horse and be ready."

"*Oui*, M'sieur," I answer, managing to get one more slug of the wine down my neck. "Right away."

As I exit the place, I hear Marshal Lannes dictating:

"*Excellency, the fog has lifted, and from a hill above the town, we are able to make out at least forty thousand Prussian troops spread out on the plateau east of this town. I believe we are in excellent position to—*"

And then I don't hear any more because I am outside, getting my Mathilde ready for yet another arduous ride. I pick up the reins and give her lovely muzzle a bit of a rub, because I know she likes it. I'd managed to stuff my pocket with a couple of apples from a plate on that table so I hold one up to her mouth and she takes it ever so gently.

"Come on, girl, one more ride. Yes, I know, it's hard, but we must do it. Good girl. Let's go…"

An hour later we pull up next to the Emperor's coach. I don't see Colonel Dupré so I just pass the letter through an open window. A hand takes it and a face looks up at me. *Oh, God…no, I ain't all that blasé yet.*

I retreat to the messenger pool to give them the news, and there is great excitement.

*Forty thousand Prussians!*

*Don't worry, we shall take them!*

*It must be tomorrow!*

*It will be tomorrow!*

*Glory for all!*

I don't say anything. I just dismount to give Mathilde a bit of a rest and lean my face into her heaving sides. *Good girl…*

———

After a short while the conversation stops as we see Bona-parte's spirited gray Arabian stallion, Marengo, brought up. The door of the carriage opens and *l'Empereur* steps out. He mounts his horse and announces to us gathered about him, "The veil has lifted. We march to Jena."

It's plain that nobody's gonna get any sleep this night. And I know with a terrible certainty that for many…this will be their last night on this earth.

I shudder and turn to my duties.

# Chapter 40

We have been on forced march since the Emperor received that message from Marshal Lannes. He gave the order to move forward and move forward we did—all that night the Army was crammed into narrow ravines, marched through woods and over endless hills and fields. The worst of it was when we had to grope our way in the dark along the edge of a precipice, keeping complete silence, for we knew the enemy was near. Incredibly, on one of my return trips, I saw the Emperor, himself, holding up a lantern and personally supervising repair work on a road so that his artillery could pass. The light shone on his face as he directed his engineers, most of whom were mere common soldiers. It is an image I shall never forget, should I live through this. In one of my few idle moments, I've tried to imagine our King George doing that, but, of course, could not.

Our pool of riders has been provided with fresh horses so my Mathilde will be given a much-needed rest. Loyal and steadfast as she has been, there are times, I'm sure, when she wishes she were back in her snug stall in Paris. I'm thinking that 127, rue de Londres, room number seven wouldn't look too bad to me, either. And a nice cup of coffee and a plump croissant at *Café des Deux Chats* along with maybe a steaming plate of…*stop that, you. Here's another message slapped in your hand, so mount up and get back to work.*

I wonder and worry about where my Clodhoppers are in all this seeming confusion. And Randall…and Bardot… and…

…and Jean-Paul de Valdon. Ah, yes, I do manage to see him once more this night. As I am galloping out of Murat's camp with yet another report to the Emperor on his Cavalry's state of readiness, I spy another rider, who is spurring his horse to follow me, and I know that it is he.

He pulls up beside me and says one word, "Jacqui," and I answer with the same brevity—"Jean-Paul," but it is enough. It's a dark, moonless night, so we dare a kiss on horseback, each leaning over into the other on our mounts.

"You be careful now, do you hear me?" I warn, as our lips part. I put the palms of my hands to either side of his face. "No stupid heroics. No seeking of empty glory. Please, Jean-Paul, promise me…"

"Yes, I promise," he says, his breath coming as ragged as mine. "But what about you?"

"Don't worry about me. I know how to keep my head down and my tail covered. I've been doing it all my life. Now, one more kiss and I must fly."

I leave my palms on his smooth cheeks while I bring my mouth once again to his and flick my tongue between his lips and then *oh, God!* and then I push him away. *We can't be doing this.*

"*Adieu,* Jean-Paul," I say, turning my horse's head. "Go with God. My prayers are with you."

"And mine with you, Jacqui. I have never loved anyone as I have loved you. If I go to my grave, I go there happy, having known such as you."

I put my fingers to his lips. *Hush, now*...and we part there in the blackness of the night.

When I return to the Emperor, I see that his tent has been set up and he is in it. *Well, I guess this long night is at last over.* I turn in the horse I have been riding and reclaim Mathilde. I find a patch of grass, tie her reins to my ankle, and lie down on the ground beside her.

I am instantly asleep.

# Chapter 41

*James Fletcher*
*On Board the* Nancy B. Alsop *and*
*Under Way with All Sails Set*

*Dear Jacky,*

*Something is afoot. Higgins returned from a meeting at the Admiralty in a state of, for him, high agitation.*

"We must be away," he says. "We are to take station off a certain desolate coast of France. Our American registry and colors will protect us from any interference, America still being neutral in this conflict. More than that, Captain Fletcher, I am not at liberty to say. Except that an arrangement has been made and we just might be getting our girl back, at least for a while."

I, myself, throw the first line off, and the ship's bell is rung and the *Nancy B* is off.

*I can only hope.*

*Jaimy*

# Chapter 42

With a groan I turn over and open my eyes. It is dawn and Mathilde is munching the grass next to my cheek, and for a moment I think I am back on Boston Common, dozing in the tall grass as my dear Gretchen grazes nearby. I reach up and stroke her muzzle, and then it comes to me that I am not there in some peaceful meadow but rather here on the edge of what is sure to be a battlefield that will soon be soaked in blood. I sit up and rub my eyes. I figure I've been asleep for maybe an hour, two at most.

Looking about, I see that the Emperor is already awake, standing next to a table his aide-de-camp has set up. His tent has been struck, and Marengo, saddled, stands by. I get to my feet and try to make myself presentable.

Messages are flying in and flying out, but a heavy fog once again covers everything. Napoléon clasps his hands behind him and looks out into the mist.

"It has been a good thing, this fog," I hear him say to the officers who stand by his side. "It has covered our movements. Now, if it'll oblige us and just go away..."

I can't see much of anything beyond fifty feet. But then

again, the Prussians can't see me, either, so I figure that's all to the good.

Since nothing is happening, except some far-off thuds of cannon fire—they must be shooting at shadows in this thick mist, for surely they can see nothing—I head off and get something to eat. The sound of the artillery sets my cowardly belly butterflies to fluttering again, and I need to calm them.

A table has been set up with steaming pots of coffee and plates of hot food, and I reflect that it is a good thing to be even a very junior member of the Emperor's staff. *Ummm...what is this? Goose liver pâté spread on a warm slice of bread...ummm...The mind worries, and the heart yearns, ah, but the belly rules.* The coffee is hot and good and it restores me.

As I am stuffing it all in, I feel a presence beside me. *Oh, Lord.*

I edge nervously away, trying to make myself invisible, but he notices me and says, "No, lad. Stay and eat." He reaches down and takes something for himself. A servant hands him a cup and he drinks. "Bouvier, is it not?" he says, looking down at me. "Are you not the one who captured the first Prussian flag? Ah, I thought so. I am glad you are still with us. Eat. You will need your strength later." He lifts his cup to me and says, "Soldiers of France, all of us, eh?"

I gulp and nod and raise my own cup, my hand shaking such that some of the coffee sloshes over the rim.

"It is to be devoutly hoped," says Napoléon to the officers that surround him, "that when the mist clears, we will all be in proper position."

Murmurs of assent are heard and then, as if on cue at a Fennel and Bean Production of *Macbeth*, the curtain is pulled aside, the rising sun burns into the fog, thinning it, while a good breeze sweeps the rest of it suddenly away.

"Now that is *much* better," I hear Napoléon remark, plainly pleased with what he sees.

I can only gasp as I look on the Plain of Jena. There are ranks upon ranks, divisions upon divisions—battalions stretching out in every direction—shining helmets and breastplates, lances, muskets, cannons. *Oh God, it's gonna be murder!*

The Emperor reaches out his hand and a long glass is put in it. He raises it to his eye. I reassure myself once again— *You are only a messenger... You will deliver the messages and then you will get out of the way when the real fighting starts. That's what will happen... calm down, you.*

"So. The Prussians have massed themselves there. Very well. We must force them into the open." He turns to his aide-de-camp. "Message to Marshal Lannes: Attack Close-witz now, and take it. Message to Marshal Augereau: Wheel the VII Corps left and make for Cospeda. Message to Marshal Soult: Support Lannes's right flank."

He snaps his long glass shut as the orders are written out, sealed with the Imperial stamp in hot blue wax, and handed to the messengers to be delivered. I have come to know my fellow gallopers during the long night past—there goes Charles, and then Émile, and now Hercule. I am not one of those chosen to deliver these messages, but I get on Mathilde and wait, for I know it will be my turn soon.

The deep boom of artillery begins, and it comes from both sides. Napoléon clasps his hands behind him and says,

"We have ninety thousand men. They have a hundred thousand. We shall see."

*Oh, my God...Almost two hundred thousand men...Yes, and boys, too...Denis Dufour is out there somewhere with the rest of the Clodhoppers—two hundred thousand standing on this plain, ready to do their best to kill one another!*

All seems to be going the way Napoléon wants it to go, and that gives me some comfort, but then, in the midst of all the trumpet calls, the shouted orders in the field, the hammering of the artillery, there comes one single trumpet call and the Emperor's head jerks up at the sound and the long glass is again to his eye. The unmistakable trumpet call was for a frontal assault—a charge.

"Damn! The impetuous fool!" He snaps his glass closed and turns to his staff. "Without orders, Marshal Ney has charged the Prussian lines from the center! It is too soon. The Prussians will close upon him and the VI Corps will be overwhelmed! Damn!" The Emperor of all France bites his knuckle, thinking. Then he straightens and looks directly at me.

"You there! Messenger! You know Murat, and he knows you?"

"*Oui,* Excellency," I say, nudging Mathilde over to him.

"You know what has just happened?"

"*Oui,* Excellency."

"Good. No time for long written orders. Take this seal..." His aide-de-camp takes a stamp and presses the Imperial *N* into a ball of hot blue wax on a piece of paper. I see the wax squishing out to the side of the stamp as Napoléon takes a pen and scrawls his signature and the word *Charge.* "...and inform Murat of Ney's rash move and tell him that

I order him to immediately charge the Prussian lines with his Reserve Cavalry. Lannes and Augereau will move forward on his flanks. Do you have that?"

"*Oui*, Excellency."

"Good," he says, taking the seal from his man and pressing it into my hand. "Fly, Lieutenant, as fast as you can."

I shove the Imperial Seal in my jacket front, turn Mathilde's head, and pound off.

There is a curious quiet on the field as I gallop across the plateau toward Murat and his cavalry. Yes, there is the far-off thump of artillery, but I see no effect here, and as I ride worrisome thoughts begin to worm into my mind, thoughts I know I should have dealt with long ago but did not.

*Just whose side am I on? I was sent here as a spy to benefit my own country, and here I am with a message that could change the outcome of this battle. Napoléon has caused the death of thousands, and he will probably be responsible for the deaths of thousands more. If I do not deliver this message, Murat will not charge and Ney's Corps will be destroyed and that might cause the whole battle to be lost. I have a woman's dress and wig in my knapsack and I could change direction and head for the rear of the Army and change back into a girl and then no one would take me for a deserter. I could easily make it back to Paris…or maybe somewhere else. I have money—I could head to some northern port and book passage back to London…back to Jaimy…Damn! I just don't know!*

I go across the front of Lannes's V Corps and see that they are not yet ready to move, and there, on the near edge of the massive formation of twenty-two thousand men, I spy the Clodhoppers. *Oh, Lord, there's Dufour with his* drum. And Laurent off to the side. And, yes, there, in charge of several companies is Bardot, mounted, with a cigar clamped in his teeth.

What I do know is that if I fail to deliver the message, the Prussians, after they dispose of Ney, will charge over that low ridge, and the poor Clodhoppers will be slaughtered... my men will be butchered.

No. I cannot let that happen. Call me a traitor, if you must, but I will deliver the message.

I spur on Mathilde to go faster. *Come on, girl, give me your best now.*

Often Murat and his Reserve Cavalry are referred to as Napoléon's Bloodhounds because of their ferocity in tracking down and harassing the Emperor's enemies, who are generally skirmishing on the edges of the infantry. This time, however, the cavalry must charge straight down the center, and it's gonna be bloody.

Murat had his fourteen thousand men arrayed as a blunt wedge, with himself at the point, with three ranks of heavy cavalry behind and the Light Cavalry on either side. I spot Jean-Paul as I ride up, and I know he sees me, for he lightly fingers my scarf, which he wears about his neck. Murat, the brave idiot, will lead the charge himself with his staff beside him. *And there, of course, as a member of that staff, is Randall Trevelyne.*

I catch his eye and he mine as I pull up to Murat. *Oh, Randall, you always wanted to see what it was like and you're gonna find out right now, and I hope with all my heart that you live through it, but this is gonna be such awful, horrible carnage, I just know it!*

I whip out the Imperial Seal and hand it to him. "From *l'Empereur*! Marshal Ney has charged the Prussian line and will be trapped without your help! Lannes and Augereau have been ordered to attack on your flanks! You must attack up the center! Now!"

Murat calmly takes the seal from me and then hands it back. "Take this and put it back in your coat. I have many of these, and it will be something for you to show your grandchildren." There is a good breeze now, and it blows his curly hair about his face. He smiles. "Ney has jumped the gun, eh? I thought he might do such a thing someday. He is brave, but he is also a fool." He shakes his head. "Well, we shall see if we can save his foolish *derrière*."

I thrust the waxed seal back in my jacket and prepare to take myself off, but such is not to be.

"We ride to glory," says Murat, preparing to give the orders, "and you, young Bouvier, shall ride by my side, for I will need a messenger to inform the Emperor of our great victory when the battle is won! There will be glory enough for all!"

*What? Glory?* I think, stricken and starting to shake. *Just what I wanted. To die a hero for France.* If I had planned to slink off to the side and wait this thing out in relative safety, I was dead wrong in thinking that, for it is not going to happen. I'm caught up in it now and I know there is no escape. Ninety thousand Frenchmen on this plain…and Jean-Paul…and Randall…and my Clodhoppers…and me… and one hundred thousand Prussians over there. *Oh, Lord, what am I doing here?*

"CAVALERIE…," bellows Murat, and his voice rolls across the still eerily silent battlefield. The man next to us has a guidon, a regimental flag, and he thrusts the staff straight up, so all of the fourteen thousand Reserve Cavalry can see, and all down the line I can hear the generals, in charge of their regiments, and then the colonels with their companies, echoing the preparatory command, and so the impending order is passed down to the ranks. "SLOW... MARCH!" Beside Murat is a trumpeter who trills out a series of notes, and we all kick up our mounts and move forward as a mass. I can see the Fusilier columns of Lannes and Augereau moving up beside us as we go, twenty-two thousand in Lannes's V Corps, twenty thousand with Augereau's VII Corps.

"DRAW...," shouts Murat, and the guidon goes back up and the echoing calls go out again. "...SWORDS!" The flagstaff whips down and fourteen thousand sabers come hissing out of their scabbards. With a barely suppressed sob, mine comes out, too. Poor, pathetic little pig sticker... and poor, pitiful little Jacky Faber, whiner, deceiver, and abject coward who is about to charge into the ranks of one hundred thousand Prussians at the side of Marshal Murat.

"IN ORDER OF RANKS... ADVANCE..." Murat raises his sword high above his head and fourteen thousand horses and their riders change from the trot to the gallop and the plain thunders with the sound of their hooves as they surge forward.

"*POUR LA FRANCE*... CHARGE!"

And we gallop toward the waiting Prussians, swords on high.

Their artillery, which up till now has been mostly silent, begins to spit out flame and smoke and death, and, dimly, I hear our own cannons dealing out the same. I hear screams of horses and men both as the shells slam into us on either side, but we keep driving on. Terrified beyond thought, I see the ranks of the Prussians getting closer and closer, and I sense, rather than see, someone beside me, but I know it is Randall and *Oh, Randall, we are surely far from Dovecote now!*

The part of my mind that is still working says to me, *Rein in a bit, girl! Fall back to the second rank! No one will think less of you for it!* And I start to do it, pulling back on the reins ever so slightly to let the first rank pass me by. *I'm sorry, Randall, you will see me for the coward I really am, but I don't care. I just want us all out of this. I just—*

But I don't get to fade back at all. Up ahead, I can see a platoon of Prussian Fusiliers raising their muskets and pointing them at me and *Oh, God, no!* and they fire and my shako is torn off my head, to dangle by the chin strap at my neck, but no bullet thuds into me *thank you, God!* but that ain't the end of it, oh, no, 'cause Mathilde screams as one hits her on her left flank and she, in pain like she has never felt before, tears off straight for the Prussian lines. *No, Mathilde, not that way! The other way!* but I can't turn her head, no, she won't listen, and so, with my sword still held up, I pull out ahead of Murat's cavalry, screeching at the top of my lungs in absolute and complete terror, and plunge through the Prussians' first rank of soldiers.

Having shot off their first round, the Prussian Fusiliers are hurriedly reloading as I burst into their midst, and one of them has the presence of mind, when he sees me there among them, to reverse his hold on his musket and swing it like a club at my head. I lift my sword to deflect it, but I do not have the strength to turn the heavy musket butt and it hits me and I am knocked sideways out of my saddle.

My back is on the ground and I look up to see the Prussian soldier, his musket again turned in his hands so to present not the butt with which he had knocked me out of the saddle but the gleaming bayonet at the other end. He lifts it and prepares to plunge it into my helpless gut as I put my hands up in a fruitless effort to ward off the descent of that awful blade that will end my life...*please, no!*...but I know it ain't gonna serve...*oh, God, help me, please!*...and then the soldier's neck spouts a fountain of blood as a saber comes down upon him. *Randall? You?*...and then the rest of the Cavalry comes roaring through and there are more shouts and shrieks of pain and agony and cries for mercy, but there is little of that to be had and then...

*CRASH!*

There is a shattering blast of an artillery shell right next to me, and for a moment I know nothing but even more confusion and terror. Then I come to my senses enough to know that my right foot is caught in my stirrup as Mathilde, still crazed, is running away, and I am being dragged across the ground. I reach up to try to get my foot loose, but it's wedged in there and I can't...I can't...

And then my head bounces against something hard and I can't see...I can't hear...I can't...and then comes an almost welcome, warm, velvety...

Darkness.

# Chapter 43

"Is she dead?"

"No. Not yet, anyway. I can hear her heart beating." Through the pain that pulsates through my head like the tolling of a cathedral bell, I can tell that a head is laid on my chest. "And stop calling the lieutenant *she*, Dufour, you stupid little blabbermouth! You'll get her...*him*...in trouble!"

I manage a groan. *Oooh, my poor head!*

"Look! She's comin' around."

I open my eyes and see that it is Corporal Laurent's ear that has been pressed to my breastbone to listen for signs of life.

"Lieutenant Bouvier...Can you hear me?"

"Yes...I can, Laurent. Thank you. Please...help me up."

I feel his strong arm slide under my shoulders and he pulls me up such that I might sit to look about me, and dazed though I am, I realize I am in the back of the Clodhoppers' wagon, with Papa Boule up forward on the reins and the men grouped about me while Dufour is holding my hand and...

...and there are two still forms next to me, their faces covered with their uniform jackets.

"Who?" I ask, dreading the answer.

"Dubois and Vedel," says Laurent. "A shell exploded next to them. They died instantly. Chaisson was wounded."

*Oh, God, please take them to you, for they were good boys... And spare Chaisson, if you can, for he is a good boy, too.*

I rub my eyes as I look out over the land, and all I can see is mile upon mile of dead soldiers lying still on the ground. Some French, but many, many more Prussian. It is so curiously quiet. I can even hear birds sing, and it seems so strange to hear them trilling on this killing field.

"The engineers are digging trenches for the dead, over there," remarks Laurent, pointing.

I look over to see men toiling at shovels and picks and others stripping the dead of their jackets and weapons and tossing their bodies into the end of the trench as fast as it can be dug.

"We were going to take ours over there, too," says Laurent. "Do you so order?"

"*Non,*" I say, digging into my pocket for some coins. "Our men shall not be buried in a common grave. Dufour, take this money and find us a pick and shovel, then get back here as fast as you can."

The boy takes the coins and dashes off. I heave myself up to stand next to the wagon. I am bruised and scratched but otherwise unhurt, my good stout Hussar jacket having taken the brunt of most of the punishment. I button it back up—Laurent had unbuttoned it to listen to evidence of my beating heart—and I lean back against the wagon, take a deep breath, and let it out, and yes, the heart still does beat.

While we wait for his return, I note with gladness that Mathilde is tied to the back of our wagon and has found some grass to graze upon. I shall have to look after her wound. *Poor baby, I am so hard on my friends...*

I ask, "So where is Chaisson?"

"In that hospital tent over there," says Laurent.

He does not have to point it out. I hear the screams, and I know that ruined arms and legs are being hacked off in generally vain attempts to save the lives of their owners, but the efforts must be made. Some will live, most will not.

Dufour comes back panting with a pick and shovel. "They were only too glad to give them up, Miss...M'sieur."

"Thank you, Denis," I say. There is a nice shady spot over there by that tree. "Dig the graves there. Take off their jackets and their shakos, so they might be given to their families."

The preparations are made and the pick and shovel dig down into the earth.

Standing by, I'm startled to hear a pistol shot from over the crest of a nearby hill. One...then another. I give Laurent a questioning look and he goes to investigate. *I thought this damned battle was over...*

He comes back and says, "There is an officer down there, drunk...shooting at the scavengers. I think you might know him, Lieutenant. He came upon us a while ago when we were loading you onto the wagon. I believe he thought we were detailed to pick up the dead and that you were one of them. He looked at you, saluted, and galloped off."

*Ah, yes, the scavengers, robbers of the dead, who creep out from the shadows after every battle since David met Goliath on the field of Elah, to strip the honored dead of their belongings as they lie silent on the ground.*

I leave the Clodhoppers to their sad task and run over

the low hill. I see an officer dressed in the uniform of the Light Cavalry standing there, pistol raised. In his other hand he holds a bottle. I slide down the embankment as he fires off another round.

"Take that, you filthy bastards!"

I step in front of him.

"Randall. Stop it. You are still alive. You should be glad of it. Now stop acting the fool."

He looks at me in astonishment and then throws back his head and laughs. "So. The cat really does have nine lives. How many have you used up so far, Jacky?"

"Why are you here, Randall, and not with Murat?"

"Ah. Well, I was sent off to deliver the news of the Marshal's victory to the Emperor. It seems that Murat had lost his chosen messenger in the ah...scuffle, shall we say?"

"You must get back to Murat's staff. Do you want to have survived the war only to be shot for desertion?"

"Let 'em wait. Let 'em shoot me, for all that. The war's over, anyway," he says. "Look! There's another one of those dirty vultures!" He fires off a shot, and I see a man scurry back into the woods. "Run, you piece of *merde*!" he shouts, and then reloads.

"Randall, please! You must take control of yourself! Please! For me, if nothing else!" I plead, clasping my hands together and beginning to cry. "This is war! What the hell did you expect?"

Randall goes quiet and looks about him. Grave trenches are being dug on this side of the hill, too, and men are hauling the dead into long lines and getting them ready to go into the ditch.

"I did not expect this," says Randall. "I expected...

honor…glory…a chance to test myself. Not this…not this…slaughterhouse."

"You acquitted yourself with honor, Randall, you must know that. You saved my life today. If you had not done that, my body would be one of those being dumped into that ditch."

He looks off. "You know, for all my swaggering about and dueling with the lads back at college, that was the first man I ever killed. All the other nonsense was just boys' games we played, thinking ourselves men." He looks down at his hands. "I killed many more than just that one this day, though. We hounded them and ran them down, then we killed them. We slashed at them and shot them with our pistols. Our lancers ran them through with their spears. Our cannon blasted them to bloody pieces. We killed them as they tried to stand and fight, and we killed them when they tried to run. We just…killed them."

He is silent for a while, then he lifts the bottle again. "Here, have a drink. Drink to love and war and honor and glory and all that."

I uncork it and smell it—it is very strong brandy.

I take it and say, "To love and to peace and to no more war." I upend it and knowingly break my vow, thinking it better to take a small taste to seal the truth of what I have just so devoutly wished for, and then I toss the half-full bottle against a rock, where it shatters. "You must be presentable when you report back to Murat. You know that."

He says nothing and then chuckles. "Oh, the ever-so-right, ever-so-bright, ever-so-clever Jacky Faber, Hero of the Great Race at Dovecote Downs, Hero of Trafalgar, Savior of the *Bloodhound,* Hero of the Battle of Jena, tells me to be . . . presentable."

"Come on, Randall. None of that is true, and you know it."

"You led the charge today, you can't deny it. It is the talk of all the camps. There you were, out in front of us all, waving your sword above your head and screaming for Prussian blood just like any Viking Valkyrie."

"I didn't lead anything. My horse ran away with me. I was screaming in terror."

"That is not how the stories will be told."

"I can't help that."

He sighs and goes on. "Dovecote seems so very far away, doesn't it, Jacky? Never thought I'd say that I miss the place, but I do."

"So do I, Randall."

Again a scavenger creeps out of the woods, and once more Randall levels his pistol.

"Randall, don't. It won't help anything."

He aims carefully, but he does not fire. He lowers the gun.

"You are right. The dead are dead and they do not care." He stands still for a while, his pistol pointed at the ground. "You know, Jacky, when I was at Napoléon's headquarters today, I learned that we lost five thousand men and the Prussians lost twenty-five thousand. *Thirty thousand men . . .* think of that . . . *thirty thousand . . .*"

There are corpses strewn all across the plain, and there are bodies that lie close to Randall and me. He gazes down at one of them, a young Prussian soldier whose lifeless face is pressed into the dust next to the road. "He was hardly more than a boy."

"Aye. His mother probably knitted his socks for him before he left home."

Randall nods and puts his pistol into its holster. He goes to his horse, which is tethered to a tree nearby, and takes up the reins. I follow him over.

"I will do my duty, and I'll follow Murat to the end of this campaign, and then I will give up my commission and return to Dovecote. If you get there before I do, you may tell them that. A kiss, Jacky, and good-bye."

He leans down to take the kiss, and then swings into the saddle. He spurs his mount to a trot and rides off. I watch him till he is out of sight.

*Good-bye, Randall. I hope we'll meet again, and in a better place than this.*

I return to my men and see that things are ready. The bodies of Dubois and Vedel are laid in the grave, I say the words, and the dirt is put over them.

"Now," I say, brushing back the tears, "let us see to Chaisson."

My remaining Clodhoppers and I walk toward the hospital tent, followed by Papa Boule in the wagon, and as I go I wonder, *Jean-Paul, what has become of you? Where are you now?* I offer up a quick prayer and then duck my head to go into Hell on earth.

Amongst the dead and dying, amid the shrieking and the quiet, we find Chaisson and are glad to discover that his wounds are minor, and if infection does not set in, he should recover completely. I give him a pat on his shoulder and compliment him on his bravery and hope that he is comfortable. In fact, the doctors demand we haul him out of there to make room for others in more need. We do it and get Chaisson out to the wagon, and then I go back in to see if I can find word of Jean-Paul...but it is not him that I find.

As I corner a doctor to ask if he has word of a Lieutenant Jean-Paul de Valdon, he looks at a list he holds in his hand and says no. Then I feel Dufour, who has seldom left my side since my return, tugging at my sleeve.

"What is it, Denis?" I ask, irritated, as I am so very, very tired, and really hurt, and sick of all this.

"Look, Lieutenant," says Dufour, pointing to a man stretched out on a cot. "It is our Captain."

*What? Whose Captain?*

And then I see.

*Bardot? Oh, please, no!*

But it is.

I rush to his side, sit down by him, and take his hand. His jacket has been taken off and lies on the ground next to him. His sword leans against the wall of the tent behind his head. His midsection is covered with blood. There is a doctor next to him looking at another man and I say, "Doctor...?" and he peers over at me and then down at Bardot. He shakes his head, and then walks away to the next cot.

*Of all of them, the one I thought the most indestructible!*

"Oh, Captain, I am so sorry!" I wail, and squeeze his hand and Bardot opens his eyes and looks at me.

"Ah, Bouvier," he says, his voice hardly above a whisper. "Good to see you. Glad you made it through."

I am unable to say anything.

"I want you to have my sword, Bouvier. It's right there. And my jacket...there are letters for my family in there... and some money...and for God's sake, stop crying."

"I can't, Sir, I'm sorry."

He sighs. "It's not so bad, this dying business. I am not in great pain, not like some of these poor devils. I am a soldier, after all, and I lived as one and now I die as one and that is as it should be—and my wound is on the front, so I die with some honor." He pauses, and then goes on. "Trouble is, as a soldier goes to leave this world, he always has some regrets—he still wants one more smoke, one more drink, one more song..." His breathing is becoming more labored and I know he is weakening. "...and one more girl."

I give his hand a squeeze and rise.

"Dufour," I say. "Go to my knapsack and bring me the bottle that is in it."

While the boy scurries out to get it, I kneel down and reach into Bardot's jacket pocket, where I know he keeps his cigars and matches, take one, stick it between my lips and light it. Coughing, I slide it over Bardot's own lips. He clamps down on it with his teeth and takes a long, deep drag of it. "Ahhh...," he breathes, and slowly lets the smoke out.

Dufour runs back in, clutching the bottle. I take it from him and say, "Go back out and get the lads. I need them here. To say good-bye to our Captain Bardot."

Wide-eyed, he rushes back out to fetch the Clodhoppers, while I uncork the bottle, and put my arm under Bardot's shoulder to raise him up a bit so that he might drink from the opium-laced cognac that I hold to his lips.

He manages to get some down.

"Oh, that is good," he murmurs. I put the neck of the bottle once again to his mouth and lift it. He chokes, and some spills out over his chin, but some goes down his throat. *This time, Bardot, drink as much as you want—it will ease your passage, my friend.* It is not called Soldier's Joy for nothing. I suspect that similar potions are being poured down the necks of other sufferers here in this tent because the place grows quieter and quieter.

"That's enough, Bouvier, thank you," he says, and I let him sink back down. Even though he grows paler and paler, the drink seems to have restored him a bit.

He cuts his eyes to me and grins. "That's the smoke, and the drink, Bouvier. Can you provide the song...and the girl?"

My men come in and group themselves about the cot. *Sorry, Captain...sorry, M'sieur...*

Though I know their sentiments are sincere, I cut them short with, "Clodhoppers, form a screen about this cot and face outward, such that none can see in."

Some look mystified, but Laurent does not, and he directs the rest to do my bidding.

When I am looking at the backs of all of them, I start to sing to Bardot, very low, as I unbutton my jacket...*Plaisir d'amour, ne dure qu'un moment...*

> *Pleasure of love,*
> *Lasts but a moment long....*

I open my jacket and begin to unlace the front of my undershirt.

"There is the song...," says Bardot, looking at me with all the intensity he can muster on his dying bed, "but where is the girl?"

I finish undoing my shirt, baring my breast, while continuing to sing... *Chagrin d'amour, dure toute la vie...*

> *Pain of love,*
> *Endures the whole life long.*

"Ah," says Bardot, looking at me, his eyes glazed and amazed but still bright. "The girl at the tavern, with that boy..."

"Yes, Bardot, that same girl," I say.

He chuckles, shaking his head. "The last smoke, the last drink, the last song... and now... the last girl..."

I again lift him up and he looks at me and he smiles... he even manages a grin. "It is so very, *very* good to know... Bouvier...," he whispers, such that only I can hear, "...that God has a sense of humor."

I press his face to my chest, and he tries to lift his hand to touch my breast, but he is too weak and his hand sinks back down.

*I hope that this cheers you on your way, Captain Bardot. You were a good friend when I needed one, and I love you for it.*

I hold him there, tears streaming down my face, till I feel the life slip from him and then I lay him back down. With my two fingers, I bring his eyelids down to close his eyes for the last time, eyes that once had gazed fondly upon me, and upon this world.

Rising, I button up my jacket. The Clodhoppers still stand looking away. *Good boys...* All except Dufour, who in his youthful innocence did *not* turn around, and who did not miss a thing. He stands astounded.

"Dufour," I say, the tears still coming on hard, "go find a stretcher. Lads, the Captain is dead. Go prepare another grave. Next to Dubois and Vedel. I pray that they all rest easy, being comrades in arms and all."

There is no checkout, no paperwork, no nothing. What do they care about one more dead soldier? Nothing. I gather up Bardot's jacket and sword and I follow the stretcher with its sad burden out of that place.

The grave is dug and Bardot laid in it, and Bouchard again takes up the shovel. I look down at Bardot's face and say, "Wait a moment," and go to my knapsack and pull out my remaining silk scarf. Kneeling, I kiss my fingertips and lean down into the grave and place them on Bardot's lips and say, "Good-bye, Pierre Bardot, my Bonny Light Horseman." Then I spread the kerchief over his face. "All right, Bouchard, but, please, gently at first."

He picks up a shovelful of dirt and lightly sprinkles it in, and then another, and another. The ones to follow come quicker and not so light, as the job must be done. I turn my face away, unable to watch.

When the last of the dirt is formed into a mound and I am about to rise, I hear a great pounding of horses' hooves and look over to the road where a column of mounted Imperial Guards is marching by not twenty feet away.

They pass by, and then comes a carriage—*the* carriage, the one with the big *N* surrounded by golden garlands of acanthus embossed on the sides. I stay on my knees next to the grave, thinking not to be noticed by the high and the mighty, and not caring overmuch about any of all that at this moment, when I hear a general halt called.

Reins are pulled in and horses snort, and the procession comes to a stop, plainly upon the orders from someone in the coach.

Then I hear a voice that has now come to be somewhat familiar say to someone inside, "Look. It is our bold American messenger. The one who led the charge of the Cavalry. Come here, Lieutenant!" he calls to me. "I have one more message for you to deliver!"

An Imperial Guard officer leaps off his horse, strides up to me, and says, "*L'Empereur* wishes to speak with you! Get up, put on your shako, and get over there!"

I get to my feet before he can kick me and I put my hat upon my head, fasten the strap under my chin, and walk over to the carriage and stand there and salute. I am unsteady on my feet, for I have not slept for more than an hour in the last two nights.

The door to the coach opens, and he looks down at me and says, "I see that you mourn for a friend..."

I nod and say nothing.

"I am sorry, but he and many others died today for the glory of France. It is how we all, as soldiers, hope to go someday."

Again I nod.

"I think you have had enough of battle for a while, Lieutenant. I will send you with a message...to the Empress... in Paris."

"*Oui*, Excellency," I say, and lift my dirt-covered and tear-streaked face to him. "But first, if I may say good-bye to my men..."

The door flies open and a man looks out and shouts, "You would make the Emperor of France wait upon you? Incredible! You get yourself—"

"Monsieur," interrupts Napoléon, and I can see his gray eyes flash in anger. Monsieur immediately falls silent. "You are a very good secretary, and I value your services, but you have very little idea of what holds an army together, what makes some men follow others into battle. You will be quiet. I do not need anyone to protect me from the honest words of my men."

The secretary, very chastened, slumps back into his seat.

To me, Napoléon says, "Go say farewell to your men and then come back here."

I salute and turn away to return to my Clodhoppers. As I go, I can hear Napoléon say, "Meneval. Take a letter: *My dearest Joséphine...I send this messenger to you to bear the news of a glorious victory that I dedicate in honor of you, dear one...*"

"Clodhoppers. Form up," I say when I get back to them. "The cruel war is over but still you need to report back to your division for mustering out, and I must go in a different direction. I am being sent to Paris, and I will probably not see you again."

They get themselves in a line, muskets at Parade Rest.

"Dufour. Go unsaddle my mare and put my gear on one of the captured horses. Mathilde is weary from dragging my sorry self all over this field and needs a rest. And don't look so unhappy, boy—you survived this battle, after all, and many did not."

He goes to do it and I address the others. "Men. You have served me and your country well, and now it is ended. I heartily advise you to go back to your village to spend the rest of your days there and vow that you will never join any army ever again. I know that some of you will do that and some of you will not, but that is up to you, not me. I thank you for your service and your kind protection of me."

I take a deep breath and start at the end of the line. I shake each hand and give each a kiss on the cheek. It is allowed, in France, for men to kiss each other on the cheek.

"Michaud, Simon, thank you both. Lambert...Guerrette...Gobin...be sure to tell the people of your village of the bravery of Vedel and Dubois...break the news to their families as gently as you can. Chaisson, you are able to stand, and it gives me joy to see that...Bouchard...Pannetier... Bertrand...go back...go back and be the good plowboys you are. Papa Boule, return your lads to the village, and return to your bakery to make good bread and leave all this fighting to others. Good-bye, all of you."

Then I stand in front of Laurent and look up into his eyes. "Laurent. I know you will stay with the Army. Maybe this army, maybe another. The quiet pleasures of the farmyard are not for you, I know that. Once a poacher, always a poacher, eh? But I will leave you with this, David, to tell your fellow soldiers when you gather together in a tavern, or around a campfire."

I stand on my tiptoes and whisper in his ear, "You have heard, perhaps, of *La Belle Jeune Fille sans Merci*?"

He looks at me, surprised. "The pirate? But she is dead..."

"Not yet she isn't, David Laurent," I say, giving him the big, knowing eyes, and an even bigger wink.

He laughs. "Well, I'll be damned. That will be a story to tell."

"Farewell, Corporal Laurent. I wish you a life of adventure."

With that, I turn to Denis Dufour, who has just brought up Mathilde and a fine gelding, the best of the horses we took from the Prussians. I see that my saddle and my gear are on the back of the gelding, as ordered. I take Mathilde's reins and place them in the boy's hands.

"Mathilde is my own mare, you see, as I bought her in Paris, and she does not belong to the Army. I now give her to you, Dufour, with the hope that you will be kind to her. When you are released from service, take your pay and your horse and go back home. Treat her gently, for she has a gentle nature. Do not use her harshly, do not use her to plow. Instead, get on her and ride around the hills and fields of your countryside, in the springs and summers of your youth, and later, well, maybe a girl will ride behind you, with her arms around your waist. If you and she have children, pile them on Mathilde's back to take them to church on Sunday, and when she grows old and weak, put her out to pasture and let her live out her days in peace. Good-bye, Dufour."

I go over and lean my head against Mathilde's neck. *Good-bye, baby. I know I was hard on you, but things will be better for you now.*

I give her a last pat, and then, choking down a sob, I turn away from them all, and with the gelding's reins in my hand, I return to the side of Bonaparte's carriage.

"Ah. You are ready, now, yes?" he says. "Good. So are we.

Tie your mount to the rear of the coach. You will ride with me till the road divides."

Nothing surprises me anymore. I do as I am told and then, taking off my shako and putting it under my arm, I climb into the carriage. There is only one open seat and I sit in it. It is, of course, next to Napoléon Bonaparte. A command is given and we rattle off.

I settle in, suffering the glares from the staff that sit opposite me. I don't care. I am too tired to worry about them.

The Emperor looks down at me. "So. The one who led the charge that saved the day."

I shake my head. "No, Excellency. My horse panicked and ran away with me. I led nothing."

He chuckles. "Well, I am sure Murat will be glad to hear that. I shall tell him. He was a bit miffed that you seized the glory of the day." He picks up my shako and peers at the bullet hole punched in the metal shield just above the head band, then puts it back down. "Well, that surely must have parted your hair."

"How is Marshal Murat?" I ask, as if I were asking after the health of a favorite uncle of mine. I endure more glares from the others for that.

"He is well," says Bonaparte.

"I am glad," I say. "He was kind to me."

"He is that way," says the Emperor. "Meneval. Give me one of those medals."

"But, Excellency…"

Again, the slate eyes flash.

"Yes, Excellency," answers Meneval. He thrusts his hand into a valise and draws out a glittering medal wrapped in a red, white, and blue ribbon, and hands it to Napoléon, who takes it and unwinds the ribbon.

"Bow your head, boy," says Napoléon Bonaparte, so I do it and he puts the ribbon around my neck, such that the medal rests on my chest.

"What is it?" I ask, dumbfounded.

"It is a new medal I have had struck. I call it the Legion of Honor. You have the first."

"Thank you, Sir."

"Ah, it is just a bauble. They are all just baubles, after all, *n'est-ce pas*? But it is with such baubles that men are led."

I nod in agreement, my eyelids starting to droop. What is a medal compared to a life? It is nothing…I think about the girls Bardot will not love, the woman he will not marry, the sons and daughters he will not raise up straight and strong. *Non…Ça ne fait rien.* It means nothing…absolutely nothing.

…and then I slump over and slip into sleep.

"Boy, wake up."

My eyes open and all I see is white fabric. My mind clears and I realize that I am looking down at Napoléon Bonaparte's trousers and that I have fallen asleep with my head in his lap.

I sit up and rub my eyes and say, "I'm sorry. I—"

"Don't worry, Lieutenant. It is the fatigue of war. But now our ways must part, as I turn north to take the Prussians' surrender, and you must go south to bear this letter to the Empress."

He hands me the letter and I stick it in my jacket.

"Yes, Excellency."

"The letter with my seal on it will be your safe passage. Deliver it in person, with my compliments."

"Yes, Excellency."

The coach stops and I crawl out. I shove my shako back on my head, tighten its strap, take up the reins of my horse, and climb aboard.

I salute, and the coach pulls off, followed by the rest of the Imperial Guard escort.

I sit there for a while, till silence falls on the field and I am alone. My war is over, evening is falling, and I'm very weary.

> *Brokenhearted I will wander,*
> *Brokenhearted I will remain*
> *For my Bonny Light Horseman,*
> *In the wars he lies slain.*

Then I put my heels to my mount and head off toward the setting sun and on to Paris.

# Epilogue

I trudge back to my old neighborhood, the rue de Londres, go into *Café des Deux Chats,* and plunk down my knapsack. The familiar smells envelop me like an embrace from an old friend. Because of my uniform, I am greeted by great cheers, and I'm thinking that I must soon get back into my female garb, else I might get shot as a deserter when the glow of this great victory wears off. But I do have that other Imperial Seal, the one that Murat insisted I keep, so that should hold me in good stead.

I sit down and order a great bowl of bouillabaisse, and when it comes I tie my napkin around my neck and bury my face in its goodness, spooning up great mouthfuls. I rip chunks off the bread given me and dip it in the stew and shove it in my mouth. *Oh, God, it's good!* Wine, yes, wine, too, and more of it.

No matter what happens to Jacky Faber, her belly still rules.

On my way here I took a detour to a small town, Château Thierry, figuring the Empress could wait a bit for her good news, and delivered news of another sort to a family who lived there. It was a nice house by a river and I pulled up and dismounted, and then Jacky Faber, the Angel of Death, went up to the front door and knocked, with my sad burden in my hand.

My knock was answered by a tall man with gray hair and beard, who nevertheless looked very much like Bardot, and who, as soon as he saw me and what I held in my hands, knew what awful news I had brought. A woman came into the room, and seeing the tears pour down my face, immediately sat down and buried her face in her hands.

"I...I am sorry to tell you this, but your son Captain Pierre Bardot is dead. He was a brave man and a good friend to me." I was gasping for breath then, but I pushed on. "I was with him when he died and I want you to know that he died easy. He told me of letters to you that he had in his pocket and I swore to him that I would deliver them. Oh, God. I can't stand it!"

I fell to my knees on the floor and covered my own face with my hands. "I saw him die and I saw him buried proper, and here is his jacket and his sword," I wail. "He...he gave the sword to me, but you should have it...I..."

The father puts his hands on my shaking shoulders and says, "No. You shall keep the sword, boy. I want no other son of mine to take it up and go off to war. One son for France is enough. Thank you for coming to us this way. I know it is hard for you, for it is plain that you loved him as we did. It...it is good to know that he had a friend as constant as you. It will be a comfort to us later."

I picked myself up and staggered out and left them to their grief.

———

When I got to Paris, I took myself, and my horse, whom I had named Rudolf, in honor of his German heritage, to *Le Palais de Tuileries* and marched Rudy straight up the front steps, scattering various overdressed minions, and announced that I had a message from the Emperor Napoléon to the Empress Joséphine, and was met with much derisive laughter, considering the state of my clothing and general dishevelment.

"Not long ago, I was on the battlefield of Jena, next to *l'Empereur*," I say to the man guarding the door. "What were you doing on that day, M'sieur? Powdering your bum?" With that I whip out the safe passage with the big blue *N*, signed by Napoléon himself. He doesn't say anything after that, so I dismount and am ushered into the palace. Rudy, however, has to stay outside. Pity, that.

It is, of course, a glorious place, but I think I am done with glory and glorious things and all that so I am not cowed by it all.

I am asked for the letter, but I wave them off and I tell them that *l'Empereur* desired that I place the letter directly in Joséphine's own hand, and that they should all bugger off as I am growing impatient with mincing, groveling courtiers.

I am told to wait, so I flop myself down in a gilt chair that, if sold, I know could keep the London Home for Little Wanderers going for at least ten years. My eyes range over the paintings on the wall, the fine tapestries, the elegant statues, and I find myself falling asleep again.

Eventually I am roused and escorted into the Empress's inner chambers. She, dressed beautifully, of course, is seated at a desk and surrounded by ladies of the court. She looks up, I bow, present the letter, accept her thanks, and then walk backward out of the room, 'cause that's what you do with royalty—you ain't never supposed to show 'em your ass is why.

Funny, I thought as I left the place, she looked like any ordinary woman, under all that finery.

I had taken Rudy to the stable where I had bought Mathilde—was it only three weeks ago that I did that?—as the people there seemed to have been kind to Mathilde when she was a resident here. 'Course, I only get ten sous on the franc, but what the hell, it will be enough to hold me for a while and I am getting hungry. The bridle and saddle go with him, too, the saddle being well polished by my bottom over these past weeks. I keep my pistols and shove them into my knapsack and shoulder it. Bardot's saber, which is too long for me to wear about my waist, as it would drag the ground, I have strapped to my back such that the hilt rides above my right shoulder and the scabbard does not get in my way. I had lost my other sword in the battle, when I was thrown from my horse. Never had much of a chance to name that other one, and I ain't named this one yet as I've got to think hard on that, what with it being given to me by Bardot and all. Looking like a proper Tartar, I headed off to my old neighborhood.

I have no idea just what is going to happen to me now and where I will be going. Probably back to Madame Pelletier's and, well, there are worse things in the world than that. And it will be good to see Zoé and the girls again. I don't know, I'll just wait and see what happens.

I knew they would find me here, and sure enough, Jardineaux comes through the door just as I am finishing up, and sits down before me. I signal for a glass of wine for him, as it would look suspicious otherwise. I am learning this game.

"So," he says, ignoring the wine. "Report."

"The Grand Army is in Berlin. Kaiser Friedrich Wilhelm III has capitulated. The Fourth Coalition is shattered. Except for Russia, there are no more anti-Napoléon forces out there. Not to the north anyway. I hear Lord Wellesley is kicking up a fuss in Spain, though, but I'm sure you know about that. I believe Bonaparte intends to move his army north and fight Czar Alexander next year. I heard this from Marshals Lannes and Bertrand and Murat." I pick up a mussel shell from the stew and suck on it. "That Prince Murat is quite a fellow. We should have a few like him ourselves."

He gives a bit of a choke. "And just where did you meet these men?"

"In Napoléon's camp, and at the head of their various Corps. At Jena. Before, during, and after the battle."

"But how...? You...?" He now takes a drink of his wine.

"I was a messenger, remember? Of course I would be there. A fly on the wall, as it were, but there all the same. I do hold a commission as a Second Lieutenant in the Sixteenth Fusiliers. I have my papers in my pocket." I tap my breast pocket, but I do *not* tell him of that special message I had delivered at the start of the battle.

I take the napkin from my neck and dab at my lips.

"*Mon Dieu*," exclaims Jardineaux, seeing the medal on my jacket. "What the hell is that?"

"What? Oh, that is the Legion of Honor Medal. Apparently *l'Empereur* thought I fought bravely at Jena. He was wrong. I was not brave, but I did do my duty for my men, I think, and so I shall keep it. Another glass of wine with you?"

His eyes bug out in amazement. "But how did you get it?"

"The Emperor put it around my neck in his carriage as we were leaving the battlefield. He had offered me a lift, you see, and—"

"You were in the same carriage with that monster?" Jardineaux's face is becoming quite red.

"Yes," I say, and polish off the last of the bread. "I thought that was where you wanted me to be. Actually, I fell asleep in his lap on the way." I chuckle, well beyond caring about what Jardineaux thinks. "I am here because he wanted me to deliver a letter to the Empress. Which I did. Earlier today. She was quite gracious."

Jardineaux fixes me with his eye. "Let me get this straight. You were in the same carriage with Napoléon Bonaparte. I know you carry a knife up your sleeve. Why did you not kill him then? Were you afraid for your miserable little life? Did you think you counted for all that much that you could not do that simple thing and rid the world forever of the greatest tyrant it has ever known?"

"He did not seem like such a monster. He takes care of his men. He takes care of his people."

"I think you have been turned, girl. I suspect your loyalty," he says, his voice low, even, and hard. "…and I believe we are done with you."

"My loyalty? To what? To crazy old King George who never did nothin' for me 'cept send his men to hunt me down like some poor fox what ain't done nothin' to him?

428

And done with me? Fine. I did my best. If it wasn't good enough for you, I am sorry, but, no, not really—I dislike you and I hate this business. Now let me go home."

"Oh, you shall go home all right," he says, ominously, "and you shall go there today. Get up."

A coldness comes over me. *What does he mean by that? What have I done that was so wrong? Could it be…*

"Get up, I told you!" he snarls and, furious, he gets to his feet. He grabs me by the arm and hustles me out of the place. Startled faces watch us go and some speak up.

*Here, here, Sir! You cannot treat a soldier so!*

*Soldier? Ha! This is not a soldier! It is a deserter, a damned traitor! Get out of my way!*

He drags me to the street, and I see Armand waiting there with the carriage and I am taken up and thrown in. My knapsack follows.

"To the docks!" roars Jardineaux, and the coach rattles off.

I get off the floor and crawl up into the seat and turn around and my jaw drops open in surprise as I see Jean-Paul de Valdon is sitting in the seat opposite me, dressed, once again, in his civilian clothes.

"Jean-Paul!" I exclaim. "I am so glad to see that you are safe! I searched everywhere for you after the battle but could not find you! Oh, I am so glad!" I reach for his hands.

But he does not take them. Jean-Paul's face is set, stony, devoid of expression. He leans across, yes, but not to embrace me; no, instead he pushes my hands away and reaches up my sleeve to take out my shiv. He tucks it into his jacket and then he looks out the window as we start off. He does not look at me, he does not meet my eyes.

"Jean-Paul, I—"

"It would be better, girl, if you said nothing," he says, his voice cold, disinterested.

My mouth is open in disbelief.

*Jean-Paul, no! This cannot be! Not you!*

"You see," says Jardineaux, smiling, "we have had word of your actions at Jena; oh, no, not from Monsieur Valdon here. He was otherwise occupied, but we had other operatives in the field and they informed me that you had conveyed many messages back and forth between the commanders of Napoléon's cursed Corps, and thus had many opportunities to cause them great confusion, but you did not. No, no, you did not."

He keeps smiling, and I can only think that he had that same smile on his face that day when he handed up that poor girl to the executioner to have her head cut off in my place, and now I know that it is my turn and I know he will smile when he does me, too.

"And then," he continues, "what is most damning, is that we learned that it was you who delivered the message to Murat that ordered him to charge the Prussian line...the order that probably turned the battle in Napoléon's favor. Do you deny it?"

I don't say anything.

"Valdon," asks Jardineaux, "did you see her deliver the message?"

Jean-Paul flicks a piece of lint from his lapel, then he answers, "Yes, I saw her ride up with it, waving it about and making a great show of it." He returns to looking out the window.

I know I am done, and I can do nothing about it. I can

only sit there, stunned. *Oh, God, I was such a fool! To think I loved you, Jean-Paul!*

"What do you have to say to that, girl?"

"Sod off," I say, revertin' to me Cockney ways, as I always do in cases like this.

"Watch your mouth, girl."

"Watch my mouth? Why, when what you're gonna do is take me off somewheres and murder me 'cause I didn't kill Boney when I had the chance? 'Cause I delivered that message to Murat 'cause I didn't want t'see me mates killed? Why the hell should I watch my mouth when I'm gonna be dead in a few minutes?"

He don't say nothin' to that. He pulls out a pistol and points it between my eyes and smiles. "You really are a piece of gutter trash, when all is said and done, no matter what the people in England think of you. And don't even consider using that sword strapped to your back. Your brains would be splattered before you could get it even halfway out. Understand?"

My chest starts in to heavin' and my eyes would start streamin' but I don't think I've got any more tears in 'em. All dried up, now.

"What I understand is that you're done with me now, right? And now you're gonna kill me 'cause I didn't do what you wanted me to do, but I don't care, you hear me? You can all go to Hell, you and *him* and all your sorry lot!"

"Shut up, girl."

"And you, Jean-Paul," I say, turning to him, "to think I loved you. Jacky Faber always thought she was clever, smart, but she was neither of those when it came to you. No. She was nothin' but a foolish, gullible girl. So stupid to be taken in that way…" I look down at my hands and think about putting my face in them and bawling for the rest of the journey to my killing ground. But I shall not. I will not give them that satisfaction. I have faced death too many times in the last weeks to tremble now. Let them do to me what they will. "Betrayal…such an awful word…" is the last thing I say. "…and the worst betrayal of all is to be done in by someone you loved."

I face straight ahead and close my eyes, and I remain that way for the rest of the journey.

*Once again I'm sayin' g'bye to you, Jaimy, and this time I think it's for real 'cause I don't see no way out o' this one. I hope you'll be able to put me out of your mind and find another girl and raise a fine family and all. I know you won't be able to name one of the kids after me, 'cause your wife'd raise a fuss and I don't blame her, 'cause I'd raise a ruckus, too… Maybe one of the dogs…or one of the horses…that's it—one of the horses, a nice little mare. See what you can do for the kids at the Home for Little Wanderers and the people who work for me at Faber Shipping…Higgins and Jim Tanner and Clementine and Solomon and Daniel and John Thomas and Smasher and all…Funny, ain't it, Jaimy, how that little dream of mine almost happened?*

Armand pulls the coach to a stop. We are at the edge of a body of water—is it the ocean? The mouth of the Seine? I don't know…all I know is that I am about to die. I am yanked out of the carriage and taken to the shore and shoved down to the water's edge. It is a deserted shore— there is an old wharf, rotting away, but nothing else—

nothing…no boats, no fishermen, no people, no nothing… there is no sound, nothing but the squawk of seagulls wheeling overhead.

*So this is where it all ends—at the end of some muddy dock in France. A deserted beach, with no one to hear the pop of the pistol that will send a bullet into my brain and so end my life, with no one but the wild birds to see and no one but them to mourn.*

I fall to my knees, sobbing. "I don't care, I don't care, just do it," I say, and I feel the barrel of his gun against the back of my head. *I don't care, I just wanna go home.* Now the tears do come, for my lost life, for my lost future, for my lost everything.

"Look out there, girl, and tell me what you see," says Jardineaux. I sense Jean-Paul standing behind him, but I don't care. I lift my head.

I lift my eyes and look out over the water. Through the tears I see…what? A ship? Could it be? I wipe my eyes to clear them. *Oh, dear Lord, it is the* Nancy B! *Yes it is, her sails slacked, and her American colors snapping in the breeze!* I see a boat being lowered and…

Jardineaux grabs my hair and pulls my head back. "You see that? You know who that is?"

I gasp out, "How could you be so cruel? How could you—"

"There are telescopes trained on us right now, you know that, don't you?"

I don't have to reply, 'cause I know it's true.

"They came here to rescue you, and we knew about that, yes we did, and we were prepared to let you go, but then you did what you did, and now they shall see what happens to turncoats. They came for you, but they shall not have you—what they shall get will be your dead body, and I want them to see it happen!"

He shoves the barrel at the back of my head, and I wait for the sound of the hammer being brought to full cock. *Dear God . . .*

But I don't hear it.

What I do hear is a sharp intake of breath, a groan, and then Jardineaux pitches forward, his face slammed in the mud next to me. I look up and see my shiv sticking out of his back, the rooster on the blade's handle starin' directly into my crazed eye.

I am stunned beyond any attempt at speech.

"I knew what he was going to do to you. I could not let that happen," says Jean-Paul, standing above Jardineaux's still form.

I get to my feet.

"Jean-Paul . . . but what about Armand?" I look over to see the man approach.

He shakes his head and looks at me. "I told you before that Armand is from my village. He is my man and will not say anything . . . Armand!"

Armand bounds over.

"M'sieur?"

"Get his identification," says Jean-Paul. "We will let the ocean take care of him."

"*Oui*, M'sieur," says Armand. He pulls out my shiv and runs it through the wet sand to clean it, then hands it to Jean-Paul, who, in turn, gives it back to me. Without thinking, I shove it up my sleeve into its sheath. Armand rolls Jardineaux onto his back and strips him of his wallet and anything else he might have had on him. The tide is coming in and seawater is already washing about the dead man's face.

"He was a cruel man with much hatred in his heart," says Jean-Paul, looking down at the body. "I, too, once had a heart full of nothing but hate...then I met you." He lifts his head and looks out over the water. "Your friends are out there, Jacqui, and you must go to them."

"Jean-Paul...," I say, putting my hand on his arm, "I..."

"No, Jacqui, you did not want to come here, and this is not where you belong. I know that." He pauses, takes a breath, and then goes on. "I am quitting this game. Armand and I will go back to our village. Without Jardineaux, his organization will fall apart. Someone will eventually bring Bonaparte down, but it will not be him...or me."

"Jean-Paul..."

He puts his hands on my shoulders and looks down into my eyes and says, "My family's estate, what is left of it, is not far from Paris. I will go back and tend to it now. My father grows old and needs my help." Another pause, as he puts his fingertips under my chin and looks deep into my eyes, a slight smile on his lips. "I may meet a girl, and I may marry, for there is room in my heart for that now, because of you. But I tell you this, Jacqui. Every time I come to Paris, I shall go to the *Café des Deux Chats* and I will order a glass of wine and I will sit there quietly, and whether it is tomorrow, or next month, or years and years from now, I will lift the glass and think of you, Jacqui, and the short time we had together in Paris. And now, you must go."

"One more kiss, Jean-Paul, one more..." I lift my tear-streaked face to his and our lips come together and when they part, I say, "Jean-Paul, I do hope you will meet that girl and that she will make you ever so happy and that you and she will have many fine children and...oh, I just wish the *very* best for you!"

"*Adieu,* Jacqui."

"Good-bye, Jean-Paul."

I turn to the water, and, though I see the boat approaching the shore, I begin wading out toward it, my eyes streaming, my arms open wide.

As it grows close, I see that it is Jim Tanner who holds the tiller and that it is John Thomas and Smasher McGee who man the oars, but it is Jaimy Fletcher who leans over the side of the boat and lifts me aboard and hugs me to him, and he holds my wet, dripping, sobbing self to him all the way back to the *Nancy B.*

*I have come home.*

ML                    12/08